The Lost
Echoes from the Past
Book 9

By Irina Shapiro

Copyright

Table of Contents

Prologue

It took a long moment for reality to sink in. It felt strangely surreal, as if the scene were playing out on stage rather than in his own house, the sharp blade in the assailant's hand a stage prop rather than a deadly weapon. He'd have only one chance to overcome his attacker, and he'd have to time it perfectly if he hoped to even the odds and save the woman he adored from a horrific fate.

He had thought he'd be afraid, but all he felt was an all-consuming fury, the bloodlust he'd read so much about surging through his veins as a red mist descended before his eyes. It was now or never. He charged. At first, all he felt was a pinch. Staring downward, he was surprised to see the blade buried deep in his side, only the plain black hilt visible. Then came the shock, and the pain. He continued to struggle, but his limbs grew leaden and his thoughts slowed to a crawl, his body shutting down as the lifeblood drained out of him. He would have died a happy man knowing he'd made a difference to the outcome, but some remote part of his brain that was still functioning cruelly reminded him of the truth. He hadn't been able to prevent the inevitable.

All was lost.

Chapter 1

March 2018
London, England

A sweet silence descended on the house, the kind of silence one could only hope to enjoy when two children under the age of five went down for their afternoon nap, and the third was still at school. Quinn closed the door to the nursery softly behind her and returned downstairs, eager to enjoy an hour of peace. She turned on the electric kettle, then went into the lounge, where she picked up several toys and fished Mia's still-full sippy cup from beneath the sofa.

Having marginally tidied up, she made herself a cup of tea and settled at the kitchen table with her laptop, ready to catch up on her emails and work on an article she was writing for a well-known periodical. She'd meant to finish it this morning while the children were at nursery school, but she'd had several errands to see to and then stopped by the institute to meet Gabe for a quick lunch, which was as close as they got to date night these days.

Quinn had always meant to return to work after Mia was born, but since the baby's arrival, she'd found it hard to commit to a regular schedule and missed the flexibility of working on the *Echoes from the Past* series. If she were honest, she missed other things as well, including using her gift of experiencing a dead person's memories by holding an object they had owned. She missed the highs and lows, the anxiety that coiled in her belly as she neared the final act of the person's life, and the joy of sharing what she'd learned with the viewers. She missed working with Rhys as well. They still saw each other socially, but their get-togethers were infrequent, and nowadays, mostly with the kids. Rhys's daughter Vanessa was almost the same age as Mia, so the adults enjoyed lunch in the garden or a quiet takeaway in the lounge while the children played.

She was happy, though. These days, her family was the heart of her, and her income from *Echoes* had been replaced by royalties from Gabe's bestselling book, *A Traitor's Heart*, which dealt with the plight of noble-born women during the Wars of the Roses. It had started out as a work of non-fiction, but the narrative had taken on a life of its own and become something of a crossover, the history of the period seen through the eyes of two families whose loyalties lay on either side of the political divide. Gabe had been surprised and elated by the success of his first book and was considering a follow-up outing into the literary world. Quinn was more than happy to support him and help him in any way she could and secretly hoped he might come across some artifact in his research that would allow her to use her gift to give him that much-needed edge.

Having dealt with her professional correspondence, she turned her attention to private emails. There was a message from Jude, who was currently stationed in Germany, and a brief missive from Brett, who was in his third year at Louisiana State University at Baton Rouge, pursuing a degree in business management. Brett sent Quinn an occasional email, and she always replied, feeling it her duty to maintain contact with her brother. According to their father, Brett had really turned his life around. He was doing well in school and seeing a girl Seth and Kathy heartily approved of. Quinn hadn't seen Brett since just before Jo died and hoped he wouldn't be in a hurry to return to the U.K. An occasional email was one thing; seeing him in person would be quite another. She wasn't ready to take their relationship to the next level, not after what she'd suffered at his hands.

Thoughts of Jo always made Quinn sad. It'd been two and a half years since her twin had been killed in a hit-and-run accident outside her building in East London. No one had been charged, and the investigation had been closed soon after the funeral, since the police had found no evidence to lead them to the driver of the vehicle. Quinn and Gabe no longer spoke of Jo. In fact, no one mentioned her much at all, not even their birthparents, Sylvia and Seth. Jo's nomadic existence and her lone-wolf nature had precluded her from forming lasting relationships, and the people who had tried to get close to her had paid for their attempts in spades.

But it still rankled that Jo's death had been so meaningless. Had she died while on assignment in some war-torn country or even from an unexpected illness, Quinn would have had an easier time accepting the tragedy, but knowing that Jo had been mowed down while standing in the street and left there, mangled and bleeding, with only the distant stars for company as the life drained out of her, still had the power to devastate. What sort of person would hit a woman and just drive away, not stopping to help? What sort of monster went on with their life, going about their business and enjoying themselves as though nothing had happened, while Jo was gone, her life snuffed out at the age of thirty-two, all her potential squandered?

Quinn didn't think she'd have ever forgiven Jo for what she'd done to hurt her, but some small part of her still missed the sister she'd never truly had a chance to know. She still mourned the relationship they might have enjoyed had they known each other since childhood rather than meeting only a year before Jo's death. Jo's adoptive sister, Karen, had offered Quinn a keepsake when she'd cleaned out Jo's flat, but Quinn had refused, not trusting herself not to let a misplaced need for closure drive her to delve into Jo's tortured psyche. She hadn't taken a single thing, not even a photo. She had several on her mobile that she and Jo had taken when they'd finally met at the military hospital in Germany, and that was the way she wished to remember her, as the amazing long-lost sister she'd finally found, not the jealous, competitive, and cruel woman Jo had turned out to be.

Quinn sighed and closed the laptop. She had at least another half hour until Alex and Mia woke from their nap, and she was eager to begin reading a book she'd downloaded yesterday. She had laundry to do and dinner to start on, but the chores would wait. She had just settled in her favorite spot on the sofa with her Kindle when the doorbell rang. Quinn sprang to her feet and hurried to the door before the caller could wake the children by ringing the bell again.

"Rhys!" Quinn exclaimed, surprised to see him on her doorstep. Rhys wasn't the type of person to just come round, not anymore. He always rang first. Not that he came over by himself very often. "This is a surprise." The dark shadows beneath Rhys's eyes and his pursed lips weren't lost on her.

"Any chance of a coffee?" Rhys asked as he followed her into the kitchen.

"Of course."

Rhys leaned against the worktop and crossed his arms, looking pensive.

"Are you all right?" Quinn asked.

"Just tired," Rhys said. "Vanessa's been having nightmares. I haven't slept through the night in at least a week. I try to let Katya sleep," Rhys explained. "She needs her rest."

"So do you," Quinn replied. Although nearing his mid-fifties, Rhys didn't look a day over forty-five. Marriage and fatherhood agreed with him—most of the time, anyway. Quinn stood across from him, imitating his pose, and smiled. "Is there something you're not telling me?"

Rhys's tired smile said it all. "We're expecting. Katya hasn't been feeling well, physically or emotionally. She's convinced this one is a boy, and I think she's right. This pregnancy is so different from the first one."

"Is that why Vanessa is having nightmares? Jealous of a new sibling already? Surely she's too young to understand."

"It's not the baby," Rhys said. "We haven't told her yet. Katya wants to wait until the second trimester to tell Vannie. It's a Russian thing, apparently. Telling people too soon might cause a miscarriage."

"But you just told me," Quinn pointed out.

"And you will never reveal my indiscretion to Katya," Rhys replied as he accepted a mug of coffee. "I think it's a silly superstition, but she truly believes it."

"My lips are sealed."

They took their coffees into the lounge, where they settled comfortably, Rhys on the sofa and Quinn in the armchair. "What's up?" she asked him, sensing his hesitation. Rhys wasn't one to mince words, but there was something in his eyes that put Quinn on guard.

"I need to ask a huge favor, Quinn," Rhys began. He exhaled loudly. "You know what they say about the road to hell, right?"

"Yes, it's paved with good intentions," Quinn replied, wondering where this was going.

"Katya loves to swim," he said, as if that was meant to explain everything.

"So?"

"So, I decided to put in a swimming pool at the new house. I wanted to make her happy. The workers broke ground last week." Rhys took a sip of his coffee and glanced toward the window, his shoulders sagging against the back of the sofa. "They had to cut down two old trees and extract the roots in order to clear the space."

"Oh, God. Don't tell me," Quinn said. Now she saw exactly where this was going.

Rhys nodded miserably. "I am telling you. They found skeletal remains trapped amid the roots. Of course, the police were called in, but they ruled it a historic burial, filed a lengthy report, and happily left me to deal with the situation."

"And have you?"

"Not exactly."

"Why not?" Quinn asked, arching her brow. Generally, any human remains that were not the subject of an ongoing investigation or a cold case were left where they had been found or reburied at a local cemetery. There were countless dead sleeping peacefully beneath every corner of Britain, many of them having lain undisturbed for centuries.

"Vanessa was there, playing in the garden, when they found the skeleton. She saw the whole thing."

"Did she understand what she was looking at?"

"She understood enough to be frightened. I would have been able to talk her round if Katya hadn't become hysterical."

"Why?" Quinn asked. Ekaterina Velesova Morgan was one of the calmest, most rational people Quinn had ever come across. She was intelligent, resourceful, and confident enough to put up with a man like Rhys, who didn't suffer fools gladly. Quinn couldn't reconcile the Katya she knew with a woman who'd give in to superstition or become hysterical at the sight of a skeleton.

"Katya's grandfather's younger brother had gone missing during the Second World War. They lived near Kiev then, in an area occupied by the Germans. Oleg was fifteen when he disappeared. His parents searched everywhere for him, asked all their neighbors and even approached the German command, but no one seemed to know anything. They eventually came to believe that Oleg had run away to join the Partisans."

"Did they ever find out what happened to him?" Quinn asked.

Rhys nodded. "It was more than ten years after the war ended that ground was broken for a new block of flats. The site was half a mile from Babi Yar. Have you ever heard of it?"

Quinn nodded. "Sounds familiar, but I can't recall the details."

"It's a mass grave where more than thirty-three thousand Ukrainian Jews had been executed and buried. There's a monument there now, but at the time, the Soviets wanted to obliterate any sign of what had taken place there and were building on the bones of the people who'd been murdered."

"And Oleg was one of them?" Quinn asked.

"Oleg wasn't Jewish, but he must have been caught in the vicinity of the killing ground. Perhaps he'd witnessed some of the atrocities, or maybe he was just in the wrong place at the wrong time. They found his remains trapped in the roots of a tree they'd cut down to clear the ground for the building site," Rhys said.

"How were they able to identify him after all that time?" Quinn asked, ever the archeologist.

"His wallet was still in the pocket of his trousers. His identity card was legible enough to make out his name."

"Had he been shot?"

"No. All his fingers had been smashed and his neck was broken, a leather belt still tied around it. He'd been tortured and hanged, then buried in a shallow grave beneath the tree."

"That's a dreadful story."

"Katya feels strongly about giving this person a proper burial and maybe even finding his or her descendants and notifying them. It's very important to her. Finding Oleg's remains was tragic, but it gave the family closure, and they were able to bury him and mourn him properly."

"Are you asking me to investigate?" Quinn asked, feeling an unexpected flutter of excitement in her belly.

"I'm asking you to investigate," Rhys replied, his gaze holding hers, a pleading look she wasn't accustomed to seeing in Rhys's eyes.

"Have you found anything that had belonged to the deceased?" Quinn asked, her mind already on the case.

"Yes." Rhys reached into his pocket and pulled out a small plastic bag. He handed it to Quinn.

Quinn lifted the bag to the light, eager to see the contents. A tarnished, dirt-encrusted silver band lay within.

"This was the only item found with the remains," Rhys said.

Quinn set the bag on the coffee table, her gaze drawn to the dull glint of the ring. "Was there nothing else? No buttons, buckles, bits of leather?" she asked.

"No. Just this."

Quinn nodded. "The deceased must have been buried in a shroud, which would explain the lack of metal objects since the body was most likely stripped naked before being wrapped."

"That would make sense," Rhys agreed.

"So, that would suggest that the person had been buried with some care. And if that were the case, why would they bury the body beneath a tree rather than in a graveyard? Is there a graveyard nearby?" Quinn asked.

"Yes. There's the parish church."

Quinn nodded, ideas already taking root in her mind. "This person might have been a plague victim, but then again, a plague victim would most likely have been buried in whatever clothes they died in. Or perhaps it was someone who wasn't of Christian faith and wouldn't wish to be laid to rest in a Christian graveyard. What have you done with the remains?"

"I've asked the workers to cordon off that bit of the garden. The remains are in situ, waiting for you to examine them."

"Good. Will you be there tomorrow?" Quinn asked. She'd speak to Gabe tonight, but was in no doubt that he wouldn't object to her excavating the remains.

"I will be there whenever you need me to be."

"What about Katya and Vanessa? I wouldn't want them more upset than they already are."

"They're at our London flat. Katya will not return until the skeleton has been removed, so you have free rein."

"All right. I'll see you tomorrow, then. Around ten?"

"Perfect. Quinn, are you all right with this?" Rhys asked. "I wouldn't want to pressure you into something you don't want to do."

"Yes, I'm all right," Quinn replied, and meant it.

"All right enough to agree to an *Echoes from the Past* Christmas special?" Rhys asked, grinning wickedly.

"Now you're pushing it." Quinn laughed. "You know what, let me see what I'm dealing with, and we'll go from there. If there's an interesting story here, then I might be persuaded to come out of retirement for one more episode."

"Deal," Rhys said. He set down his mug and stood. "I really do appreciate this, Quinn. More than you know."

"I'm happy to help. I can understand the need for closure," she replied.

"I know."

Rhys kissed her cheek and headed for the door, looking a lot better than he had when he'd arrived. "See you tomorrow."

"See you."

Chapter 2

Hertfordshire, England

Saturday morning found Quinn and Gabe driving to Hertfordshire. The village of Potters Cove, where Rhys and Katya had settled after Vanessa was born, lay a few miles north of Potters Bar and was as picturesque as only an English village could be. Rhys had purchased and renovated an eighteenth-century manor house and had spared no expense to make it both modern and beautiful. The drive was lined with stately trees that directed the visitor's gaze toward the lovely house that sat upon a gentle slope, its buttery façade golden in the spring sunshine.

"Thanks for coming with me," Quinn said as Gabe parked the car on the gravel drive in front of the house and turned off the engine.

"Some couples go see a film on their date night; we excavate a burial site," Gabe replied with a grin. "Normally, I'd tell you to think twice about getting involved in this type of case again, but I can see you're excited about this."

"I am," Quinn admitted.

"I am too. I miss getting my hands dirty," Gabe said. "And I love hearing the stories." He turned toward Quinn and removed his sunglasses, looking at her intently. "Promise me you'll stop if you find it too destressing."

"I promise. But to be honest, I don't think any case can be as heartbreaking as that of Annie Edevane. I still dream about that poor little girl."

Gabe nodded. That case had led to Quinn's refusal to commit to a third season of *Echoes from the Past*. She simply couldn't bring herself to delve into any more tragic deaths, especially those of children.

"Well, this one is an adult," Quinn said. "Shall we?"

Gabe got out of the car and opened the boot, taking out their kit. He slung one of the bags over his shoulder, hefted the other one, and followed Quinn around the back of the house, where the area in question was clearly marked with yellow and black tape. Rhys stepped out through the French doors at the back and walked toward them, smiling in welcome.

"Quinn. Gabe. Thank you for coming. I'm at your complete disposal. Tea? Coffee? Sandwiches? A curry?" he asked as he followed them to the site. "There's a decent Indian restaurant in the village."

"Curry sounds great, Rhys," Gabe replied as he eyed the upturned roots of the ancient oak. "But for now, a bottle of water will do."

"On it," Rhys replied. "I'll keep you fed and watered for as long as this takes."

Gabe set down their cases and pulled out two pairs of latex gloves, handing one pair to Quinn. The skeleton was clearly visible, the skull peeking through the gnarled roots as if it were playing hide-and-seek. No wonder Vanessa had been terrified. The scene resembled a particularly ghoulish Halloween display.

"What do you think?" Gabe asked as soon as Rhys headed back toward the house to fetch the water.

Quinn tilted her head to the side as she lowered the camera, having taken a dozen photos of the remains in situ.

"If I had to guess, I'd say this is an adult male. Of course, it could just as easily be a tall woman or a well-developed teenager. We'll know more once Colin Scott gets it on the slab. Rhys has already called him, so he'll be expecting me."

Gabe nodded. "I'm glad you'll get to work with Colin again. I know you miss him."

"I do," Quinn admitted. She hadn't seen Dr. Colin Scott since he and her brother Logan had broken up for good nearly two years ago. Their first split had come in the summer of 2015, but they'd reconciled after Jo's sudden death. The relationship hadn't lasted, however, and it had been Colin who'd ultimately walked away, giving Logan the space he'd needed to find his way forward. As far as Quinn knew, Colin and Logan hadn't spoken since, and she looked forward to seeing Colin and catching up with him.

Quinn put away the camera and crouched next to the remains. "I think we're going to have to cut this skelly free," she said. "Some of the thinner roots have grown through the ribcage and skull. The bones are too brittle and will break if we apply even the slightest pressure."

"I agree." Gabe took out industrial-size secateurs from his case. "We'll cut around it and then extract the trapped bits."

It took nearly three hours to free the skeleton from the suffocating embrace of the web of roots. Once the support of the latticework had been removed, the skeleton began to come apart, since the bones were no longer held together by joints and ligaments. Quinn spread plastic sheeting on the ground and reconstructed the skeleton, labeling the bones while Gabe excavated the area beneath the grave, using a trowel and brush to sift for any artifacts that might have belonged to the deceased but had become embedded in the soil or stuck to the wood.

"Anything?" Quinn asked as she labeled the last bone and stood up, stretching her aching back.

Gabe shook his head. "Not a bloody thing. Not even a button or a strip of leather."

"Any evidence of a shroud?"

"Not that I can see, but it would have rotted away by now," Gabe replied. "This tree was probably no more than a seed when this person was buried. Any organic matter would have decomposed years ago."

"So, what would you say?" Quinn asked, taking in the girth of the tree stump. "About two hundred years?"

"At least."

"Any indication of how he died?" Rhys asked as he emerged from the house with steaming mugs of tea.

Quinn shook her head. "Nothing obvious. Some bones are cracked, but I would think that happened postmortem, once the roots began to spread. We'll have to wait for Colin's assessment."

"Rhys, when was this house built?" Gabe asked.

"The house was completed in 1727. It had been commissioned by Lester Lowell, whose descendants lived here until two years ago, when the last surviving scion of the original family passed away at the impressive age of one hundred and two. A cousin from Canada inherited the estate and promptly sold off everything, including every stick of furniture and heirloom that had been in the family for generations. No sense of history," Rhys scoffed, clearly disgusted by such blatant commercialism.

"Did you purchase any of the contents of the house?" Quinn asked, wondering if the person whose bones were about to be packed in a large rectangular box might have been a Lowell.

"No. Katya wouldn't want any of those moss-eaten sofas and dusty tapestries," Rhys replied with a grin. "She loves everything modern, my Katya."

"Can't say I blame her," Gabe said as he pulled off his gloves. "There's something to be said for surrounding yourself with modernity and comfort. I didn't want to keep any of the furnishings from my parents' home either. My mum took a few items that possessed sentimental value, but the rest went at auction."

Rhys laughed. "I've never been faced with the choice, being descended from dirt-poor Welsh farmers. Not everyone can trace their roots to the Conquest," he teased Gabe. "No antique cabinets or Aubusson carpets for us. Or medieval swords, for that matter."

"I don't know about you, but I'm ready for that curry now," Gabe said. "I'm starving."

"Me too," Quinn agreed. "I asked Nicola to order a pizza and watch a movie with the children before putting them to bed. She has no other plans tonight, so we needn't rush."

"Excellent. Would you like to get a takeaway or go into the village?"

Quinn looked down at her mud-stained jeans. "Let's do a takeaway. You place the order, and we'll finish up here and clean up a bit. It really is lovely here," she said, taking in her peaceful surroundings. "I can see why you fell in love with the place."

"Oh, it wasn't me," Rhys replied as he collected empty water bottles and sandwich wrappers. "Katya had dreams of living in the country. I'll take London over this any day."

"Too peaceful for you?" Gabe joked.

"Something like that," Rhys replied with a grin. "But, now that we've dug up a skeleton, things are looking up."

"Have you already pitched the Christmas special to the network?" Quinn asked, amused by Rhys's enthusiasm.

"Of course. They love the idea."

"What if this bloke was totally vanilla?" Quinn asked, borrowing one of her American father's turns of phrase. She loved American expressions. They were so—for lack of a better word—expressive.

"Have no fear. Vanilla can always be doctored until it's chock-full of nuts and bits of chocolate," Rhys replied. He always knew what made for good television.

"Now you two are making me even hungrier," Gabe said. "Rhys, grab some ice cream while you're picking up that takeaway."

"And a bottle of wine," Quinn added.

Rhys chuckled. "I have plenty of wine, and there's ice cream in the freezer, at least three different flavors, if I'm not mistaken."

"Compliments of Katya?" Quinn asked.

"She allows herself half a cup of ice cream every night," Rhys said with an indulgent smile. "And it has to be a different flavor every time."

Quinn laughed and nudged Gabe in the ribs. "And you thought I was high maintenance."

Chapter 3

On Monday morning, having dropped off the children at nursery school, Quinn presented herself at the mortuary, the box of bones in her hands. She and Gabe had discussed the skeleton at length on their way back to London on Saturday, coming up with possible stories for their nameless passenger, and were curious to see what the tests would show. Dr. Colin Scott came out to greet her, a warm smile lighting his handsome face.

"Quinn!" he exclaimed. "It is so good to see you."

"And you," Quinn replied as she followed Colin into his office. "It's been too long."

"I do miss working on your cases," Colin said. "The mystery added a little spice to my otherwise uneventful workdays. I hear there's to be a Christmas special."

"Yes. Rhys is quite excited about it."

"Are you?"

"A bit," Quinn admitted. "It's been a while since I got involved with a case. I do miss the practical side of archeology, but it'll be a while until Gabe and I can sign up for a dig."

Colin nodded. "How are Emma and Alex?"

"They're well. There is also Mia. She's going to be two this month."

"Congratulations," Colin said. "What's she like?"

"A handful," Quinn replied, smiling. "I didn't know Emma as a toddler, and Alex was such an easygoing baby that I wasn't quite prepared for the terrible twos, which, technically, have yet to begin. But what about you? You look well," she said as she settled herself in the visitor chair and set the box of bones on Colin's desk.

"I am to be married in June," Colin said.

"Congratulations! I'm so pleased for you. Who's the lucky lad?"

"His name is Adam, and he's a florist," Colin replied with a happy smile. "We met when I stopped in to order flowers for my mum's birthday."

"Have you a photo?"

Colin pulled his mobile out of a desk drawer and showed Quinn a picture of his intended. Adam had to be in his mid-forties, his broad face framed by an artfully trimmed beard and his soft brown eyes looking into the camera. Logan referred to stocky, bearded middle-aged gay men as teddy bears, and Adam certainly fit the bill. Although handsome in his own way, he was nothing at all like Logan, who, at thirty, still looked like a wild child and often acted like one.

"We are well suited," Colin said, sounding as if he were trying to convince himself. "Adam is ready to settle down."

"I'm happy for you, Colin. Truly," Quinn said.

"How's Logan?" Colin asked at last. "Is he still working at the London Hospital?"

"Logan is well. He transferred to A&E. He likes working the trauma cases. In fact, that's where he met his new partner. Rafe brought in his mate, who'd been stabbed during a mugging outside a club."

"Is it serious between them?" Colin asked. Quinn could see the pain in his eyes. Logan had hurt Colin badly, but it was clear to Quinn that Colin still carried a torch for Logan. She was glad he'd found the strength to move on and find happiness with Adam.

"Yes, it's serious," Quinn said. "They're expecting their first child in April. It's a boy," she added.

"Are they using a surrogate?"

"Yes, and a donor egg, but the baby is Logan's biologically. He's so excited," Quinn said, smiling at the memory of Logan's joy when he'd first seen his son on an ultrasound scan.

"I'm happy for him," Colin said. "That was what ultimately broke us up, you know," he said conversationally.

"Was it?" Quinn had assumed it was Logan's infidelity.

"Logan wanted children."

"And you didn't?"

Colin shook his head. "I like my life, Quinn. I have my job, my partner, my hobbies. I like to go out to nice restaurants and travel. Babies change all that, and frankly, I never felt the urge to be a dad. It's not for everyone. I had initially agreed to think about having a child, because it was so important to your brother, but ultimately, I couldn't get behind the idea. I simply wasn't ready for that kind of lifestyle change."

"I see. Well, you've made the right decision, then. For both of you."

Colin nodded. "Yes, I think things have worked out for the best for us both. And I hear Gabe is doing well," Colin said, changing the subject. "I read his book. Very insightful. It's almost as if he'd been a woman during the Wars of the Roses himself," Colin joked.

Or as close as he could get, Quinn thought, trying not to giggle.

"Now, tell me about this skelly," Colin invited.

Quinn filled him in on the details of Rhys's find. "Will Dr. Dhawan be working with you on this?" She hadn't seen Sarita Dhawan since they'd worked on the crucifixion case from Ireland and wanted to say hello.

"Sarita is long gone," Colin said. "She's a Home Office pathologist now. Works out of a lab in East London. It was your cases that steered her toward working homicide. I have a new assistant—Shannon McCardle. She's very competent," he added.

"I look forward to meeting her."

Colin stood and scooped up the box. "I'll ring you in a few days."

"Thanks, Colin. I hope you're able to glean something useful. There was nothing buried with the skeleton except a silver ring that the deceased must have been wearing at the time of death, so whatever information we obtain will have to come from the bones."

"I'll do my best."

Quinn left the mortuary and stepped outside into the mild March morning. Spring was in the air, and a few buds had already appeared on the birch trees near the exit. Quinn inhaled deeply, thinking she'd take the children to the playground after school. And then, once they went down for their nap, she'd spend some time with the ring found with the remains.

Chapter 4

October 1777
Long Island, Colony of New York

The morning was breezy and cool, bright sunshine flooding the kitchen as soon as the shutters had been opened. Ben gulped down a cup of milk and stepped outside, needing to see just how much damage last night's storm had wreaked. The gale had come out of nowhere, gaining in intensity and raging through the night, the tempest ripping through Long Island like some crazed giant who'd torn out trees and smashed outbuildings in his fury. The yard was littered with broken branches, and several felled trees lay on their sides across the fields. He'd chop them up and use them for firewood once the wood dried out.

"Ma?" Ben called out as he stepped into the dim interior of the barn.

"Here, son," Hannah Wilder called. "I'm just milking Tansy."

"Where's Derek?" Ben asked. The house had been empty when he woke, his brothers already gone.

"Derek's gone to the Blanchette farm."

"How much longer does she have to wear the splint?" Ben asked. Their closest neighbor, Barbara Blanchette had recently been widowed, and to make matters worse had taken a fall and broken her leg. Her three daughters, all under the age of twelve, did their best to help their mother, but some jobs were beyond them. Derek stopped by nearly every day to chop wood, help Mistress Blanchette up and down the stairs, and fetch any supplies the girls might need from town.

"A fortnight more, at least," Hannah said. "And once it comes off, she'll have to take it easy for a while. I feel for the poor woman. There's so much to do with winter just around the corner."

Ben nodded. "And Josh?"

"Ran down to the beach first thing this morning," Hannah said as she rose from the milking stool and lifted the pail of milk.

Josh loved to scour the beach after a storm, looking for beautiful seashells and anything else the sea may have decided to expel from the depths of its roiling cauldron. Unfortunately, Ben didn't have the luxury of strolling on the beach. The wind had torn at least a dozen shingles from the roof and wrenched off a shutter just outside his mother's window. A section of the chicken coop enclosure had been flattened, and there were broken branches and leaves in the well. He'd start with the chicken coop, then reattach the shutter and replace the shingles. Hannah would have to see to the well.

Ben had just positioned the ladder against the front of the house when he saw Josh running across the field, waving his arms like windmills.

"Ben!" he screamed. "Ben, you've got to come. Quick!"

"What is it? What's wrong?" Ben cried as he hurried toward Josh. At twelve, Josh was small for his age. His limbs were like birch twigs, white and narrow, and his face had an elfin quality, the ears just pointy enough to attract attention and make him the subject of endless teasing.

"There's been a shipwreck," Josh exclaimed, trying to catch his breath as he hunched over, hands on his knees. "There's stuff all over the beach." Josh pulled a watch from his pocket, dangling it in front of Ben's face. "That's solid gold, I reckon," he said, grinning impishly.

Ben reached for the watch and looked closer. The mechanism had stopped, due to exposure to water, no doubt, but the casing did look like gold. Was it wrong to take it? Ben turned the watch over, marveling at the fine craftsmanship.

"I'm keeping it," Josh said defiantly, and held out his hand for the watch.

Ben returned the watch to him. "Are there any survivors?" he asked.

Josh's mouth opened in shock. It hadn't even occurred to him that victims might wash up on the beach. He'd never seen a shipwreck, had never been part of the aftermath of a tragedy.

"I don't know," Josh muttered. "I haven't seen any."

Ben took off at a run, Josh trotting behind him.

"Wait!" Josh wailed. "I hardly had time to catch my breath."

"I'll meet you there," Ben called over his shoulder.

He got to the beach in record time. Several people were walking along slowly, hunched over as they peered down at the sand. Some already had bulging pockets, having found something of value, others still searching for something worth keeping. Ben felt a twinge of irritation. How quickly human beings turned to scavenging, lining their pockets with the possessions of the dead. He looked out over the Atlantic. It sparkled in the bright sunshine, the water a silvery blue, a mirror image of the clear sky. Seagulls screamed overhead and dived for fish as waves rolled onto the beach in the age-old rhythm of land and sea.

Ben squinted and shielded his eyes with his hand. A mast rose out of the water about a mile off the coast. His gaze followed the dark wood downward, his imagination supplying the rest. He could almost see the ship resting on the bottom, its hull smashed, its contents disgorged on the ocean floor. How many people had been aboard? How many had survived? Had any of them tried to get to shore, or had they thought they could ride out the storm and continue on their way? Where had the ship been going?

Leaving the scavengers behind, Ben walked along the beach. He wasn't looking for loot; he was looking for dark shapes in the water—sailors and passengers who'd been aboard the ill-fated vessel. He heard a cry behind him and turned just in time to see Tom and Rob Painter drag a limp shape onto the sand. Given their unhurried manner, he could only assume the person was dead.

Ben walked on, unsure where he was going. He wanted to help, but the thought of pulling bloated, lifeless bodies from the sea made him queasy. And there would be bodies. There had to be.

He saw something just up ahead and hurried over. It was a woman lying lifeless on the sand, her dark green skirts sodden, and her legs clad in bright yellow stockings. There was nothing he could do for her, so he left her where she was.

"Ben! Wait!" Josh called as he exploded onto the beach. He ran after Ben, his feet kicking up clouds of sand.

Ben stopped and waited until Josh caught up with him. The boy stared at the dead woman, his mouth opening and closing in shock as he inched past her.

"Is she—?" Josh whispered.

"Yes. Come away."

They walked on in silence. "We should go back," Ben said at last. "There's work to be done."

"Wait, not yet," Josh pleaded as he spotted something in the sand and dove for it. Josh turned the object over in his hands, looking to Ben for an explanation.

"I think it's some kind of navigational tool," Ben said, hoping he was correct.

"Didn't help them navigate through the storm," Josh pointed out.

"No, it didn't."

Josh's eyes widened in surprise, and he took off, darting into the dune with a strangled cry. "Ben! Quick!"

Ben followed his brother, his heart pounding when he realized that what he'd taken to be a bit of flotsam was in fact a leather-clad foot. Ben stopped next to Josh, who was staring down in awe. A young woman lay on the sand, partially hidden from view by scraggly grass. She wore a gown of apple-green wool, and her fair hair was spread about her head like a halo. Her eyes were closed, her skin nearly translucent, and her lips had a bluish tint, but Ben thought he saw movement beneath the pale lids and sank to his knees, reaching for her wrist. It was limp, and he couldn't locate a pulse. He let out the breath he'd been holding.

"I think she's gone, Josh."

Josh shook his head. "No. Try again. I think she's breathing."

Ben stared at her chest. Josh was right. It seemed to rise and fall ever so slightly. Ben pressed his hand against her neck. It was cold and clammy, but he did feel a faint pulse. He turned her onto her side and watched in horrified fascination as seawater poured from her mouth. He supposed that was a good sign, so he held her head until the stream became a trickle, then rolled her back onto her back, tore off his coat, and used it to cover the woman. He rubbed her hands to get the circulation going. "Josh, get Dr. Rosings," Ben added. "And be quick about it."

Josh took off running down the beach. The number of would-be rescuers had doubled in size since Ben had arrived on the scene, word of the shipwreck having spread through the town. He could now see several lifeless bodies laid out on the sand and was sure more were soon to follow. He bowed his head and said a prayer for the souls of the lost, asking God to spare the young woman before him. She was so lovely, and so young. Had the circumstances been different, she'd have so much living to do before her time came to an end. Ben sat down next to her and reached for her hand, leaving his thumb on the inside of her wrist. It reassured him to feel her pulse.

The woman's color had improved, and her pulse had grown stronger by the time Dr. Rosings came huffing and puffing toward them. He was an older man, his complexion ruddy and his hair nearly white but still as thick as that of a young man. His round spectacles slid down his narrow nose, which was slick with perspiration, and he nudged them back absentmindedly as he crouched next to the young woman and pushed aside Ben's coat.

He performed a brief examination, then turned to Ben. "She must be kept warm and dry. Help me get her to town."

"No!" Ben said, the refusal erupting before he had a chance to think it through. "We're taking her back to our house. We'll look after her."

Dr. Rosings looked surprised but didn't bother to argue. He had been widowed several years ago, and even though he had Carrie, his Negro servant, to look after him, he did not have anyone who could nurse the young woman properly.

"I'm sure your mother will take good care of her," Dr. Rosings said. "I'll come by later, after I've seen to the others." He was in no rush. The bodies laid out on the beach were not in urgent need of care.

Ben lifted the woman into his arms and cut across the beach, bypassing the townsfolk he'd known all his life. He was in no mood to answer any questions or have them gawk at her as if she were a curiosity. He felt strangely protective of her, and although he didn't consider himself a fanciful man—Derek always teased him that he sorely lacked imagination—Ben felt she would play a vital role in his life.

"Derek won't like it," Josh said as he walked alongside, trying to keep up with Ben's long strides.

"Derek doesn't have to look after her."

"Ma won't like it either," Josh continued. "It'll be extra work for her. You should have let Dr. Rosings take her. His servant could do whatever needs doing."

"Ma won't mind," Ben replied gruffly.

"It's because of Kira, isn't't?" Josh asked, nearly stopping Ben in his tracks.

Yes, it was, Ben admitted silently. Kira had fallen overboard when she and her younger brother had taken out their father's skiff without permission, just for a lark, not realizing a storm was brewing off the coast of Connecticut. Kira had drowned a few weeks before they were to be married, her remains carried out to sea, leaving her grief-stricken parents with no body to bury and a son whose guilt had nearly driven him mad. Ben's thumb went to the silver band on his finger. It was to have been Kira's wedding ring, but he still had it, the ring a constant reminder of his loss. He was only twenty-two, but he felt so much older, especially on a day like today, when he unexpectedly came face to face with the cruel randomness of death.

"It's for God to decide if she lives or dies," he said gruffly, "but if she does die, let it be in a clean bed surrounded by good people. No one should die alone."

Josh shrugged as if Ben's reasoning didn't really make much sense to him but didn't bother to disagree.

Chapter 5

"Goodness me! What's all this?" Hannah Wilder exclaimed when she saw her sons from the window and rushed out to meet them. "What's happened?"

"There's been a shipwreck, Ma," Josh exclaimed. "We found her on the beach. She's still alive."

"Well, let's get her inside, then. Take her to one of the attic bedrooms, Ben."

Ben carried the woman up the narrow stairs to the attic. There were two small bedrooms there, each with a sloped ceiling and a dormer window. They had once been intended for the children his parents were going to have, but two girls had died in infancy, and no babies came after Josh, whose birth had nearly killed Hannah. The bedrooms remained empty, used only when their uncle and his family had come to stay, but no one had visited since their father's death three years before.

Hannah pulled back the woolen blanket on the bed, then eyed the woman's dress. "Wait," she told Ben. "Set her down here." She pointed to the braided rug covering the wooden planks. "Now step outside," she instructed him.

"What for?"

"Her clothes are wet, and there's sand everywhere. Out with you," she said with mock severity.

Ben left the woman on the floor and stepped outside, closing the door behind him. Of course, his mother was right. She couldn't be put to bed in wet garments. When he was called back in, the woman was clad only in a cotton shift, her arms and legs bare. Ben tried not to stare, but the outline of her breasts was clearly visible through the thin fabric, and he could make out her nipples and a dark shadow between her legs.

"Quit gawping and lift her onto the bed," Hannah admonished him.

Ben lifted the woman and laid her down gently, standing back and watching as his mother brushed the woman's hair out of her face and covered her with the blanket.

"There now," she said softly. "You just rest now. Take all the time you need. You are welcome here."

"She can't hear you, Ma," Josh said. He'd come upstairs and was leaning against the doorjamb, watching his mother with a look of consternation on his face.

"And how do you know that?" Hannah asked. "You can hear things when you're asleep."

"No, you can't," Josh replied stubbornly.

"No? Just the other day, you told me that the wind and the sound of the rain woke you," Hannah reminded him. "Isn't that so?"

Josh rolled his eyes. "I suppose. Well, I hope she hears you and wakes up soon. I want to hear about the shipwreck."

"I doubt she'll want to talk about it. It must have been horrible," Hannah said as she ushered Ben and Josh out the door. "Poor thing. I can't begin to imagine what she must have been through."

Ben followed his mother downstairs and into the kitchen, where he sat at the table. He hadn't had his breakfast that morning and was now ravenous. Hannah set about frying bacon and eggs while Ben buttered a piece of bread and gulped down a glass of cold milk. Josh followed his example, grinning at his brother from across the table. He took out the watch and held it up by the chain, watching it swing slowly from side to side like a pendulum.

"Think it'll work once it dries out?" he asked.

"I don't know."

"What's that you got there?" Hannah asked, turning just in time to see a ray of sunshine reflect off the gold casing and send a beam of light onto the wall.

"I found it on the beach. It's made of gold," Josh gushed. "I want to keep it."

"Well, you can hold on to it for now," Hannah said, "but if there are more survivors, you might have to give it back. It may belong to one of them."

"Yes, Ma," Josh muttered.

Ben took another bite of bread. He didn't think there'd be any more survivors. Just the one.

Chapter 6

The sunlight streaming through the window seemed unbearably bright, forcing her to squeeze her eyes shut. Her temples were throbbing, the pain bringing tears to her eyes, and a dull ache seemed to radiate from the back of her skull, making it painful to lie on her back. She carefully turned onto her side, facing away from the window, and gingerly opened her eyes. She was in a small room in what appeared to be an attic. There was just the narrow bed, a three-legged stool in place of a bedside table, and a pine chest of drawers. An unlit candle stood on the stool, the holder made of pewter.

She reached out and touched the back of her head, instantly yanking her fingers away. She had a lump the size of an egg that was tender to the touch, the pain shooting into her head like a bolt of lightning. Her eyes felt gritty, and there was an odd taste in her mouth, like she'd eaten something very salty and hadn't washed it down with a drink, leaving her mouth and lips unbearably dry. She allowed her hand to trail downward, her fingers brushing the soft linen of the well-worn shift and resting on the thick wool blanket. Where was she?

Who was she? The question came unbidden but required an immediate answer, one she didn't seem to have. No name sprang to mind. No place of residence floated up from the murky depths of memory, and no faces of loved ones materialized before her eyes to offer comfort. She tried to pull up a memory, but her thoughts seemed to bounce off an impenetrable barrier, her questions unable to breach the brick wall her mind seemed to have erected.

"What's my name?" she whispered into the silence of the room, but no answer came. She wanted to call out, to summon whoever had brought her here, but she didn't know who they were or what they were called. She didn't even know if they were friend or foe. She wasn't sure why that thought had popped into her head, but it made her hesitate. Perhaps it wasn't a good idea to alert them that she was awake just yet. She had to try to remember as much as she could, but first, she had to remember herself. The very notion was absurd. How could she not remember her own name?

Forcing herself to concentrate, she mouthed a few names, hoping one of them would feel familiar, right, but they all sounded hollow and alien.

"Elizabeth, Mary, Abigail, Jane," she muttered. Nothing. No sense of recognition. "Anne, Amelia, Sally." Silent tears ran down her cheeks, sliding down her nose and dripping onto the embroidered pillowcase. She felt helpless and scared, but most of all completely adrift. At sea.

How had she come to be here, in this room? Had she undressed herself, or had someone taken the liberty of removing her clothes? Had they touched her? Violated her? Her body felt battered and bruised, but she didn't think it was from a beating. Her hair smelled briny, her eyes were irritated, her lips cracked and dry. She noticed a few grains of sand on the pillow. Where had they come from? Her hair? She lifted a hand and touched the tangled mess. Her hair was matted and damp, sand sprinkling the sheet as she pulled on a curl.

She must have been in the water. Seawater. But why? She shut her eyes and tried desperately to bring forth an image, but nothing came. Nothing at all. It was as if her life until that moment had been completely erased from her memory. She covered her face with her hands and wept silently into the sand-covered pillow.

Chapter 7

It must have been about an hour later that the door opened and a middle-aged woman stepped into the room, accompanied by an elderly man with bushy gray whiskers. They had been speaking softly but grew silent when they saw her watching them. The woman smiled brightly and came toward the bed.

"Praise the Lord," she said with great feeling, clasping her hands before her. "I'm so glad to see you awake. I'll leave you two to talk."

"Thank you," the man said, and approached the bed slowly. "Hello, my dear. My name is John Rosings. I'm a doctor, so you have nothing to fear from me." He had a kindly face and gentle manner, and she relaxed somewhat, hopeful that this man would be able to help her.

"May I sit down?" the doctor asked. "Oh, I do hope you speak English," he said. "Do you?"

She nodded. For some reason, she couldn't bring herself to speak.

"Good. Well, that's one hurdle out of the way. How do you feel?" he asked.

Terrified, battered, nauseated, lost, she wanted to scream. "My head aches." Her voice sounded hoarse, and her throat felt like sandpaper.

"Well, let's have a look, then." He reached out and very carefully examined her skull, his cool fingers settling on the throbbing bruise at the back of her head. She let out an involuntary gasp as he pressed a little harder. "I'm sorry for that," he said, and removed his hands. He then pulled up her eyelids and stared deep into her eyes. "You must have sustained a severe blow," he said, watching her. "Do you remember being struck?"

She tried to shake her head, but instantly regretted it as arrows of pain shot into her temples. "No," she whispered.

"What about your name?" he asked softly as he used a bell-shaped tube to listen to her chest. "Can you tell me your name?"

"I don't know it," she replied tearfully. "I can't remember my name. I can't remember anything!" she cried, her desperation mounting. "How did I get here?"

The doctor reached out and took her hand, patting it in a paternal manner. "There was a terrible storm last night. A ship was wrecked just off the coast. You washed up on the beach."

She drew a complete blank. She had no recollection of being on a ship or of the terrible events the doctor was describing. Surely, she'd be able to remember a shipwreck. One didn't easily forget something like that.

"Are there any other survivors?" she asked hopefully.

"We haven't located any yet," the doctor replied softly. "But there are people scouring the beach even as we speak."

She glanced toward the window, wincing at the light. The doctor had said the storm had happened last night. The sun was high in the sky, so it had to be close to noon. If they hadn't found any other survivors by now...

"Everyone must have drowned," she said under her breath, blown away by the scope of the tragedy. Her shoulders sagged in defeat as all hope drained away. She had survived, but she couldn't recall the most basic of facts. Yet she remembered how to speak, she thought desperately, and understood the ramifications of a ship going down in a storm. How was it possible to remember some things and forget others so completely, especially anything that pertained to her own life?

"Why can't I remember anything?" she asked desperately.

Dr. Rosings' gaze was warm with sympathy. "I have no first-hand experience of memory loss, but the body and the mind are surprisingly resilient. You've suffered a blow to the head and a near drowning. Perhaps your mind is dealing with the trauma by blocking out painful and frightening memories. After a period of rest, I think your memories will begin to return. All you need to know right now is that you are safe and there are people who want to help you."

"What people?" she asked, needing to know their names and something of who they were.

"Ben and Joshua Wilder were the ones who found you this morning. They brought you to their house. Their mother, Hannah Wilder, is a kind, God-fearing woman. She has volunteered to look after you until you recover."

"That's very kind of them. Where am I, exactly?"

"You are in the town of Milford on Long Island. Does the name mean anything to you?"

"No."

"What about New York City?" the doctor asked.

"Yes, I recall the name, but have no memory of being there," she replied.

"Not to worry. Recalling the name is great progress in itself, in my professional opinion," he said, smiling at her. "I will come back to see you tomorrow to check how you're getting on. In the meantime, I suggest we give you a name. Is there a name you particularly like?"

She shrugged. "Nothing comes to mind."

"How about Alice? I've always liked that name."

"All right," she agreed hesitantly. The name didn't feel right. It was like putting on someone else's shoes that were too small and pinched one's feet, but the doctor meant well, and Alice was as good a name as any.

"Very well, then, Alice," Dr. Rosings said, rising to his feet. "Small meals, bed rest, and quiet."

"Yes, Doctor," Alice replied, and watched him leave.

Desolation swept over her once again as soon as the doctor left. She closed her eyes and willed herself to rest, as he'd instructed, but her mind refused to comply. Her mind spun like a top, thoughts forming and splintering, and dissolving without making any sense. If she closed her eyes, bright colors formed behind her eyelids, overwhelming her with their strange hues. She felt frantic, her frustration at not being able to quiet her mind mounting until she thought she would scream with desperation.

It was then that her rescuer came.

Chapter 8

March 2018
London

Quinn set the ring aside when she heard a little voice over the child monitor.

"Mum? Mama?"

Mia was awake. Quinn sighed regretfully, wishing she could have spent a few more minutes in the past. Being able to see two people's memories from one artifact was very rare. It only happened when the artifact had belonged to both people, but the ring had been on Ben's finger, and he'd just met Alice. Or had he? Quinn looked forward to finding out, but Ben and Alice would have to wait.

Mia was sitting up in her cot, her dark gaze anxious, when Quinn walked through the door. Alex was still asleep, his mouth slightly opened and his hand clutching a toy car.

"Come on, my girl," Quinn said as she lifted Mia into her arms. The little girl wrapped her arms around Quinn's neck and rested her head on her shoulder, her body solid and warm in Quinn's arms. "Did you have a nice nap?"

Mia nodded into Quinn's neck. "I'm hungry."

"Let's get you a snack, then. What would you like? How about an apple?"

Mia looked up, her feathery eyebrows knitting in displeasure. "Biscuit. No, three biscuits," she quickly amended. For someone who was just beginning to speak in complete sentences, she was very good at negotiating.

"Two biscuits and two apple slices," Quinn said, her voice firm.

"Okay," Mia muttered. Quinn was sure Mia would eat the biscuits first and then just nibble on the apple. She wasn't a big fan of fruit and veg.

Having had her snack, Mia ran off to the lounge in search of her favorite toy, a pink Barbie computer that Seth had sent her last month. Quinn was partly amused and partly annoyed by the number of parcels that showed up on her front step. The grandparents made up for not being able to see the children regularly by sending toys, outfits, and books, despite Quinn's pleas to not spoil them so. Quinn did like the educational toys, though. The Barbie computer was for a child of at least three years old, but Mia had figured out how to work the toy in a matter of minutes.

Quinn settled on the sofa and watched her daughter at play. She really was amazed by Mia's progress these last few months. Alex hadn't begun to construct proper sentences until he was closer to three and hadn't been interested in pretend play unless it was rolling cars on the carpet and making *vroom-vroom* noises, but some people said girls developed faster at this age. That was certainly evident in Jill's daughter Olivia, who seemed to have come out of the womb as a tween.

As if reading her mind, Mia looked up. "I want to play with Olivia," she said imperiously. She was a right little madam sometimes, Quinn thought, a smile tugging at her lips as she looked at her daughter's impatient little face. "Today," Mia stated.

"Sorry, darling, but you'll have to wait until Saturday. Olivia's mum works, so Olivia can only have playdates on weekends."

"What day is today?" Mia demanded.

"Monday."

Mia shrugged and went back to the computer, Olivia momentarily forgotten. Quinn reached for the plastic bag containing the ring and examined it more closely. She had cleaned it very carefully, using mild soap and bits of cotton to clean away the grime. The band was wide, made of solid silver and etched with a pattern that resembled a woven braid. The ring would have been too big for Alice's delicate fingers. Had she ever worn it? Quinn wondered as she turned the bag over in her hand.

Based on her brief foray into the past, Quinn thought Gabe had been right when he'd said the skeleton was about two hundred years old, give or take a few decades. Judging by the fashions and implements Quinn had seen in the Wilder household, it had to be sometime in the eighteenth century, possibly around the time of the Revolutionary War. She hadn't had much interest in American history before meeting her biological father, but having witnessed the events that had led to the death of Madeline Besson just before the American Civil War, Quinn had decided to make more of an effort to learn about her father's country's history. She found that she enjoyed it, all the more so after she'd visited the newly formed colony of Virginia through the eyes of Mary Wilby, who'd been one of the first Englishwomen to set foot in the New World.

Might Alice have been British? The American accent had evolved over the centuries, but in the 1700s, the two accents would have still been virtually indistinguishable from each other. If Alice had, in fact, come from England, that might explain how the ring came to be in Hertfordshire. It stood to reason that the skeleton now occupying one of Colin's slabs was Ben Wilder, but Quinn wasn't about to take anything for granted. She was just at the beginning of this story, and she knew from experience that she should avoid drawing hasty conclusions.

Chapter 9

"Did you see Colin today?" Gabe asked once the children were in bed and he and Quinn had settled in for their nightly chat.

Quinn leaned against the armrest of the sofa, her legs outstretched, her calves resting on Gabe's thighs. "Yes. He's getting married soon. He seems happy."

"Good for him," Gabe said. He took a sip of his beer, looking thoughtful. "Did he ask about Logan?"

Quinn nodded. "I think he still misses him."

"Do you think Logan ever regrets the way things ended?" Gabe asked.

"I'm not sure. He never talks about it. He's all about the coming baby right now," Quinn said.

Gabe didn't say anything, which was telling in itself. He tried to follow the old adage, *If you have nothing good to say, don't say anything at all.*

"What?" Quinn asked. They didn't often discuss Logan's domestic situation, but she could see Gabe's reservations.

"It's not for me to judge. I certainly hadn't been ready for fatherhood, but it's an odd situation, don't you think?"

"How so?"

"Well, Rafe seems to be in denial about the whole impending fatherhood thing, which is not an easy thing to do given that the surrogate is living with them. What happens once the baby is born? Will she simply pack her bags and leave? And are Logan and Rafe prepared for the changes that will need to take place once they have a newborn?"

Quinn shrugged. "I have no idea. Logan hasn't really outlined their plan, and it doesn't seem right to ask. I'm sure Sylvia will help them out. Perhaps she'll even move in for the first few weeks."

"She had better. There needs to be at least one adult in that household," Gabe remarked.

"Gabe, that's unkind."

"The truth is rarely kind," Gabe replied. "You did ask. So, what did Colin say about the skelly?" he asked, clearly ready to change the subject.

"Not much. He'll ring me in a few days. And how was your day?"

Gabe shrugged. "The usual. Staff meeting, followed by a lecture hall full of students who'd rather watch videos on their mobiles, several complaints from staff that the ladies' bathroom had run out of toilet rolls, then a heated argument in the teachers' lounge that almost ended in blows."

"Oh dear," Quinn said, trying to hide her smile. "What did they argue about?"

"An article that appeared in the new issue of *Archaeology Today* about the black sarcophagus that was discovered in the Valley of the Kings. I never did figure out what the issue was. They were screaming and swearing so much, I couldn't make out a word of the actual argument."

"What did you do? Put them in timeout?" she joked.

"Basically. I banished them to their respective classrooms to cool down." Gabe's sigh sounded like a deflating balloon. "I've just about had it, Quinn. I was elated when I was offered the position of department head, but I feel like all I do is try to keep a bunch of rowdy children from pummeling each other on the playground."

"And then you come home and try to keep a bunch of rowdy children from pummeling each other in the lounge."

Gabe laughed. "I can honestly say that our children are more mature and better behaved than most middle-aged archeologists."

"They are certainly cuter," Quinn said. "And speaking of children, Mia's birthday is coming up next month."

"I hope you don't mind, but my mum wants to come down for a few days."

"Of course, I don't mind. Why would I? She can stay here with us," Quinn suggested, but knew Phoebe would refuse. She preferred to stay in a hotel, where no one woke up crying during the night or argued loudly about what to wear to school in the morning. Phoebe had trouble sleeping and often slept well into the morning to make up for the time she'd lost during the night.

"She'll stay in a hotel," Gabe said predictably. "She misses the children, though, and she's been so lonely since my dad passed away."

"I can certainly understand that," Quinn said. "Getting old isn't for the faint of heart."

"No," Gabe agreed. "It isn't, but there's actually some good news. My mum's sister, Flora, is thinking of selling up and moving into Mum's community. That would be ideal. They bicker like an old married couple, but they love each other to bits, and it would be nice for them to be so close to each other."

"You mum must be thrilled," Quinn said.

"Let's just say she's cautiously optimistic. Flora can still change her mind."

"Why would she?"

"Seems there's a gentleman friend that has arrived on the scene," Gabe said, smiling. "Flora is smitten."

"How sweet. How would you feel about your mum finding herself a boyfriend?" Quinn asked. Phoebe had been resolutely alone since Gabe's father had died, but as Gabe had said, she was lonely.

"I'd be thrilled. I hate that she's all alone, but she'll never consider moving down to London to be closer to us. She wants to remain close to my dad, so that she can visit the memorial park. She goes every week. But getting back to Mia. What do you think she'd like to do for her birthday?"

"If the weather is good, maybe we can go to the zoo and then have a little party for her at the house. We can invite Jill, Brian, and Olivia, and Rhys, Katya, and Vanessa. And I'm sure Sylvia would like to come. And Logan and Rafe, of course."

"Sounds great. Okay, I'm off to bed," Gabe said. "You coming?" he drawled, giving her a look that would melt an iceberg.

"I am," Quinn replied softly, and wrapped her arms around his neck as he lifted her off the sofa and captured her lips in a kiss.

Later, once Gabe had fallen asleep, Quinn reached for the plastic bag on the nightstand. She usually fell asleep before her head hit the pillow, especially after making love, but tonight she felt strangely awake, her mind eager to learn more about Alice. She felt the familiar fog descend on her as an image of the Wilders' farm replaced the shadows of the bedroom.

Chapter 10

"Hello. I'm Ben."

He wasn't classically handsome. His nose was a trifle too long and his eyes deep-set and slanted above sharp cheekbones. He was a big man, tall and broad, and his hands, which hung limply at his sides, were large and capable, the hands of a working man, the hands that had touched her and lifted her off the ground when she had been half dead. He grinned shyly, and Alice knew it to be a genuine smile, one that reached the eyes and made them glow with warmth.

"You were the one who found me," Alice said. She hadn't realized she was smiling, but the bewilderment she'd felt since waking receded, replaced by curiosity about this man who'd cared enough to bring her into his home and offer her shelter. "I've been christened Alice by Dr. Rosings," she added, trying to make light of a situation that left her trembling with fear.

"I heard. It's a lovely name," he added. "How are you feeling?"

"Sick to my stomach," she replied, focusing on the physical discomfort instead of the panic she was trying desperately to keep at bay. Hannah had offered to bring her some soup, but she couldn't imagine eating anything. Not yet.

"I expect you'll feel that way for a while. You probably swallowed a lot of seawater. Is there anything you need?"

Just someone to talk to, Alice thought, but she didn't want to put him out. He probably had things to do. She couldn't help noticing the calluses on his hands. A farmer, she guessed, or maybe a carpenter.

"I could bring you a book," he offered. "Do you like to read?"

"I don't know," she answered truthfully. "I don't know anything about myself," she said in a small voice.

"Just think how exciting it will be to discover everything anew."

"Will it? I suppose that's one way of looking at it."

He smiled again, a slow, warm smile that made her feel marginally less scared. "You survived. That's all that matters."

She tried to keep the tears at bay. Yes, she had survived, but what was she meant to do now? Where was she to go once she was strong enough to leave in a few days?

Ben shifted from foot to foot, watching her as if he could read her mind. "We'll figure out who you are. I promise," he said.

Alice nodded, unable to speak. How could he make such a promise? But it didn't matter. Just knowing that he was willing to help her made her less afraid.

"Thank you," she said, gazing into his dark-green eyes. "Thank you for helping me, Ben."

"It's my pleasure," he said, his gaze warm on hers. "I'll come back to check on you later."

Alice watched him leave, her initial gratitude replaced by wariness. There had been obvious male interest in Ben's gaze, but there had also been something else. If she had to put a name to it, she'd say he'd looked at her in a proprietary way.

Chapter 11

"Why did you bring her here?" Derek demanded, his eyes dark with anger. He'd finally returned in time for supper, having spent several hours making repairs to Widow Blanchette's roof and helping her girls put the place back to rights after the storm, and then heading down to the beach to help the townspeople who were still hauling the dead out of the sea. Josh had told him about Alice as soon as Derek walked in, stopping him in his tracks. If Ben knew his brother, he hadn't worked himself up into a fury because Ben had offered shelter to Alice, but because he hadn't been consulted, a respect due him as the head of the household.

"Because she needed help," Ben snapped. "Was I supposed to leave her to die?"

"I didn't say that," Derek countered. "Dr. Rosings would have taken her, or Mercy Greaves. She's all alone in that big house since her husband passed, and she has experience nursing the sick."

"And what's wrong with us?" Ben asked, his voice low and angry.

"There's nothing wrong with us, Ben, but did you ask Ma how she feels about this added responsibility? It's not as if you or I are going to be nursing this woman. Ma's got enough to do, especially with me not here half the time."

"Well, maybe you shouldn't spend so much time at Barbara Blanchette's house," Ben countered. He knew he was being unfair, since Hannah had been the one to ask Derek to help their neighbor in her hour of need, but he couldn't help lashing out. Derek was always so righteous.

"What are you suggesting?" Derek demanded, his voice dangerously low.

"She is an attractive woman and has a good-sized farm."

"I *have* a farm," Derek snapped. "Maybe you should start going over there, given that you're looking for a place to call your own."

Ben would have decked him had their mother not come between them. "Stop arguing this instant," she said, looking from one son to the other. "I don't mind looking after Alice. My heart goes out to her. She is so frightened, the poor girl. I'm sure her people will come looking for her."

"And if they don't?" Derek asked, but the anger had left his voice. He was resigned to the situation. "How would they even know to look here?"

"Magistrate Tate will send word to New York, and they can print an account of the shipwreck in the papers. Now, sit down. Supper is getting cold."

"Ma," Derek began patiently as he took his seat at the head of the table, "we don't know the name of the ship, where it was going, or where it came from. There are seventeen bodies laid out in the church, but no other survivors. It would be a very short account," he pointed out.

"Once Alice recovers her memory, she'll tell us what she knows," Hannah replied patiently.

"And if she doesn't?"

"And if she doesn't, we will treat her as part of our family," Hannah said. "I'm still mistress of this house, Derek, and I will decide what happens here. I have raised you to be kind and charitable, and I would ask you to respect me in this." Hannah had spoken quietly, but her tone brooked no argument, and Derek had the decency to look shamefaced.

"Yes, Ma. I'm sorry," he muttered. "I will go up and introduce myself tomorrow morning, and I'll ask Lydia if she might have some castoff gowns she'd like to donate to our guest."

"Any excuse to see Lydia," Ben needled him. Lydia Blackwell was the daughter of Harold Blackwell, the owner of the Blackwell Arms. They all knew Derek was sweet on her, but the courtship that seemed to have blossomed over the summer had stalled of late. Ben didn't think it was because Derek had lost interest, so perhaps Lydia had experienced a sudden change of heart.

"So, now you think I'm courting both Barbara Blanchette and Lydia Blackwell?" Derek asked, glaring at Ben.

"Barbara is newly widowed, Ben, and in need of our help. Your insinuations are untrue and unkind," Hannah said archly. "And as for Lydia, she'll come around, Derek. Just give her a bit of time."

"Time to do what?" Josh piped in. "Find herself an officer?"

Everyone turned to Josh. "What are you talking about, Josh?" Derek asked.

"I saw her walking in the woods with Lieutenant Reynolds yesterday. She seemed to be really enjoying his company," Josh said, grinning and wiggling his eyebrows.

"And how would you know that?" Hannah demanded, glaring at her youngest.

"Because I saw them kiss," Josh announced triumphantly.

Derek's hand froze as he reached for the bowl of mashed potatoes. "He kissed her?" he asked incredulously.

"Right. That's enough of that, young man," Hannah chided him. "Eat your supper. I'm sure you misunderstood what you saw."

"I doubt it," Josh muttered under his breath. "Pass the mash, Derek."

"I do hope Lydia has something to spare. I'll ask Mercy Greaves tomorrow, as well. I'd lend Alice one of my gowns, but she's taller and thinner than I am."

"I'm sure we'll find something for her to wear," Ben said, eager to steer the conversation away from Alice. "Seventeen bodies, you say?" he asked Derek. "You think there will be more?"

"Hard to say. It's possible, I suppose."

"Derek, was there nothing on the victims to indicate who they were?" Hannah asked, her expression sorrowful.

"Just the clothes they'd been wearing at the time of the storm," Derek replied. "Several appear to be sailors, and the others looked prosperous enough, but they could have been anyone, from anywhere."

"Were there any women or children?" Hannah asked, her voice cracking with distress.

"There were two women," Derek replied. "Both of middle years. No children, thank God."

"One of those women may have been traveling with Alice," Hannah pointed out. "They might have been her mother, or mother-in-law, or even her servant."

Derek raised an eyebrow at that. "What makes you think she had a servant?"

"Oh, I don't know," Hannah replied. "It was just a thought."

"Was she wearing a fine gown? Silk stockings? Jewelry?" Derek inquired, his interest piqued. Hannah paused in thought for a moment.

"Mother?" Ben asked. "Did you notice the quality of her clothes?" He hadn't paid much attention to what Alice had been wearing, his only objective to get her warm and dry as soon as possible.

"I soaked the gown and stockings in cold water to get the salt and the smell out," Hannah said. "The stockings are plain cotton but good as new. They'd never been darned. And the gown is of fine wool, the color not yet faded. She wasn't wearing any jewels when I undressed her, except for a silver chain with a small cross," she added as an afterthought.

"No wedding ring?" Derek asked.

"No, but I suppose it might have slipped off when she went in the water."

"The other women still had theirs," Derek pointed out.

"I certainly hope no one has helped themselves to any of their valuables," Hannah said. "I wouldn't put it past some to steal from the dead." Josh chose this moment to apply himself to his food, hoping his mother wouldn't bring up thewatch he found on the beach.

"No, of course not," Derek rushed to assure her. "They will be buried with whatever they had on them at the time of their death. They will be given every respect. Mr. Tate has asked that everyone attend the funeral, as a mark of respect."

"When is it to be?" Hannah asked.

"Tomorrow. They've already started digging the graves," he added.

"Will they have individual graves for them?" Hannah asked. Seventeen graves made for a lot of digging.

"There will be three mass graves," Derek replied. "With markers."

Hannah nodded, her eyes filling with tears. "How sad to be buried in a strange place, with not even a name to put on a marker. The families of these people will never know what became of their loved ones."

"Ships are lost at sea all the time," Derek said. He pushed away his plate. He'd hardly eaten anything, Ben noticed, which was unusual. Maybe his pragmatic, stoic brother had been more affected by the disaster than he was letting on.

"Has Alice eaten anything?" Ben asked.

"I took up a bowl of broth and some bread," Hannah replied. "Dr. Rosings said she was to eat lightly for the next few days. She managed some broth and a few bites of bread, but then she began to feel ill."

"Did she puke?" Josh inquired, his face alight with curiosity.

"No, she didn't," Hannah answered him. "But she was tired, so I let her sleep. I left the bread and a cup of water, should she wake in the night."

"I do wonder who she is," Derek said. "Imagine not being able to remember anything about your life, not even your name."

"She's very fragile," Hannah said. "Be mindful of her feelings, boys."

"Yes, Ma," they answered in unison.

Chapter 12

Alice woke to find sunlight streaming through the dormer window, bathing the small room in golden light. She suddenly realized that she didn't even know what month is was, much less what day. She'd lain awake long into the night, struggling to recall something of her life, but after hours of frustration had finally succumbed to sleep. She did feel marginally better. Her head still hurt, and her stomach roiled as if she were standing on the deck of a ship, but she felt a little stronger. A wave of dizziness assailed her when she tried to get up to use the pot, her legs folding beneath her as if they were made of straw.

"Come on," she said through gritted teeth. "You can do this." She couldn't bear the humiliation of having to call someone to help her, so she sat back down, waited for the dizziness to pass, then tried again. She even managed to wash her face and hands in the basin Hannah had left for her on the chest of drawers.

Climbing back into bed, she stared at the patch of sky visible through the narrow windowpanes. So blue. So clear. Had the sky been clear and blue the day she'd boarded the ill-fated ship? Where had she been going? she asked herself for the hundredth time. Alice turned her face toward the door when she heard footsteps. There was a light knock, followed by Hannah.

"Good morning. How are you feeling today?" Hannah asked brightly.

"Better," Alice assured her, her gaze fixed on the man who'd followed Hannah into the room, a wooden tray in his hands. Alice sat up, wondering who he was. He was clearly related to Ben and Josh, who'd peeked through the open door but hadn't come to speak to her. The man's hair, a deeper brown than Ben and Josh's sandy hue, was pulled back and secured with a black ribbon, and his eyes were a darker green. In fact, he was a taller, leaner version of Ben. He also appeared to be a few years older. Alice put him at around twenty-five.

"Hello," he said, giving her a respectful bow, the tray still in his hands. Alice couldn't help noticing the glimmer of curiosity in his gaze. He was as intrigued by her as she was by him. "I'm Derek Wilder."

"My eldest," Hannah supplied.

"Alice." The name felt wrong on her tongue, so wrong, in fact, that she almost preferred not to be called anything at all.

"I'm glad to see you feeling better this morning," Derek said.

"Thank you."

"There's porridge, bread, and a cup of warm milk. I hope you feel up to some breakfast," Hannah said.

"You're very kind," Alice replied. She was surprisingly hungry, and the promise of something hot in her belly made her mouth water.

"Can you manage on your own?" Derek asked as he carefully set the tray in her lap. Sunlight glinted off the silver ring on his finger. It looked just like the one worn by Ben.

Why? Are you offering to feed me? Alice bit her tongue as the flirtatious words nearly spilled from her unbidden. "Yes, thank you," she said instead.

He smiled into her eyes, his gaze strangely intimate and uncomfortably familiar, then took a step back, taking up a position behind his mother, the warmth of a moment ago replaced by silent watchfulness.

Mother and son watched her as she took a sip of milk followed by a spoonful of porridge. It was good, flavored with butter and maple syrup and bits of apple. She felt strange eating as they looked on, as if she were some sort of entertainment, but continued to bring the spoon to her mouth until the bowl was empty.

"That was delicious," she said truthfully.

"I'm glad you liked it," Hannah replied. She seemed genuinely pleased. "I've washed out your things. There's a stiff breeze today, so they should dry quickly."

She was about to say something else when a bell tolled in the distance, then again. "Is it Sunday?" Alice asked.

"It's Wednesday," Derek Wilder replied quietly.

"So, why are they ringing the bell?"

"There's to be a funeral today, for the victims of the wreck," he replied, his gaze never leaving her face.

"No!" Alice cried. "I must be there. I need to see—" The words died on her lips. It sounded morbid to say she needed to see their faces before they were lost to her forever, but this was her last chance. "Please, I need to see them," she pleaded.

"My dear, it would be too distressing for you," Hannah said, but Derek nodded in agreement.

"I think she should see them, Ma. I will escort Alice to the funeral. It is to be held at eleven o'clock. Can you find something for our guest to wear?" he asked.

"Of course. And I will help you with your hair. Don't worry, I will be very gentle," Hannah promised, noting the look of alarm on Alice's face.

"I'll tell Josh to take a message to Reverend Paulson, asking him to leave the faces of the dead uncovered until Alice has had a chance to say goodbye," Derek said. "We'll go to the church early so you can view them privately."

"Thank you," Alice said, grateful for his understanding.

She had to see if she recognized any of the victims. Perhaps seeing a familiar face would jolt her awareness, be that stray thread that would unravel memories that had taken a lifetime to knit.

"It'll be all right," Derek said softly once Hannah had left with the tray. He was looking at her intently, almost as if trying to work something out. Perhaps he was wondering why she had been the one to survive, or how long she meant to stay.

"Derek," Hannah called from downstairs.

Derek looked like he was about to say something but seemed to change his mind and left without another word.

Chapter 13

The gown Hannah had brought was several inches short and too large in the bosom, even with the laces pulled tight, but it was dry and sufficiently somber. Hannah had given her a starched cap to cover her freshly washed hair and a woolen shawl to ward off the chill of the October morning. The shoes and hose were her own, since they'd had sufficient time to dry.

October is such a beautiful month, Alice thought as Derek handed her into the trap. The trees were crimson and gold against the backdrop of aquamarine sky, the air fresh and crisp, the field they passed dotted with dozens of fat-bellied pumpkins. The bell tolled again in the distance, and Alice dragged her mind back to the task at hand. She didn't care to admit it to Derek, but she was frightened. She must have seen corpses before, most people had, but these were victims of drowning. She could so easily have been among them. Had Ben and Josh not found her in time, she might have died there on that beach, just slipped away without ever regaining consciousness. Gooseflesh broke out on her arms, fingers of fear stroking her spine.

"Are you all right?" Derek asked, glancing sideways at her. "You've gone pale."

"I'm fine."

"You don't have to do this," he said. "I know you think seeing their faces will help you remember, but if it doesn't, the only thing you'll be left with is a memory of seventeen bloated corpses." Alice winced, and he looked instantly contrite. "I'm sorry. That was thoughtless of me."

"It's all right," Alice assured him. "You've simply spoken the truth. Even if I do recognize someone, I'll still be left with a memory I'd sooner forget. There's no escaping it."

"I will be right there by your side. You can lean on me," he said, giving her a reassuring smile as the town of Milford came into view.

Town was too grand a name for what lay ahead. There were about two dozen clapboard buildings, some lining a wide street, others set further back. The church, with its tall spire, was easily recognizable, as was the tavern that bore a green and gold sign proclaiming it to be the Blackwell Arms. There was an official-looking building at the end of the street that might have been the town hall. The rest were small shops and private residences. Most had yards enclosed by picket fences, complete with outbuildings and neat vegetable patches.

The people all seemed to be going about their business, women hanging out laundry, two men unloading casks from a wagon parked in front of the tavern, and children playing a game of ball and hoop on a patch of grass near the town hall. Several people were already heading toward the church, and they nodded and tipped their hats to her, as if she were some visiting dignitary rather than a woman spit out by the sea before it had a chance to claim her soul. She nodded back but didn't make eye contact with anyone, except for an auburn-haired young woman who stared at her openly, her face tight with displeasure.

Alice turned to Derek in her confusion but, when she saw the look of dismay he bestowed on the woman, thought she understood. This woman had a claim on Derek Wilder. He should have been escorting her, not some stranger who was now living in his home. Alice tried to smile, to let the woman know that Derek was simply being gentlemanly, but the woman bristled like a cat, probably mistaking Alice's smile of apology for one of smugness.

"Don't worry about her," Derek said softly, a note of pride in his voice. He clearly liked that the auburn-haired beauty was jealous. Her passionate reaction was firewood for the pyre of his ego.

"I didn't mean to—" Alice began, but couldn't finish the sentence. She had nothing to apologize for. She was going to church to see people who'd been alive a mere day ago. People she must have met, spoken to, even laughed with. She wasn't here to steal anyone's admirer, or intended, if that was what Derek was to that woman. She had no interest in him. The only person she was interested in right now was herself. She was like a porcelain doll, pretty on the outside but completely hollow on the inside, devoid of thoughts or feelings outside of fear and confusion. She wasn't a threat to anyone, only to herself.

Derek drove up to the church and stopped in the wide rectangle reserved for the carts and wagons of the parishioners who lived too far to walk, then helped Alice down and offered her his arm, in case her steps should falter. The reverend was standing outside. He was a tall, thin man with a balding pate and soulful dark eyes. He appeared to be waiting for them.

"I'm very sorry," he said softly, his sympathy nearly bringing Alice to tears. "Go on in. I will make sure you are not disturbed."

"Thank you," Alice muttered.

Now that the moment was upon her, all she wanted was to leave. Her heart was pounding with terror, her hands were ice-cold, and she felt faint, but she forced herself to walk into the church and headed up the nave toward the row of bodies laid out before the pulpit. The bodies were tightly wrapped in coarse shrouds, making them look like giant maggots. Alice supposed a town the size of Milford had only one carpenter, who couldn't possibly make seventeen coffins on such short notice. Linen was easier to come by, and the dead would take up less room in the graves they were to share. These people might not have known each other well in life, but they would lie together for eternity in a place no one would ever think to look for them.

Alice cautiously drew closer. The fabric was parted just enough to reveal the features and hair color of the victims. She felt ill, and a tightness in her chest made it difficult to draw breath. Derek wrapped his arm about her waist, offering silent support, and she leaned against him, afraid her knees might buckle.

"Do you wish to leave?" he asked softly.

"No."

"Then how about you sit down for a moment?" he offered.

"No."

"All right, then." He led her slowly along the row of corpses, allowing her to stand silently in front of each body for a number of seconds before moving on. It took no more than five minutes to reach the end of the line, but it felt like five hours, each face burning into Alice's brain, their features familiar yet completely foreign at the same time.

"Do you recognize anyone?" Derek asked as he escorted her to a pew and sat down next to her.

She was breathing raggedly, trying to keep the nausea at bay, but it seemed to roll over her, like the crushing waves that had sunk the ship. She shook her head. These people were strangers to her. She'd stood longest before the women, trying desperately to remember their faces. The women on the ship likely would have spoken, banded together in the company of men, but they were as unknown to her as the rest. There had to have been others who hadn't washed ashore. Or maybe they'd washed up somewhere further down the coast. Maybe someone had survived and was out there even now, telling their story, naming the ship, sending a message to someone who'd spread the news.

Would someone come for her if they knew where she was? Did she have parents? Siblings? A family of her own? She didn't even know how old she was. She'd seen her reflection in the hand mirror Hannah had lent her. She was pretty, she supposed, except for that haunted look in her eyes. And young. Twenty? Twenty-two? She was old enough to be someone's wife, even someone's mother. Did she have children out there somewhere? A husband who'd be grieving for her? Alice stole a peek at her left hand. She wore no wedding ring, but that didn't mean anything. She might have lost it, or someone could have slid it off her finger. Perhaps they'd found her first and helped themselves to the one thing of value.

Two women hurried into the church and approached the row of bodies, carefully covering their faces before the mourners came inside. *They must have prepared the dead*, Alice thought, watching the no-nonsense way the women handled the deceased.

"Alice, are you all right?" Ben asked as he sat down heavily next to her. Hannah and Josh slid in next to him, the pew now nearly full.

"I'm fine. Thank you, Ben," she said.

"Did you recognize anyone?"

"No."

"That's a shame," Hannah said. "It might have made it easier for you, knowing you'd said your goodbyes."

"Yes, I suppose so," Alice agreed. She had been partly relieved not to have recognized any of the victims. Maybe she hadn't known them. Maybe none of them had belonged to her in any personal way.

The funeral service began, and she allowed her mind to drift, unable to listen to the words of Reverend Paulson. She didn't want to hear about death in the midst of life. She wished she could just walk out of the church and wander outside among the golden trees and the bare fields, the fresh wind caressing her face and tugging at her hair, making her feel gloriously alive.

At last, the service ended, and all able-bodied men trooped to the front, each pair lifting one of the bodies off the floor. They carried them out into the graveyard, and everyone else followed, their heads bowed as they watched the nameless victims lowered carefully into the waiting graves. Alice excused herself and walked away, unable to watch. She stood with her back to the graveyard, facing the town.

A tremor of fear ran through her when two British soldiers stepped out of the tavern, heading toward the church. They were young, mere boys, and they walked along at an unhurried pace, their posture relaxed, but they were armed, their muskets slung over their shoulders, the bayonets gleaming in the autumn sun.

Both men tipped their tricorns to her when they spotted her, muttering, "Good day, madam."

"Good day," Alice replied woodenly. Why did she fear them? They'd barely looked at her.

She found Derek's trap and leaned against it, needing its solid support at her back. She wanted to go back to the farm, to hide in the attic room, to sleep. She felt weak, her stomach heaving as her mouth grew dry, then black spots appeared before her eyes, and the world around her grew silent.

"Alice. Alice." The voice came from far away, insistent and high-pitched. "Alice, can you hear me?"

Alice opened her eyes. She was lying on the ground beneath the wheels of the trap, her face shadowed by the conveyance. Hannah was leaning over her, her face anxious. She laid a cool hand on Alice's brow.

"There now," she said soothingly. "You'll feel better soon. Help me, Derek," she ordered.

Derek, who'd been hovering behind his mother, stepped forward and lifted Alice into his arms, settling her on the bench of the trap. "All right?" he asked, his gaze searching her face. She nodded, but a wave of nausea overtook her as soon as she moved her head.

Derek climbed onto the bench and took up the reins. "Lean on me," he said as he wrapped an arm around her shoulders.

Alice looked around but didn't see the auburn-haired woman, so she nestled against Derek's side, grateful for his solid warmth. She felt better once they left the churchyard.

"It's off to bed with you," Derek said, his tone that of a father sending a child to bed. "This was too much for you."

"Yes," she agreed. "It was. I feel lightheaded."

"I'd give you a stiff drink, but Dr. Rosings would have my head. No spirits, he said."

Alice thought a glass of sherry or even Madeira might bolster her sagging spirits and waning strength. "If we get back before the others—"

Derek looked at her and grinned. "We'd best hurry, then."

He slapped the horse's rump with the reins, and it broke into a trot, making the trap sway from side to side. Alice gripped the bench, feeling nauseated again. She tried to breathe through her nose and fix her gaze on a distant point instead of looking around. That seemed to help, and soon the sickness passed.

"We're going to look after you," Derek said. "Don't worry."

That's not what you said yesterday, Alice almost blurted out. She'd heard his objections through the thin walls, his voice indignant as it floated up to her attic room. And Ben's deeper, softer voice, challenging him, ready to take him on should Derek decide to cast her out. He'd changed his tune. Was it because he'd seen her? Did he find her beautiful? Did he think she was there for the taking?

Alice shifted away from Derek, making sure they were no longer touching. Was that what this was about? She'd thought he was being chivalrous, but perhaps he was just using her weakened state to touch her, to get her used to being touched by him.

No! The word exploded in her brain like a shot fired from a cannon. No! No man was going to touch her without her say-so.

Chapter 14

After a nearly silent midday meal, Derek and Ben went off to see to their chores, and Josh was sent to the parlor to read for an hour, while Hannah busied herself with clearing and washing the dishes. Alice would have helped, but the funeral had left her physically weak and emotionally overwrought, her mind still refusing to come to terms with the tragedy she'd been part of.

"Go sit outside for a spell," Hannah said. "The fresh air and sunshine will do you good."

Alice nodded and stepped outside, glad to be alone. She closed her eyes and turned her face up to the sun, trying desperately to find a pleasant image to replace the one she had in her mind, but the yawning graves were not so easily displaced, the cocoon-like bodies with their bloated faces swimming before her eyes, silently blaming her for not being able to recall their names.

"Good day," a haughty voice said, startling Alice. She hadn't heard anyone approach. She opened her eyes to find the woman she'd seen before the funeral standing before her, her gaze narrowed as she studied Alice. She was very beautiful, her auburn hair shining like copper in the sunlight and her wide blue eyes the color of cornflowers, but the hostility Alice had noticed earlier was still there, and it made Alice deeply uncomfortable.

"I'm Lydia Blackwell," the woman supplied.

"Eh… Good day, Mistress Blackwell," Alice muttered. "Hannah is inside."

"It's you I've come to see," Lydia said, sitting down next to Alice without being invited to.

"What can I do for you?" Alice asked warily.

Lydia smiled solicitously. "It's what I can do for you," she replied. "Seeing as you've lost all your possessions, I thought I'd bring you a couple of things. It's not much, just one of my older gowns and some petticoats. Oh, and a pair of hose. They've been darned, but I'm sure they'll do in a pinch." She handed Alice the bundle she'd brought.

"Thank you," Alice said. "That's very kind."

"Christian charity begins at home, I always say. I was going to give these to my slave girl, but you are in greater need. Hetty can wait." She cocked her head to the side, as if expecting Alice to thank her again, but Alice remained silent, wishing Lydia would take the hint and leave.

"They say Ben found you on the beach."

"Yes, he did."

"Strange that he brought you here," Lydia observed. "I would have thought you'd be better off at Dr. Rosings', where he could keep an eye on you."

"I believe he'd offered to take me," Alice replied, wondering what Lydia was getting at.

"Your people must be worried sick about you. Have you sent word?"

"Not yet," Alice replied, not wishing to explain to this unpleasant woman that she couldn't recall anything of her past.

"Well, you shouldn't tarry. No doubt they'll be happy to have you back."

"No doubt," Alice agreed.

"Had you been traveling with your husband?" Lydia asked, watching Alice with those cool eyes.

"Oh, Lydia, what a surprise," Hannah said as she stepped outside, saving Alice from having to reply. "What brings you by?"

"I brought some things for your guest," Lydia said sweetly. "Seeing how bedraggled she looked at the funeral, I thought I could easily spare one of last year's gowns. You might need to take it in a bit in the bosom, but the length should be just right."

"Your kindness knows no bounds," Hannah said, disguising the sarcasm with a knowing smile. "Derek is not here. He's in the lower field."

"I'll see him later. He promised to come by," Lydia said smugly as she cast a look of triumph at Alice.

"I'll be sure to mention your generosity to him," Hannah said.

Lydia waited a moment, perhaps hoping she'd be invited in for a cup of tea or cider, but when Hannah failed to issue an invitation, Lydia said goodbye and left.

"Don't take anything she said to heart," Hannah said. "Lydia can be a bit high-handed, especially when made to feel insecure."

"She has no cause to worry," Alice said, and stood. A part of her wished she could throw the bundle of clothes into the pigpen, but the more practical part asserted itself, and she took the clothes up to her room. Despite Lydia's arrogant attitude, a spare gown was always welcome.

Chapter 15

March 2018
London

The afternoon was mild, the hazy sunshine bathing the playground in golden light. Several children in colorful coats climbed on the monkey bars and went down the slides while their parents stood nearby or sat on the benches, watching them play. Quinn pushed the swing harder, and Mia squealed with delight, her dark eyes bright with excitement.

"Me too," Alex cried. "I want to go higher."

Quinn gave him a push and reached into her coat pocket. Her phone was vibrating. It was Colin.

"Hi, Colin," Quinn said, surprised to hear from him so soon. "You have news for me?"

"Can you come by the mortuary?" Colin asked without preamble. "In an hour or so?"

"Sure, but I'll have to bring the children with me."

"If they don't mind, I don't mind," Colin replied. He sounded distracted, his mind already on something else. "I'll see you soon."

Taking Alex and Mia to the mortuary wasn't ideal, but it made no sense to ring Nicola. Whatever Colin had to tell her probably wouldn't take long. Quinn let them play for another half hour, then settled Mia in her buggy and took Alex by the hand. Alex didn't protest, but Mia looked upset.

"I want to stay," she complained.

"We can come back again tomorrow," Quinn replied.

"I want to stay now," Mia countered.

"I'm sorry, but someone is waiting for us."

"Who? Daddy?" Alex asked, looking up at her.

"We're going to see Colin Scott. Do you remember him?" she asked as they left the playground. Of course, Alex wouldn't remember Colin, Quinn realized. He hadn't seen him in years.

"No," Alex replied. "Are we going to his house?"

"No, his workplace."

"What's his job?" Alex asked.

"He's a pathologist," Quinn said, sorry she'd started this conversation.

"What's a pathol—. What's it again?"

"Pathologist. It's a kind of doctor. He sees people after they've died."

"I don't want to go there," Alex said, his gaze fearful.

"I don't want to go," Mia cried from the buggy.

"You two can wait in his office while I speak to him. It won't take long."

"Want to go home," Mia whined. "Watch *Trolls*."

"I don't like *Trolls*," Alex protested.

"Trolls are funny." Mia giggled, and Alex relented.

"Fine, we can watch *Trolls*," he grumbled.

Quinn looked at the children and made an executive decision, hailing a passing cab. She'd bill Rhys for the expense. After all, this was work related, and it'd be easier and faster than taking two small children and a buggy on the Tube. The taxi got them to Colin's mortuary in less than fifteen minutes.

"Bye." Mia waved to the cabbie, who waved back.

"Bye, darlin'," he said. "You too, little lad."

"Bye," Alex muttered under his breath.

Quinn smiled down at him. "There's nothing to be frightened of."

"You said there'd be dead people," Alex protested.

"I said Colin works with dead people. I didn't say you'd have to see any of them."

"Still."

"Don't worry," Quinn said, using her best soothing mum tone. "You don't have to come inside."

Colin came to meet them at the door, his mask hanging around his neck, his hair covered by a surgical cap. "Well, hello there," he said to the children, who stared at him in horror.

"Colin, do you think Shannon might come out here and mind them while we talk?" Quinn asked. "Alex is frightened, and Mia is upset about having to leave the playground."

"Of course. Not to worry."

Colin disappeared down the hall and returned with his assistant, whose purple and pink streaked hair instantly captured Mia's attention. Alex looked intrigued as well.

"Hi, guys," Shannon said, looking from one to the other. "Who wants to go for a walk?"

Neither child responded, but Alex shook his head stubbornly and took a firmer hold of Quinn's hand while Mia crossed her arms.

Shannon looked to Quinn, then tried again. "Who wants to take a walk to the vending machine? I just happen to have some coins in my pocket. Oh, let's see, enough to buy a bag of M&Ms."

"I like the red ones," Alex said.

"I like the green ones myself," Shannon said. "What color do you like, Mia?"

"Pink."

"I'm afraid they don't have pink ones, but I'm sure we can find you something." She took hold of the buggy and wheeled Mia off down the corridor, Alex walking beside her.

"Well, that was easy," Colin said as he looked after them. "Come on in."

He led her to the lab, where their skeleton was laid out on a table, bright lights illuminating its grinning countenance.

"I didn't expect you to get back to me so quickly," Quinn said as she stood next to Colin, looking down at the remains.

"I'm sorry to disappoint you, but I don't have much to share with you, hence the rapid turnaround time. There's very little to go on."

"Surely you must have learned something from the remains," Quinn protested.

"Yes, but not nearly enough to build a picture of this person's life and death. What we have here is an adult male. He could have been anywhere between mid-twenties to mid-thirties at the time of death. Carbon-14 dating indicates that he lived roughly two hundred to two hundred and fifty years ago, so the latter part of the eighteenth century. The ridges on his wrists and ankles would indicate that he worked with his hands and probably did a lot of walking. He'd broken the radius bone in his arm at some point, but it had healed cleanly, so it would have been years before his death, possibly when he was still in his teens. Given his height and the condition of his teeth, I'd say he enjoyed a plentiful diet. Mostly meat based. He was in reasonably good health before he died."

"What? Is that it?" Quinn asked, gaping at him.

"I'm afraid so. I wasn't able to extract any usable DNA. Having been buried without the benefit of a coffin and in soil that's moist and rich in nutrients, the body would have decomposed quickly, all organic tissue and hair completely broken down within a year."

"And the nails?"

"Rotted away."

"But he has a mouthful of teeth," Quinn persisted.

"Extracting DNA from a tooth is a time-consuming and costly procedure. Rhys was unable to authorize funding. Budget cuts." Colin smiled at Quinn in a sympathetic manner. "I know it's not much to work with."

"What about the manner of his death?"

Colin shook his head. "I can't say with any certainty what killed him. Most of the ribs are fractured and the pelvic bone is splintered. I think the damage was done postmortem, by the spreading roots, but I can't be certain. The arms and legs are intact, as is the neck. There is something I found, but again, I don't know if this happened before or after death."

"Show me," Quinn said.

Colin reached out a latex-clad hand and pointed to the left temple. "There's a hairline fracture right here. Do you see it?"

Quinn leaned in and peered at the skull but couldn't see what Colin was pointing to.

"Here," Colin said, handing her a magnifying glass. "Look again."

Quinn could see a tiny crack, the width of a hair. "You think this is significant?"

"It could be. A blow to the temple can lead to an intercranial hemorrhage, which can be fatal; however, I have no way to ascertain when the skull was fractured."

"This doesn't look like much," Quinn said. "Would this really be enough to kill someone?"

"You don't need to cave in someone's skull to kill them, but I can't confirm this was the cause of death. The skeleton is too badly damaged to allow for anything more than an educated guess."

"Thanks, Colin," Quinn said as she handed back the magnifying glass and accepted the nearly empty file folder from Colin. All his findings fit on one sheet of paper.

"I'm sorry I couldn't be of more help," Colin said. "Let me know if you find anything that was buried with the body."

"There was nothing. He must have been buried naked, which is odd."

"Why do you say that?" Colin asked as he walked Quinn to the door.

"Historically, people were uncomfortable with nudity, especially in England. They bathed, made love, gave birth, and were examined by doctors while almost fully covered up. It's only in films that you see characters in historical dramas disrobing without a second thought. Nudity was synonymous with sin, and shame. To bury someone naked would be a sign of disrespect, indifference, or even hatred. Whoever this person was, he hadn't endeared himself to those who'd been left to bury him. No clothes, no proper grave, no marker."

"It's as if they'd wanted to erase him," Colin said.

"Precisely. One day he was there, and then he wasn't."

"Well, that should tell you something, I suppose," Colin said. "Not a pillar of the community, or a beloved husband or father. Or son. Someone who wouldn't be missed."

"Sometimes I think that's the most tragic fate of all," Quinn said, forcing a smile to her face when she spotted Shannon and the children at the end of the corridor, walking toward them. Mia had chocolate smudged on her cheek, and Alex looked almost relaxed.

Shannon handed Quinn a half-empty packet of M&Ms. "Don't worry, Mum. I didn't give them too much. Only four pieces each. And I might have had a few," she added, grinning impishly. "Could never resist chocolate, me."

"Thank you. I appreciate it."

"Got what you came for?" Shannon asked.

"Not nearly as much as I'd hoped for, but yes. Thank you both," Quinn said, and pushed the buggy toward the exit, the folder beneath her arm. Rhys would not be too happy with the lack of factual information, but Quinn had enough to update Katya. She took out her mobile and selected her number.

"Quinn, hi," Katya said cheerily. "How are you?"

"I'm all right," Quinn said. "Actually, I was just leaving the mortuary."

Katya's voice instantly changed. "Was Dr. Scott able to learn anything?"

"Tell you what. Why don't you bring Vanessa by for a playdate tomorrow afternoon, and you and I can chat? How does that sound?"

"Sounds great, actually. I'm going mad with boredom. This stay-at-home mum thing is not quite what I had envisioned."

"It does get lonely," Quinn agreed.

"See you tomorrow," Katya said.

"Vanessa is coming over to play tomorrow," Quinn announced, getting happy smiles from the kids. "Now, let's go home and get dinner started. Daddy and Emma will be home soon."

Chapter 16

"Nothing?" Gabe asked as he stacked the dishes in the dishwasher. The children were in the lounge, watching *Trolls*, with Emma in charge. For the moment, all was quiet.

"He says the skeleton was too badly damaged by the roots to be able to determine the cause of death."

"Well, we did think as much," Gabe said, his expression thoughtful. "I suppose we can work backwards."

"How so?" Quinn asked.

"We did not find a bullet buried with the skeleton, which means he wasn't shot," Gabe theorized.

"He may have been. Without soft tissue, we have no way of knowing if there was an entry or an exit wound."

"True. Well, we know he wasn't hanged," Gabe suggested, smiling guiltily because he knew that was another erroneous supposition.

"We don't. Not every hanging breaks the neck."

"So, what do we know?" Gabe asked.

"Absolutely nothing. Impossible to make out if there are nicks from a sword or any evidence of a knife wound. If he was shot, he may have died instantly or bled to death. If he was hanged, we have no tangible proof, and if he died of any other cause, such as a fever, poisoning, or even a heart attack, we have no way to discover that either. All we know at this stage is that he was a well-fed, youngish man who was most likely not of noble birth, given the ridges on his wrists and ankles."

"But you think the remains we've excavated are those of Ben Wilder?" Gabe asked. Quinn had filled him in on everything she'd seen in her visions.

"Or Derek. They wore identical rings, and even though I'm seeing Ben's version of events, it's entirely possible that Derek had been wearing his brother's ring at the time of death. They could have easily mixed them up."

"Yes, I suppose so. But what would a farmer from Long Island be doing in Hertfordshire?"

"That is the million-dollar question," Quinn replied.

"And I might have the answer," Gabe said, leaning against the worktop, his arms crossed as he ran with his theory. "If either brother was a royalist, he might have been forcibly sent back to England. Many royalists were victims of a mob. They were dragged from their homes and forced onto a departing ship in nothing but the clothes they stood up in. They arrived in England with not a penny to their name and a substantial debt for their passage and meals."

"Milford was a small colonial town. It had no port, hence no departing ships," Quinn pointed out.

"No, but there's nothing to suggest one of the brothers might not have been taken in New York. Were they involved in anything untoward, do you think?"

"I haven't seen enough to make that determination. All I saw was an ordinary family thathappened to be living through a turbulent time in their country's history."

"And Alice? Any ideas about her?" Gabe asked.

"Not yet. I should ask Colin what percentage of people who develop amnesia as a result of blunt force trauma recover their memories."

"It would have to be a significant number, or a good portion of the population would have no recollection of having lived before getting struck on the head."

"Do you think that many people sustain head injuries?" Quinn asked.

"More than you imagine. I have," Gabe said, grinning.

"When was this?"

"When I was fourteen. On a school trip to Berwick Castle. My mates and I were roughhousing and then a real scuffle broke out. I don't even remember what brought it on. All I know is that this boy named Billy Barnes shoved me with all his might, and I went crashing down onto the stone walkway. I hit my head pretty hard. Had to be taken to A&E. My mum was frantic."

"Did you lose your memory?" Quinn asked, surprised she'd never heard the story before.

"No, but I remember feeling stunned. I wanted to call out, but my mouth just wouldn't cooperate. I couldn't make a sound. And there was this weird silence. I could see people looking down at me, could see the teacher's mouth opening and closing, but it was as if the sound had been muted."

"How long did it take for that to pass?"

"By the time the ambulance arrived, my hearing had begun to come back, but it took me about an hour to finally say something. My parents were terrified I'd sustained permanent brain damage."

"What happened to Billy Barnes?"

Gabe's satisfied smile said it all. "He got grounded for a month. No TV, no hanging out with his mates, no football practice. He blamed me, of course. We never made it up, Billy and I. Kept our distance from each other until I left for uni."

"Well, we don't know how hard Alice was hit, or with what. And she came near to drowning. That might play a role, as well. She's fighting hard to recall any small detail she can, though, I can tell you that."

"I suppose we'll just have to let her story play out and see what develops," Gabe said.

Quinn chuckled. "And so we should. If only Rhys didn't ask for hourly updates."

"Sod Rhys," Gabe said with a grin. "He'll just have to wait. He's getting awfully territorial over this skelly. You'd think he was the one who buried him."

"He's just worried about Katya."

"Do you really think that learning what happened to this person will put Katya's mind at rest?"

"Probably not."

"I am looking forward to hearing more of what happened," Gabe said eagerly.

"Give the children a bath, and I'll have the next installment for you by the time they're asleep," Quinn offered, grinning at him.

"You're on!"

Chapter 17

October 1777
Long Island

Alice had barely enough time to grab for the chamber pot before her stomach emptied itself. It had been more than a week since the shipwreck, but she still felt unwell, her head aching and her body sore and strangely unfamiliar. She tended to feel better toward the evening, but her head injury made itself known in the morning, after she'd been lying down during the night, unwittingly putting pressure on the still-fresh bruise. Despite the bouts of sickness that came several times a day, she felt hungry and secretly relished Hannah's attempts to feed her up. She wasn't terribly thin, but her pallor and weakened state were enough to convince Hannah that all would be well if Alice would only eat.

Putting on her own gown over Hannah's spare chemise, Alice gingerly brushed her hair and plaited it loosely, so as not to pull on the skin at the back of her head, then made her bed and presented herself downstairs. She was surprised to find a visitor waiting in the parlor. He was enjoying a cup of tea and one of Hannah's corn muffins.

"Alice, this is Lieutenant Reynolds," Hannah said. "He'd like a word."

Hannah patted Alice's arm reassuringly but did not follow her into the parlor, returning to the kitchen instead to allow them to speak privately. Alice wished Ben or Derek were there, but they must have already eaten and left, given that only Josh's piping voice could be heard coming from the kitchen.

"Good morning," Alice said. She felt a flutter of nervousness as she stood across from the man. What did a British officer want with her?

The man brushed crumbs off his hands and stood, bowing to her politely. He would have cut a fine figure in his red tunic and white breeches if only someone had thought to place a bucket over his head. His dark eyes bulged like those of a bullfrog, and he had pockmarked skin, a souvenir of some adolescent illness, no doubt, probably smallpox. His long, thin nose formed an almost perfect triangle if viewed from the side. He also seemed nervous in her presence, which made Alice feel marginally less afraid.

"Mistress…eh, well, Alice," he began, not knowing her surname. "Won't you have a seat?"

Since the lieutenant stood before the settee, Alice perched on the wingchair Derek favored. Her fingers nervously smoothed down the fabric of her skirt as she waited for the officer to state his business. She had no reasonable cause to fear him, but something about that bright-red tunic made her uneasy.

"I trust you're feeling better," Lieutenant Reynolds said, watching her intently.

"Yes. Thank you."

"That must have been a terrible ordeal for you," he said, shaking his head as if envisioning what Alice had gone through.

"I suppose it must have been, but I don't recall anything that happened before waking up in the room upstairs," she replied carefully.

"Nothing at all?"

"Nothing."

"Shame. I was hoping you might at least be able to tell me the name of the ship you'd been traveling on."

"I'm sorry, Lieutenant, but I can't even remember my own name, much less the name of a ship."

"Do you think you might recognize the name of the ship if you heard it?" he tried again.

"I can't promise anything," Alice said, wishing the man would just leave. What was he after?

"*Essex*?" Lieutenant Reynolds asked softly. "*Lady Anne*?" he tried again.

"Sorry, no. They don't sound familiar at all."

"*Peregrine?*" the major intoned, his gaze pinning her head to the back of the chair.

Something inside Alice recoiled, a cold dread spreading from her belly to her extremities. *Peregrine.* There was something about the name that frightened her and caused her to suck in her breath as her heartrate accelerated, her palms sweating.

"Are you all right, Mistress Alice?" Lieutenant Reynolds asked.

"You must excuse me, Lieutenant. I haven't been well. I fear I'm going to be sick," she mumbled, and bolted from the room. The major found her around the side of the house, wiping her mouth with the back of her hand. She felt marginally better but needed to lean against the wall for support.

"I do apologize," he said, sounding genuinely contrite. "Mistress Wilder informs me you're still suffering the ill-effects of the tragedy."

"I am," Alice said, wishing fervently her legs didn't feel like jelly.

"Can I help you back inside?"

"Thank you, but I think I'll stay out here for a few minutes. The fresh air helps."

"As you wish. I'll bid you a good morning, then." He bowed from the neck and turned on his heel, walking away as if on parade, his hat beneath his arm.

Odious man, Alice thought as she watched him put his hat on his head and mount his horse before cantering out of the yard. She waited until he disappeared from view, then reentered the house.

"Are you quite all right, Alice?" Hannah asked when Alice walked into the kitchen. "Did Lieutenant Reynolds upset you?"

"Not at all," Alice lied. "I wasn't feeling well when I woke up."

"Let's get some breakfast into you, shall we?" Hannah said, setting a bowl of porridge before Alice and adding butter and honey without asking. "Cup of tea?"

"Yes, please," Alice replied, spooning some porridge into her mouth. She began to feel better as soon as the warm mass reached her stomach, settling with a comforting weight.

Hannah poured them both tea and sat down across from Alice, watching her eat.

"Where is everyone?" Alice asked.

"Derek went into town, and Ben is fixing the fence in the lower pasture. Josh was meant to be helping him, but he came back saying his belly hurts. He went upstairs." Hannah took a sip of tea and set the cup carefully on the table. "You don't seem to be getting any better," she said.

"I am," Alice protested. "My head doesn't hurt as much," she lied. She wasn't sure why, but she felt the need to reassure Hannah that she was improving.

"I think perhaps the blow was more severe than you imagine. A head injury can often cause nausea and headaches for months afterward. My brother fell out of a tree when he was twelve. Hit his head on a boulder that was half-buried in the ground. He never lost his memory, as you have, but he became temporarily blind."

Alice gasped. "Did he recover his vision?"

"Once the swelling went down, his vision gradually returned, but he was never the same afterward. Suffered with terrible headaches and double vision for years after the accident."

"And now?" Alice asked.

"They still trouble him, but not as frequently. I'm glad Dr. Rosings is due to look in today," Hannah said. "I'm worried about you."

Alice felt the prickle of tears, deeply touched by Hannah's concern. If she had to rely on the kindness of strangers, she was glad it was the Wilders who'd found her and not someone who'd see her as nothing more than a burden, another mouth to feed. Derek had kept his distance since the day of the funeral, but Hannah, Ben, and Josh treated her with understanding and kindness. They would help her get well, if only by the sheer force of their will, but she was worried. What if she had sustained permanent brain damage, the full extent not yet apparent?

Alice spent the morning in a fog of fear and doubt. After feeding the chickens, she came back into the house, ready to help Hannah prepare the midday meal, but kept her head down, reluctant to engage in conversation, her anxiety getting the better of her. She wanted Dr. Rosings to say she was well and reassure her that her memories would return in time, but how could he promise such a thing? He was a country doctor, used to treating the usual range of ailments and farm-related accidents. This was beyond the scope of his experience; he'd said so himself.

"*Peregrine*," Alice whispered under her breath when Hannah stepped out to use the privy. Once again, the name brought forth an instant reaction. Fear, loneliness, but also a surprising sense of relief. How was it possible to experience such conflicting emotions?

Alice bent her head over the mindless task of peeling potatoes. "*Peregrine*," she said again, louder. The emotions the name invoked sparked a tiny flame of hope, a light that dispelled some of the impenetrable darkness caused by her lack of memories to rely on. Unpleasant memories were better than none, she decided.

"Did you say something?" Hannah asked as she walked through the door. "It sounded like peregrine."

"A megrim," Alice said, blurting out the first thing that came to mind that sounded somewhat similar.

"Go have a lie-down," Hannah said. "You look pale. I'll finish here."

A part of Alice wanted to assure Hannah that she was all right, but the opportunity to escape her watchful gaze was too tempting to resist. She climbed up to her attic bedroom and shut the door, then closed the shutters, plunging the room into near darkness. Alice lay on the bed and closed her eyes, focusing all her inner energy on that one word.

"*Peregrine*," she mouthed into the silence of the room. "*Peregrine*." But try as she might, she couldn't bring forth an image of the ship or recall any details of her voyage.

By the time Dr. Rosings knocked on the door, she was ready to take a break from her self-imposed exile. She would tell him about the feelings the name stirred in her and see what he thought.

Entering the room, Dr. Rosings placed his medical bag on the chest of drawers and opened the shutters before sitting down on the side of the bed. Alice squinted as gray light filtered into the attic, making her eyes water after several hours of darkness.

"Hannah tells me you haven't been well," Dr. Rosings said as he studied her. "Is there no improvement?"

"Not really," Alice admitted.

"Tell me exactly what you're experiencing," the doctor invited, his kindly face serious.

"My head still hurts, especially in the mornings. As soon as I turn my head or try to sit up, I feel bilious. The nausea doesn't abate until I vomit, and then I feel better, and hungrier. I'm achy and tired, and there are pains in my stomach," Alice complained.

"What kind of pains? Is it stomach gripes? Do you need to go to the privy?"

"No. It comes and goes, and sometimes it's quite sharp, but only for a moment or so, and at other times, it's a pulling sort of pain."

"Pulling?"

"Stretching," Alice amended.

"I see," Dr. Rosings said. "I'm going to have to examine you again, Alice. Can you sit up for me?"

"Of course."

Dr. Rosings examined her head by pressing lightly on the spot at the back of her skull, then parted the hair to get a closer look at the skin.

"The swelling has gone down, and the bruise is not as livid. Lie down, please."

He listened to her chest, took her pulse, then palpated her belly, his expression thoughtful as he exerted gentle pressure. "Do your breasts feel swollen or tender?"

"Yes," she replied.

"And do you feel the need to relieve yourself often?"

"Yes."

"Have you had your courses since the shipwreck?"

"No," Alice replied. "Not yet. What does any of this have to do with my head?"

"Nothing," Dr. Rosings replied. "Alice, I believe you're with child," he said, sending her tiny, confusing world crashing down around her.

"Are you sure?" she whispered.

"It's difficult to say with any certainty since you can't recall when you last had your courses, but the symptoms fit. Your womb is enlarged, your breasts are sore, you experience morning sickness followed by hunger, and you make water often. And the headaches can also be related to the pregnancy."

"Is there any way to know for certain?" Alice asked. A pregnancy was sure to change a woman's life forever, be it her first or her tenth, but for a woman who had no recollection of her life before a week ago, it was catastrophic. Alice was trembling with agitation, her hands ice cold as she reached out to Dr. Rosings. "Please, I must know for sure. There must be a way to tell."

Dr. Rosings' brow furrowed in thought. "I've never used this method; it's quite old, goes back to ancient Egypt, if you can believe that, but I read about it when I studied medicine. And it's said to be quite accurate."

"How does it work?" Alice muttered. She couldn't begin to imagine how they'd tested for pregnancy in ancient times and wondered if some sort of sacrifice might be required, or bloodletting at the very least.

"It's simple, really. Take a small amount of wheat and barley seeds and put them in a glass jar. Urinate on them several times over the next two days and leave the jar in a spot that's exposed to sunlight. Then wait for something to happen. If the seeds begin to sprout, you are pregnant."

"That's all?"

"That's all."

"I don't want anyone to know," Alice said.

"I understand," Dr. Rosings said. "You have much to contend with just now, and you need time to come to terms with this new development."

"You said the swelling has gone down. Does this mean I'll start to remember?" Alice asked, her gaze searching his for any kind of confirmation.

Dr. Rosings shook his head. "I'd like to think so, but I can't make any promises. When dealing with the brain…" He lifted his hands in a universal gesture of uncertainty. "We must wait and see. But you mustn't lose hope. This observation has no scientific merit, but I've noticed that patients who are determined to get better usually do, while the ones who lose hope tend to deteriorate."

"Is there anything I can do?" Alice asked. She was desperate to get better, but determination didn't seem enough. She had to act, to do something to extricate herself from the deadlock she found herself in.

"I would think that seeing or hearing something from your past might jolt your memory and accelerate the recovery process, but since we don't know anything about your past, we can't facilitate that type of experiment. Perhaps some random phrase or image will trigger a memory," Dr. Rosings suggested. "Don't give up hope, my dear. Not ever."

Alice nodded, grateful to the man for his support and for the fact that his supposition fit in with what she'd experienced upon hearing the name of the ship

"And let me know how that other thing turns out," he said quietly as Hannah peeked into the room.

"How's the patient?" she asked, walking in once she saw that the consultation was over.

"Getting stronger every day," Dr. Rosings said. "As long as Alice remains calm and gets plenty of rest, I have hope for a full recovery."

"Thank you, Doctor," Alice murmured. Calm. How was it possible to remain calm in view of what he'd told her?

"Dinner is ready," Hannah announced. "Come downstairs. Dr. Rosings, would you care to dine with us?"

"Thank you, Mistress Wilder, but I still have several patients to see. I'll be home in time for supper, if I'm lucky," Dr. Rosings grumbled.

"But you must eat," Hannah protested. "How about I give you a nice buttered corn muffin to take with you? I made a fresh batch only this morning."

"I wouldn't say no to one of your muffins," Dr. Rosings replied, grinning. "They're a treat."

Dr. Rosings followed Hannah downstairs, leaving Alice blessedly alone. She wrapped her arms around her middle and leaned forward, her head almost touching her knees. Of all the things she'd expected to hear, that she might be with child hadn't been one of them. The possibility made her feel caught in a vortex of uncertainty and indecision. What was she to do now? How was she to go on?

"Alice, are you coming down?" Hannah called from below.

Alice forced herself to leave the sanctuary of her room and trudged downstairs, her stomach in knots. She'd have to wait for Hannah to leave the house so she could help herself to some wheat and barley seeds. And then, she'd have to live through several agonizing days before she'd know for certain, or as certain as some arcane Egyptian method could guarantee.

**

When Gabe came into the bedroom, having put the kids to sleep, Quinn was on her phone.

"What are you doing? I thought you were going to spend an hour with Alice," Gabe said as he climbed into bed and lay down next to her.

"I did. And now I'm Googling Egyptian pregnancy tests," Quinn replied, her gaze glued to the screen.

"What?"

"Ha!" Quinn cried. "I found it."

"Found what, exactly? What does Egypt have to do with anything?"

"Dr. Rosings spoke of an ancient Egyptian way to check for pregnancy. And I've found a reference to it. It was called the wheat and barley test. Evidently, the ancient Egyptians realized that something happened to a woman's urine once she became pregnant. Says here they even thought they could tell if the baby was a boy or a girl depending on which seeds began to sprout after being soaked in urine."

"You've lost me," Gabe said, trying to see over her arm as she scrolled through the article.

"It seems Alice was pregnant at the time of the shipwreck," Quinn announced, gratified by Gabe's astonishment.

"Was she? That must have come as a shock."

"You bet. Can you imagine not being able to remember something like that?" Quinn exclaimed, setting the phone on her bedside table.

"Maybe she hadn't known," Gabe suggested.

"Maybe not. Oh, that poor girl," Quinn said, dismayed. "It's earth-shattering enough to find out you're pregnant in the here and now. Imagine what it was like in the eighteenth century, especially if you had no idea whose baby you were carrying."

"Surely she'll remember," Gabe said.

"I hope so, for her sake," Quinn replied, and turned out the light.

Chapter 18

March 2018
London

When Katya and Vanessa arrived the following afternoon, the two women took the kids out into the garden, where Gabe had set up a swing and a slide, and let them play while they watched them over a cup of tea and chocolate biscuits. Katya looked stylish as ever, but lines of fatigue were etched into her lovely features, and her hair was scraped into a bun. She'd lost weight, and her jeans hung loosely around her long legs. She reached for a biscuit and bit into it gingerly.

"I know Rhys told you about the baby," Katya said as she continued to nibble. "He's so excited, he just can't help himself," she added affectionately.

"Congratulations. How are you feeling?" Quinn asked, glad the cat was out of the bag and she didn't have to pretend she didn't know about the pregnancy.

"The morning sickness has been awful," Katya said. "I never felt this sick with Vannie. It's as if my insides are trying to turn themselves out. I've been living on tea and dry toast for weeks. Rhys keeps trying to tempt me with all kinds of goodies, but just the thought of eating them makes me ill."

"He's worried about you," Quinn said.

"I know. He's a dear man," Katya said with a tired smile. "But women have been having babies since the beginning of time. I know this is temporary, and then I'll have a beautiful child to love. I just have to get through the next couple of weeks."

"How far along are you?"

"Nearly twelve weeks," Katya said. "I don't have to tell you, Rhys is thrilled. He'd have a dozen children if he could. He dotes on Vannie. The kid is spoiled rotten."

"He's waited a long time for this, but I've never seen him happier," Quinn said. She didn't think Rhys would ever forget the baby he'd lost with his previous partner, but Vanessa had filled the gaping void, bringing out Rhys's paternal side.

"I'm happy too. It's as if we were made for each other," Katya said dreamily. Her expression suddenly changed. "Vanessa, I saw that!" Katya exclaimed, shaking her head in exasperation. "Say sorry to Mia for pushing her off the swing."

Vanessa gave her mother a defiant look, but promptly mumbled, "Sorry, Mia."

"I wonder what it will be like to juggle two kids. Vannie can be a handful."

"So can Mia. She's so different from Alex," Quinn said. "He was such an easygoing toddler. I wasn't prepared for this little hellion."

"It's because she's a girl. Girls are so much more temperamental, I find. Speaking of which, how's Emma?"

"She's all right. Moody. She's only going to be nine, but it's like she's already a teenager."

"I think these days they go straight from being a toddler to becoming a tween. There's nothing in between," Katya joked. "Vannie is already giving me a hard time about clothes and my choice of playmates for her. She has very definite opinions about what and whom she likes."

"That's as it should be," Quinn said. "They have their likes and dislikes, same as us."

Katya took a sip of tea and turned to face Quinn. "So, tell me about this skeleton. Was Dr. Scott able to learn much?"

"Well, the good news is that he wasn't a victim of a recent crime. Colin dated him back to the mid-to late-eighteenth century, so he's been sleeping beneath that tree for over two hundred years."

"But was he murdered?" Katya asked, her gaze filled with apprehension.

"It's hard to tell. The roots have done a lot of damage to the skeleton."

"You must think me mad to worry about what happened to him. I mean, it's your job to unearth secret burials, but I can't bear the thought of someone being disposed of like that. It gives me nightmares."

"I don't think you're mad," Quinn said. "Archeology might be my chosen profession, but I wouldn't like to find someone's remains in my garden. It's disturbing, to say the least." Quinn sighed and looked out over her peaceful garden, the silence disturbed only by the giggles of the children.

"There's something profoundly cruel about denying someone a proper burial. It's almost as if they'd tried to erase them from the annals of history. Sure, most people are only remembered for a time, and only by those who'd loved them in life, but their names live on, if only on their gravestones or in parish records and family legends. When someone is buried in secret, as this person must have been, there's no closure, no dignified end to their story."

"Exactly," Katya said. "Rhys thinks I'm being silly, but I'd like to give this person a proper burial. It would bring me peace. Is there any chance you could find out who he was?" Katya asked, smiling at Quinn in a manner that could only be described as guilty.

"He's told you, hasn't he?" Quinn asked, interpreting Katya's look the only way she knew how. Less than a handful of people knew about Quinn's psychic gift, and Quinn preferred to keep it that way. People still scoffed at preternatural ability and would brand her a fake or a kook if they knew her secret. Her professional rivals especially would question her every find, her every conclusion, and try to destroy her academic legacy, turning her into a laughingstock in the archeological community.

"Katya, it's not common knowledge," Quinn said, hoping Katya hadn't shared the information with anyone else.

"Of course. I completely understand. I would never betray your confidence," Katya swore, her hand on Quinn's wrist. "But I do think it's amazing, what you're able to do. To give these people their identities back and to tell their stories."

"It's not as simple as you think," Quinn replied, annoyed with Rhys for divulging her secret.

"Please, don't be angry with him. I sort of badgered him into telling me. I just knew there was something he was keeping from me," Katya said.

"I'm not angry," Quinn said. "It's just that I feel a responsibility to these people, a duty to learn their stories, and they rarely have a happy ending. It takes a toll, you know?"

"I can only imagine. I can see why you didn't want to continue with the program, especially while you were pregnant. You need to guard your peace of mind while you're carrying a child."

"I'll do everything I can to give your man a name," Quinn said.

Katya gave her a sidelong glance. "You already know his name, don't you?"

"I can hazard a guess as to who he was, but I won't know for sure until I see his story to the end. Can you wait till then?"

Katya nodded. "Thank you, Quinn." She seemed more at peace somehow.

They chatted for a while longer, and then Katya called to Vanessa. "Come, Vannie. Time to go home."

"No!" Vanessa moaned. "I want to stay!"

"Daddy will be home soon," Katya said. Vanessa's face instantly transformed, as if Katya had just told her Father Christmas was coming. Vanessa slid down the slide and ran over to Katya, ready to go.

"Bye," she called out to Mia and Alex.

"She's going through a daddy phase," Katya confided to Quinn quietly.

"Hey, whatever works," Quinn replied, amused.

Chapter 19

November 1777
Long Island

The waves rolled onto the shore with increasing frequency, the surf foaming as it saturated the sand and claimed more and more of the beach, the tide coming in fast and hard. The water was a charcoal gray, nearly the same color as the sky that seemed to hang so low it pressed on Alice's aching head. Seagulls perched on the rocks jutting out of the water, some taking flight just long enough to dive into the waves in search of fish. They didn't appear to be successful and returned to their perches, eyes watchful, feathers ruffled.

Alice drew the shawl closer about her shoulders. She was freezing, the sand beneath her skirts cold and damp. But she couldn't bring herself to leave. She sat staring out over the churning water, her face turned into the wind as storm clouds gathered on the horizon, their underbellies an ominous shade of violet. She placed her hand on her stomach, still unable to believe there was life within.

Half the seeds had sprouted, leaving Alice to deal with the knowledge that she was indeed with child. Now her symptoms made sense. The pulling sensation in her growing womb, the nausea, the tender breasts, and the frequent urge to use the chamber pot were all easily explained. The smell of bacon turned her stomach inside out, but the nausea was quickly replaced by a gnawing hunger that seemed to come out of nowhere and sometimes shortly after she'd eaten.

Alice got to her feet and ran toward the water's edge. The wind whipped her hair about her face, its intensity stealing her breath, but she hardly noticed. She'd lain with a man and now carried his child but had no idea who he might have been or where he was. Did he lie at the bottom of the sea? Had he waited for her at the end of a journey she'd now never complete? Had she left him behind when she'd boarded the ship, promising to return?

She wrapped her arms around her middle, sheltering her unborn baby from the incoming storm, but the wind had a life all its own, the gusts strong enough to push her backward, making her stagger. She wished the tempest had the power to make her forget her troubles, but the questions kept coming, their relentless assault on her memory making her want to howl with frustration. Had the child's father been her husband? Had she loved him? Had he loved her? Was he grieving for her even now, or was he dead, torn from her like a healthy limb, the amputation leaving her bleeding and broken? Had he known about their child? Had she? Dr. Rosings couldn't tell her how far along she was so early in the pregnancy, when he couldn't feel the child within her womb and assess its size. How much time did she have before her condition became obvious? What would she do once the baby was born? So many unanswered questions. So many gaping holes in the fabric of her life.

"Who am I?" Alice hollered into the raging wind. "Who am I?"

And then a voice, quiet and gentle, a voice she'd heard before, spoke from somewhere deep inside her damaged mind. Her own voice. "Jocelyn Sinclair."

"Jocelyn," she repeated, stunned by the revelation. "Jocelyn." Now she understood why Alice had felt so wrong. It sounded nothing like Jocelyn. Had it been Jesse, or Lynn, she might have warmed to it, but it had grated on her like a strike of tinder on flint. Not Alice—Jocelyn. The name felt so right, so true. It slotted neatly into one of the gaping holes, filling it perfectly.

"Jocelyn!" she cried into the wind. "My name is Jocelyn."

She beat a retreat as a rogue wave came at her, reaching the tips of her toes and nearly soaking her shoes. Fat drops of rain fell from the leaden sky, the icy tears of the stormy heavens making her shiver.

"You're going to catch your death out here," Ben yelled over the wind as he ran toward her. There was genuine fear in his eyes as he grabbed for her, pulling her away from the hungry tide.

"I wasn't going to…" she began. Why would he think that? Did she seem that desperate to him?

Ben took her face in his big, warm hands and looked deep into her eyes. "Alice, please, don't do anything foolish. It will be all right. I will make it all right."

"What will be all right?" she snapped, annoyed by his naivete.

How could anything truly be all right? At least seventeen people were dead, buried in graves that would never bear their names. More probably rested at the bottom of the sea, their remains picked over by fish and whatever creatures made their home beneath the frigid waves. Their families would never know what had become of them, would never have a grave to visit, their farewells left unsaid. And she was here, on Long Island, alone and pregnant, and utterly dependent on the Wilders, who bore no obligation to her. They were kindly strangers, but how long could she abuse their hospitality?

"I don't know where I come from, Ben. I don't know where I was going," she cried, his ridiculous chivalry having unleashed something feral in her. "I may have been traveling with someone, but I can't even recall their name. It might have been one of the men buried in the churchyard, or someone who went down with the ship. It may have been my mother, or sister, or friend," she wailed, now nearly hysterical. She was shaking from both cold and emotion, desperate to release some of the feelings bubbling away inside her, but she couldn't tell Ben about the child, not yet. She couldn't share her secret with anyone, not until she clearly recalled its father and the circumstances that had led her to the doomed ship. *Peregrine*, her mind supplied helpfully.

Ben drew her to him and held her close as she wept, her fists pressed into his chest. His body was warm, his tone soothing as he tried to reassure her again and again that he'd look after her and keep her safe. After a time, she stopped shivering, her tears drying as the storm of emotion passed and hope began to raise its head, like a lone crocus pushing through the snow. She had recalled her name. She supposed that was a huge step toward regaining her memory, but nothing more had come with the knowledge, at least nothing concrete. *Peregrine* might be the name of a ship she'd seen before, or a vessel her impaired memory associated with the man who'd fathered her child. He might have been a sailor, a man of business, or even a soldier, for all she knew. Or maybe her father had gone to sea on a similarly named ship. The Peregrine could even be the name of a tavern. The name by itself meant nothing without the context in which she'd known it.

"Come, let's get you home. You are soaked through," Ben said gently, as though sensing that the worst of her grief had passed. He took her hand and pulled her along, their feet sinking into the damp sand and leaving deep footprints. "Ma was worried about you," Ben said. "She thought you looked upset when you left the house. Has something happened?" he asked carefully.

"No. I suppose it all got to be too much," Jocelyn replied.

"You can't give in to despair," Ben said. "I won't let you."

Jocelyn forced a smile to her lips. Ben was so kind, so steady. Her heart instinctively warmed to him.

"It was just a moment of weakness," she said. "I'm glad you were there."

"I'll always be there for you, if you let me," he replied, his voice husky, his eyes pleading with her to let him in.

"Ben, I—" she began, pulling away from him.

"Don't say it. I understand. I'm a patient man, Alice," he said gently, but she could see she'd wounded his pride. What was she supposed to have done? Jocelyn fumed inwardly. She was in no position to make promises, and he had no right to ask anything of her, not when she couldn't recall anything of her past. Surely he understood that she might not be free, or did he think the shipwreck had erased all her previous commitments and she could simply start over? *Oh, if only it were that easy*, Jocelyn thought as she trudged after Ben.

By the time they returned to the house, thunder clapped in the distance and flashes of lightning split the sky. Jocelyn's teeth chattered with cold, and her feet were wet and muddy, her hair hanging in wet sheets.

"Get out of those wet clothes and get warm," Ben ordered, his tone gruff, then turned on his heel and walked toward the barn.

Jocelyn walked into the house and ran up the stairs before anyone could ask her any awkward questions. She hadn't done anything wrong, but she felt as if she'd let Ben down somehow, had disappointed his hopes. She'd have to tread even more carefully now that he'd made his feelings clear.

Chapter 20

Having seen Alice safely home, Ben made a dash for the barn to make sure the animals weren't spooked by the storm. The cows hardly seemed to notice, but the horses were restless, snorting and neighing miserably. Ace, in particular, hated storms and was pawing at the floor with his front leg, breathing hard and shivering as if terrified. He'd bolt given half a chance and would probably knock himself silly if he tried to headbutt the door. Ben entered the stall and laid a hand on Ace's neck, talking to him softly until the horse began to calm down, its nostrils no longer flaring or its eyes rolling in fear.

"There you go," Ben said softly, almost murmuring. "Nothing to fear. Just a bit of weather. Not nearly as bad as that last one."

Ben finally left the horse and settled himself on a bale of hay. He knew he should go inside, change into dry clothes, and join the family for supper, but he needed a few minutes to himself. The thunder crashed outside, and flashes of lightning lit up the sky, suffusing the barn in an unnatural glow before growing dark again. Ben leaned against the wall and exhaled deeply, suddenly tired, his mind reliving the moment he'd seen Alice running toward the waves, her hair flying in the wind as it tore at her shawl. She'd looked wild, like a witch running from a mob. What had she been screaming? He wished he'd heard, but her words had been lost on the wind. Had she been calling for her dead love? Had she meant to join him?

Gut-wrenching pity bloomed in Ben's chest, nearly stealing his breath. He could understand how she felt. He'd been so angry and lost after Kira's death, so despondent. The loss of one person could make all the difference, change one's life irrevocably, mercilessly. Alice must have had someone special in her life. She was so lovely, her manner so pleasant and demure. There had to have been a man, and he was either dead or searching for her, probably in all the wrong places.

Ben had felt a fool, running across the fields as the wind picked up and the first rumbles of thunder echoed across the darkening horizon, but he didn't care. He'd wanted to save her, again, if only from getting drenched. He'd wanted to envelop Alice in his arms and hold her tight, to promise her she'd never be alone, and he'd given in to the urge, doing exactly the wrong thing at the wrong time. He'd wanted to assure her that he'd never question her about her past, even if she managed to recall it. He'd never reproach her, never be unkind, but Alice wasn't ready to hear anything he had to say. She couldn't look to the future until she clearly saw her past. As usual, he'd rushed things and made a fool of himself, and now he'd have to wait and hope that he hadn't put her off permanently with his ill-timed promises and earnest declarations.

"What's the matter with you?" Derek's voice came to him on the wind as his brother walked into the barn, his hair dripping, his coat soaking wet.

"Nothing. What are you doing here?"

"Came to check on Ace. You know how he fears thunder and lightning. I take it you're here for the same reason."

"Ace is fine. I talked him down."

"So, why are you sitting here looking glum?" Derek asked, his tone softening.

"I was just thinking about Alice."

"What about her?" Derek removed his coat and hung it on a nail protruding from a beam, then sat down next to Ben and shook out his hair, spraying water like a dog.

"She walked down to the shore. I think she meant to do away with herself."

"What? What makes you think that?" Derek asked, clearly alarmed.

"I saw her, Derek. She was running toward the water, this odd look on her face. And just before that, she'd been shouting something. She looked wild, unhinged."

"That doesn't mean she wants to die."

"Maybe she does. She's all alone in the world."

Derek turned to face Ben, who was staring straight ahead. "Look at me," Derek said forcefully.

Ben reluctantly turned to face his brother. "What?"

"Ben, don't get ideas. I know you want to help, but Alice is not yours for the taking. There are people out there who care for her. She just has to remember who and where they are."

"I found her," Ben replied stubbornly, knowing how ridiculous he sounded.

"She's not a stray puppy. She's a woman who had a life before all this, and she will wish to return to her people once she remembers them."

"What if she has no people?" Ben asked, refusing to acknowledge that Derek was probably right. "She might be all alone."

"Ben, everyone has someone. Parents, siblings, friends, her husband's people, if she was married," Derek said. "I know you still mourn Kira, but Alice is not Kira. She's not some wounded bird you can nurse back to health and keep locked in a cage."

"She needs me."

"*You* need her," Derek snapped. "Don't be a fool."

"I'm not the fool," Ben spat, truly angry now. "I'm not the one sniffing around Lydia Blackwell. You think it's you she wants? She was seen leaving Lieutenant Reynold's lodgings the other night."

Derek stilled, his brows knitting together in anger. "Seen by whom?" Derek demanded.

"By Josh. He's taken it upon himself to keep an eye on her. For your sake."

"Stay out of my affairs, you two," Derek said, his voice dangerously low. "I can look after myself."

"So can I. Alice is mine," Ben hissed.

"Is she, indeed?"

"You heard me," Ben said. He jumped to his feet and faced Derek, his hands balled into fits.

"Oh, I heard you," Derek retorted. "I heard you loud and clear."

He stood, grabbed his coat, and strode from the barn, a gust of wind slamming the door in his wake.

Chapter 21

Jocelyn did not go down for supper. Instead, she peeled off her wet garments and climbed into bed in her chemise, pulling the blanket over her head. It did little to muffle the sound of thunder and rain lashing against the shutters, but she did feel warm and relatively safe. She'd nearly admitted to Ben that she had remembered her name, but something had stopped her from telling him the truth. Perhaps it was an innate sense of self-preservation. As soon as she made mention of recalling something of her past, the questions would start, and possibly the hints. The Wilders owed her nothing, and if she recalled her life before the shipwreck, she'd be expected to figure out where she'd come from and return there with all due haste. She hoped that the knowledge would come in time, but tonight, the secrets of her past were just as indecipherable as they had been that morning. Only now everything had changed. She knew her name, and she had a child to think of.

Had she wanted a baby? Had it been conceived in love? She shut her eyes and loosened her limbs in an effort to relax, then tried again to conjure the face of its father, but nothing came. It was like being in a stone cellar with no candle. Pitch black, not even the faint outline of a window or a sliver of light beneath the door. But there was something in that darkness, and if she stared at it long enough, her eyes would adjust and shapes would begin to emerge, until the faint light grew brighter, like a torch igniting from the smoldering embers of memory, illuminating every murky alcove in the dungeon of her mind.

Eventually, the house grew quiet. Everyone had gone to bed, but the storm outside continued to rage, the wind howling in the rafters as Jocelyn courted sleep. Tomorrow was a new day in which some small but important tidbit might come to her, she reassured herself. She just had to have patience and keep her own counsel.

She sucked in her breath when she heard stealthy steps coming up the stairs and moving toward her room. The door opened, the well-oiled hinges making nary a sound as her visitor entered the room and shut the door behind him. She was in no doubt it was Ben. Hannah wouldn't be creeping around at night, and neither Derek nor Josh would have any reason to come to her at night. Perhaps Ben meant to return to their earlier conversation, now that he'd had time to see her reply for what it was and understand that she hadn't meant to hurt him.

Jocelyn sat up and pulled the covers to her chin, the thick wool of the blanket her only protection, should she need it. With the shutters closed, she couldn't see his face, but she could hear his even breathing. He wasn't nervous, then—always a good sign. Whatever had brought him to her room hadn't been precipitated by impulse or desire. The mattress sank as he sat down, leaning forward until she could feel his warm breath on her face. A gentle hand rested on her hand, the strong fingers brushing against her wrist.

"What do you want, Ben?" Jocelyn asked, unnerved by his silence. Did he think this was what she wanted? Had she unwittingly given him the wrong idea when she'd allowed him to hold her down at the beach?

"Take all the time you need to recover, but don't toy with my brother."

She didn't need a light to recognize who it was, and the note of warning in his tone left her trembling.

An involuntary gasp escaped her lips. "Why would you think I'm toying with your brother?" she demanded. She meant to sound indignant, but her voice was reedy with apprehension.

"Because I know who you are, Jocelyn Sinclair," Derek said. He lifted his hand to stroke her cheek. "Even if you don't."

The trembling intensified as he moved his hand downward, tracing the column of her neck. Jocelyn thought he was going to touch her breast, but he allowed his hand to fall, getting to his feet instead. "I'll say goodnight, then," he said, his voice silky, yet all the more intimidating for it. "Sweet dreams."

She heard the door close softly behind him and let out the breath she'd been holding. Her whole body shuddered with shock, her teeth chattering as she wrapped her arms about herself, her pulse accelerating until it felt as if her heart was hammering against her ribs, her breath coming in short gasps. How could he know her name when she'd only just remembered it this afternoon? The beach had stretched in either direction as far as the eye could see, the shoreline bare and desolate, her shout snatched away by the wind and carried out to sea.

Was he threatening her, and if so, with what? Did he mean to ask her to leave, or was there something else he wanted from her? Was it possible they'd known each other before the shipwreck? If they had, Derek had shown no signs of recognizing her in those first few days. Had he been waiting for her to remember him, to acknowledge him? And why hadn't he said anything before tonight? Was there a reason he'd kept her identity a secret this long? Whatever his motives were, she had to stay clear of him until she had a firmer grasp on the reality of her situation. She had nowhere to go, no one to turn to for help. Derek hadn't asked her to leave, only not to encourage Ben, but she hadn't done anything to give Ben the wrong idea. Had she?

Jocelyn lay awake for hours, listening for footfalls on the stairs or the stealthy turning of the doorknob, but the house was quiet, everyone asleep, or pretending to be. She must have dozed off eventually because suddenly she was on a ship, the sky nearly black despite the early hour, the wind howling with rage as it tore at the canvas sails and rocked the great vessel as if it were a toy. People were running across the deck, calling out to each other as they tried to secure the ship. Several sailors were up in the rigging, holding on for dear life as they went about furling the sails. The captain was on the bridge, his lips pressed into a firm line, his expression tense as he surveyed the tempest raging around them.

"Get down below!" he hollered over the wind, his command directed toward the passengers who'd come up on deck.

The storm had come on suddenly, the sky darkening in a matter of minutes and the waves swelling as if some giant hand were stirring the ocean and whipping it into a frenzy. The water towered higher above the ship with every new wave, crashing onto the deck and covering it with at least a foot of water.

Jocelyn heard a muffled cry as a sailor lost his grip on the rigging and fell hard, his agonized scream of pain immediately drowned by another gush of water. He sputtered and coughed as he tried to raise his head, but went white with pain, unable to shift his back off the slick boards.

"His back is broken," someone cried. Jocelyn stared in horror as the man's face contorted, tears rolling down his already wet cheeks as his mates tried to move him from beneath the mast. They didn't get far. Another crushing wave knocked them off their feet, their burden landing with a heavy thud and a piercing scream.

"Get down below!" the captain yelled again, but none of the passengers paid him any mind. They gripped the sides of the ship until their knuckles were white, watching in terrified fascination as wave after wave built and crashed, battering the ship and forcing it to tilt precariously on the starboard side.

Jocelyn looked around in panic. Her mind was sluggish, uncooperative. Her skirts and cloak were soaked, her feet barely managing to maintain purchase on the slick wood of the deck. Someone was crying and praying, someone else was cursing the captain for not anticipating the sudden change in weather. She looked around again, searching, craning her neck, when she heard the crack. It seemed to go on for a few seconds, the sound raw and jagged. One of the masts had cracked under the strain, the spar falling, dragging the rigging and the half-furled sails with it.

Jocelyn screamed as she was pitched forward by the rush of seawater flowing over the side, and then she felt the impact, the pain in her head blinding as the force of the blow sent her hurling over the side and into the bubbling cauldron beneath. She never felt the ocean's watery embrace. She was nearly insensible by the time she began to sink, her skirts blooming about her as if she were a giant jellyfish.

Chapter 22

March 2018
London

"What does your day look like?" Quinn asked Gabe as he came into the kitchen, his hair still damp from the shower. Quinn popped several slices of bread into the toaster and spooned coffee into the cafetiere.

"Surprisingly light," Gabe replied. "I have a lecture in the morning, and then I hope to catch up on some paperwork. What about you?"

"I have some errands to run, and I'd like to speak to Colin about the effects of a head injury on memory, for one," Quinn replied. "Alice has remembered her name. It's Jocelyn Sinclair, but she doesn't seem to recall anything else. Not yet."

"That's a lovely name," Gabe said. "And fairly unique. Think there might be something about her online?"

"It's worth a try, I suppose."

Quinn didn't expect to discover much. Unless Jocelyn Sinclair had done something to distinguish herself, her name would be lost in the annals of history. She did wonder how long it would take for Jocelyn to fully recover her memory. Given her situation, she hoped not too long. Quinn couldn't begin to imagine how she would feel if she found herself in Jocelyn's situation. Jocelyn had been lucky to have people who were willing to care for her, but given what Quinn had seen, the situation was about to turn toxic.

"The wheat and barley test confirmed that Jocelyn was pregnant at the time of the shipwreck," Quinn said. She tried to sound matter-of-fact but couldn't keep the emotion out of her voice. "Oh, Gabe, can you imagine not being able to remember who the father of your child was or any other details of a life you'd had before it all happened? I can't even begin to wrap my mind around that."

"Losing your memory must be difficult enough in this day and age, but I can't imagine what it must have been like in the eighteenth century, when there was no information to go on, save the person's word for who they were and where they'd come from," Gabe said.

"She was completely bewildered," Quinn agreed.

"Did she think the child's father might have been lost in the wreck?"

"She hadn't seemed to recognize any of the men who'd washed up on the beach," Quinn pointed out.

"Which doesn't mean one of them couldn't have been her husband. Memory can play strange tricks, especially after such a harrowing experience. Her mind might have been protecting her from more trauma."

"I can't help hoping he was alive and waiting for her somewhere. Perhaps she'd been on her way to join him."

"Or maybe she'd been trying to get away from him," Gabe suggested. "Not every marriage was a happy one."

"No, I suppose not," Quinn said. She smiled brightly as Emma walked into the kitchen, putting an end to the discussion. In either case, it was time to wake Alex and Mia and get them ready for school.

"I'll see you both later," Quinn said. "Have a good day."

"You too," Gabe and Emma said in unison.

**

Quinn returned home just before noon to find a large Amazon box on her doorstep. She grinned when she saw the name of the sender. Seth Besson. He'd sent a gift for Mia's birthday. He always made sure to send something a few weeks early in case Quinn didn't approve and the present needed to be returned or exchanged. Quinn brought the box inside and opened it carefully, gasping with delight at the beautiful dollhouse Seth and Kathy had chosen. It came with about fifty pieces of furniture and a family that had a mum and dad, an older sister, a middle brother, and a little girl, just like the Russell family. Quinn hid the gift in the cellar and went to call Colin.

"Hello there," Colin said cheerily. "You caught me just in time. I was about to begin a postmortem."

"Hi. Colin, I was wondering if you might help me with something."

"Certainly. Did you find anything else that had belonged to the victim? Assuming this person was a victim," he added. "We really don't have anything concrete to support the theory that he was murdered."

"No, we haven't been back to the burial site. My question is more hypothetical. If a person were to lose their memory as a result of a blow to the head, how long would it generally take to regain it?"

Colin considered this for a moment. "I'm not an expert on memory loss, Quinn. Why do you ask? Have you learned something that might suggest our man had been hit on the head?"

"No. This is for a different case," Quinn lied. She could hardly share her findings with Colin. "An educated guess will do," she prompted.

Colin considered his answer for a moment. "This type of memory loss would fall under psychogenic or dissociative amnesia. It's usually caused by severe trauma and can last from hours to years."

"What does that mean, exactly?" Quinn asked.

"Dissociative amnesia is the loss of episodic memory. A person will still remember language and be able to perform everyday tasks but won't be able to recall any personal details, such as their name, their past, relatives and friends, or their work. Generally, this type of amnesia is treated by exposing the person to familiar faces and places to jumpstart their memory."

"And would the memory come back all at once, do you think?"

"Probably not. It would start returning with brief flashbacks, I should think, and not necessarily the important bits first. Perhaps the brain would release images that were easy for the patient to handle. But again, this is pure conjecture on my part. You would have to consult a specialist if you were after a more scientific explanation."

"Thanks, Colin. I appreciate it."

"Anytime. Happy to help. Regards to Gabe," he said as he rang off.

Quinn didn't think she needed to seek an expert opinion. If Colin's hunch proved correct, then within the coming weeks, Jocelyn should begin to recall events from her life. Quinn would just have to be patient and allow the story to unfold. In the meantime, she had the children to collect.

Chapter 23

Having finished their snack, the children went down for their afternoon nap, and Quinn returned downstairs, where she settled on the sofa with her laptop. She had some time until she had to start on dinner, and she was ready to delve into the history of Long Island, and Milford in particular.

She had visited the Hamptons once, years ago, and remembered the seaside community as being peaceful and picturesque, with multi-million-dollar homes and gorgeous boats moored off the piers. She hadn't liked its residents nearly as much as she had liked the views, finding their snobbery and sense of entitlement off-putting in the extreme. But that was the way of the rich the world over, and despite her standing in the scientific community and Gabe's newfound status as a bestselling author, Quinn could never see herself rubbing shoulders with people who were drawn to the Hamptons' overpriced shores.

But this was now. In the eighteenth century, Long Island had been a rural community, a backwater sparsely populated by farmers and fishermen. It had encompassed what were currently known as Brooklyn and Queens as well as Nassau and Suffolk counties that made up modern-day Long Island. Brooklyn, known as Kings County, had been the setting for the Battle of Long Island, the largest Revolutionary War engagement between the British and the Continental Army, but the rest of Long Island had seen virtually no military action. It had been occupied by the British during the latter years of the war, and relations between the colonists and the occupiers were for the most part cordial.

The locals had been ordered to provide housing and meals for the British and Hessian troops stationed in Queens and Suffolk counties, not an arrangement they relished, but they had put up with the invaders to protect their homes and loved ones. Quinn didn't find any references to the town of Milford, possibly because it no longer existed or may have been renamed or absorbed into a larger township of a different name. And given what she'd seen of the town and shoreline, it was impossible to tell which part of Long Island it had been located in. The only thing she thought she knew for certain was that it hadn't been on the shore of the Long Island Sound.

Likewise, there was no mention of either Jocelyn Sinclair or Ben and Derek Wilder, but she hadn't really expected there to be. Few civilians made it into the history books unless they had done something heroic or met with a gruesome end that had resulted in repercussions that couldn't be ignored, sparking change or outright rebellion. Disappointed, Quinn shut the laptop and was about to put the kettle on when the doorbell rang.

A young woman stood on the step, a curtain of hair obscuring her face as she looked down at her phone, a bag slung over her shoulder. She looked up when Quinn opened the door, her gaze anxious. Quinn smiled, her heart simultaneously leaping with nervousness and joy. The visitor was a few years older than the last time Quinn had seen her, her hair now had coppery streaks, and her face was no longer that of an adolescent girl but a young woman, but Quinn would know Daisy Crawford anywhere. At first glance, she didn't resemble her birth mother, but the tilt of her head, the direct way she looked at Quinn, and the defiant angle of her chin were pure Jo.

"I'm sorry," Daisy began as she shoved the phone into the pocket of her jacket. "I don't know if you remember me." Daisy looked lost for a moment, probably second-guessing her decision to come.

"Of course I remember you. I'm so glad to see you, Daisy. Do come in. I was about to make a cup of tea. Have you eaten?"

"No," Daisy said softly, visibly relieved that Quinn wasn't angry with her.

"Come through to the kitchen," Quinn invited as they entered the house. "I can make us some sandwiches, or an omelet, if you prefer." Quinn had eaten a yogurt before going to collect the children and suddenly realized she was quite hungry.

"It doesn't matter," Daisy said. "Whatever you were going to have is fine with me." She set her bag down on a chair and came to stand by the worktop, leaning against it just as Jo had done when she visited Quinn.

"Ham and cheese?" Quinn asked. "I got a taste for it while I was in America. They really do go well together, especially with a slice of tomato and a bit of mustard or mayonnaise."

"Sure. Sounds good."

"Are you in London by yourself?" Quinn asked. Daisy should have been at school, but Quinn didn't want to sound accusatory or overly maternal. It wasn't her place.

"I'm meant to be home sick," Daisy replied. "I'm not, though," she added hastily. "You don't have to worry about me being around the children."

Quinn nodded. The thought had crossed her mind, but she didn't want to admit it. "So, what brings you to London?" Daisy would have taken the train from Leicester, so she must have had a plan when she set off.

Daisy averted her eyes, her cheeks turning a lovely shade of rose. Quinn noticed that she was clasping her hands anxiously. "I needed to speak to you. I hope you don't mind me showing up like this."

"Of course not," Quinn said, although she was a bit baffled by Daisy's sudden arrival.

Daisy took a deep breath. "I don't even know where to start."

She looked so nervous; Quinn felt a wave of sympathy for her. She couldn't begin to imagine what had brought Daisy to her door but didn't want to rush her. She'd tell Quinn the reason for her visit in her own time. They hadn't seen each other since Jo's funeral, two and a half years before, and even then, they hadn't really spoken to each other. The Crawfords had left immediately after the burial, and there'd been no contact since. As far as Daisy was concerned, Quinn was her absentee aunt's long-lost sister, not someone she'd have reason to seek out.

Daisy took a deep breath and tried again. "My dad gave me Aunt Jo's camera. I like photography, you see, so he thought I might want it. It's very expensive, the type of camera professional photographers use. I could never hope to buy a Leika for myself or wheedle one out of my parents for my birthday or Christmas." She sounded breathless as she spoke. "I was happy to have it, especially since I'd never really known my aunt, so I felt no sense of loss," Daisy explained. "I'd never even met her in person."

"I'm sure she would have been glad to know that someone was using it. She loved that camera."

Daisy nodded. "Leikas take amazing photos."

Quinn finished making the sandwiches and handed the plates to Daisy, who set them on the table. She then poured them both mugs of tea and brought them over. Daisy sat down across from Quinn but made no move to touch her sandwich. Her face was flushed, and she looked even more anxious. It wasn't the lack of welcome she'd been worried about, Quinn realized. Her stomach dropped, her heart beating faster as an unsettling idea took hold and made her reevaluate Daisy's pained expression.

"Daisy, you can tell me anything," Quinn invited, trying to keep her voice even.

"Can I?" Daisy asked. Her gaze was searching Quinn's face, as if she were trying to decide if she could trust her.

Daisy picked up half a sandwich and took a bite, chewing slowly, as if stalling for time. She swallowed and took a sip of tea. Quinn took a bite of her own sandwich, giving Daisy time to compose herself.

"I saw things," Daisy blurted out. "I saw awful things."

"When you held the camera?" Quinn asked.

Daisy nodded, her head going up and down like a bobblehead's. "I don't know what it means. I thought I was going crazy. Every time I picked it up, I saw these scenes. It was like watching a film, only I knew all the actors from my own life."

Quinn experienced a sudden chill as she tried in vain not let Daisy see her shock. Her pulse was galloping, and her breath came in short gasps. Daisy was biologically related to Jo, and to Seth, through whose line the psychic ability had been passed, although it had skipped his generation. Daisy had the gift.

"What did you see, Daisy?" Quinn finally asked, overwhelmed with sympathy for the girl. It must have been shocking, to say the least.

"I saw Jo and my dad," Daisy said, her voice barely audible. "I saw them...you know."

Quinn nodded but didn't interrupt.

"I saw, and felt," she added vehemently, "what Jo had felt. She was Quentin then. Quentin Crawford," Daisy spat out with disgust. "My dad's sister and *my* mother," she cried, tears spilling down her cheeks. "My biological mother, who gave me up without even looking at me, without ever asking what had become of me."

Daisy's eyes flashed with anger, and a shiver of recognition surged through Quinn. At that moment, Daisy was her mother's daughter. "Dad never told me," Daisy spat out. "He'd lied to me my whole life."

"Daisy, he was only trying to spare you pain," Quinn said. "Had you known, you might have hoped for a relationship with your mother, but Jo wasn't interested, at least not then."

Grabbing a napkin, Daisy furiously blew her nose and buried her face in her mug of tea, taking several sips in an effort to calm down. She set the mug down and took a shuddering breath before trying again.

"I saw it all, Quinn. I saw her whole life play out before my eyes. I hate her. I hate her so much." The tears began to flow again, but this time Daisy angrily wiped them away with the back of her hand. "She was horrible. Cruel. Selfish. Indifferent to the feelings of others."

"I'm so sorry, Daisy. It must have been an awful shock," Quinn said, her sympathy inadequate in the face of Daisy's suffering.

"That's the understatement of the year," Daisy scoffed. She sniffled loudly, then gasped for air, as if she'd forgotten to breathe and only now remembered she needed oxygen. She exhaled slowly, trying to calm herself. "But then I saw you," she said at last, and her expression brightened somewhat. "She cared for you, even loved you, I think," Daisy said.

"She had a strange way of showing it," Quinn said archly, and wished she hadn't.

"She feared you. You had forced her to take a long, hard look at herself and she hadn't liked what she'd seen. She wanted to punish you," Daisy explained. "She wanted to hurt you because she was hurting."

"I'm sorry you had to see that," Quinn said again for lack of anything more insightful to offer.

"But there were nice moments too," Daisy said, her face taking on a wistful expression. "There was your reunion in Germany, and the time you took turns with that gold amulet. Hamsa, you called it. And when she told you about me."

"She regretted what she'd done."

"Yeah, for like five minutes," Daisy replied, curling her lip in derision.

"She wanted to find you, to get to know you. She had no idea you'd been there all along, living with your dad."

"She had known," Daisy said, shocking Quinn into silence. "Granddad had written her a letter. He'd known she'd come looking sooner or later. He was a clever man. I miss him."

"How long had she known?" Quinn asked, wondering if the whole quest to find her daughter had been some sort of a ruse. But no, it couldn't have been. It wasn't until the lawyer, Mr. Richardson, had passed on a letter from her father that Jo had suddenly changed her mind about continuing with the search. Of course, now it all made sense, including Jo's sudden flight from the country. She'd known Daisy was her daughter at the time of her death, but she'd never shared that knowledge with Quinn, or anyone else.

"She was ashamed," Daisy said, as if replying to something Quinn had said. "She didn't want you to know."

"Had she contacted you?" Quinn asked.

Daisy shrugged. "She sent me a friend request on Facebook, and I accepted, thinking my aunt finally took an interest in me. She must have been stalking me on social media, like a peeping Tom. I feel gross just thinking about it."

"Do your parents know you know?" Quinn asked, wondering what Michael Crawford would make of this new development.

"No, but they'll have to tell me eventually. Jo left everything to me in her will. I heard them talking about it. They decided to invest the money and tell me the truth once I turn twenty-one. I don't want her money," Daisy said defiantly. "I don't want anything of hers. I don't even want that bloody camera now. Not like I can touch it without connecting with her," she said angrily. "I'm going to sell it on eBay. Just because I know she would have hated that."

Daisy picked up the sandwich again, but her hands were trembling as she took a bite. She chewed slowly, her mind elsewhere. She replaced the half-eaten sandwich on her plate and fixed her gaze on Quinn.

"Would you have forgiven her for what she'd done?" Daisy asked, her cheeks flaming with embarrassment. It must have been mortifying to see her mother's attempts to seduce Gabe. Jo hadn't been shy in her efforts. The video evidence Gabe had sent to Quinn had been graphic and brutally honest, the pain of Jo's betrayal still sharp enough to take her breath away when she allowed herself to dwell on it.

"I don't think so," Quinn replied truthfully. "I like to think I'm a forgiving person, but what Jo did was beyond the pale. She'd set out to destroy my marriage, my family. She didn't deserve forgiveness."

"I wouldn't have forgiven her either," Daisy said. The blush had faded, leaving her looking pale and scared. "Am I like her?" she asked. "Am I going to be just like her?"

The pleading look in Daisy's eyes nearly undid Quinn. She wanted to take Daisy in her arms, to comfort and reassure her, but she didn't think Daisy would appreciate that. She wanted an answer, not Quinn's pity or charity.

"Do you think you're like her now?" Quinn asked instead, pinning Daisy with her gaze.

"No."

"Then it's not very likely you will become like her later on. You are you, Daisy. You are the product of your DNA, but you've also been molded by your environment and upbringing, which I think was very positive," Quinn suggested, hoping she was right.

Daisy nodded in agreement as she considered Quinn's reply. "My dad is great. And I love my stepmum. She's amazing. I've always thought so. She loves me way more than that bitch ever did."

"My adoptive mother loves me with her whole being. She's the one I think of as my mum, not Sylvia."

Daisy thought about that for a moment. "Yes, I saw Sylvia in the visions. She's a piece of work."

"That she is," Quinn agreed.

"Do you keep in touch with her?"

"We see each other from time to time, but our relationship is very casual. I no longer blame her for giving me away; she had her reasons, but I can't find it in my heart to love her."

"Do you think she loves you?"

"I think she loves me as much as she's able to, which is not saying much. She's just not a very giving woman."

"Does she love her sons?" Daisy asked.

"She does, but she raised them from babyhood. She's invested in them in a way she can never be with me."

"Jo didn't like her much, probably because she saw so much of Sylvia in herself," Daisy pointed out astutely. "I think they would have forged a bond had Jo lived."

"Perhaps, although I'm not sure that Jo could forge a lasting bond with anyone."

"No, probably not. Sylvia's my grandmother, though," Daisy said, her nose wrinkling with something like distaste.

"Would you like to meet her, judge for yourself?" Quinn asked. "You can meet your grandfather too. He's really cool," Quinn said, meaning it. She'd come to love Seth and appreciate his involvement in her life. "And his wife Kathy is very nice."

Daisy went silent, staring at her sandwich again. "I don't know," she said at last. "I'm just not ready."

"You don't have to make any decisions now. Just know that it's an option you can exercise at any time."

"Any time?"

"Any time. You can meet Logan and Jude as well," Quinn added.

Daisy instantly brightened. "I liked them."

"I like them too. They're not at all what I would have wished for in my brothers before meeting them, but I love them both, and I'm glad to have them in my life."

Daisy nodded, but her mind seemed to be on something else. She pushed away her plate and clasped her hands together, almost as if in prayer. Her young face suddenly looked determined, and a little scared.

"Quinn, there's something else. I wasn't sure if I should tell you, but I really think I should."

Quinn felt a moment of apprehension, her pulse quickening again. This was it. This was what had brought Daisy to her, she realized with a jolt. Everything else had been a buildup to what Daisy had come to share with her.

Daisy lifted her face slowly, her gaze resolute. "Quinn, I saw Jo's killer. It was Brett Besson."

Chapter 24

Quinn huddled in the corner of the sofa after Daisy had rushed off to catch the train back to Leicester. Her head ached and she was trembling, but her eyes were bone dry, her mind spinning like a centrifuge. Daisy's revelation had been shocking but made a twisted kind of sense. Brett had come to London after his release from prison to make amends. He'd said he'd make it up to Quinn, whatever it took, and had been there when Quinn had received the video of Jo trying to seduce Gabe. Brett had been privy to one of the most private, hurtful, and all-around earth-shattering moments of her life, had watched as the carpet of security was yanked from under her feet, and had witnessed the unmasking of the sister she had come to love in all her mind-blowing naivete.

Brett had seen her distress, had felt the depth of her shock. Any other person would have offered sympathy and comfort, but Brett was not just any person. Years ago, when she'd finally found her biological father and met the brother she hadn't known she had, Brett had locked her in a cemetery vault when she'd unwittingly threatened his way of life by revealing a truth he'd tried to hide not only from those around him but also from himself. He'd been willing to sacrifice both Quinn and her unborn child, to walk away without a second thought, his conscience untroubled by the knowledge that she would die a slow, agonizing death in a place where no one would ever find her.

He'd begged for her forgiveness afterward, had sworn he was a changed man, but people didn't change. Not really. Brett may have proclaimed his devotion when he'd come to see her, but he'd simply shifted his focus from Quinn to Jo. He'd made amends to Quinn by killing the woman who'd threatened her marriage, then blithely boarded a flight to the States the next day, certain that no one would ever connect the hit-and-run accident that killed Jo Turing to him. He'd got away with it, too. He'd been living his life, attending college, going out with his friends, and spending time with his parents without ever giving himself away.

He'd committed the perfect crime, and even though Quinn now knew the truth, there was precious little she could do about it.

She could hardly walk into a police station and announce that her niece, who shared her psychic ability, had seen the face of the man who'd mowed her mother down two and a half years before. Quinn would be laughed out of the station. Worse yet, her professional name would be dragged through the mud. She could just see the headlines: *TV Host Fancies Herself a Psychic Crime Fighter*, or something equally vicious.

Quinn's initial instinct had been to tell Gabe what she'd learned. She'd almost called him at work after Daisy left, but something had stopped her. How could she tell him? Gabe had been the innocent victim of Quinn's quest to find her birth family, the events that had threatened his family not easily forgotten.

Now, after more than two years, things had finally calmed down. Gabe had come to accept Quinn's family. He tolerated Sylvia and was friendly with Seth, Logan, and even Jude, who'd managed to earn his grudging respect. He still thought Brett belonged in prison, but as long as there was no immediate threat to his family, Gabe was willing, if not happy, to live with the fact that Brett had been freed on a technicality and would never serve his time for what he'd done to Quinn.

Using every ounce of will, Quinn left the sofa and trudged into the kitchen to start on dinner. She took out several potatoes, fished a peeler out of a drawer, and went at the potatoes as if they were in some way responsible for her dilemma. She didn't want to bring this up with Gabe; she could only imagine his reaction, but she had to. They had no secrets from each other, and this newfound knowledge was like a hand grenade that had lain dormant for years until Daisy pulled out the pin. An explosion was inevitable, and the only thing Quinn could do was try to minimize the carnage, if such a thing were even possible.

She'd talk to Gabe tonight, she decided, once they were alone and she could speak freely without any danger of being overheard by Emma, who seemed to have a radar for private adult conversations. Once finished with the potatoes, Quinn put them in a bowl of water, dropped the peeler and splayed her hands on the worktop, bowing her head as the magnitude of what she'd learned hit her like a two-ton truck. Once she told Gabe, there'd be no going back, no pretending that Jo's death had been an accident. Once again, she was thrust into an impossible position, all because of the damn psychic ability that Seth had unwittingly passed on to his children, and Jo had passed on to hers.

Turning abruptly, Quinn yanked open the fridge and took out a half-finished bottle of wine. If ever there was an occasion to drink alone, this was it. Once she felt a little calmer, she fetched the ring from her bedroom, and turned on the baby monitor. Getting out of her head for a little while might help her get through the rest of the day. Dinner would just have to wait.

Chapter 25

November 1777
Long Island

"Alice! Alice, it's all right. You're safe." Ben's voice was soothing and warm, his embrace comforting as he pulled her close. Jocelyn buried her face in his chest. Her heart was still pounding, her breath coming in short gasps.

"What's wrong?" Hannah came rushing into the room, her candle shining a light on the pitch-black corners of Jocelyn's mind.

"Nothing, Ma. Alice had a nightmare is all. She's all right now. Aren't you?" Ben held her away from him for a moment, studying her tear-stained face. "Were you dreaming about the shipwreck?" he asked, throwing her a rope she was happy to grab hold of. She nodded.

"Is it coming back to you, then?" Hannah asked. Her face looked harsh in the eerie glow of the candle, her plait snaking over her shoulder.

"Not all of it," Jocelyn replied truthfully. "Just the terror of it."

Hannah nodded. "I can't imagine how frightened you must have been, but God has chosen you for some purpose known only to himself," Hannah said.

I wish I knew what it was, Jocelyn thought.

Ben gazed into her face, his eyes warm with concern. "Would you like me to stay with you until you go back to sleep? I'll sit by the door," he added when Hannah glared at him.

"There's talk enough already," she snapped. "Off with you. I'll stay with her for a while."

"What sort of talk?" Jocelyn asked once Ben had been shooed from the room.

"Just the usual kind," Hannah said as she settled at the foot of the bed. "Young woman, two unmarried men. You know the sort of thing people say."

"I haven't—" Jocelyn began.

"I know you haven't done anything wrong. But people will talk." Hannah sighed. "It's high time the boys were married. I worry about them, Alice. Ben lost his intended a year ago, and Derek fancies Lydia Blackwell, Lord knows why. I think she might have her sights set on someone who can offer her more than the life of a farmer's wife. Got ambition, that one. Why, I wager she'd gladly marry that homely Lieutenant Reynolds if he'd have her. I hear he comes from money and will inherit a sizable estate in Hertfordshire, or Oxfordshire, or some such once his father is gone. I don't want to see Derek hurt. Or Ben." Hannah sighed, giving Jocelyn a meaningful look. "Well, if you're all right, I'll go to my bed now," she said, rising to her feet. "I don't mean to burden you with my problems. You've got your own to contend with. Goodnight."

"Goodnight," Jocelyn muttered, glad to be left alone.

The room was plunged into darkness once again, leaving Jocelyn to reconstruct the dream that had terrified her. She gingerly touched the healing bruise on her head. She could still feel the blinding pain and the sheer terror of hurtling overboard into the nearly black waters of the roiling sea, but there had been something else, something before that. She couldn't conjure up the details or the context, only the terror that had left her shaking and helpless.

She was running, her footsteps unbearably loud in the eerie silence of the night. Someone was after her, someone who terrified her. She could almost taste her panic and fear and feel the erratic beating of her heart. She couldn't see him, but knew he was gaining on her, the thudding of his boots getting closer. There was no getting away, and nowhere to hide. A hand closed over her arm, yanking her back forcibly and dragging her back the way she'd come. *All is lost*, her mind screamed. No one could help her now. Tomorrow she would hang.

Jocelyn wrapped her arms around herself, rocking back and forth in her distress. Her mouth was dry, her heart racing as if she were still trapped in the dream, running for her life. Had it been a random dream or a memory of something that had happened before she'd boarded the ship? Had her mind dredged up a terrifying reality from the murky depths of her damaged memory?

Jocelyn rested her forehead on her knees, wrapped her arms around her legs, and screwed her eyes tightly shut, but the images raced across her mind, the panic making her breath come in choking gasps. The fear was real, and it was raw, and she instinctively knew that the threat was still out there, only, for the life of her, she couldn't remember what it was.

Chapter 26

The bright light of day brought new clarity. The storm had passed, and so had Jocelyn's resolve to steer clear of Derek. Even if he meant her no harm, he clearly possessed vital information that would help her identify the threat against her. She needed to discover what he knew and how he'd come by the knowledge. Jocelyn washed and dressed and presented herself downstairs, her heart racing. Would Derek acknowledge last night's visit? Would he tell her what she needed to know?

"Good morning, Alice. How are you feeling today?" Hannah asked solicitously when Jocelyn walked into the kitchen. Hannah was setting the table for breakfast.

"I'm well. Thank you," she said demurely. "Can I help?"

"You can slice the bread." Hannah gave Jocelyn an inquiring look as she set the dish of butter on the table. "Ben says you went down to the beach yesterday," she said nonchalantly. "He saw you running toward the water."

It wasn't really a question, but Jocelyn felt an answer was expected. Hannah and Ben were clearly worried about her.

"I thought looking at a stormy sea might help me remember," Jocelyn explained.

"And did it? Is that what brought the nightmares on?" Hannah asked, her eyes filled with sympathy.

"Yes, I think so," Jocelyn replied. She had no wish to tell Hannah about her dream.

Hannah nodded. "Dr. Rosings did say something trivial might trigger your memory."

"Good morning, Ben," Jocelyn said brightly, grateful for the interruption as Ben came in from the outside. He smelled strongly of cow, and there were bits of straw on his boots.

Josh was right behind him, carrying a bucket of water. "Here you go, Ma," he said.

Hannah nodded her thanks and set the bucket aside, the water to be used later for washing up. Everyone took their seats at the table.

"Where's Derek?" Jocelyn asked. "Should we not wait for him?"

"Derek left early this morning," Hannah said as she set the pot of porridge on the table.

"He went to New York City," Josh exclaimed. "I wish he'd take me with him," he said wistfully.

"He doesn't need you getting underfoot," Ben said as he ladled porridge first into his own bowl and then into Josh's. He passed the ladle to Jocelyn, who took a healthy helping.

"What's in New York City?" she asked.

"We need supplies for the coming winter," Hannah said. "Derek will trade some of our corn and barley for items we can't purchase locally. And Mistress Blanchette asked him to trade a few jars of honey. She has a beehive," Hannah explained. "The girls have been looking after it."

Jocelyn stole a peek at Ben. He finished his porridge and reached for a piece of bread, which he buttered liberally and spread with some honey. He didn't seem tense or upset, nor did he regard her with suspicion. Derek didn't appear to have shared his misgivings about her with his brother, but the sudden trip to New York City was concerning. What if Derek's true mission was to inform someone that she was here? Jocelyn sighed warily. If she went on like this, she'd worry herself into the grave, but how could she be sure she was safe?

"Is there anything I can help you with today, Hannah?" Jocelyn asked. She needed to keep busy in order to safeguard her sanity.

"I could use your help with the laundry," Hannah replied. "We'll get it done in half the time with the two of us working. I think I'll make us an apple pie for dessert," she mused as she took a sip of tea. "I have a hankering for something sweet."

"Yes, please," Josh cried. "We haven't had pie in forever."

"If by forever you mean a few weeks, then yes, it's been forever," Hannah teased him. "You can help peel the apples."

Josh shrugged. "I don't mind, as long as I can eat the peelings."

"Are you a pig?" Ben asked, and made oinking sounds.

Josh smacked him on the arm. "I like peelings," he said defensively. "They're sweet."

"Nothing wrong with peelings," Hannah jumped to his defense. "I like them too. I'll tell you what. We'll make two pies," she said. "That way, everyone can have a second helping."

"Sounds good to me," Ben said as he rose from the table. "Well, I've got chores to see to. Maybe if you have time, you can help me out as well." He winked at Jocelyn in a conspiratorial way.

Jocelyn nodded but made no promises. She had no wish to be alone with Ben until she confronted Derek.

The day seemed to go on forever, every hour dragging with maddening slowness. Jocelyn peered into the distance every time she stepped outside, as hopeful as she was fearful to finally spot Derek. But there was no sign of him. She had no idea how long it took to get to New York City but didn't ask for fear of showing too obvious an interest.

"Would you like to take a walk?" Ben asked when he came in around four o'clock. "We don't have to go far if you don't feel up to it."

Jocelyn's first instinct was to refuse, but the waiting was driving her mad, and she could use the exercise. She'd been on the go all day, helping with the laundry and various other household chores, but she longed to just walk out in the open, the fresh breath of the November breeze gentle on her face.

"Yes," she said. "I'd love to."

"Go on," Hannah called from the kitchen. "Take my cloak, Alice."

The cloak was made of thick, coarse wool, but it was warm and kept out the chill. Ben and Jocelyn skirted a field and walked across a meadow, the still-green grass covered in a carpet of fallen leaves. The reds, golds, and persimmons of autumn were gloriously vibrant, a living canvas painted by nature's hand.

"I thought you might want to talk," Ben said gently. "After what happened yesterday."

"I wasn't trying to drown myself," Jocelyn said defensively.

"You just seemed so…" He let the sentence trail off. "I just want to help," he tried again, his expression earnest. "You can talk to me. About anything."

Jocelyn nodded. He was only trying to be kind, but she didn't want to talk. She wasn't ready. Talking would only make her feel lonelier and more frightened since she didn't have answers, only questions. "How about we talk about you instead?" she suggested, smiling up at him.

"Me? Surely there are more interesting topics of conversation."

"I would like to know more about you," Jocelyn said shyly. *And about Derek*, she added silently.

"Well, what would you like to know?"

"Do you and Derek get on?" she asked, hoping he'd reveal the source of the tension she'd noticed between the brothers. Was it just normal sibling rivalry, or was there more to their bickering?

"We do, for the most part. We're just very different."

"In what way?" Jocelyn asked.

"Derek is more like our father. Mother always says so, at any rate. He's driven, and passionate in his beliefs. He has no patience for other people's feelings or fears."

"And what are these beliefs that he's so passionate about?" Jocelyn inquired carefully.

Ben's face clouded with displeasure. "I think you'd better ask him, if you really want to know. I thought you were interested in me."

"Your relationship with your brothers is about you," Jocelyn replied, hoping to tease him out of his sulk. "Being the middle son must be hard. Derek is the man of the house, Josh is the baby, and you? What are you?"

"I'm the one who gets things done," Ben replied, somewhat mollified by her renewed interest in him. "Derek will inherit the farm, but he's not a farmer at heart. He doesn't love the land. And Josh, he just wants to run around and explore. Chores are just that—a chore."

"But you enjoy farming?"

"I do. I love watching things grow. I'm happy living my life according to the laws of nature. Knowing that morning follows night, that one season comes after another, there's beauty in that, and a sense of peace. Whatever happens, no matter what manner of insanity men get up to, the sun will still rise in the east, and spring will come after winter."

Jocelyn wondered if he was referring to the war for independence but decided not to press him, since she wasn't sure what her own position had been before the shipwreck. The thought of war momentarily stopped her in her tracks. No political discussions took place around the dinner table in the Wilder household, and aside from the small number of soldiers who were billeted in town, there was nothing to indicate that a conflict with the colonists was in progress, but she'd remembered there was a war on and had felt a momentary surge of something she couldn't quite name. Excitement? Apprehension? Uncertainty? She was getting used to that last one, but the other emotions came as a surprise.

"Are you all right?" Ben asked, watching her with concern. "You had this odd expression on your face."

"Yes. I'm fine," Alice assured him. "Tell me about these rings you wear," she invited, eager to distract him.

Ben grinned, his eyes lighting with humor. "There's a funny story behind the rings. Well, maybe not funny, exactly, but amusing. Typical of me and Derek, I suppose."

"Tell me," Jocelyn said, glad she'd hit on something that had the power to brighten his mood and distract him from her own.

"Derek and I always went to the beach in the summer once we'd finished our chores. We'd sun ourselves and swim until it was time to go home for supper. Well, one day—this was about ten years ago now—we were coming out of the water after a nice dip and spotted something shiny in the sand. We both ran for it, laughing and pushing each other out of the way. It was just something we did, always keeping an eye out for anything that might have washed up on the beach, and pretty shells to bring for mother."

"What was it?"

"It was a shoe buckle. And a thing of beauty it was. Very finely wrought, almost delicate. We argued about who'd get to keep it until we got home and showed the buckle to Father. He examined it and proclaimed it to be silver. So, of course, now the argument escalated. We both wanted to hold on to it, although what we planned to do with a single shoe buckle never really figured into our reasoning. So, Father, very King Solomon-like, passed down a judgement. He said we'd have to split the buckle down the middle. That silenced us pretty quick. We just looked at each other, wondering what we were supposed to do with half a buckle. That's when father suggested melting down the silver and making it into rings. He said we could keep the rings for ourselves or give them to our future wives as a symbol of our love for them."

"So, he had the rings made for you?"

"In time. Once our hands were the hands of men and not boys. And there was enough silver left to make a cloak pin for Mother."

Jocelyn's hand went to the pin at her throat. "What? This one?"

"The very one," Ben replied.

"Must have been some buckle," Jocelyn joked.

"It was. Must have belonged to someone wealthy. We often wondered if the man had drowned." Ben grew quiet, as though realizing what he'd just said. "I'm sorry," he muttered. "I didn't mean to—"

"It's all right," Jocelyn said, but the mention of drowning instantly brought her back to reality, reminding her that she had no idea what had happened to the father of her child. She couldn't bear to focus on that now, so she thought back to something Hannah had mentioned last night. "Your mother said you'd lost someone," she said softly.

"I was to be wed," Ben said quietly. "She died weeks before we were to be married. Drowned," he added apologetically.

"I'm so sorry, Ben," Jocelyn said, gazing up at him. She could see the pain in his eyes. He must have loved her.

"Life goes on," Ben replied stoically. "I mean to find another love." He looked at her in a way that suggested he already had, but thankfully refrained from saying anything that would put her on the spot.

"So, what about Derek, then? He's what, twenty-four?" Jocelyn asked, desperate to wheedle out some information about Derek using any means necessary.

"Twenty-five." Ben's face grew serious. "Derek was married. His wife, Amy, died in childbirth three years ago, the child with her. A boy. Derek hasn't taken an interest in anyone since, well, not until Lydia."

Learning that Derek had been married came as something of a surprise. No one had mentioned Amy or the baby, but it was a painful subject, especially if Derek was still grieving, so completely understandable. Derek's feelings for Lydia Blackwell, on the other hand, were an entirely different matter.

"Does Derek love Lydia?" Jocelyn asked.

Ben shrugged. "I've no idea. I think she's holding out for something better," he said, reiterating the sentiment Hannah had expressed last night. Ben smiled wryly. "We're not lucky in love, us Wilders."

"Will Derek marry her, do you think?" Jocelyn asked. Perhaps Ben's view of Lydia was colored by his own feelings and the effect Derek's marriage would have on him and his stake in the farm.

"How should I know?" Ben snapped, glaring at her. "Why are you so interested in Derek all of a sudden?"

Jocelyn sighed, suddenly bone tired. "I find myself living in your house, dependent on Derek's goodwill. I'm worried he'll ask me to leave, I suppose," she said softly, hoping Ben would let go of his anger and see her side of it.

"We'll look after you, Alice," Ben said vehemently. "Derek can be headstrong and impatient, but he's not unkind. He'd never throw you out, but once you figure out where you belong, you'll leave us. I know you will."

"You'll be glad to see the back of me by then," Jocelyn said, trying to tease Ben out of his somber mood.

"No," he said softly as he looked down at her. "Never."

"Ben, you hardly know me. I hardly know myself," Jocelyn added, smiling bitterly.

"I know enough," Ben replied.

"Shall we go back? I'm tired."

"Of course."

They walked back in companionable silence, but Jocelyn's mind was busy turning over what she'd learned. She had to tread carefully, even more so than she'd initially imagined. Ben was bitterly jealous of his brother, and she didn't want to be the next shoe buckle to come between them. Ben was already staking his claim and would fancy himself in love with her if Derek paid her any undue attention. Ben was the type of man for whom it was essential to feel needed and recognized. He was a caretaker, a protector, a defender of what was his, or what he perceived to be his. He wanted the farm for himself, and he wanted her. It didn't require a great deal of perception to notice his territorial attitude toward her.

Jocelyn huddled into the cloak as the wind picked up. She was shivering, but it wasn't just from the cold. Just then, she wasn't sure which brother she feared more.

Chapter 27

By the time Derek finally returned, Jocelyn's nerves were so frayed, she thought there might be jagged tears in the fabric of her sanity. She couldn't be bothered with subtlety or caution; she needed answers. She ran across the yard toward the stable, hoping Josh hadn't beaten her to it, eager to see his brother. Derek was alone. He had already unhitched the horse and was pouring oats into a bucket as Jocelyn slipped inside.

"How do you know my name?" she blurted out, coming as close to him as she dared. Her heart was hammering in her chest. Having worried about it all day, she still wasn't sure what outcome she hoped for. If Derek really knew her, he could be the key to regaining her lost memories, but the knowledge would also give him power over her, which he might decide to abuse. She didn't know him well enough to predict what he might do or how much danger she was in.

"So, you do admit that's your name," Derek replied, infuriatingly calm.

"I admit no such thing. I can't remember my name. But you obviously do. How do you know me?" she demanded, hoping her false bravado masked her fear.

"I saw you."

"Where?"

"At the John Street Theatre in New York City," Derek replied, watching her carefully.

Jocelyn absorbed this information, her mind trying desperately to conjure up an image of herself attending a performance in New York. It failed. She studied Derek's expression. She didn't get the impression he'd known her personally. Perhaps he'd known her husband. A tiny sliver of hope pierced the gloom in her heart.

"Who was I with?" she asked, her voice pleading. "Was I there with my husband?"

"Only if your husband was the leading actor," Derek replied, his narrowed gaze fixed on her.

"What do you mean?" Jocelyn asked, taken aback.

"I mean, you were on the stage. You played the lead."

"What was the play?" she asked, stalling for time as her brain scrambled frantically to make sense of what Derek was telling her.

"I can't recall."

"But you remember my name?" Jocelyn persisted. "Do you remember the names of all the actors you see?"

Derek smiled, his grin seductive. "I remember your name because you were the only one I saw that night. You were exquisite."

Jocelyn felt heat rising in her cheeks and was glad Derek couldn't see her reaction in the dim confines of the stable. "Are you making fun of me?" she asked, suddenly realizing Derek could be making the whole thing up just to test her reaction. It was his turn to look surprised.

"No. Why would I do that?"

"I don't know. Maybe for the same reason you snuck into my room in the middle of the night to warn me off. Don't worry, I won't stay a day longer than I have to." She was close to tears and hated that Derek could see her distress.

He looked instantly contrite. "I didn't mean to frighten you. I'm sorry. I was just—"

"You were just what?"

"Never mind," Derek said. "I shouldn't have done that. Please forgive me."

"Your brother is a grown man. He can look after himself," Jocelyn said. "And for your information, I don't have any designs on him. I just want to go home," Jocelyn wailed, the stress of the day catching up with her as her vision blurred with tears.

"I know. I'm sorry," Derek said again, his tone soothing. "What can I do to help?" He reached out to touch her arm, but Jocelyn stepped back and crossed her arms in front of her chest. The defensive posture helped her regain some control over her feelings.

"Why didn't you say you knew me right away?" she demanded.

"Because I wasn't sure where I'd seen you. It took me a couple of days to work it out," Derek replied.

She blinked away the tears. "Will people know me if I go back to this theater?" she asked.

"All productions have been suspended since the occupation," Derek replied. "The theater is closed."

Jocelyn leaned heavily against the side of the stall, her head dipping in misery as her arms fell to her sides. She hadn't expected to feel such bitter disappointment, but it was as if a door had just slammed in her face. She was right where she started. This time, she didn't push Derek's hands away. He pulled her into an embrace, and she allowed herself to be held, resting her cheek against his chest, silent tears sliding down her face. He stroked her hair and kissed the top of her head, the gesture strangely paternal.

"It'll be all right," Derek said softly. "In the meantime, you are safe here with us."

Jocelyn lifted her tear-stained face to his, reassured by the sympathy in his eyes. "Derek, Dr. Rosings says I'm with child. I can't remember the man I love. I don't even know if he's alive or dead," she confessed, her voice breaking. "I've never felt so lost, or so afraid."

Derek's arms tightened around her. "Let me help you," he said into her hair.

"How can you help me?" Jocelyn asked desperately.

"I can take you to New York. You might recognize something you see, remember someone you knew."

Jocelyn bit her lip. She was flooded with apprehension at Derek's suggestion, but she had to admit, it was a reasonable one. If he had truly seen her in New York, chances were she'd lived there. Seeing familiar places might trigger a memory of her past.

"Thank you. I think that's a good plan. But Derek," she said, looking up at him.

"Yes?"

"Please don't tell anyone. Not yet."

"Don't worry. Your secret is safe with me. I will invite you to come to New York with me and suggest that the change of scene will do you good. If you're as good an actress as I think you are, you'll have no trouble convincing everyone that my offer is unexpected and even a little inappropriate."

"Why would it be inappropriate?"

Derek's eyebrows lifted in surprise. "A young woman spending hours with an unmarried man, driving through thickly wooded areas where he could force his unwelcome attentions on her, would be viewed by some as unseemly."

"Are you planning to force your unwelcome attentions on me?" she asked, unable to keep the smile out of her voice.

"Would you like me to?" he asked, smiling at her in a way that made her insides quiver.

"I'd better go back inside before I'm missed," Jocelyn said instead of answering, although she wasn't exactly sure who'd be missing her.

"Yes, I think you'd better," Derek agreed. "I still have to unload the supplies I brought back."

Jocelyn hurried from the stable, relieved to be away from Derek. For the first time since the shipwreck, she felt a flicker of hope for the future, but she couldn't allow herself to get too secure or give in to the spark of attraction she'd felt when Derek held her. She had to remain loyal to the father of her child, even if she couldn't remember his name. She might not recall the life she'd led before the shipwreck, but she didn't think she was the type of woman who'd give herself to a man without loving him. She was wed; she was sure of it, just as she was suddenly sure that he hadn't been on the ship with her when it sank.

Chapter 28

March 2018
London

Gabe stared at Quinn in utter disbelief, his eyes wide with shock. Quinn made to approach him, but he held up his hand, warning her off, then turned abruptly and left the room, his feet pounding on the stairs.

Quinn followed him. He was in the kitchen, pouring himself a shot of whiskey.

"Gabe," she began.

Gabe turned to her. The shock had been replaced by anger, his eyes flashing dangerously as he tossed back the shot, never breaking eye contact.

"I know what you're going to say—" Quinn began in her most placating tone.

"Really?" Gabe demanded as he slammed the shot glass on the worktop. "Do you?"

Quinn couldn't blame him for being upset. She was absolutely gutted herself, but they had to talk about this. This wasn't some minor infraction Brett had committed, this was murder, and it hadn't been a crime of passion. He had thought it through, had planned it meticulously, and got away with it. "You are going to tell me to let this go," Quinn said, bracing for a full-scale row.

"You are damn right I will," Gabe snapped. "Do you even comprehend what you're suggesting?"

"What about what you are suggesting?" Quinn countered. "You are proposing we let him get away with murder."

"He already has," Gabe reminded her brutally. "Nothing you do will bring Jo back, but if you pursue this, you will be drawing his attention to yourself, to our family, and to Daisy. Do you still not understand what he's capable of?"

"Oh, I do," Quinn cried. "That's why he must be stopped. Brett is a sociopath. He feels no genuine guilt or remorse. He told me he'd changed in prison, had found God, then promptly murdered his own sister over something that had nothing whatsoever to do with him, and walked away without a moment's hesitation."

"And all you have for proof is the word of a teenage girl," Gabe replied.

"Everything Daisy said was accurate. She knew it all, Gabe, had seen every sordid detail. She'd watched Jo die. Brett can't be allowed to simply get on with his life. It's my duty to stop him."

"No, it's not. Let someone else stop him," Gabe exclaimed. "For once in your life, take off your superhero cape and consider what you're proposing."

"I can't believe you're saying this." Quinn didn't mean to raise her voice, but she was so angry, she could barely breathe. "I've never known you to be a coward."

"Coward, am I?" Gabe replied, his voice dangerously low.

"I didn't mean that," Quinn backtracked.

"Yes, you did. Well, you are right. I am a coward. I don't want to see my family decimated. And I never want to feel the way I felt when I saw you lying broken and nearly lifeless in that tomb. Meeting Brett almost cost you your life and the life of our son. You didn't know him then, but you do now. You know he'll do anything to protect himself."

"He need never know where the information came from."

"Of course he'll know. As far as he's concerned, you are the only person who might know the truth. He gambled on you being hurt and angry enough to not want to touch any of Jo's possessions. He took a chance, and it paid off. Had Daisy not walked into your life today, you'd have remained in ignorance, and you would have been better off. We all would have."

"But she has walked into my life, and I'm no longer ignorant of what happened. I mean to get the case reopened."

"And how do you propose to do that?" Gabe demanded, trying a different tack. "Will you simply walk into a police station and tell them Daisy's had a vision? Who will believe you? You need evidence to convince the police to reopen a case. You need proof, which you thankfully don't have."

"I can find proof," Quinn said stubbornly, refusing to acknowledge that Gabe was probably right.

"How? It's been over two years. Let it go, Quinn," Gabe shouted. "Please, for all our sakes."

"She was my sister," Quinn said, her voice breaking.

"She was the sister who would have destroyed you had she lived. She was poison, Quinn. You are well rid of her."

"Maybe so, but she didn't deserve to be murdered," Quinn countered.

"Maybe not, but it's not your job to avenge her murder. She's gone. Brett is out of our lives. Please, for once, listen to me."

Quinn swallowed hard, trying to dislodge the lump in her throat. Everything Gabe had said was true, but she couldn't bring herself to capitulate.

"Promise me," Gabe demanded, his gaze nailing her to the wall. "Promise me you won't go to the police."

She nodded miserably.

"Say it," he insisted.

"All right."

"All right, what?"

"All right, I won't go to the police. And I'm sorry. I didn't mean to hurt you," she mumbled.

Gabe's expression softened. He could never stay angry for long. "I know you're hurting, Quinn," he said. "I do understand."

"So, you are not angry with me?" Quinn asked tearfully.

"Of course I'm angry, but not with you."

Quinn walked into Gabe's arms and buried her face in his chest. "I'm sorry," she muttered again. "You are the bravest man I know."

"I'd have to be to be married to you," Gabe said, but the heat had gone out of his voice. He wrapped his arms around her and held her tight. "I'm sorry, Quinn. I really am. It's a terrible moral dilemma you've been presented with, but in this case, you must do the wrong thing."

"So, you admit it's the wrong thing," Quinn said, giving him a watery smile.

"Yes, I do, and I'm prepared to live with that."

"Come to bed," Quinn said. She needed to feel Gabe's arms around her, to know he'd truly forgiven her for branding him a coward, but Gabe shook his head.

"I need some air. You go on up."

Chapter 29

The night was cool and crisp. Wispy clouds floated across the overcast sky, casting eerie shadows across the hazy moon. Gabe walked down the street, his step so quick he was almost trotting. Several cabs slowed down as they passed him, probably expecting him to hail them in his hurry to get to nowhere. He didn't care where he went. He just needed to burn off some of his anger, frustration, and guilt. Blood roared in his veins and his heart thumped painfully against his ribs, his mind mercilessly replaying the conversation with Quinn, holding up a mirror to his fears and motivations.

He'd had no right to tear into Quinn the way he had or to imply that she was on some sort of superhero crusade. She had reacted the only way she could have to the information Daisy had shared with her. She'd come to him, looking for understanding and support, and instead of sharing her horror, he'd made it sound as if the whole situation was her own fault. She was right; he was a coward. His gut reaction had been to protect his family, and himself. He wanted to bury his head in the sand and pretend nothing had happened, but there was no turning back, no unlearning what he'd learned tonight.

Jo had not been a pleasant woman, her death no great loss to anyone, it seemed, but no matter how badly he wanted to protect his family, he couldn't ignore that a brutal crime had been committed, a crime he'd be happy to ignore. What sort of person did that make him? As much as he didn't want to kick the hornet's nest that was Brett Besson, he couldn't simply walk away from the truth. Brett had committed murder, Daisy had seen it, and now they had to act on the information she had presented them with.

Quinn had nothing to take to the police, but there was someone who could help. Drew Camden. For all his outward reserve, Drew was like a bloodhound who wouldn't give up until he either found the evidence needed to support Daisy's claim or confirmed once and for all that they needed to let the matter drop. Gabe would be happy with the latter outcome, but if Drew proved successful, then sooner or later, Brett would learn of the threat against him, and then what? Would he go to ground in the States, or would he try to flee? How easy would it be for British police to bring a case against an American citizen? Gabe had no idea, but with today's level of cooperation between the two nations, he didn't think the police in the United States would put up too many obstacles if presented with solid evidence. And what of Kathy and Seth Besson? Would they try to help their son at any cost? They'd done so once, but now the stakes were higher, the implications more dire. Brett had actually killed his own sister, Seth's daughter.

Dear God, how was it possible to spawn such a monster? Gabe wondered as he gazed up at the unsympathetic moon. Kathy and Seth weren't bad people. In fact, he liked them both immensely. They were "salt of the earth," as his father would have said: solid, dependable, compassionate. How had they produced such a sociopath, and had they really not known what Brett was capable of?

And Jo… She was still haunting them from the grave, wreaking havoc on their lives. Would they ever be able to fully move on from the events that had led to her death? Would Quinn ever be able to expunge those awful memories, or would Jo be forever linked to Gabe in her mind? Probably not, but as Gabe turned for home, he asked himself the one question he still didn't have an answer to. Was it wrong to love someone enough to let a murderer go free in order to protect them?

Chapter 30

Sleep wouldn't come. Quinn couldn't even bring herself to summon the past. She was still worked up, her emotions raw. Gabe was right in everything he'd said; she knew that, but how could she simply let this go? Brett had mowed down Jo in cold blood, and he'd killed her because of Quinn. So, indirectly, she was responsible for Jo's death. And what if there had been others, before or after he'd murdered Jo? Who was to say that Brett hadn't disposed of other people who'd threatened him or simply got in his way? How could she live with herself if she allowed him to walk away as if he'd done nothing wrong?

If only his conviction hadn't been overturned, Quinn thought angrily. Brett would still be in prison, removed from society for several more years. Would prison have changed him? Probably not. In order to change, you had to see the error of your ways, to repent and want to be better. But Brett was unrepentant, his conscience clear.

Of course, no one would take her seriously; Gabe was right in that as well. Without fresh evidence, the case would remain closed, just another file collecting dust in an out-of-the-way cabinet until enough time had passed and it was moved to some basement archive, where it would never see the light of day again.

Quinn sighed heavily. She needed expert advice. She had to know if she had a legal leg to stand on. She'd promised Gabe she wouldn't go to the police, but she hadn't promised she wouldn't consult Drew Camden. Drew had helped her find her twin when everyone else thought Jo had dropped off the face of the earth, and he had been able to make inroads into finding Daisy before Jo had abruptly decided to abort the search. Drew was clever, determined, and most importantly discreet, and, being a retired police detective, would know exactly how to proceed and what evidence would stand up in court.

The bedroom door opened, and Gabe came in. He undressed quickly and got into bed. Realizing she was still awake, he pulled her into his arms, and Quinn melted into him, thinking he wanted to resolve their differences the old-fashioned way, but Gabe didn't respond to her obvious willingness. His gaze was troubled, his breathing ragged. He was still upset.

"I'm sorry," he said softly. "I'm so sorry for everything I said. You were right; we can't ignore this. We don't have enough to involve the police, but we can speak to Drew. He'll advise us. I'll stand by you, Quinn, no matter where this takes us."

"I'm sorry too," Quinn said softly. "Now, shut up and make love to me."

Their joining was urgent and intense, the feelings that had been simmering for the past few hours finally boiling over in a culmination of love, forgiveness, and mutual acknowledgment that nothing would ever truly be the same. This day had changed everything, regardless of the eventual outcome. Like Adam and Eve, they'd taken a bite of the apple and now possessed knowledge they could no longer ignore that could lead to their expulsion from paradise. And their life had been paradise before she went and cocked it all up, Quinn thought bitterly. She'd brought the serpent into their lives.

Unable to rest even after Gabe had finally dropped off to sleep, Quinn reached for the ring, desperate to escape a reality she couldn't have imagined only twenty-four hours ago.

Chapter 31

November 1777
New York City

The ride into New York City took several hours, but Jocelyn didn't mind. She was warm and snug in Hannah's cloak, her hair kept out of the grip of the playful wind by a linen cap. They'd left before the sun had come up, but Jocelyn had been more than ready to go, glad no one would see them on the road at such an early hour. She had no desire to fuel the gossip that had spread like a forest fire over the past few weeks, the nasty insinuations fanned by Lydia Blackwell and based on her unfounded belief that Jocelyn was making a play for Derek. Derek seemed unperturbed, no doubt pleased by Lydia's jealousy, nor did he ever address the rumors at home, not even when Ben had brought up the subject over supper last night.

Jocelyn found Ben's anger more telling than anything he might have said to her outright. He resented her name being bandied about in relation to his brother, who'd been nothing but chivalrous and respectful since their conversation in the barn, keeping her secrets as if they were his own. Ben hadn't spoken to her of his feelings again, but the intensity of his gaze when he looked at her and his constant attempts at getting her alone had become wearying. She'd said nothing to encourage him, but he took her every smile and comment as a sign of interest and repaid her friendly gestures with romantic overtures. He'd left a bouquet of late-blooming roses in a jug by her bed and had sewed her a handsome leather purse, which hung empty from her bedpost since Jocelyn had nothing of her own to put in it. Ben was kind, solicitous, and respectful, but the intensity of his feelings terrified Jocelyn, more so because she didn't return them.

"Do you normally go into the city on your own?" Jocelyn asked Derek, who'd been silent far too long, his gaze fixed on the road shrouded in early morning haze.

"Most of the time," he replied.

"Do you not find the journey lonely, especially at night?"

"No. I like being on my own. I have plenty to think about."

"Such as?" Lydia? Jocelyn wanted to ask but stopped herself.

"We live in extraordinary times," Derek said. "The decisions we make today will reverberate through the centuries."

"Do you think the Continental Army stands a chance against the might of Britain?" Jocelyn asked, eager to draw Derek into a political discussion. The Wilders scrupulously avoided talking about the rebellion, but she'd never heard them proclaim their devotion to the king either. Were they afraid to say too much in front of her, not knowing where her loyalties lay, or did they simply not care either way, believing themselves immune to the winds of change that blew outside their small rural community?

"I do," Derek replied.

"But the Americans are sorely outnumbered, if what the newspapers say is anything to go on."

"Maybe so, but they're more committed."

"How do you mean?" Jocelyn asked.

"A paid soldier fights differently than a man who's defending his family and his homeland."

Jocelyn nodded. There was truth in that. "The British will never surrender New York," she said.

"No, but they will be driven out," Derek replied.

"You seem awfully sure."

"It's what I believe," he said.

"Have you ever considered enlisting?" Jocelyn asked, wondering just how committed Derek was to the cause of freedom.

"There are many ways to fight," Derek said evasively.

"What about Ben? Does he share your conviction?" Jocelyn asked, not ready to let the matter drop.

Derek turned to look at her. "Does it matter?" he snapped. "Ben rarely sees past the end of his own nose."

The statement might have been humorous had his scowl not been so thunderous. Jocelyn had a feeling politics were a sore subject between the brothers, among other things.

"And what about you?" Derek demanded. "Where do you stand?"

"What? Me? I don't take sides," Jocelyn replied, uncomfortable now that the focus had turned to her.

"Don't you?" Derek asked.

"What's that supposed to mean?"

"Nothing. I just think every person should have an opinion on issues that affect them directly."

"Even women?" Jocelyn teased. Most men didn't value women's opinions, even if they were well informed and often more intelligent than that of their menfolk.

"Especially women," Derek replied.

"Why's that?"

"Because women are sorely underestimated as weapons of war. They're clever and brave and can go places men can't."

Jocelyn bit her lip. Something of what Derek said resonated with her, but she couldn't be sure what her views had been before the shipwreck. What of her husband? Had he been a revolutionary or a royalist? Had she agreed with him? Had they debated openly, or had she kept her views to herself, outwardly supporting him? She wished she could remember.

"Let's change the subject, shall we?" Derek said.

"All right. Are you planning to propose to Lydia Blackwell?" Jocelyn blurted out, and instantly regretted asking.

Derek turned to face her, a smile tugging at the corners of his mouth. "Would you mind if I did?"

"Eh, no, of course not. It's just that everyone seems to expect it."

"Who's everyone?" Derek asked, clearly amused by the turn the conversation had taken.

"Lydia, for one."

"Has she said so?" Derek asked, looking very pleased with himself.

"Not in so many words. I think Ben is hoping you will."

"Ben wants the farm. He doesn't care who I marry as long as I leave the running of it to him."

"Would you?" Jocelyn asked. She'd assumed Derek would bring his wife to live at the farm, but perhaps he intended to live with Lydia in town and work at the Blackwell Arms.

"I hate farming. I'm not cut out for it," Derek replied with a shrug.

"What are you cut out for?"

"A life of adventure," Derek joked. "And heart-pounding romance."

"You're not going to marry Lydia, then," Jocelyn said.

"And how did you arrive at that conclusion?"

"Because the only heart that's pounding is hers," Jocelyn replied. *And not necessarily for you*, she added mentally.

"Don't presume to know my feelings," Derek said, but there was no heat in his voice. He was enjoying their banter.

"I'm right, though. Aren't I?"

"You might be," Derek teased, that maddening smile playing about his lips. "By the same token, I don't think there'll be wedding bells for you and Ben."

"I've never done anything to encourage Ben. You know that."

"He doesn't need much encouragement. A damsel in distress is enough to set his heart aflame."

"That's not saying much for my charms," Jocelyn said, smiling despite herself.

"Nothing wrong with your charms as far as I can see, Mistress Sinclair. Nothing at all."

Jocelyn looked down at her hands clasped in her lap, a slow smile spreading across her face. It wasn't a flowery compliment by any means, but coming from Derek, it meant a lot.

Chapter 32

Ben brought down the hammer so hard, the wooden post split right down the middle. He cursed under his breath. Now he'd have to replace it. He threw the hammer to the ground and stalked off, too angry to deal with mending the fence. At this very moment, Alice was alone with his brother, traveling to New York City for reasons he didn't quite understand.

When Derek had announced last night that Alice would be joining him, Ben had opened his mouth to protest, but his brother had silenced him with a look. Ben had no claim on her, the look had said. He supposed it was true that she needed to get away from the farm for a bit, and the change of scene might help her recall something of her past. Dr. Rosings had said as much the last time he'd called, but Ben could barely contain his rage.

It wasn't that he didn't trust Derek with Alice. Derek was an honorable man. He'd never do anything to hurt her, but he couldn't help being better looking or more enigmatic than Ben. Ben was an open book; his mother always told him so. He wasn't good at playing games or pretending he wasn't interested, not when his heart was engaged in ways it had never been with Kira. He wanted Alice, and not just because she was vulnerable and alone. He wanted her because she was charming and clever and clearly needed a man, her lush beauty too sensual to be wasted on sleeping alone. He wanted to be that man. He wanted to offer her his love and protection and to plant his seed in her belly, proclaiming to the world that she was his, but he had no right to act on his feelings. Just because Alice had no memory of a husband didn't mean the man didn't exist. He may have gone down with the ship, but he could just as easily be alive and well somewhere, grieving the loss of his wife.

Alice wasn't able to marry, not until she knew for certain that she was free. But he would wait. He was a patient man. And she would come around to the idea of spending the rest of her life with him, more so if Derek finally made up his damn mind and made an offer to Lydia Blackwell. Ben was sure that her attempts at making Derek jealous by showing an interest in Lieutenant

Reynolds were nothing more than clumsily executed ploys to force his hand.

Stomping across the frostbitten landscape, Ben wondered miserably what was holding Derek back. Lydia was beautiful, wealthy, and willing. What more could a man want?

Love, his heart replied. A man wanted love, and Derek was halfway in love with Alice.

Chapter 33

Jocelyn gripped the bench as Derek guided the cart onto the ferry that would take them from Long Island to New York City. There were three other wagons loaded with casks of ale and cider, potatoes and pumpkins, baskets of apples, and even fish. The wooden conveyance didn't seem sturdy enough to get them across the river, but Derek appeared calm, and the other men exchanged greetings and casual comments, clearly unafraid the flimsy wooden platform would tip over or collide with one of the bigger boats.

The traffic on the East River was surprisingly heavy, with several other ferries making the crossing from points further down the shore, at least three naval ships offloading supplies and troops at the South Street Port, and half a dozen merchant ships flying British flags. Once the ferry left the dock and glided toward the center of the river, Jocelyn spotted several ships anchored close together. They were in a state of advanced dilapidation, and a strong smell of human waste and decay carried on the breeze, forcing her to cover her nose and mouth with her handkerchief.

"What's on those ships?" she asked Derek, who glared at the ships, his mouth compressed in a grim line.

"Prisoners. The British use decommissioned ships as floating prisons for anyone they perceive to be a rebel soldier or spy. The conditions aboard are hellish. People are dying by the dozen every single day, on every ship. It's an outrage."

"Does anyone ever get pardoned?" Jocelyn asked.

"There's only one way off a prison ship," Derek said angrily. "Wrapped in canvas and tossed over the side."

"That's barbaric," Jocelyn said.

Derek didn't reply. He turned away, his gaze fixed on the southern tip of the city.

The rolling of the ferry and the vile smell made Jocelyn feel sick, so she began to count the ships on the river to distract herself from the nausea that threatened to overwhelm her, but the exercise didn't help. The ferry was downwind of the prison ships, and the reek intensified as they reached the center of the river.

"Are you all right?" Derek asked. "You look awful."

"I'll be fine once we dock," Jocelyn managed to reply, hoping she wouldn't vomit on his boots. Derek reached for her hand and squeezed it in a reassuring manner.

"Almost there," he said. "Just hang on."

It took some time to get off the ferry and then twice as long to make it to the next corner. The street leading away from the dock was thronged with wagons and carriages, and there seemed to be people everywhere. British soldiers in their red tunics stood out of the crowd, sailors crowded the decks of their ships, and stevedores called out to each other as they unloaded the merchantmen, cargo lowered using pulley systems that suspended the heavy crates directly over their heads in a most precarious manner.

At last, they reached Broadway Street, and Derek turned right, leaving the worst of the congestion behind. This street was wider, paved with gray stone and lined with handsome brick houses, some of which were fronted by neatly trimmed bushes and russet-leafed trees. Well-dressed pedestrians strolled leisurely along or hurried about their business, but it was the soldiers who drew Jocelyn's eye. They were everywhere, walking in pairs with muskets slung over their shoulders, delivering messages, and, in some instances, standing guard, their grim faces shadowed by tricorns pulled low over their eyes to keep out the bright sun.

A young soldier exited a house on the corner of Broadway and Crown Street and waited for the cart to pass before crossing to the other side. His pale blue eyes met Jocelyn's gaze and widened with interest, his mouth stretching into a friendly smile. She quickly looked away, uncomfortable beneath his scrutiny.

"Where are we going?" Jocelyn asked, wondering why Derek had brought her to this part of town. She felt deeply uneasy since most of the houses appeared to be occupied by British officers. Their presence made her stomach clench with fear, even though most of them paid her little mind.

"To the theater at John Street," Derek replied patiently. "We're nearly there."

"I thought you said it was closed," Jocelyn said as the cart slowed down yet again to let an expensive-looking carriage pass.

"It is, but I thought it might help you to see it for yourself. Do you recognize anything?" Derek asked, looking at her intently, as if willing her to say yes.

"I feel a sense of familiarity," she said truthfully. "But I suppose this looks like any other street in any other city."

"Yes, but if you had performed at the theater at John Street, you would have walked down these streets, possibly even lived somewhere nearby," Derek pointed out.

Jocelyn paid closer attention to the individual facades, wondering if she had come this way. Was it possible that she had lived in one of these grand houses? She didn't think so. If she had been an actress, she would not have been able to afford extravagant lodgings, unless she'd married one of the theater's patrons, but this new theory didn't feel right, so she dismissed it. Could her husband be one of the actors in the troupe? Or might she have had a lover rather than a husband? Was she the type of woman to live with a man without the benefit of marriage? All she knew was that she was carrying someone's baby, but the man's identity eluded her.

The wall her mind put up whenever she thought of her child's father made her tremble with frustration, so she forced her thoughts down a different path. The theater had been closed since the occupation, so for just over a year. What had she been doing since then? Had she had to earn a living, or had she been supported by her man? And where had she been going at the time of the shipwreck? Had he been with her? Was he now dead? Jocelyn nearly screamed as the questions crowded her mind, each inquiry bringing her closer to tears.

Everything hinged on remembering the father of her child. If she could do that, then she could unravel the rest of this impenetrable web and finally see a glimmer of light. He was at the center of everything, but she couldn't conjure up even a twinge of emotion or put a name to her feelings for him. Surely if she had loved him, she'd feel a deep sorrow, an instinctive sense of loss, even if she couldn't envision his face. How was it possible to draw a complete blank when it came to the most important person in her life?

"How far away are we from the theater?" Jocelyn asked, tearing her mind away from the futile questions that threatened to overwhelm her.

"Not that far. It's just down John Street, to the right."

She peered down the length of the street as the cart laboriously turned the corner, hoping against hope she'd recognize the theater. Derek stopped in front of a squat brick building and turned to her, clearly expecting a reaction.

"This doesn't look much like a theater," Jocelyn said, deeply disappointed by the factory-like appearance of the place and her failure to recognize it.

"I think it was a brewery before it became a theater."

Jocelyn wrinkled her nose. She'd imagined red velvet curtains and gilded balconies filled with beautifully dressed people who'd come to see a professionally mounted performance. This place probably boasted a makeshift stage and wooden benches.

"What was it like inside?" she asked.

"Not very impressive, I'm afraid. But the quality of the acting was top notch," Derek assured her. "Does it look familiar?" he asked, his voice filled with hope.

Jocelyn shook her head. "No."

"Have you been able to recall anything at all?" Derek asked as the cart moved away from the shut-up theater.

She'd experienced several flashbacks in the past few weeks, but they had all been scenes of ordinary life: kneading bread, washing linen, shopping for produce, walking with a basket slung over her arm, but she hadn't seen anyone's faces clearly. It was as if she had been completely alone, going about her life in a city full of people without truly belonging to anyone.

"Not anything that matters," Jocelyn replied miserably. "Where to now?"

"There's a tavern not far from here. Let's get something to eat and then we'll continue our tour of the city," Derek suggested.

"All right."

Ned's Ale House was crowded. Derek found them a table in the corner and went up to the bar to order a drink—a tankard of ale for himself and a half-pint of cider for Jocelyn. She was hungry and tired, not having slept well last night in anticipation of today's journey. As soon as Derek returned to the table, she took a long sip of cider, then excused herself to go to the necessary before ordering the food. Weaving through the crowd of mostly men, Jocelyn made her way toward the back door of the building. She was just about to push it open when the blue-eyed soldier she'd seen earlier stepped into her path, his back blocking her from Derek's view.

"Good day, mistress," he said, smiling down at her.

"Eh, good day," Jocelyn replied. "Please excuse me."

"Don't you remember me?"

"I'm afraid I don't," she replied, wondering if she'd really met him in the past or he was just trying it on with her.

"It's Robert. Robert Sykes."

"I'm sorry, Mr. Sykes, but you mistake me for someone else."

He gave her an odd look but took a step back. "I'm sorry to have troubled you, ma'am." He gave her a curt bow and allowed her to pass.

Jocelyn stepped out into the yard and hurried toward the privy, hoping the soldier wouldn't follow her outside, where she'd be defenseless. Finishing her business in record time, thanks to the eye-watering stench inside the tiny outhouse, she returned to the dining room and made her way toward the table and Derek.

"Come have a drink with us, darlin'," a handsome young soldier beckoned as she passed the bar. "Got a face like a thundercloud, yer man. We'll show ye a better time," he joked. His friend winked at her, and she couldn't help smiling. They were just having a bit of fun.

"Do you know that man?" Derek asked, his narrowed gaze fixed on the soldier who'd invited her for a drink.

"No. He was just being cheeky."

"Let's get some food. I'm famished."

"What's good here?" Jocelyn asked.

"Roast beef and potatoes and turkey with chestnut stuffing. They serve it with cranberry sauce and mashed potatoes."

"That sounds good," Jocelyn said, suddenly ravenous.

She didn't protest too loudly when Derek ordered two slices of apple pie and cups of strong coffee. By the time they finished their meal, Jocelyn felt pleasantly full and considerably less agitated. Derek escorted her from the tavern, tossed a coin to the boy who'd been looking after the cart and horse, and helped her up onto the bench. The wind had picked up since they'd arrived in New York, and fat drops of rain fell from a now-leaden sky. Jocelyn pulled up the hood of her cloak, but the wind blew it off, tearing at the flimsy linen cap and whipping her hair around her face. Derek grabbed for his tricorn, which was about to fly off, and jammed it forcibly on his head before pulling up the collar of his coat.

"We'll have to stay the night if the weather doesn't improve," he said grimly.

"What? Why?"

"The ferry can capsize in such strong wind, and it's not exactly pleasant traveling weather," Derek pointed out.

"But where would we stay?" Jocelyn asked.

"I have friends who live just off Water Street."

Jocelyn felt a twinge of panic. She had no wish to stay in New York. The place made her nervous, and how safe would she be with Derek's friends?

"Jocelyn, my friend's wife is a kind and respectable woman. She'll act as chaperone, if that's what worries you."

Jocelyn tried to pull up her hood again, more to hide her embarrassment than to keep out the rain. She was being ridiculous. She had been sharing a house with Derek and Ben for weeks. How would this be any different?

"Whatever you think is best, Derek," she cried over the wind.

"Let's get out of this rain," he said. The wind and rain precluded further conversation, so they drove in silence until they arrived at Derek's friend's house nearly an hour later.

Chapter 34

"Please come in," Fran Cox said, ushering Jocelyn into the parlor. It was cozy and warm, a merry fire burning in the grate and thick curtains drawn to keep out the draft. "Get that wet cloak off and make yourself comfortable."

Jocelyn turned to look for Derek, but he'd disappeared somewhere between the front door and the parlor, leaving her alone with their hostess.

"Jim and Derek went to see to the horse and cart," Fran explained as she draped the cloak over her arm. "Would you like some tea? You must be chilled to the bone after that wet ride."

Jocelyn nodded. "Yes, thank you. Tea would be wonderful."

Fran left the room to hang up the cloak and make the tea while Jocelyn held out her hands and feet to the fire, enjoying the lovely warmth that spread through her body. It had begun to rain in earnest soon after they left the tavern, the weather halting the already slow-moving traffic along Queen Street. By the time they'd finally made it to the Cox's door, both Jocelyn and Derek had been wet and shivering from the cold wind gusting off the East River. Despite her misgivings, Jocelyn was glad of the shelter and the offer of a bed for the night.

"Are you all right?" Derek asked as he followed Jim Cox into the room. He'd taken off his sodden coat and hat, but his face was still ruddy with cold, and his hair was damp where it had been exposed to the lashing rain.

"Yes. Fran is making tea," Jocelyn said.

"Splendid," Jim said, rubbing his hands together. "There's something I'd like to show you in the meantime," he said to Derek, and the two men disappeared again.

Jocelyn leaned back in the chair and stared into the flames. The Coxes seemed like a nice couple. They were in their mid-twenties and had that lived-in look some people achieved once they settled into married life. Jim's fair hair was already thinning at the front, his face still tanned from the summer months, when he'd obviously spent much time outdoors. He was thin and wiry and had the nervous energy of someone who was always moving about. Fran was short and plump, her nose and cheeks sprinkled with freckles, and her eyes a warm brown. She was about eight months gone with child, her belly swelling beneath the brown skirts of her somber gown.

"Here we are, then," she said as she bustled into the room, bearing a tea tray. "Where have Jim and Derek got to?" she asked, looking around.

"Jim said he had something to show Derek," Jocelyn said.

"Oh, that would be his new acquisition. He's mad for maps, my Jim," she said affectionately as she poured the tea. "Sugar and milk?"

"Yes, please. What sort of maps?" Jocelyn asked.

"Local maps and maps of the colonies. He loves to compare the earlier versions to the more recent ones and note all the new towns and landmarks that've sprung up over the years."

"How do you know Derek?" Jocelyn asked. She was curious about Derek's life, since he'd shared so little of himself.

"I grew up in Milford. Didn't Derek tell you? I was sweet on Derek when I was a girl," Fran confessed with an embarrassed giggle, "but when Jim walked into town, I just knew."

"What was he doing there?" Jocelyn asked. Milford wasn't the type of place people just walked into. It was too small and out of the way to be much of a draw for businessmen or visitors.

"It was the maps he was after. My father used to be a sea captain in his younger days and had some old maps. He'd met Jim while in New York and had invited him to visit. Jim was more than happy to pay for the maps, but Father gave them to him as a gift. He had no use for them, and he liked the man. I did too," Fran added. "What about you? Where are you from?"

"Born and bred in New York City. My father used to teach philosophy at King's College," Jocelyn said without thinking. She felt a jolt of excitement as she realized that the words had come from somewhere deep inside her mind, an unbidden memory of her past swimming to the surface when she'd least expected it.

"And your mother?" Fran asked.

"Died when I was fifteen. I have a brother in Virginia," Jocelyn said, the words tumbling out like marbles from a bag.

"Oh? And what does he do?" Fran asked. She sipped her tea delicately, her left hand on her belly.

"He teaches at the College of William and Mary," Jocelyn replied, happiness pumping through her veins. "In Williamsburg," she added. *Gregory Sinclair*, her brain supplied helpfully. Greg.

Jocelyn crashed back to earth, her joy at recalling something of her past quickly replaced by dismay. If her brother's name was Sinclair, as her father's had been, she now recalled, that meant she wasn't married. There was no husband who was either grieving for her or resting at the bottom of the sea. She was alone, unmarried, and pregnant. This revelation seemed to settle over her shoulders like a mantle of marble, pushing her deeper into the chair, her breath catching in her throat.

"Are you all right, Jocelyn?" Fran asked, all concern. "You look unwell."

"I'm fine. Really," Jocelyn lied. "I'm just tired. It's been a wearying day."

"I'm sure it has. It's quite a distance from Milford to New York. Jim and I never attempt to go there and back in one day."

"Do you go to Milford often?" Jocelyn asked, eager to shift the conversation to anything but her past.

"Several times a year, to visit my parents. You might know them. John and Anne Garrett."

"Yes. Yes, of course," Jocelyn said. "I've met them at church. Lovely people. And you have a sister, I believe."

"That's right. Felicia. Do you know her?"

"We've met," Jocelyn said. Felicia Painter was one of the women who'd laid out the victims of the shipwreck. She was kind, and one of the less judgmental matrons of Milford, who seemed to regard Jocelyn with suspicion.

"Do tell her we've met," Fran said. "I miss her sorely, especially now." Fran's gaze slid to her belly. Felicia had to be the older sister, Jocelyn decided, since she already had three children, all boys.

"Is this your first?"

"Yes. I'm a little nervous, truth be told. I wish my mother and sister were nearby. It's nice to have other women to talk to, to ask questions. I don't have many friends hereabouts."

Jocelyn's hand went to her own belly, but she instantly moved it up to the bodice of Lydia's cast-off gown, adjusting the plain cotton tucker even though it was in place. She wished she had someone to talk to as well, someone who wouldn't think badly of her.

"Ah, here they are. So, what did you think of Jim's newest acquisition?" Fran asked, smiling up at Derek.

"It's very eh…detailed," Derek replied with a roll of his eyes, making Fran laugh. "I'm afraid I'm not the enthusiast Jim is. Is there any tea left?"

"Of course. Come and join us."

The men pulled up two chairs and sat down, Derek moving as close to the fireplace as he could without setting his boots aflame.

"I'm afraid I'm going to have to leave you to it while I see to supper," Fran said, rising to her feet with obvious reluctance.

"Can I help?" Jocelyn offered.

"You're a guest," Fran protested. "You just rest. You look done in, if you don't mind me saying so."

Derek turned to look at her, his eyes brimming with concern. "Would you like to lie down before supper?"

"No. I'm fine here," Jocelyn lied. She was exhausted, and she would have liked a few minutes of solitude to gather her thoughts. Everything she had come to believe had suddenly shifted, her perception of life before the shipwreck taking on a whole new light. She had been an actress, and since she now recalled that her father had passed away five years ago and her brother currently lived in Virginia, she must have lived alone or with the man who'd fathered her child. And since she wasn't married, the man must have been her lover.

Jocelyn couldn't explain how she knew, but she now felt certain that he hadn't been with her on the doomed ship. She'd been alone, she suddenly recalled with unflinching clarity. And she had been going to Virginia, to Greg. She had been running away, but from what?

Chapter 35

November 1777
Long Island

The rain had stopped sometime during the night, leaving behind a brilliant blue sky. A pleasant breeze moved stealthily through the flaming canopy of autumn leaves and had made the crossing a little more bearable, since the prison ships had been downwind this time. The cart swayed from side to side, the wheels squelching in the mud as Derek drove down a well-traveled road that bypassed some of the larger towns and settlements on southern Long Island. Fran Cox had given them breakfast and had even prepared a bundle of food for the trip, insisting they would get hungry well before reaching home, but the thought of food made Jocelyn ill, the hours stretching before them until they reached Milford a test of endurance.

Derek had been right in thinking that bringing her to New York would jog her memory. Little by little, starting with the information she'd shared with Fran, tiny bits had begun to swim to the surface: childhood memories, cherished moments with her mother, happy hours spent reading in her father's study, and later, the desolation of losing her parents, the falling out with Greg, and the gesture of defiance that had led her to the theater. But at the end of the parade of images, that quaint and often heartbreaking collection of experiences that had made up her life, came the truths her mind had tried so valiantly to suppress.

She'd spent a sleepless night in the Cox's tiny spare room, tormented by a relentless stream of images, her heart hammering against her ribs as the memories came hard and fast, the events that had driven her to board the *Peregrine* on the afternoon of October nineteenth more visceral than she could have imagined. She'd broken out in a cold sweat as she lay in the dark, shivering and weeping, not only because she now recalled everything, but because she was terrified of what was to come. The revelations of last night had changed everything, and she was glad of Milford's remoteness and the sanctuary it offered to someone who needed to disappear. And now that she knew she had no loving husband who'd be grieving her passing or desperately searching for her, she had to make use of the opportunities fate had chosen to offer her. She needed protection for herself and her child. She needed a man.

"Are you going to tell me what's troubling you?" Derek asked after his attempts at conversation fell flat when Jocelyn barely managed to offer more than monosyllabic answers.

"What makes you think anything is troubling me?"

"If you have to ask that, you're not as good an actress as I imagined," Derek said, only half-teasing. He looked worried, his gaze searching her face anxiously. "What is it, Jocelyn? What have you remembered?"

Jocelyn was about to deny that she'd remembered anything of significance. Some part of her wanted to hold on to her secrets, to build a wall that would keep anyone from getting in, but she couldn't get through this alone. Not after what had happened yesterday at the tavern. But she couldn't tell Derek about that. Not yet.

"You were right," she said at last. "Seeing familiar things helped me remember."

Derek watched her silently, waiting for her to speak. She sucked in a shuddering breath. She'd tell him what was safe to share, play for his sympathy.

"I grew up in New York City. My father was one of the first tutors to join the staff of King's College when it opened. He taught philosophy." Jocelyn looked down at her lap, trying desperately not to cry. Now that she remembered her father, she felt like she'd just lost him all over again, her grief as all-consuming as it had been when he passed. "He died five years ago," she choked out.

Derek reached out and placed his hand over hers. "I'm sorry. And your mother?" he asked gently.

"Two years before him."

"Have you no one?"

"I have an older brother. He lives in Williamsburg, Virginia."

"Is that where you were going?" Derek asked softly.

Jocelyn nodded, unable to speak. She'd been running away, going to the only person who'd be willing to help her, protect her, but she'd only made it as far as Long Island before the storm that had seemingly come out of nowhere put an end to her journey.

"Was there anyone traveling with you?" Derek asked, too polite to ask outright about the father of her child.

"No," Jocelyn whispered. "I was traveling alone."

That was why she hadn't recognized any of the people she'd seen laid out in the church. She hadn't known them, having only just come aboard a few hours before. Some of the passengers had introduced themselves and had struck up a conversation, but Jocelyn had kept apart, wanting only to stay invisible for as long as she could for fear of being recognized.

"What about your theater friends?" Derek asked. "Is there anyone you'd like to contact?"

"They're gone," Jocelyn said quietly. "After the theater closed, they waited for a while, hoping the British might change their minds and reopen the theater, but when that didn't happen, the troupe took their act on the road."

"But you didn't go with them," Derek said, still watching her.

"No, I remained in New York."

"Why?"

She couldn't tell him the truth. Not yet. Maybe not ever, so she improvised. "Anna, that was the only other woman in the troupe, had decided not to go. She lived with another woman, down by the Battery—her partner," Jocelyn said, hoping Derek would take her meaning. "Had I gone, I would have been the only woman among eight men."

"Had any of them ever behaved inappropriately toward you?" Derek asked, probably assuming she'd had a failed affair with one of the other actors.

"No, but being on the road, sometimes sleeping rough or having to share rooms in a tavern…" She let the sentence trail off, allowing Derek to form his own conclusions.

"I understand. So, what did you do?"

"I found employment as a maidservant. I'd looked after my father and brother since I was a girl. My mother was often ill, so the running of the household fell mostly to me. Housework didn't frighten me."

"Why did you not go to your brother after your father died?"

"Greg can be a bit…" Jocelyn bit her lip as she tried to come up with the right word. "Autocratic, I suppose," she finally said. "He'd try to control everything I did. I had grown accustomed to my freedom."

She could see that Derek wanted to ask more questions, such as why her brother had permitted her to remain on her own in New York, or whom she'd lived with while working as an actress. She supposed he might have wanted to know if she'd had a partner and had lived with him in sin, but he didn't ask.

"Jocelyn, you're welcome to stay with us, but if you still wish to join your brother, I can arrange passage to Virginia."

Had she not been with child, she might have asked him to do just that, but Greg would not make life easy for her once her condition became obvious. Of course, she could lie and tell him she'd been wed and her husband had gone down with the ship. He'd believe it too. His imagination didn't stretch to the type of life she'd led or to the terrible events that had forced her to flee. She had a bit of time before her pregnancy began to show in earnest. She'd stay with the Wilders through the winter and then decide what to do come spring. She might not have to leave, Jocelyn reasoned, if another alternative presented itself.

"You've been much kinder to me than my brother has ever been," Jocelyn said at last, realizing Derek was still waiting for an answer.

"It's decided, then," Derek replied, his warm fingers wrapping around hers. "But I do think it's time you allowed us to use your real name."

Jocelyn recoiled from the idea. Revealing her name would mean that she'd have to confess other things as well, and possibly have to come before Lieutenant Reynolds and answer his questions about the shipwreck. An account might be published in a New York newspaper, listing her as the only survivor. She couldn't allow that to happen.

"Derek, I—" she began. "Please don't make me," she croaked.

Derek removed his hand from hers, the gesture leaving her feeling vulnerable. "I think there's much you're not telling me, Jocelyn," he said, all the gentleness and understanding of a few minutes ago now gone. "We all have our secrets, but if you want me to keep yours, I think you'd better give me a reason."

Jocelyn scrambled for a plausible story, but Derek's gaze was like a beam from a lighthouse, shining a light into her darkness and leaving her exposed to his scrutiny. She supposed she owed him the truth, or at least part of it.

"Can I count on your discretion?" she asked, matching his direct gaze with her own.

"Yes." It was one simple word, but there was so much imbued in those three letters. She had no choice but to trust him, since the alternative was much riskier.

"All right," Jocelyn said, but it wasn't. Not really.

Chapter 36

March 2018
London

Quinn experienced a moment of apprehension when the doorbell rang but pushed it down and went to answer the door. It'd been a while since she'd seen Drew, but he hadn't changed much. A few more gray hairs perhaps, and several more inches around the middle, but his gaze was just as keen and his smile just as warm.

"It's good to see you, Quinn," Drew said as he came in out of the rain, his mac dripping onto the tile floor.

"It's good to see you too, Drew. Coffee?" Quinn asked, knowing he preferred it to tea.

"Please. It's really pissing down out there."

Drew took off his mac and tossed it over the banister before following Quinn into the kitchen. They made small talk while she made coffee, neither one of them ready to get down to business until they could give the case the attention it deserved.

"So, tell me," Drew invited once they were seated at the kitchen table, a plate of almond biscuits between them.

"Drew, I have reason to believe Jo was murdered," Quinn said. She'd wrapped her hands around the mug, finding the warmth radiating through her fingers comforting.

"What reason is that?" Drew asked.

Quinn took a deep breath and plunged in. She'd never told Drew what had happened in New Orleans. There'd been no reason to, but she had to begin at the beginning, when all the trouble with Brett had started.

Drew looked at Quinn thoughtfully as he stirred sugar into his second cup of coffee. He'd listened to her attentively, resisting the urge to pepper her narrative with questions. Now it was his turn to talk.

"First of all, let's get something straight," Drew said, his dark gaze speculative. "I know there's something you're not telling me, and I can only assume you've chosen to leave out some vital bits because you're covering for someone. Now, I am not going to press you, but if you want me to help you, I need to know as much as possible."

"I've told you all I can," Quinn replied, cringing inwardly. She hated lying to Drew, but that was all she could give him without revealing where the information had come from.

"So, let us say that what you are suggesting is true and Brett killed your sister. What exactly do you hope to accomplish, Quinn?"

"I want to see him pay for what he's done."

"You do realize that you've given me nothing to work with?" Drew asked conversationally.

"Yes, but if we know who did it, surely we can work backward and try to establish some connection between Brett and Jo's death."

"Possibly," Drew conceded, and took a sip of his coffee. He set down the mug and drummed his fingers on the table, a faraway look in his eyes.

At last, Drew took out a battered notepad and a biro pen and opened the notebook to a fresh page. "I'm going to need some information from you."

"I will give you whatever I can."

"I doubt that," Drew said, obviously still put out with Quinn's refusal to name her source. "I need the dates, the name of the hostel where Brett stayed, and anything you can recall of his itinerary. Where did he go? Whom did he meet? Did he mention making any new friends while in London?"

Quinn thought back to that tumultuous week in her life, wishing desperately she didn't have to relive those awful days. "He arrived in the UK around June twenty-sixth and stayed at the Intercontinental House Hostel near Victoria Station, if I remember correctly. I know he went sightseeing, but I have no idea which sites he visited. We didn't exactly indulge in a friendly chat. I think he may have met with Jo at some point. Sorry, that's all I know."

"Did he rent a car during his stay?"

"I don't believe so."

"So, whose car was he driving that night?"

"It had to be a rental car," Quinn replied.

"Yes, but who rented it?" Drew asked. "If it wasn't registered in Brett's name, it'll be damned hard to connect it to him."

"Sorry, I don't know," Quinn said. "Might he have stolen it?"

Drew shrugged. "Anything is possible, I suppose. And it has been more than two years. Any physical evidence would have been washed away by now."

"I realize that," Quinn said. "But what if I could provide you with the registration number of the car that killed Jo?" Quinn asked.

"First, I'd wonder why you hadn't given this information to the police at the time, and second, I'd want to know how you had come by this useful nugget."

"Would you believe me if I told you I had an anonymous tip-off a few days ago?" Quinn asked.

"No, I would not, but that's neither here nor there."

"I know this is an impossible task."

"I'll say. You might as well have asked me to get you the moon." He suddenly smiled, his gruff expression replaced by one of boyish mischief. "You do keep me on my toes, I'll give you that," he said. "Now, that registration number," he prompted.

Quinn pulled a slip of paper out of her pocket and slid it across the table. Drew unfolded it and took a photo of the number with his phone.

"I'll see what I can find out." He drank the remainder of his coffee and set the mug on the table.

"Drew, do you think I'm making a mistake in pursuing this?" Quinn asked.

"What does Gabe think?" Drew asked instead of answering.

"Gabe would have been happier had I let the matter drop," Quinn replied truthfully. "But he's supporting me in this."

Drew looked thoughtful for a moment. "Perhaps you should. This is not a TV program, Quinn; this is real life, and in real life, justice is rarely served. Even if you can prove that Brett Besson did this, the charge will be involuntary manslaughter since no one will be able to prove he did it intentionally. His lawyer will claim that it was an unfortunate accident, and Brett panicked and left the scene of the crime. He'll get a few years in prison and be out in half the time for good behavior, if he's smart enough to keep his head down. Or, if his lawyer is really clever, he might get off with nothing more than a slap on the wrist and maybe a couple of hours of community service."

"So, you think I should let him get away with murder?"

"No, I don't, but you need airtight evidence to present to the police if you hope to get this case reopened. I don't know that I can offer you that."

"Are you willing to try?" Quinn asked.

"You know I like a challenge," Drew replied, grinning at her. "But I do suggest you keep this under your hat, especially where your father is concerned."

Quinn nodded. "I won't say a word."

She couldn't begin to imagine what this knowledge would do to Kathy and Seth. Learning that Brett had murdered Jo in cold blood would present them with a moral dilemma they wouldn't be able to resolve simply by hiring a top-notch lawyer for their son. They had been able to move past what Brett had done to Quinn, labeling it a crime of passion, but this new revelation would finally force them to acknowledge that their son was a danger to society and to make a decision that would change the rest of their lives.

Drew rose laboriously to his feet and winced when he put weight on his damaged leg. He'd been shot in the knee during the course of duty, prompting his early retirement and leading to a career in private investigation and security.

"Damn knee acts up when it rains," he said gruffly, trying to mask his pain.

"So, every day, then?" Quinn joked.

"If I had the sense I was born with, I'd move to a warmer, sunnier climate, like your folks," Drew said.

"Marbella has its charms," Quinn agreed. "But I think you'd be bored out of your mind."

"You're probably right. I need to keep busy."

Quinn handed him the mac, and he shrugged it on. "I'll be in touch."

As Quinn returned to the kitchen, Drew's warning echoed in her head. How she wished Daisy had never come to her. Sometimes ignorance really was bliss.

Chapter 37

For the next few days, Quinn tried valiantly to concentrate on the case Rhys had tasked her with, but all she could think of was Brett, imagining him attending classes, hanging out with his friends, visiting his parents and talking about his life as if he were any normal college kid, not a coldblooded killer. She avoided speaking to Seth for fear of giving something away, letting his calls go to voicemail. Seth was a perceptive man, and he'd hear something in her voice and question her. How could she lie to him and pretend all was well?

She went about in a haze, checking her phone several times every hour to see if there might be a message from Drew. There was none, but Daisy had called, anxious to know if Quinn had acted on the information she'd shared with her. Quinn promised to keep her updated, but that would be the extent of Daisy's involvement. She meant to do everything in her power to keep Daisy safe. Daisy wasn't on Brett's radar, and Quinn would make sure he never learned of her connection to Jo.

"Can you get Alex and Mia to bed?" Quinn asked Gabe a week after she'd met with Drew. "I want to speak to Emma." Emma had just gone upstairs, having eaten little at dinner.

"Sure," Gabe said, and lifted Mia out of her highchair. "Come on, guys. Time for your bath."

Quinn loaded the dishwasher, then headed upstairs, having given Emma enough time to take a shower and change into her pajamas. She found Emma curled up on her bed, her arm around Rufus. The pup whoofed happily when he saw Quinn.

"Get off, Rufus," Quinn told him, and sat down in the spot he'd reluctantly vacated. She reached out and smoothed Emma's damp hair away from her face. Emma looked tired and worried. "Em, are you okay?" Quinn asked. "Is everything all right at school?"

Emma nodded.

"Getting along with your friends?" Quinn asked carefully. She knew how quickly kids could go from being the best of friends to not speaking to each other and refusing to sit together at lunch.

"Everything's fine, Mum," Emma replied warily.

"Then what's bothering you? You've been awfully quiet these past few days, and you've barely touched your dinner."

"I wasn't in the mood for chicken."

"Is there something you'd like me to make for dinner tomorrow?" Quinn asked.

Emma shrugged. "Whatever you want. It doesn't matter." Her eyes filled with tears as she met Quinn's gaze. "Mum, are you ill?" she blurted out.

"What? No. Why would you think that?" Quinn asked, taken by surprise.

"Because I see the way Dad watches you. He's scared. I can tell," Emma said quietly. "I've seen that look before."

"You have? When?"

"When we took you to the hospital the night Alex was born, and then when you were pregnant with Mia. When you had high blood pressure," Emma said, watching Quinn intently.

Quinn sighed. She knew Emma was observant, but she hadn't realized how much she was internalizing.

"Em, I am absolutely fine. I promise," Quinn said, stroking Emma's hair.

Emma's eyes widened as some thought popped into her head. "Are you going to have another baby?" she demanded.

"No. Were you hoping I was?"

"No. I don't want you to have any more babies."

"Really? Why?" Quinn asked. Emma adored Alex and Mia, so her answer was surprising.

"Because you're always busy. Every time I ask you to help me with something or to take me somewhere, you tell me that Alex has a playdate or it's time for Mia's nap, or someone has a doctor's appointment. If you have another baby, you'll never have time for me."

"I'll always have time for you."

Emma gave her an accusing look, and Quinn realized, quite guiltily, that she hadn't spent much one-on-one time with Emma in weeks.

"How about we do something this Saturday? Just you and me. We can go to the cinema or go shopping, if you like."

"I want to go to the British Museum," Emma said, surprising Quinn yet again.

"Great. Sure. Was there any particular exhibit you were interested in?"

"I want to see the Egyptian stuff. Do they have a mummy?"

"I think so. I haven't been in a long while. Why the sudden interest?"

"Miss Spencer told us about Howard Carter and how he discovered King Tut's tomb. It was interesting," Emma said, looking a little more animated.

"Are you getting the archeology bug?" Quinn asked, smiling. Emma had expressed her reservations about what her parents did for a living, upset that they often desecrated someone's final resting place during the course of a dig. It was only natural given that her birth mother, Jenna, had died when Emma was quite small. Emma worried about death more than other children her age, which was understandable, so Quinn and Gabe never dismissed her concerns and assured her that they would always be respectful of the dead.

"No," Emma said. "I want to be a doctor when I grow up," she said matter-of-factly, "but I would like to see a sarco—. What is that thing called again?"

"Sarcophagus," Quinn replied.

"Yes. That. And I'd like to see what an actual mummy looks like. Since I'm not the one digging it up, I think that's okay," Emma reasoned.

"All right, then. We will go to the museum on Saturday, followed by lunch at an eatery of your choice. Deal?"

"Deal," Emma agreed, looking distinctly more cheerful. "I'd like to try something new."

"Okay. Whatever you want."

"And maybe we can go shopping after," Emma said, now in full flow. "I need some new tops for school, and I want new shoes. Two pairs," she quickly amended.

"You got it. Now, it's time for bed."

"I'm going to read for a little while."

"Don't stay up too long," Quinn said, not wanting to ruin a nice moment by being too strict. Emma looked worn out. She'd be out like a light.

Having left Emma and Rufus, Quinn walked into the bedroom and changed into her favorite comfy pajamas. She was tired and upset by her conversation with Emma. She hadn't realized how much her emotional state pervaded the household and affected the children. She'd have to do a better job of keeping her feelings to herself, she thought, especially since Drew's inquiries might come to nothing in the end.

"Emma okay?" Gabe asked as he came in and sat down next to her on the bed.

"She asked if I'm ill, Gabe," Quinn said miserably. "She thinks you're watching me because you're worried."

"I am," Gabe replied. "I just never realized it was that obvious."

"Emma notices everything. She's very astute."

Gabe pulled Quinn close, resting his chin atop her head. "You still haven't heard from Drew, then?"

"No. He would have rung had he discovered something useful," Quinn said.

"It takes time. This happened over two years ago."

"I know. I'm just so—" Quinn couldn't find the right word for how she was feeling. She was angry, sad, worried, and afraid of what this newfound knowledge would do to her and Gabe, especially if Drew wasn't able to find anything useful. To live the rest of their lives with the knowledge that Brett had escaped justice would weigh on them in ways she couldn't imagine, especially when they'd come face to face with Brett sooner or later.

"I know," Gabe said soothingly. "Me too. And I wish Daisy had never been exposed to any of this. I can't imagine how difficult this must be for her, especially when she can't even tell her parents or siblings."

Quinn sighed. "Being psychic is a lonely business. People rarely take you seriously once you tell them the truth. That's why I never told my parents, or even Jill. I just didn't think our relationship would ever be the same."

"If there was a way to stop the visions, would you do it?" Gabe asked.

Quinn thought about it for a moment. "I've been privileged enough to see life as it was in the past, not as the historians or filmmakers would have us believe, and so fortunate to be able to use my ability in conjunction with my chosen profession, but this thing with Brett has made me wish this gift, or curse, had died with Madeline Besson. I would not stop my visions because I have learned to control them, but I very much wish they wouldn't manifest in future generations. I'm sure Daisy would gladly forego this ability in favor of peace of mind."

"Yes, I'm sure she would," Gabe agreed. He gave Quinn a sidelong glance. Someone who didn't know Gabe well wouldn't notice the subtle change in his expression or the dipping of his voice, but she was instantly aware of the change in his demeanor, and her heart went out to him.

"What is it?" she asked him as she reached for his hand, but she could already guess. They'd never discussed it, but now the possibility couldn't be ignored.

"Quinn, when will we know?" Gabe asked, his voice thick with apprehension.

"I don't know, but we'll be ready," she promised. "We'll see the signs and address the situation right away. We have a few years, though. We can still protect them."

"But we won't be able to protect them forever," Gabe replied. "Only one of them might inherit your ability. Or both."

"Or neither," Quinn said. "Seth is not psychic, so it does skip a generation here and there."

"One can hope," Gabe said.

Quinn turned out the light and snuggled against Gabe. He wrapped his arm around her and fitted himself to her body, offering silent comfort. She didn't want to think anymore or worry about something she couldn't control that might not be an issue for years to come. She allowed her mind to drift, but one final thought registered before she succumbed to sleep. She would ring Drew in the morning.

Chapter 38

Having dropped off the children at nursery school, Quinn walked to a nearby café, ordered a cappuccino, and took a seat at a table by the window. She felt a desire to be around people, even though she didn't know anyone. The upbeat atmosphere of the café helped to dispel some of her nervousness as she pulled out her mobile and selected Drew's number.

"Morning, Quinn," Drew said when he finally answered. "Sorry I haven't been in touch."

"Does that mean you haven't had much luck?" Quinn asked, her stomach clenching with anxiety.

"On the contrary. I've made some real progress," Drew reassured her.

"Really?"

"Yeah."

"Can you tell me what you've been able to discover?" Quinn asked, her cappuccino forgotten. There was a noise on the other end and then what sounded like the creaking of springs.

"Are you still in bed?" Quinn asked. She glanced at her watch. It was nearly nine thirty, and she'd assumed Drew would be up and about.

"Thought I'd have a bit of a lie-in," Drew grumbled. "Been under the weather."

"I'm sorry to have disturbed you."

"Don't worry about it. I actually need to get to the office. One of my clients is demanding an urgent meeting." Quinn waited patiently until Drew's mind returned to the case.

"Right. Sorry. I digress. So, I paid a visit to the hostel where Brett stayed and was able to learn that he shared a room with a Swedish student named Swen Persson. With a little persuasion, I was able to get Swen's contact information."

"Have you spoken to him?" Quinn asked breathlessly.

"I have. Swen remembers Brett quite well. Thought him a total wanker," Drew said. He was huffing and puffing, as if he were getting dressed while speaking on the phone.

"Was he able to provide you with anything more useful than that?" Quinn asked.

"He was, actually. Swen had rented a car for the duration of his stay. A silver Nissan Sentra. He doesn't recall the registration, of course, but he was able to provide me with the name of the rental company. He said that on the morning Brett checked out, he thought the car was parked in a different place than he'd remembered leaving it, but he also admitted that he had been drinking the night before and might have forgotten exactly where he'd parked it. He did, however, mention that the car appeared to be cleaner. He assumed it must have rained heavily during the night."

"Is that enough evidence to go on?" Quinn asked, disappointed. She'd expected something a little more promising than a drunken tourist's hazy version of events from more than two years ago.

"It's a start. I was able to run the registration number, and the make and model came up as a silver Nissan Sentra. It stands to reason that Brett had borrowed the car without Swen's permission and had it cleaned before returning it."

"So, what now?" Quinn asked.

"Now the grunt work begins," Drew said. "I've printed out a list of carwashes located between Jo's address and the hostel, using every possible route from point A to point B. There are thirty-seven."

Quinn's mouth opened in shock. Thirty-seven. That was quite a lot. "Say you locate the carwash Brett visited on the night of the murder. How would that help?"

"If we are very lucky, they might have some sort of proof that Brett was there. A recording on their security camera, a credit card receipt with his name on it, or an employee who can recall seeing blood would go a long way to proving our case."

"And how likely is that?" Quinn asked.

"Not very. Realistically, no carwash would keep footage for that long. Most small businesses override old footage every thirty days. Also, I strongly suspect Brett was smart enough to pay in cash."

"So, is it even worth the bother?" Quinn asked, now really deflated.

"It is, because if I can pinpoint the carwash, then I can locate the CCTV cameras in the vicinity and possibly even trace his route from the scene of the crime to the carwash."

"How would that help?"

"I have a mate on the force who can be persuaded to check the CCTV footage for that night. If we could get an image of Brett driving the car, we'd have something more than just idle speculation to present to the police."

"But an image of Brett driving Swen's car proves nothing unless we can conclusively show that the car he was driving is the one that hit Jo," Quinn pointed out.

"You are absolutely correct," Drew said. "Which is why I need more time. Look, Quinn, as far as we know, Brett knows nothing about this and is blithely going about his life. Correct?"

"Correct," Quinn replied.

"Time is not of the essence."

"No, it's not," Quinn agreed.

"So, give me the space I need to work this case. I know you're anxious. Jo was your sister, and this is your brother we're talking about, but you need to let me do my job. The only way we can convince anyone to reopen this case is if we can present them with irrefutable evidence, none of which I currently have."

"I understand," Quinn said. "I'm sorry if I made you feel pressured."

"You haven't. I should have given you an update, but I've been a bit busy. Personal stuff," Drew added gruffly. "I'll ring you on Sunday, regardless of what I discover. Okay?"

"Okay."

Quinn rang off and took a sip of her lukewarm cappuccino. Drew had found quite a lot in the short time he'd been investigating the case. She had to be patient. And she had to act natural, especially when speaking to Seth. He'd called the night before and left another message, asking her to call him back. Quinn stared at her phone. She'd call Seth later. She simply couldn't bring herself to speak to him just yet. She longed for the uncomplicated company of a good friend. Perhaps Jill would be free to meet for lunch. They hadn't seen each other in weeks and hadn't even had time to catch up on the phone. The prospect of seeing Jill lifted Quinn's spirits.

Chapter 39

Quinn and Jill met in a small restaurant near her office building in the City. She'd resumed her career as a forensic accountant after her vintage clothing shop had failed and had steadily moved up the ladder in her firm. She looked smart in a business suit and silk blouse, her dark hair pulled back into a neat bun.

"Quinn!" Jill exclaimed when she hurried inside the restaurant. "It's so good to see you."

"You too, cuz," Quinn said.

Jill settled into her seat and let out a long sigh. "I'm so glad you called. I needed to take a break and actually leave the office. I've been working on an audit for weeks, and I have yet to untangle all the threads of this company's finances. I do miss the shop sometimes," she said wistfully. "It wasn't profitable, but at least my head didn't feel like it was going to explode."

"Perhaps you'll try again someday," Quinn said.

"I don't think so. The days of chasing dreams are over. I need a steady income. Not everyone's husband is a bestselling author," she teased.

"Being a bestselling author is not as profitable as you might imagine," Quinn replied.

"Is Gabe working on something else?" Jill asked once they placed their order, both of them foregoing wine, something that would never have happened in the past.

"He's interested in Renaissance Italy," Quinn said. "The Borgias and all that. I think he has a historian crush on Lucrezia Borgia. I guess it could be worse. He could have developed a fascination with Amelia Dyer."

"And who's she when she's at home?" Jill asked.

"She was a notorious serial killer who was rumored to have murdered over four hundred babies and children at a baby farm she worked at."

"Why do you think some people feel the urge to kill?" Jill asked, hitting uncomfortably close to home with her innocent question. "Although, I tell you, there are days when I come close to an act of violence myself. Brian and I had a massive row yesterday," she confessed.

"What about?"

"He's been offered an amazing new job," Jill said, the corners of her mouth dipping.

"Is that a bad thing?" Quinn asked.

"It is when it's in Beijing. The contract is for three years. The company will cover the cost of the move, provide us with a three-bedroom house rent-free, and even cover the cost of Olivia's school. At the end of the three years, Brian has the option to extend the contract for another three years." Jill sighed. "It's an incredible opportunity for him, but I don't want to go. My life is here, Quinn: my family, my friends, my own career. I mean, if this was somewhere in Europe, I might be persuaded to give it a go, but this is China," she moaned.

"I take it Brian really wants to take the job?"

"He does. He says the money we'll save while there will enable us to buy a bigger house once we return, and if I don't work for the next three years, it would be the right time to have another baby."

"Do you want another baby?" Quinn asked.

"I do, but the thought of being cut off from everything and everyone I love frightens me. What would you do if Gabe suggested such a move?" Jill asked.

"I don't know. I was reluctant to agree when he wanted to move us north to be closer to Phoebe," Quinn confessed. "Berwick-upon-Tweed is not that far, but it might as well have been on the moon. I was so relieved when Phoebe decided to sell the house and move into a retirement community. My home is here. In fact, I'm working on a new case for Rhys."

"I thought you were done with all that."

"I was, but I'm doing it as a special favor to Rhys. The skeleton was found on his property in Hertfordshire."

Jill laughed. "And I bet there's an *Echoes from the Past* special in the works."

"There is. It's to be a Christmas episode."

"That wily old devil," Jill said, still chuckling. "He always knows how to reel you back in."

"It didn't take much persuading. I enjoy teaching and doing research, but there's nothing like an archeological site to get me going. To unearth a skeleton that had been buried for hundreds of years and have the opportunity to learn about the person's life and death is like nothing else in the world. It's magic," Quinn finished.

"So, why not do it?" Jill asked. "Why not go on a dig like you used to?"

"Because we have three children," Quinn replied with a grin. "Can you imagine dragging those three along?"

"Maybe you don't need to," Jill replied as she tucked into the grilled salmon salad the waiter had placed before her.

"What do you suggest I do with them?" Quinn asked, picking at her own salad.

"Your parents would love to have them for the summer. Leave the kids in Marbella and go off on a dig, just you and Gabe. Rekindle the romance," Jill suggested, wiggling her eyebrows suggestively.

"What makes you think it needs rekindling?" Quinn demanded with mock severity.

"Aw, come on, Quinny. When was the last time you and Gabe went away for a romantic weekend or an actual holiday? When did you last go out for a meal without the kids?"

"We went to Rhys's house and dug up a skelly. That was plenty romantic," Quinn replied, grinning. "But you're right. It's been a while since we've done anything for ourselves. I do miss spending time together without having to constantly cater to the needs of the children. I'm not sure my parents can handle them for that long, though. It's a lot of work."

"Ask them," Jill suggested. "I bet they'd love it. There's only so much tennis one can play and so many boozy lunches one can have on the veranda," she quipped.

"You know, you might just have something there," Quinn replied. "There's time enough to make the arrangements before the end of the school term. And what about you? What will you do?"

Jill looked thoughtful, her earlier amusement forgotten. "The selfish part of me wants to refuse outright, but maybe China will be good for us. We both work long hours, Olivia barely sees us, and we've been putting off having another baby for a while now. Three years is not such a long time," Jill said. "Not when there's so much to be gained."

"I'd miss you."

Jill nodded. "Funny how life takes you in directions you never expected. Even a month ago, the prospect of moving to China was about as likely as us picking up sticks and decamping to Timbuktu, but suddenly it's a very real prospect and a surprisingly lucrative one."

"You're the accountant, Jilly. Follow the money."

Jill glanced at her watch. "I'm sorry, but I need to get back to the office. See you at Mia's birthday party," Jill said as she reached for her purse.

"Lunch is on me," Quinn said. "You go on. Thank you for meeting me on such short notice."

"I'll miss you, Quinn," Jill whispered, her eyes growing moist. "When did we turn into these responsible grownups?"

"When we weren't looking," Quinn replied, her own eyes prickling with tears.

Chapter 40

November 1777
Long Island

"You weren't supposed to stay the night," Ben said when he found Jocelyn alone in the yard the following morning, hanging the laundry. His displeasure was easy to detect in his narrowed gaze and gruff tone. He stood closer to her than Jocelyn would have liked, but she made no move to distance herself, shrugging off his jealousy.

"The weather had turned. Derek didn't think the ferry would be running," Jocelyn said.

"The weather was fine here," Ben retorted. "It took you a long time to get back, if you left just after breakfast, like you said," he observed, watching her closely for any sign of deceit.

They had finally arrived in Milford in the late afternoon, and Jocelyn had gone straight up to her room, claiming fatigue, but she had been desperate to be alone for a time to calm down and gather her thoughts. She couldn't bear to face Hannah or Ben in her raw emotional state and had needed to put some distance between herself and Derek, who now knew the truth, or most of it.

Derek had stopped the cart and they'd sat shoulder to shoulder, leaning against the thick trunk of an ancient oak. He hadn't interrupted or given vent to his own feelings; he'd just listened, and then held her while she cried, offering silent support and understanding. It had taken her a long time to calm down and feel ready to resume their journey, the food Derek had offered her left untouched, her stomach in knots. But she had felt better, lighter, for having told him. Somehow, knowing that he didn't judge her helped her to feel less responsible, his quiet understanding assuaging some of her guilt.

"The road was muddy after the rain," Jocelyn said, wishing Ben would just desist with his interrogation. "It was slow going."

"That's why I hate going to New York City," Ben said. "It's not worth the journey, and once you get there, it's dirty, congested, and overrun by the British. I'm happy to stay right here and leave the traveling to Derek. He grows restless after a time and makes up excuses to visit the city. Would you like to take a walk later?" Ben asked, seemingly less upset now. "I have to go into town to fetch a cask of ale from the Blackwell Arms. I would have thought Derek might like to take this opportunity to visit Lydia, but he's expressed no desire to go. Ma will be making quite a feast for Thanksgiving," he said happily. "Do you like Thanksgiving?"

"I'm sure I do."

Ben tilted his head, his gaze sympathetic. "Surely something must be coming back to you, Alice."

"Little bits, yes," she admitted reluctantly.

"It's been more than a month since the shipwreck," Ben pointed out.

"Has it? I apologize if I've overstayed my welcome."

"I think you know by now that I don't want you to leave," Ben said. "Besides, we might have more room here soon."

"How do you mean?"

"I think Derek intends to propose to Lydia by year's end. Seems her campaign to make him jealous has worked. She told Felicia Painter that her father means to offer Derek a partnership in the tavern. Derek would love that. He never wanted to farm."

"What makes you think Derek is ready to wed?" Jocelyn asked, her hand stilling on the shirt she was hanging on the line.

"Just something he said to Ma last night after you had retired."

Jocelyn felt a hollow ache in her chest at the thought of Derek marrying Lydia. He wasn't hers to lose, but somehow the idea of him belonging to another woman made her want to weep. She'd lost so much already; she didn't want to lose him too. He was the only person she truly trusted and had assumed he'd be there to protect her should the need arise. Ben cared for her, she knew that, but Ben's emotions would always get the better of him, and his mistrust and jealousy would be his undoing. He was too intent on his own needs, believing them to be synonymous with hers, and would continue to pressure her whether she was ready or not.

She admired Derek's cool reserve and clear thinking. She'd also liked the gentle circle of support his arms had offered when she'd buried her face in his chest and cried her heart out, relieved to finally be able to share her pain with someone who was willing to stand by her. When she'd lain in her bed last night, cradling her tiny bump, she'd longed for him to hold her again and tell her everything would be all right. She wouldn't be able to hide the truth from the Wilders for much longer. Already Hannah was giving her sidelong looks, probably wondering why she hadn't asked for rags to use during her time of the month, or why she still felt sick in the mornings.

"I'll be glad once he's gone," Ben said, his expression serious.

"Why is that?"

"Because then maybe you'll finally see me," Ben said, his gaze warm on her face. "I want you to see me, Alice."

"I do see you, Ben," Jocelyn said. "More clearly than you imagine."

"I'd give anything to have you look at me the way you look at him, even once," Ben continued, moving so close to her, she was forced to take a step back.

"Ben, I'm not in love with Derek," Jocelyn said with more heat than she'd intended, probably because Ben had hit a nerve. He was making her feel cornered and angry, and she wished he'd just leave her in peace.

"You just keep telling yourself that. He loves Lydia, you know," Ben said snidely. "She's got more to offer, and that matters to our Derek."

"But it doesn't matter to you?" Jocelyn asked, offended on Derek's behalf. *Would you still want me if you knew there was another man's child growing in my womb?*

"I would take you as you are, Alice, because you are enough. You would always be enough." He looked so earnest, Jocelyn almost wished she could muster some feelings for him. Ben would cherish her, would protect her. Ben would offer her a home.

"Would you like to go for a walk?" Ben asked again, undeterred by her vehemence.

"Not just now," Jocelyn replied, desperate to be rid of him. She did, however, feel the need to walk, to be alone.

Jocelyn finished hanging the laundry, returned the basket to its proper place, and grabbed the cloak off the peg, heading out.

**

It was a bright November day, mild for the time of year. Jocelyn walked across the fields, inhaling the wonderful earthy smell and enjoying the vibrant hues that made the world look so lovely, just before it shrugged off its colorful mantle and everything turned a shade of gray. Already a carpet of fallen leaves softened her steps, and the clear blue sky was visible through shedding branches, winter just around the corner.

Having walked off her initial frustration, Jocelyn slowed her steps. She had to set her feelings aside and consider her position in a rational manner, like a man, or like a general going into battle. Except for Greg, with whom she was usually at loggerheads, she was alone in the world, and she needed to make a place for herself, a home. She had nothing to her name, not even the cloak on her back. Whatever meager possessions she'd brought with her were now at the bottom of the sea, as was the tiny purse containing her life savings. She hadn't had much, but now even that small bounty was gone. She couldn't go back to New York City, not as long as the British were still there, but Milford was safe. This sleepy little town was the best refuge she could have asked for.

If she were free to follow her heart, she might allow her budding feelings for Derek to develop, but she had no right. Derek was in love with another woman. He planned to marry her and start a family. Jocelyn had already started a family, just not in the way she might have hoped and not with a man who'd be there to love her. Her only alternative was Ben, whose possessiveness and need to be loved could be just the tool she needed to protect herself and her unborn child.

Jocelyn stopped and stared up at the cloudless sky, watching several crows take flight as something spooked them. Would Ben still want her if he knew she was with child? Would he be able to get past the circumstances surrounding its conception? As with Greg, she could tell Ben her husband had drowned, legitimizing her pregnancy, but the truth had a way of coming out. She couldn't build a life on a lie, nor could she repay Ben's love with counterfeit coin.

She tried to imagine Ben's hands on her body, his lips on hers. She harbored no romantic feelings for him. Could she grow to love him for the sake of her baby and their future? Funny how she was so protective of this child. Would she love it once it was born? Would she be able to see it simply as her baby, and not *his* child? Would she be able to mold it into a good human being, someone kind and noble? *Someone like Derek,* her mind unhelpfully supplied.

Ben is kind and noble, Jocelyn argued with herself. *Ben will love us.* She knew she was trying to convince herself, to justify an act of indecency against another human being, one whose weakness she would be forced to exploit if she grew desperate enough.

"God forgive me for what I mean to do," Jocelyn said into the silence around her.

She turned for home, having made up her mind. Her steps were plodding, her heart heavy. Some part of her wished she'd told Derek the whole truth rather than the scrubbed version she'd offered up to protect those she'd promised not to betray. But in the end, it didn't matter. She was responsible for what had happened to her, and now she'd have to pay the price.

Chapter 41

October 1776
New York City

It was about a week after the theaters had been shut down by the occupiers that Richard Kinney came to see Jocelyn at her lodging house. New York was still recovering from the great fire that had consumed a quarter of the city only a few weeks before and had resulted in numerous injuries and deaths. There was an acrid smell of soot in the air that turned Jocelyn's stomach, not only because the stench seemed to cling to just about everything but because it reminded her of how close she'd come to losing her own modest home. She had watched in horror, too frightened to go to sleep, as an orange glow lit up the sky, the hungry, crackling tongues of flame reaching ever closer and devouring everything in their path. Thankfully, she still had a place to call home, but she was acutely aware of the impermanence of her position.

Richard Kinney was a stocky man with ginger hair and soulful blue eyes. In his mid-forties, he was married, had two teenage daughters, and owned a printshop on William Street. Being something of a theater enthusiast, Mr. Kinney considered himself a patron of the arts and had printed leaflets and posters for the various performances free of charge. In exchange for this service, he liked to have a drink with the actors after a performance and sometimes asked to be permitted to watch a dress rehearsal. Jocelyn had no idea what he might want with her now that the theater was closed.

She received Mr. Kinney in the tiny parlor reserved for visitors and invited him to sit, taking a seat opposite him in a worn armchair. "How have you been keeping, Mr. Kinney?" she asked.

"Very well, thank you, Mistress Sinclair." He glanced toward the open door and lowered his voice. "What do you mean to do now that the theater is closed?" he asked.

"Look for a domestic situation, one that offers room and board," Jocelyn replied, wondering why he should care. "I can't afford to remain here past the first of the month."

"What would you say if I offered to help you secure such a position?" Richard Kinney asked.

"Are you looking to hire a maidservant, Mr. Kinney?"

"Not exactly." He glanced toward the door again, but the lodging house was silent, all the women currently at work, and Mrs. Blunt, who owned the establishment, at the market, as was her daily custom.

"Look, Mistress Sinclair, I won't beat about the bush. I know you're no royalist. I've heard you express your opinions on the current conflict."

Jocelyn sank deeper into the chair, suddenly worried about what she might have said after a tankard of ale and the high of a successful performance. She'd thought she was among friends, but perhaps she'd been mistaken.

"The Continental Army is outnumbered and outgunned, so our only hope of defeating the enemy lies in outmaneuvering them. We need intelligence that comes straight from the horse's mouth, so to speak."

Jocelyn stared at Richard Kinney, seeing him in a whole new light. "Mr. Kinney, I'm no spy."

"You don't have to be. All you need to do is go about your duties as a domestic servant. If you happen to overhear a private conversation or find yourself on the receiving end of a careless comment, then perhaps you can report that to your contact. And if your employer happens to dispose of a letter or a report, throwing them in the wastepaper basket for you to empty, then he'd be none the wiser if that report wound up in our hands. We would never ask you to endanger yourself or others. Simply go about the tasks you're assigned and report what you see and hear."

"And you have someone specific in mind?" Jocelyn asked.

"Major Hector Radcliffe, a close personal friend of General Howe, will shortly find himself in need of a new servant. We would like you to fill the position."

"And what makes you think I would be hired?" Jocelyn was secretly impressed with Richard Kinney's confidence and persuasive manner, but conviction was rarely enough to get the job done.

"For one, you will have impeccable letters of recommendation. For another, Major Radcliffe is a lover of beautiful things. He has a keen appreciation for music, art, and beautiful women, particularly women who are young and fair. And you, dear Jocelyn, are young and fair. And an excellent actress to boot. Think of this as the defining role of your career."

Jocelyn gave Mr. Kinney the gimlet eye. "And is there a Mrs. Radcliffe?"

"There isn't, but Major Radcliffe is a perfect gentleman. He does not keep a mistress, nor does he visit brothels, as many of his compatriots are wont to do. If, at any time, you feel you're not safe, you have leave to quit his employ and return to the lodging house, a month's rent your compensation for your assistance. And, of course, you will be paid, quite handsomely, I might add. You will have an opportunity to put something by for when you're ready to return to your old life."

"You make it all sound so simple," Jocelyn said, watching the man for any signs of deceit.

"Jocelyn, we're desperate. We need information, and the British, who are accustomed to having a domestic staff, view their servants as part of the furniture. Who better placed to gather intelligence than a maidservant who goes about her business and often serves at dinner, where the highest echelons of the British Army are speaking openly, their uptight upper-class tongues loosened by the finest madeira and brandy? They mistrust men, but as a rule, women are completely overlooked, even though throughout history women have played a vital part in starting revolutions and toppling governments."

"How glamorous you make it sound," Jocelyn scoffed.

"There's nothing glamorous about it. It's hard, unpleasant work. You will be scrubbing pans and taking out chamber pots, but you will be ideally placed to help us. What do you say?"

"Can I have some time to think about it?"

"I'm afraid I'll need your answer now. If you won't do it, there are others who will, but the more operatives we have planted in the homes of high-ranking officers, the better chance we have of driving the British out. Would you not like to see that happen?"

"Yes, I would," Jocelyn said with feeling.

"Then, what do you say?"

Jocelyn leaned back in the armchair and crossed her arms over her chest. A part of her wanted to ask Richard Kinney to leave and never bother her again, but she already knew she wouldn't do that. What he was asking wasn't so outrageous. She'd have to find a position as a domestic in either case; her meager savings wouldn't last long. If taking out chamber pots and washing some man's drawers was to be her life, she may as well do it for a good cause and feel a sense of pride. She could make a difference, help win the war. Well, perhaps that was a bit too optimistic, but even if she could provide information that would save one life, already it would be worth it.

"And who would be my contact?" Jocelyn asked.

"I can't reveal his identity now, but I can tell you that he would come to see you once a week, as your only living kin should, and join you for a drink and a walk on your afternoons off. It would all be perfectly innocent. Just two young people spending an hour together before returning to their respective homes."

"You have it all figured out, don't you? How many operatives are you running, Mr. Kinney?"

Richard Kinney smiled in a way that suggested he was flattered by the question. "What's it to be, Mistress Sinclair?"

"Yes, Mr. Kinney. I'll do it."

Chapter 42

November 1776

Jocelyn stood in front of the imposing brick mansion, the satchel containing her earthly belongings in her hands, her heart in her mouth. Once she went inside, there'd be no turning back. When she'd first agreed to work for Major Radcliffe, she'd been excited, energized even, but then Nathan Hale had been captured and executed, and everything changed. Spying for the Continental Army was no longer a lark, an act of bravery; it was a suicide mission if you were caught. Nathan Hale had been committed, brave, and clever. No one would have expected him to fall into the trap Robert Rogers of the Queen's Rangers had set for him, but he had, because deep down he had been a trusting, idealistic man. He'd been only twenty-one, the same age as Jocelyn. Only she was more world-weary, she'd told herself as she lay sleepless last night. She wouldn't fall into the same trap. She was prepared.

"Don't do anything foolish," Richard Kinney had told her when she'd stopped by the print shop to tell him she got the position in the major's household. "You got the job, now just do it. Don't take any unnecessary risks. Become invisible," Richard had said. "Or as invisible as a beautiful woman can be in a man's household. And don't, under any circumstances, get chatting to a kindred spirit. It might be a trap."

"What if I must send an urgent message?"

"If there's something that can't wait, pass a message to John Carver, the publican at the Spyglass Tavern. He's a loyal man and will see the information gets where it needs to go."

Richard had taken her by the shoulders and looked down into her upturned face. "If you need to get out, don't wait. Go to your friend Anna Reid's house. She will look after you until we're able to get you safely out of the city. Promise me, no heroics."

"I promise," Jocelyn had said. "You can count on me, Richard. I won't get caught."

"That there is your first mistake," Richard had said angrily. "Never get cocky and think you're smarter than those who came before you. Always think, *I will get caught if I let down my guard.* It'll make you more mindful of the danger."

"I understand."

"And no confiding in your brother," Richard had added as an afterthought.

"My brother is a royalist. I'd hardly confide in him."

Jocelyn had written to Greg, as she did every month, but had left out the bit about the theater closure. If she told him the truth, Greg would instantly demand that she give up her lodgings and join him in Williamsburg, where he would no doubt try to introduce her to every eligible male under the age of sixty-five. He thought it unseemly that she lived on her own and paraded herself on stage as only a harlot would. He'd always been something of a prig.

There was some small comfort in the knowledge that she could turn to Greg in a time of crisis and he'd do his duty by her, but she was nowhere near having reached the point where she'd turn to her brother for help. In return for his financial support and protection, Greg would watch her every move, try to censor her every thought, and do his utmost to convert her to his view that the Rebels in the American Colonies were no better than a dog biting the hand that fed it.

Jocelyn supposed she could understand his position. He was a man who liked order, tradition, and continuity. He valued loyalty and honor and believed that a man should never question his allegiance to King and Country, no matter the circumstances. He was sure the rebellion would end in blood and tears and the men who'd risk all to rid themselves of the yoke of British rule would come out of the conflict much worse off than they had been when it had begun. Perhaps he was right. Richard Kinney had admitted that it wasn't a fair fight. It never would be, but it was too late to turn back now. The Rebels would see it to its bitter conclusion, and she'd be proud to say that she'd done her part.

"All right, then," Richard Kinney said gruffly. "Off you go. May God bless you and keep you."

"And you as well," Jocelyn replied, knowing deep down that Richard was putting himself in a lot more danger than she'd realized.

Her heart beat like a drum and her knees threatened to buckle as she finally approached the servants' entrance and knocked on the door, ready to report to Mrs. Johnson, the housekeeper, who would introduce her to Major Radcliffe.

Chapter 43

Despite her nervousness, Jocelyn settled into the household fairly quickly. Mrs. Johnson was a pleasant woman who wasn't too exacting in her demands, as long as the work got done. With her graying hair, florid complexion, and rotund figure, she was the epitome of a kindly grandmother and behaved like one. Because of her dodgy knees, she kept mostly to the ground floor rooms and the kitchen and asked Jocelyn to take on the cleaning of the bedrooms, the weekly laundry, and the serving of meals.

A taciturn man in his forties named John Wilcox looked after the horses, brought in firewood, and fetched water. He spent the rest of his time outdoors, pruning the bushes, sweeping the leaves, and performing any odd task that needed doing. He slept in a small room off the kitchen, which he kept neat and clean but rarely spent any time in, regardless of the weather.

The third member of the household was Private Sykes. He was a young man of about nineteen with straw-like fair hair, blue eyes, and a ready smile. He was a bit slow on the uptake, according to Mrs. Johnson, which was why he was used mostly as a messenger and general dogsbody, something he didn't seem to mind. He performed any task assigned him with a childish zeal that seemed to irritate Captain Palmer, the major's aide-de-camp, to no end. Captain Palmer was a fastidious man in his early thirties who seemed happiest when he was alone in his study. He rarely spoke to Jocelyn or even looked at her, his discomfort obvious when they met on the stairs or when she served him in the dining room.

And then there was Major Radcliffe, whom Jocelyn had finally met at the beginning of the second week of her employment, since he'd been absent from the house, possibly having traveled to Philadelphia or West Point, Mrs. Johnson speculated. The major was something of a surprise. Jocelyn had expected a gruff middle-aged man who'd bark out orders and expect them all to carry on as if on parade, but the major was mild mannered and soft spoken. He was in his thirties and had wide brown eyes, an aquiline nose, and unexpectedly full lips. He preferred to wear his own hair, which was a rich chestnut brown, when at home or attending informal functions, but donned a curled and queued periwig when going to military events or regimental dinners. Major Radcliffe treated both Jocelyn and Mrs. Johnson as if they were ladies of his acquaintance rather than household help, always thanking them and asking politely for anything he required.

Richard Kinney had instructed Jocelyn to render herself invisible, but that became more difficult as the weeks went by, since Major Radcliffe had taken a liking to her. He sometimes invited her to dine with him when he had no other engagements and regaled her with stories of his home in Kent and the Grand Tour he'd taken before his father had purchased him a commission in the army. Jocelyn couldn't begin to imagine a world in which someone was encouraged to travel for a full year, all expenses paid, the only expectation that they enjoy everything the great cities of Europe had to offer and come back a somewhat more polished version of themselves. She'd been enthralled by the major's accounts of the floating city of Venice, the sprawling hills of Tuscany dotted by vineyards and olive groves that surrounded solitary farmhouses built on verdant hills, his tour of the Bastille, and his visit to the gothic cathedral of Notre Dame.

She liked the major and felt surprisingly at ease in his company, probably more so because he never spoke of the war or revealed anything worth passing on. Sometimes, Captain Palmer joined them at dinner. Jocelyn could see why someone like him had been assigned to clerical duties rather than sent into combat. He was a conscientious assistant and wrote a fair hand, but she couldn't imagine him firing a musket at another human being, not even a Continental soldier. He was also careful of clearing his desk and destroying any documents he didn't wish to keep, throwing them on the fire in his study at the end of every day and leaving his wastepaper basket frustratingly empty.

By the time the new year began, Jocelyn had settled into a comfortable routine. She always brought refreshments when Major Radcliffe took meetings, and listened intently, lingering as long as she reasonably could, pouring the tea, setting out plates of finger sandwiches and bowls of fruit. She also served at table when the major had dinner guests, making herself as unobtrusive as possible and absorbing all that was said. She kept an eye out for anything of importance while cleaning the major's study, but like Captain Palmer, he never left any important documents or correspondence lying around. If she were to learn anything, she had to dig deeper and rifle through the drawers, which, thankfully, were left unlocked. She resorted to such drastic measures only when both Major Radcliffe and Captain Palmer were out, ensuring that she was never caught in the act.

Every Sunday, after attending church with the rest of the household, Jocelyn met with Thomas, a fair-haired youth who posed as her cousin and dutifully listened to everything she had to say, even the most minute of details. He wanted to know everything from where the major went to whom he met with, even asking her to repeat the personal stories he'd shared with her, which, to Jocelyn's mind, had no relevance whatsoever to the war effort. She did so, however, not wishing to seem uncooperative.

"Am I helping, Thomas?" she asked him one Sunday in January when the weather was mild enough to allow for a longer walk. The news she was relaying was so trivial, it couldn't possibly matter. "Is my information valuable?"

"Of course it is. You just keep doing what you're doing. Your intelligence is gold," Thomas assured her.

Jocelyn's cheeks suffused with heat at his praise. Maybe he was just complimenting her to keep up her morale, but she didn't care. She was useful. She was an integral part of the Continental intelligence network. And spying on Major Radcliffe was surprisingly easy. Richard Kinney had been right. All she had to do was go about her duties, and the rest fell into place. She was simply playing a role, but the role had become her life.

Chapter 44

March 2018
London

By the time Sunday rolled around, Quinn was on pins and needles. She'd done her level best to act normal around the children and had made sure her day out with Emma was fun and carefree, but when alone, it was impossible to drag her mind away from the case—both cases. She hadn't heard from Drew, and working on Rhys's case wasn't proving any easier. Jocelyn seemed to be regaining her memory, but none of what Quinn had seen offered a clue to how Ben's ring had come to be in Hertfordshire. The only connection—tenuous as it was—pointed to Lieutenant Reynolds, who, according to Hannah, might have hailed from Hertfordshire.

"Ben Wilder might have joined the British Army and eventually been posted to England," Gabe suggested when Quinn shared her frustration with him over a glass of wine on Sunday evening. The children already in bed, the grownups were enjoying an hour of peace after a busy day.

"I can't see Ben as a soldier, and he certainly wasn't overly devoted to the royalist cause, or any cause, for that matter. He just wanted to live in peace and farm the land," she said. "I don't think he much cared who won the war."

"Surely he'd picked a side," Gabe replied. "How was it possible to live during that time and not care?"

"I'm sure there were many people who didn't feel strongly either way, just like now. There are those who are advocating for us to leave the European Union, while others would prefer to remain. But there are those who feel their life won't change regardless. I suppose that largely depends on their line of work and their financial standing."

Gabe inclined his head in assent. "All right, let's say for argument's sake that Ben followed his lady love to England."

"I suppose that's possible, but Jocelyn was American born and bred. Why would she have gone to England? She knew no one there. And she had been spying for the Continental Army. I can't imagine she would have seen the shores of England as a place of refuge."

"Perhaps she went with her brother. You said he was an avid King George supporter."

Quinn thought about that for a moment. "I wonder if she might have been forced to leave."

"By whom?"

"There were many instances of royalists being dragged from their homes and forced onto a ship bound for England. Perhaps if Jocelyn's brother was an outspoken royalist, Jocelyn might have got caught in the fray."

"Or she may have been accused of supporting the royalist cause because she'd been employed by a British major," Gabe suggested. "Once the British were driven from New York City, she would have been fair game."

"That would be more likely," Quinn said. "Jocelyn seemed reluctant to go to her brother."

"But had she not been on the way to Virginia when the ship was caught in the storm?"

"Yes. She'd been running away from something. She was scared," Quinn agreed.

"Perhaps she wound up in England, and Ben went to fetch her home."

Quinn nodded. "That sounds like a plausible theory, but if he was wearing the ring at the time of his death, how is it that her memories were imprinted on it?"

Gabe took a sip of wine, his expression thoughtful. "They may have married, and she'd worn his ring for a time, which would account for her set of memories. Perhaps she'd given it back when she left him."

"I suppose," Quinn said. "She didn't love him; that was obvious."

"This is a curious case," Gabe remarked.

"That's only because we don't have all the facts yet," Quinn replied.

"Do you think we ever will?"

"I hope so."

"I wish I could see it all for myself," Gabe said, his expression dreamy. He was about to say something else when the doorbell rang. Gabe looked at Quinn. "Who can it be at this hour?"

She shrugged.

"I'll get it," Gabe said.

He returned to the lounge a few moments later, Drew trailing him. "I'm sorry to disturb you," Drew said. "Are the children asleep?"

"Yes." Quinn set down her glass and sat up straight. "Have you discovered something, Drew?"

"Quite possibly. At any rate, I thought I'd update you in person. I was able to locate the carwash where Brett washed the car the night Jo died. They keep a record of every vehicle they service. Of course, no one can recall anything specific, nor do they have any kind of video footage. I was, however, able to obtain an image from a CCTV camera just down the street."

He took a seat on the sofa, pulled a folded sheet of paper from his pocket, and handed it to Quinn. It was an image printed from surveillance footage, and it was grainy and colorless. It showed a car standing at a light at a street junction. It was clearly nighttime, but the driver was illuminated by the dim light of the streetlamp. Or part of him was.

"I can't tell if this is Brett," Quinn said, disappointed and relieved in equal measure. "The visor of the baseball cap is obscuring most of his face."

Drew nodded but didn't take the picture back. "Look at his hands."

Quinn's gaze slid to the driver's hands, both clearly visible on the steering wheel. Her hand flew to her mouth.

"You recognize that ring, don't you?" Drew asked. "It's rather unique."

Quinn nodded miserably. "He loves that ring. He bought it on a trip to Mexico, on Dia de los Muertos."

"Was he wearing the ring when he came to see you the day Jo died?"

Quinn nodded again.

"This is definite proof, isn't it?" Gabe asked as he peered over Quinn's shoulder. "He's wearing the ring and driving a silver Nissan Sentra. Does the registration match?"

"It does," Drew said. "I checked with Budget Rentals, and the car is still in circulation."

"Then we've got him," Quinn said, her voice cracking.

"Not quite," Drew replied. "As far as the police are concerned, this is a random person driving a random car. They have nothing to suggest that this car was the one that struck Jo and ultimately killed her. Everything I've found to date hinges on the registration number, which was provided by your anonymous source," Drew said caustically. "Unless I can give them a reason to suspect Brett Besson, this information is of no value."

"What sort of reason?" Gabe asked.

"Had Brett made a threat against Jo, or had they had some kind of row, the police would have a reason to take a closer look at his movements."

"Jo had been outside, alone, at the time of the accident. Perhaps he'd asked her to meet him," Gabe suggested.

"Or she could have been going to the shops to pick up some milk or a bottle of wine," Drew replied, waving his hand in a dismissive gesture. "Unless we can get proof that they planned to meet, we have nothing."

"Well, can't you get proof? Surely Jo's phone records would show if she'd spoken to Brett. There might even be texts."

Drew looked thoughtful for a moment. "Was he using his own mobile, or did he get a pay-as-you-go while he was here?"

"He was using his own phone," Quinn said.

"Do you have his number?"

"Yes. He left me a message to offer his condolences when Jo died," Quinn said, shocked anew by his lack of remorse. "I'll forward you the number."

"Well, that's something, I suppose. I'll have to check it out," Drew said.

"Are you able to access Jo's phone records?" Gabe asked.

"Legally, no," Drew replied, his lip curling in a humorless smile.

"And illegally?" Gabe asked. He didn't sound disapproving, just curious.

"One of my security clients can hack into literally anything. He helps me out with my investigations from time to time, and I throw lucrative contracts his way."

"Right. I don't think we need to know that," Gabe said.

"You don't," Drew replied, still grinning slyly. His smile faded when he looked back at Quinn. "Look, Quinn, once we take our findings to the police, there'll be no going back. Are you sure you want to poke the bear?"

"Are you suggesting I let him get away with murder?" Quinn asked, surprised by the question.

"I'm suggesting you consider the consequences. If there isn't enough evidence to go to trial, Brett will not only go free, but he will know exactly who had tried to get the case reopened. This is a person who's killed before."

"Drew, I hear what you are saying, but I simply can't walk away from this and live with the knowledge that Brett had taken Jo's life knowingly and willfully. I also can't ignore the possibility that there will probably be victims in the future. He's gotten away with it. There's nothing to stop him from trying again."

Drew nodded and got wearily to his feet. "All right. I'm sure you understand that I had to ask."

"We understand the risk," Gabe said.

"Goodnight, then. I'll see myself out."

"Are you off to bed?" Gabe asked Quinn once Drew had gone.

"I don't think I can get to sleep, not after that conversation. Let's finish the bottle," Quinn said.

Gabe nodded and poured her more wine.

Chapter 45

The summons from Drew came two days later. Quinn had just dropped off the children at the nursery school and was all set to return home and do some research when her mobile rang.

"Morning, Quinn," Drew said. "Are you free for an hour or two?" He sounded a lot less distracted, his tone full of determination.

"Free to do what?" Quinn asked, apprehensive.

"I made us an appointment with Detective Inspector Marshall. He works out of my old station. You could say we're mates," Drew added with a chuckle.

"What else could you say?" Quinn asked, sensing there was a story here.

"We were bitter rivals while I was still on the Met. Never saw eye to eye."

"And you think he'll be receptive to what we have to tell him?" Quinn asked, dubious.

"I know he will be. Marshall is a good cop. Old school. He doesn't care about departmental politics or projecting an image of a kinder, gentler police force to the public. He's about getting results."

"All right, then. Where should I meet you?"

"I'll collect you in half an hour," Drew said, and rang off before Quinn had a chance to ask any more questions.

Quinn tossed the phone into her bag and trudged upstairs to change. What did one wear to a police station? she wondered as she considered her choices. Her face looked pale and drawn in the full-length mirror on the door of the wardrobe, and there was a haunted look in her eyes. She'd be lying if she said she wasn't scared of what this interview would mean. If DI Marshall dismissed their evidence, Brett would walk free. Again. If DI Marshall thought they had a case, there'd be no going back, and sooner or later, Brett would find out that he was the subject of a murder inquiry. Or was that manslaughter?

Quinn chose a demure silk blouse in a floral pattern of pale pink and gray and a pair of charcoal-gray trousers. She looked stylish and professional, but inside, she felt like a little girl who'd been called before the headmaster. She didn't want to do this. She had to do this. She was the only one who could do this. And she was the one who'd be making herself a target, her inner voice reminded her.

Damn you, Brett, Quinn thought vehemently as she returned downstairs. *Damn you, you evil little bastard!*

**

The police station was modern and bright, the décor practical and minimalist. Several people nodded to Drew as they passed by, a few stopping to say hello and ask after his leg and his life as a civilian. Drew was friendly and easygoing, no hint of unease in his manner. Quinn, on the other hand, felt sick. She should have told Gabe she was doing this. He would have insisted on accompanying her, and although she'd wanted to spare him this, she now wished he were here.

I can do this, Quinn chided herself. *This is nothing but a preliminary interview. There's nothing to worry about. I'm not the one on trial here. But I might be asked some difficult questions.* If DI Marshall was as thorough as Drew had intimated, he'd want to know the source of her information.

"Drew, good to see you. And this must be Mrs. Russell. I'm Detective Inspector Dan Marshall," the man said, holding his hand out to Quinn. "Please come this way." He made a sweeping gesture toward the beige-painted corridor that led to several closed doors. "I've reserved us an interview room."

DI Marshall was tall and lean, his physique reminiscent of a professional cyclist. His salt-and-pepper hair was cut short, the haircut stylish and expensive looking, as were his gray suit and slate-blue silk tie. Next to him, Drew Camden looked like a bear who'd just awoken from a prolonged hibernation. He lumbered down the corridor, nearly filling the narrow space.

"Please have a seat," DI Marshall invited. "Tea?"

"Yes, please," Quinn said. Her mouth was so dry she could barely get the words out.

"Any chance of a decent cup of coffee?" Drew asked.

"A very good chance. We have a new machine," DI Marshall replied. He made a call and asked for two coffees and a tea. A young constable arrived a few minutes later and set the cups on the table, leaving without a word.

"Right," DI Marshall said once everyone had their cup before them. "So, what's this about? You were awfully tightlipped on the phone, Drew," he said, watching Drew as if he were the suspect.

"This is regarding the hit-and-run accident that killed Jo Turing, who was Mrs. Russell's sister."

"Yes?"

"Dan, Mrs. Russell hired me to gather evidence to support her belief that her sister was murdered."

DI Marshall's brows rose in surprise, but he said nothing.

"I have been able to recreate the timeline of events and gather enough evidence to support the allegation."

"Go on," DI Marshall said. He was leaning forward now, clearly intrigued.

Drew opened the manila folder he'd brought along and consulted the contents. "Let me begin by saying that Brett Besson, the brother of Quinn Russell and Jo Turing, had served a year at a Louisiana penitentiary for attempted murder. The conviction was overturned during an appeal trial because the confession had been illegally obtained. Brett Besson arrived in London two days after his release."

"Whom did he try to kill?"

"Me," Quinn croaked. "He tried to kill me."

"Why?"

"Because I had unwittingly threatened to expose something he didn't wish to be known."

"I see," DI Marshall said. "And you think he meant to kill Ms. Turing for the same reason?"

"No. His reasons for wanting Ms. Turing dead are unclear, although we believe he thought he was making amends to Quinn by ridding her of a sister who'd threatened her marriage," Drew interjected.

"This gets better and better," DI Marshall muttered. "All right. Proceed."

"Brett Besson arrived in the UK on June twenty-sixth, 2015, and made contact with Quinn Russell shortly thereafter," Drew began. "He'd expressed a desire to apologize for what he'd done and make amends. Quinn was not receptive to meeting with him, so he ambushed her. During his time in London, he also connected with his other sister, Jo Turing, whom he was meeting for the first time." Drew pushed a sheet of paper toward Marshall. "I highlighted the calls and texts between them."

DI Marshall lifted the paper and looked at it carefully. "This is a register of Jo Turing's phone calls. Where did you get this, Drew?"

"That's not important."

"You know this is inadmissible," DI Marshall said.

"Of course I do. But it will be if you request your own copy," Drew pointed out.

DI Marshall nodded. "Please continue."

"Brett Besson and Jo Turing met two days before her death. You can see that from their texts."

"Allegedly met," DI Marshall corrected Drew.

"Okay, allegedly met. You can subpoena the security footage from the bar where they met or check Jo Turing's credit card activity for that day. I'm sure you'll find proof. Then, Brett Besson made a call to Jo Turing on the night of her death. The call lasted less than a minute. A few seconds later, she texted him her address. It stands to reason that they'd arranged to meet again, and this time, he was coming to her place."

"Not an unknown occurrence for siblings," DI Marshall muttered.

Drew glared at the man but didn't rise to the bait. "Brett Besson shared a room at the Intercontinental House Hostel with a Swedish student named Swen Persson. Swen had rented a car for the duration of his stay, a silver Nissan Sentra. This is the registration number," Drew said, pointing to a number on the printout from the rental company. "I've checked with the car rental agency, and the vehicle is still in circulation."

DI Marshall shrugged. "All right. What makes you think this was the car that struck Jo Turing?"

"Swen said that on the morning after Jo's death, the car was parked in the wrong place and was suspiciously clean." DI Marshall's eyebrows rose comically, but he didn't interrupt. "We believe that Brett Besson borrowed his roommate's car without permission and drove it to the address Jo Turing had texted him."

"That doesn't mean he killed her."

"No, it doesn't," Drew agreed. "Jo Turing was struck by a car at approximately 10:35 p.m. At 11:05, Brett Besson had the car cleaned at this twenty-four-hour carwash, which is only a ten-minute drive from Jo's residence and on the way back to the hostel."

"So, what was he doing for the other twenty minutes?" DI Marshall asked.

"Probably driving around to make sure no one was following him, and he was in the clear."

"All right. Do you have anything else in that folder?" DI Marshall asked, a smile of amusement tugging at his lips.

His expression seemed to annoy Drew, but he didn't remark on it and continued laying out his evidence, piece by damning piece. He pushed another sheet of paper toward Marshall.

"This was taken by a CCTV camera located just up the street from the carwash at 11:15, just after the driver left the carwash."

"This man is wearing a cap that obscures most of his face," DI Marshall said. "For all you know, this is Swen what's-his-name returning to the hostel after a night out."

"It could be, yes, but the driver is wearing a ring that belongs to Brett Besson and which anyone who knows him would have seen him wear."

"So, how can you be sure Swen didn't borrow Besson's ring instead of Besson borrowing Swen's car?" DI Marshall asked.

Now he's just being an ass, Quinn thought angrily, and hid her face in her cup of lukewarm tea to hide her expression.

"Swen Persson had no reason to kill Jo Turing. They had never met. They'd had no communication," Drew said.

He was beginning to lose his patience, but DI Marshall was calm and cool, his expression difficult to read. He turned to Quinn and studied her for a long moment. "Mrs. Russell, did your brother do or say anything in the days preceding Jo Turing's death that would lead you to believe he meant her harm?"

"Brett had come to London to beg my forgiveness. He wished to make amends for what he'd done to me. He kept insisting he'd make it up to me."

"I see, and what did Ms. Turing do that would inspire him to bump her off?"

"Jo had begun sending nude photos of herself to my husband and inviting him to have sex with her." Quinn nearly choked on the words. Her face burned with humiliation, and she wished she had taken Drew's warning more seriously. If this case ever came to trial, every sordid detail of their lives would be revealed, examined, and possibly written about in the press.

"And was your husband receptive to her advances?" DI Marshall inquired.

"No, he was not."

DI Marshall looked dubious but continued. "Was Brett Besson aware of what your sister was doing?"

"He was."

"So, he thought he was doing you a favor?" he asked, sounding as if he were asking Quinn if she really believed there was intelligent life on Mars.

"He never actually said so," Quinn replied.

"Mrs. Russell, what was it you were going to reveal that had led to an attempt on your life?" DI Marshall pinned her with his steely gaze, and Quinn met it head on, annoyed by the man's insolent tone. She might not be on trial, but she felt as if she were.

"While investigating our family history, I had learned that Brett, Jo, and I are descended from a slave woman who'd been brought to America from Trinidad on a slave ship. Brett was raised in New Orleans, Louisiana," Quinn said. "Deep American South. He didn't want it to come to light that one of our ancestors had been a slave. He couldn't accept that he had Negro blood."

"Is he that much of a racist?" DI Marshall asked.

"Brett has white supremacist leanings," Quinn replied. "He expressed his views to me just before he locked me in a tomb in a deserted part of a cemetery and left me to die. I was pregnant at the time," she added.

"I see. And how did you come by the registration number for the vehicle that killed Jo Turing?" DI Marshall asked, turning to Drew.

Quinn sucked in her breath. She'd promised herself that she wouldn't bring Daisy into this, and given DI Marshall's sardonic glare, she couldn't begin to imagine what his reaction would be if she admitted that the registration number had been seen in a psychic vision.

Drew collected his papers and stuffed them back in the folder. He appeared to be buying time to come up with a reasonable explanation. He then looked up at Dan Marshall and smiled slyly. "I worked backwards, Dan. It had been mentioned in the press at the time of Jo Turing's death that she had been struck by a silver Nissan. That much was clear on the CCTV footage, but the registration number was impossible to make out. The image was too dark. I mapped out every possible route back to the hostel and hit every carwash along the way. There are thirty-seven," he added conversationally. "At carwash twenty-six, I found what I was looking for. A silver Nissan had been brought in right around the time of the accident. I then scoured CCTV footage from the two nearest cameras and was able to find the car and obtain a photo of the driver. The rest you can figure out for yourself."

"That was quite a long shot," DI Marshall observed.

"Perhaps, but since I knew I was looking to implicate Brett Besson, I was able to narrow down the area and also confirm that the Sentra had been rented by Swen Persson for the duration of his stay."

DI Marshall grinned broadly, the smile lighting up his serious face. "I'm impressed, Drew. That's solid detective work."

"Thanks, Dan. That's what I'm paid for," Drew replied acerbically. It was obvious the two men hadn't quite buried the hatchet, but they had a grudging respect for one another.

"Leave this with me," DI Marshall said as he held out his hand for the folder.

"You have enough here to reopen the case, Dan," Drew said as he handed over the folder.

"You know I can't make that decision, Drew. I will present your findings to the powers-that-be and recommend that they reopen the investigation."

"Thank you," Quinn said, grateful beyond words that Daisy's name hadn't come into the conversation.

"Mrs. Russell, I'm sorry for what happened to you," DI Marshall said, surprising her with a look of sympathy. "I meet many dysfunctional families in my line of work, but this…" He made a gesture that indicated utter disbelief. "I will be in touch."

"With Drew?" Quinn asked.

"No, with you. Drew's involvement in this is over. If we hope to get a conviction, our investigation must adhere to the letter of the law, and Drew's less-than-legitimate ways of obtaining evidence may come into question."

Drew nodded but didn't argue.

"I have one more question, Mrs. Russell," DI Marshall said as he stood to leave. "Why have you waited so long to bring this to our attention?"

"I tried to tell myself that Brett had turned over a new leaf and couldn't possibly have done such a horrible thing, but the feeling just wouldn't go away. I think I've always known deep down that Brett's attempt on my life wasn't a one-off."

"But this time his MO was vastly different," DI Marshall pointed out.

"Brett is not a serial killer, Dan. He's just someone who takes care of a problem as it arises and uses whatever means he has to hand," Drew replied.

"Do you believe there were other victims, Mrs. Russell?" DI Marshall asked as they headed toward the door.

"I don't know," Quinn said. "I sincerely hope not."

Once back in the corridor, DI Marshall held out his hand, and she took it, shaking it as firmly as she could manage given that she was trembling from head to foot.

"I'm sorry," he said again. "Drew, you know the way out."

Chapter 46

"Why didn't you ring me?" Gabe demanded once Quinn had told him of her visit to the police station. "I would have met you there."

"It's all right. Drew was there."

"Quinn, we're in this together," Gabe said. She could see he was worried, and she was doubly glad she'd spared him the experience. He'd suffered enough, thanks to her family. "Did you have to mention Daisy?"

"Thankfully, no. Drew came up with a plausible explanation, since he knew I was reluctant to reveal my source."

"Good old Drew," Gabe said. "He's the type of man you'd want at your back in a fight."

"Yes, he is. He's clever too. DI Marshall was impressed."

"I bet he was. Quinn, you can't tell anyone about this," Gabe stressed.

"I'm not going to tell Seth, if that's what you're concerned about," Quinn said defensively.

Gabe looked momentarily surprised. "I didn't think you would. Even you are not that tender-hearted."

"And what's that supposed to mean?" Quinn rounded on him. She wasn't really angry, but the interview had left her feeling edgy and fragile.

"It means that you hate what this will do to your dad and wish you could do something to make it easier for him, but forewarning him will only make things worse. Surely you know that," Gabe said, watching her for a reaction.

Quinn nodded. "I do. But you're right. I can't stand what this will do to him, and to Kathy. Another court case will finish them off emotionally."

"Do you think they'll stand by Brett this time?" Gabe asked.

"He's their son. Would you not stand by our children?" Quinn asked, already knowing what Gabe would say.

"Yes, I would. I won't always approve of their life choices, nor will I readily forgive their more spectacular mistakes, but I will always love them."

"And what if one of our children tried to kill one of the others?"

Gabe shook his head. "Quinn, how can I answer that? I hope with every fiber of my being that we'll raise good, decent people, but we both know that sometimes the most diabolical individuals come from loving homes and there was no life-shattering event that made them into who they are."

"You believe people are born evil?" Quinn asked, surprised by the suggestion. She'd always believed nurture could overcome nature and thought Gabe shared that belief.

"Some are."

"What about Jude? Your opinion of him was extremely low at one point."

"Jude is not evil," Gabe said. "Misguided, weak, yes, but not evil. He has an addictive personality, but he's doing his best to keep his addiction in check. I actually have the utmost respect for him. He's really turned his life around."

"Do you believe he's no longer susceptible?"

"No, I don't. I believe he can very easily spiral out of control if the right, or I should say the wrong, set of circumstances derail his resolve. Jude will be walking the razor edge of addiction for the rest of his life."

"Isn't it amazing that we are born preprogrammed with our appearance, level of intelligence, and certain behavioral traits and spend the rest of our lives trying to alter all three?"

"You don't need to change a thing," Gabe said, finally smiling. "You are perfect just the way you are."

"And you are the smartest man I've ever met," Quinn said, walking into his arms.

"Because of my academic achievements?" Gabe asked, grinning.

"No, because you know when to lie through your teeth."

Quinn rested her head against Gabe's shoulder. She wished she could stay in his embrace forever, safe from whatever life had in store for her. Her moment of peace was interrupted by the vibrating of her mobile on the worktop.

She reluctantly glanced at the screen. "I have to take this." Quinn picked up the phone with a shaking hand.

"Mrs. Russell? DI Marshall here. Just wanted to let you know that we are officially reopening the inquiry into your sister's death. I think it goes without saying that you shouldn't discuss this with anyone who might alert Brett Besson to our suspicions."

"Will you keep me abreast of the investigation?" Quinn asked.

"I'm afraid I'm not at liberty to discuss an ongoing case, but I will inform you if there are any important developments, such as an arrest."

"I see. Thank you."

"Goodnight," DI Marshall said.

"Goodnight," Quinn muttered. "They've reopened the case," she told Gabe. She tried to sound pleased, but her heart was hammering against her ribs, and there was a twisting pain in her stomach. "We've done it."

Gabe nodded. "We're not there yet."

Chapter 47

June 1777
New York City

As spring turned to summer and New York City smoldered in the heat and humidity of an unexpectedly warm June, the staff at Major Radcliffe's house underwent a change that instantly altered the dynamic of the household and jolted Jocelyn out of her torpor. She'd become complacent and overconfident, believing herself to be above suspicion, but the transfer of Captain Palmer to General Howe's staff changed all that. Major Radcliffe was assigned a new aide-de-camp, who arrived, ready to assume his duties, the day after Captain Palmer had moved out.

"This is Captain Palmer's replacement, Captain Denning," Major Radcliffe said when Jocelyn brought a tea tray into his study on that first afternoon. "Captain, allow me to introduce Mistress Sinclair."

The man sprang to his feet, bowing to her as if she were the lady of the house. "A pleasure to make your acquaintance, Mistress Sinclair," he said politely.

Whereas Captain Palmer had practically blended into the woodwork, Captain Denning filled the study with his presence, making the spacious room feel somehow much smaller. He was tall and lean, his inky-black hair pulled into a ponytail and secured with a ribbon, and his dark blue gaze evaluating her as if she were one of the famous paintings Major Radcliffe had spoken to her about. She saw a glimmer of surprise in his eyes, followed by obvious masculine interest.

"It's a pleasure to meet you, Captain Denning," Jocelyn said. "Please don't hesitate to let me know if you need anything to make your stay more comfortable."

"I certainly will, Mistress Sinclair," the captain said, sitting back down and accepting a cup of tea. Jocelyn couldn't help noticing that he had beautiful hands, his fingers long and elegant.

"That will be all, Jocelyn," the major said. He'd taken to addressing her by her Christian name of late, a practice Jocelyn didn't condone. It implied an informal relationship between herself and her employer, a situation further complicated by Major Radcliffe's request that she call him Hector, at least in private.

"I'm sorry, sir, but I can't do that," Jocelyn had replied, scandalized. They weren't friends. They were master and servant, Englishman and American, quarry and spy. She liked the major well enough, but she wasn't about to permit him to take any liberties. She knew he was interested in her. He made it known in the way he sought out her company, bought her an occasional present that she wished she could refuse but had to accept in order not to offend him, and spoke to her as if she were a lady rather than the woman who washed his drawers and took out his chamber pot.

The major noted Captain Denning's look of appreciation, and his disapproval wasn't lost on her. Jocelyn had no desire to get between the two men, nor did she wish for their admiration. She was passably pretty; she'd been aware of that since she was a girl of thirteen and one of her father's friends had remarked on her budding beauty, but that didn't mean she was there for the taking, by any man. As she left the study and made her way back to the kitchen, she resolved to keep her distance from Captain Denning, but the decision did nothing to ease her discomfort. Her instinct of self-preservation warned her that the man was going to become a problem.

Chapter 48

"Does your father not worry about you cohabitating with three unmarried men?" Captain Denning asked as Jocelyn set his breakfast before him the following morning. He'd risen early, eager to familiarize himself with his surroundings and get to work.

"My father is no longer with us, and I really wouldn't call this cohabitating," Jocelyn replied snappishly, irritated by the inappropriateness of the question.

"I'm very sorry about your father. What about your mother?" the captain asked, ignoring the barb.

"She's gone too."

"Have you no family? A brother to look after you?"

"I have an older brother. He lives in Virginia," Jocelyn replied, eager to put an end to the conversation and get on with her day.

"I would never permit my sister to remain in New York City on her own," Captain Denning said.

"I don't need his permission. We are estranged." She was overstating the situation, but she wasn't about to explain her relationship with Greg to a near-stranger who had no business asking her these questions.

"Your fault, no doubt," the captain said, giving her a teasing smile.

"And why would you assume that?"

"Because a man understands his duty to his family. It had to have been your decision to distance yourself from your kin."

Jocelyn opened her mouth to protest, but to her great irritation, Captain Denning had summarized the situation quite accurately. She had been the one roused to new heights of anger when Greg had disparaged her views and ridiculed her loyalty to the American cause the day they'd buried their father. He'd called her silly, ignorant, and childish. She'd called him a few choice names as well, not the worst of them being pigheaded, priggish, and cowardly. He'd threatened to force her to join him in Virginia, which was when she'd taken flight. She'd eventually written to him to assure him she was well and to give him the address of her lodging house, certain that he wouldn't bother to come back for her, and he hadn't.

"I was right, wasn't I?" Captain Denning said, correctly interpreting her expression.

"I don't need the protection of a man, Captain. I can look after myself," she said, full of bluster.

"Oh, I'm sure you can. You are not only beautiful, you're spirited, like a young filly that needs breaking in." She could tell he was teasing, but for some reason that made her even angrier with him.

"I'm not a horse, nor do I require breaking in, as you so gallantly put it, Captain. Now, if you will excuse me." She walked out of the dining room, shoulders squared, head held high.

"I apologize if I've offended you," the captain called after her, but she could hear the grin in his voice. He wasn't sorry in the least. In fact, he seemed to have enjoyed their exchange and still had a smile on his face when he walked past her to get to his office.

Staying away from Captain Denning proved harder than she'd expected. Unlike Captain Palmer, who'd remained in his office for most of the day and only came out for meals, Captain Denning was a constant presence. He stopped by the kitchen to ask for a cup of ale, stepped out into the back garden to stretch his legs just as Jocelyn was hanging out the laundry, and often sat in the parlor in the evenings, reading or just enjoying a glass of the major's madeira. He was always scrupulously polite and respectful in front of the major, but when he got her on her own, which was a lot more often than she would have liked, there were the backhanded compliments and thinly veiled insinuations that she needed a man to look after her because she wasn't quite as safe as she believed herself to be. Was he referring to the major? she wondered as she lay sleepless during those long, hot nights, or was there another threat she wasn't aware of? Had he guessed at what she was doing?

"I'd like to meet this cousin of yours," Captain Denning said one Sunday as they walked out into the stifling August afternoon after enduring a particularly dull sermon by a visiting reverend. Thomas was to meet her in an hour at their usual place.

"And why is that?" Jocelyn asked, affecting a playful tone to mask the twisting anxiety she felt inside.

"Because I don't think he's your cousin at all," Captain Denning replied, smiling at her with all the glee of a cat who'd caught a mouse and meant to play with it before biting its head off.

"And who do you think he is?" Jocelyn asked coyly.

"I think he's your sweetheart."

"What if he were?"

"I'd be jealous in the extreme," he replied. "Do you think you might forgo seeing him one Sunday and walk out with me instead?"

"I'm sorry, Captain, but I'd rather not, given that we are *cohabitating*," she said, throwing his own expression back in his smug face.

"Do you think I have less honor than some colonial hick?" he asked, clearly stung by her refusal.

"I think I'd like to keep our association professional," Jocelyn said, wishing the major would tear himself away from the verbose reverend and join them, which would put an end to this worrying repartee.

"I'm not completely without charms, you know," Captain Denning said, smiling down at her. She wondered how he managed to look so cool in his wool tunic. Her curls were limp, and there were embarrassing stains beneath her arms. The backs of her knees were moist with perspiration beneath her petticoats and the clinging cotton of her stockings, and she would have sold her soul for a cool drink.

"I never said you were, but I would ask you to respect my decision."

"As you wish," the captain said, and bowed to her stiffly. "Enjoy your afternoon, Mistress Sinclair."

"I will."

She watched as he walked away, his back straight and his red tunic like a bloody gash among the evergreens of the graveyard. Why couldn't he just leave her alone? She'd hoped the major might ask for a replacement, but he seemed pleased with the captain's work and appeared to be a lot more forthcoming with him than he had ever been with Captain Palmer. Perhaps he responded to the captain's brash and confident manner. Captain Denning never seemed to feel the slightest embarrassment, indecision, or regret.

He's not human, Jocelyn concluded as she followed Major Radcliffe through the graveyard and toward the street. Mrs. Johnson fell into step with her. Her cheeks were red as apples, and she was perspiring freely in her black woolen gown.

"He's a handsome devil," she said wistfully.

"Who? The major?" Jocelyn asked. Mrs. Johnson was always friendly and kind, but she rarely made comments of a personal nature.

"The major is a handsome man, to be sure, but it was Captain Denning I was referring to. Why, if I were twenty years younger, I'd not let a man like that get away."

Jocelyn stopped and stared at the woman, snapping her mouth shut when she realized it was hanging open.

Mrs. Johnson laughed, her eyes crinkling at the corners. "Do you think I was never young, Jocelyn?" she asked. "When I was a girl, the sight of a red tunic and beautiful eyes could always set my heart aflutter."

"Was your husband a soldier, Mrs. Johnson?" Jocelyn asked.

"Indeed, he was, and I paid for it dearly," Mrs. Johnson replied, her smile fading. "I lost my William less than two years after we were married. Didn't even leave me a child to love." She sighed. "Killed at the Battle of the Monongahela in fifty-five."

"Did you never want to remarry?" Jocelyn asked, wondering if that was an indelicate question.

"I thought I might, in time, but my heart never let go. Every time a man showed an interest in me, I compared him to my William and found him lacking. And then, before I knew it, I was an old woman."

"I'm sorry," Jocelyn said.

"So am I. Don't miss your chance at happiness, Jocelyn. Life only gives us a handful of opportunities; seize yours when it comes your way."

"Are you saying Captain Denning is my opportunity?" Jocelyn asked, surprised by the turn the conversation had taken.

"I'm saying that you're a lovely young woman who's got her pick of admirers. The major isn't indifferent to you either. It's not his way to pursue a woman aggressively, but he's smitten with you, the poor man."

"How long have you worked for him?" Jocelyn asked, surprised that Mrs. Johnson seemed to know so much about the major's feelings.

"I've been with him for more than three years now. Follow him wherever he goes, and he rewards my loyalty. I'll have a comfortable life once I'm ready to stop working."

"Where will you go?"

"I have a sister who lives near Philadelphia. I reckon I'll go to her. I'm not overly fond of her husband, but I've got years yet. He may be good and dead by then," Mrs. Johnson joked. Jocelyn didn't think it was particularly funny to wish one's sister's husband dead, but then people became selfish in their loneliness. She could see how Mrs. Johnson might not want to share her sister.

Perhaps Captain Denning is just lonely, Jocelyn thought as she followed Mrs. Johnson into the kitchen once they arrived back at the house. She helped herself to a cup of ale and fanned her face with an old newspaper until she finally felt a little cooler. She had no great desire to go walking with Thomas, but he'd be waiting for her, and she had a few important tidbits to share with him this week.

Chapter 49

"Captain Denning worries me," Jocelyn said. She had relayed the conversation with the captain to Thomas as they strolled along the Hudson River, trying to catch a cooling breeze that never came.

"I think he's just an ass," Thomas said with feeling. "He's one of those men who think every woman should fall at their feet. Does he have any reason to suspect you?"

"Not that I know of."

"Then don't fall into his trap. He's trying to unnerve you. It gives him a sense of power, of control. Is the major pleased with his work?"

"He seems to be. Captain Denning is so different from Captain Palmer, though. I think he hates this position and resents being ordered to sit behind a desk. He's a man of action, a man of blood," Jocelyn added.

"Joss, I know you're an actress, but that's pretty dramatic, even for you," Thomas said, smiling at her. "All soldiers are men of blood. They kill because they must."

"But some enjoy it more than others," Jocelyn argued.

"True, but has he ever done anything more than make irritating comments?"

"No," Jocelyn admitted grudgingly.

"Then ignore him. It's a game he likes to play to liven up his day," Thomas said. "If ever you feel threatened by him, just say the word, and we'll pull you out. You're doing great work, though. General Washington is very pleased with your contribution."

"He knows about me?" Jocelyn said, gaping at Thomas.

"He likes to know who his people are and where they're placed. He's a great admirer of yours."

"You lie!" Jocelyn exclaimed, elbowing Thomas in the ribs.

"Maybe a little. He doesn't know your name, but he knows we have a spy in Major Radcliffe's house and that spy is providing valuable intel. Isn't that enough?"

"It is," Jocelyn said, glowing with pride. "It really is."

She returned to Major Radcliffe's house feeling reenergized. Thomas was right. Captain Denning was probably bored and frustrated. Drawing up lists of supply wagons and requisitioning food and leather for boots could never be enough for a man like him. There were desk soldiers, like Captain Palmer, and battle soldiers, like Captain Denning. She couldn't help wondering if this posting was a form of punishment for crossing one of the higher-ups. Surely any commanding officer worth his salt would see that Captain Denning was a man better suited to the field.

Retiring to her room, Jocelyn threw open the window and pulled off her sweat-soaked garments before stretching out on the bed in her shift. Her thoughts turned to Major Radcliffe. What kind of soldier was he? She'd only ever seen him interacting with other officers, but he'd never mentioned any military action he'd participated in. Was he a desk soldier as well, someone better suited to strategizing and organizing supplies than actual combat? With him, it was hard to tell. He was mild mannered and well bred, but somehow, he'd made the rank of major. He must have distinguished himself at some point, Jocelyn decided. Or perhaps his parents had simply purchased the rank for him. Wasn't that what the British did? They bought their sons a commission in the army, the higher the family, the higher the rank? She wasn't sure about that, and the major's family wasn't titled, as far as she knew.

Dismissing both Major Radcliffe and Captain Denning from her mind, Jocelyn considered her own situation. Mrs. Johnson's earlier comments had struck a nerve, and now she felt compelled to examine her options. She loved acting but couldn't see doing it for decades, as Anna Reid had. One grew weary of living that kind of life, and increasingly discouraged as the plummier parts went to younger women. Actresses like Anna, who had to be at least forty, were relegated to playing the crone or the witch, and once they were too old for those parts, they became dressers or seamstresses, doing whatever they could to earn their bread.

Jocelyn didn't want that for herself. Acting had been a means to an end, not an end in itself. She wanted a home of her own, and a family. She wanted love, she concluded, as the purpling shadows of twilight finally dispelled some of the scorching heat of the day. She hoped to meet a man who'd make her feel safe and loved, someone whose warm gaze would make her shiver with anticipation, someone who'd offer her a lifetime, not one night. There'd been admirers who'd come to the theater and declared their love for her, but she'd never encouraged any of them because she meant to hold on to her innocence. She wouldn't sell herself for a good meal or a pretty trinket.

No, she wouldn't go back to acting, Jocelyn thought as she grew drowsy at last. All this was temporary. Someday the British would leave and then she would see to her own life, and her own future.

Chapter 50

"You seem very pleased with yourself this morning," Captain Denning remarked when Jocelyn served him breakfast the following morning.

"No more than usual," she replied casually.

"I don't believe that," Captain Denning replied with a smile. "Did that cousin of yours finally come to his senses and offer to make an honest woman of you?"

"I am an honest woman, sir," Jocelyn bristled. "And he is my cousin."

"Then let me take you to supper one of these days," Captain Denning said. He caught her by the wrist after she'd placed a plate of bacon and eggs before him. "Jocelyn, I'm sorry if I come across as brutish or insensitive. I don't have much experience of women, to tell you the truth, at least not the kind of women that deserve respect."

"All women deserve respect," Jocelyn snapped, and snatched her hand away.

"You are right, of course. You see, I really do need a guiding hand," the captain said, looking contrite. "My mother died when I was quite young, and I never had older sisters or aunts to instruct me. I am a novice when it comes to gently bred young ladies, and I would value your help."

"So you can woo some unsuspecting girl?" Jocelyn replied archly.

"So I can woo you," he said, his voice silky and seductive. "Teach me how to woo you."

"I'm afraid I can't do that, Captain. Now, I really must get on with my duties."

"Of course. Don't let me keep you."

"Good morning," Jocelyn said as she turned to leave the room.

"It might have been," the captain replied under his breath.

"Are you all right, Jocelyn?" Mrs. Johnson asked when she returned to the kitchen. "Might you be sickening for something?"

"No. Why?"

"Your face is flushed, and your eyes look unusually bright," Mrs. Johnson replied, and Jocelyn realized she was being teased.

"I'll be glad to see the back of Captain Denning, I don't mind telling you," Jocelyn said, bristling at the implication that he had the power to make her blush. "There's just something about him that sets my teeth on edge."

Mrs. Johnson smiled knowingly. "It's the ones who set your teeth on edge that get under your skin," she pointed out. "It's hard to be immune to someone as beautiful as he is," she said a bit too dreamily for a woman of her years.

"Wild animals can be beautiful, but that doesn't make them any less dangerous," Jocelyn replied archly.

"Is that what you think, that he's dangerous?" Mrs. Johnson asked. "Has he acted inappropriately toward you? If he's done anything untoward, you must report him to Major Radcliffe."

"He makes me uneasy, that's all," Jocelyn replied.

She was spared from having to continue the conversation by the arrival of Private Sykes, who visited the kitchen more often than was strictly necessary. Mrs. Johnson seemed to have taken him under her wing and was always sneaking him slices of cake and cups of tea. She gave him an apple and a corn muffin and sent him on his way.

"You spoil him, Mrs. Johnson," Jocelyn said, glad to have someone else to discuss for a change.

"My heart goes out to him," Mrs. Johnson said as she covered the muffins and stowed them in the bread box, where the mice wouldn't get to them. "He's as much a soldier as I am a fine lady. It's a good thing they have him delivering messages and accompanying the major when he goes out. That's all that boy's fit for. A bit soft in the head," she said, tapping the side of her own head. "He's as innocent as a child."

"I suppose," Jocelyn replied as she made a fresh pot of tea and took a seat at the kitchen table. It was time for her own breakfast. She buttered a piece of bread and reached for the egg she'd boiled earlier. She hadn't given Private Sykes much thought, but now that Mrs. Johnson had mentioned it, she supposed there was something off about the private. It was as if his maturation had stopped as soon as he reached his teens. He was kind and pliable, but not overly perceptive when it came to the nuances of human interaction. She wouldn't go as far as to call him soft in the head—that was cruel—but there was an innocence in him that made one want to be kind to him.

"Take him a cup of water after you're finished, will you?" Mrs. Johnson said. "It's so hot outside."

"Yes, it is. I can't wait for autumn. I do hate summers in New York," Jocelyn said as she sprinkled salt on her egg.

She loved the autumn months, with their shortening days and cooling nights and the bright, bold colors that made such a lovely contrast to the deep blue sky. And this year, she didn't fear the coming of winter. Major Radcliffe was generous with firewood, allowing everyone a fire in their room when the temperature dropped. She wouldn't freeze, nor would she starve. She was doing her bit for the war effort, but she wasn't suffering in the process, not like the poor soldiers who'd be freezing in their tents come winter and subsisting on meager rations. She was truly blessed.

Chapter 51

March 2018
London

"You're a hard woman to get ahold of," Seth said when Quinn finally called him back. "I left you three messages."

"Sorry, Dad. I was really busy," Quinn said, cringing at the falseness of the statement. She hadn't been busy, at least not in the real sense of the word. She'd escaped from worrying about the potential outcome of the inquiry by losing herself in Jocelyn's memories, preferring to journey to Revolutionary War America rather than dwell on what DI Marshall might be doing to tighten the case against Brett.

"How are the children?" Seth asked. "I sent Mia a little something for her birthday."

"Little is not how I would describe it," Quinn said, recalling the size of the box she'd received. Seth's gifts were always elaborate and ridiculously expensive.

Seth chuckled. "Do you think she'll like the dollhouse?"

"I'm sure she'll love it," Quinn said. She was on autopilot, wishing she could bring the conversation to a close, but Seth seemed eager to chat.

"Will you be having a party for her?"

"Just a little one. She's too young to appreciate anything grander than cake, balloons, and a pile of presents to open."

"Wish I could be there," Seth said wistfully. "I feel like I'm missing out. Hey, Kathy and I were thinking of paying you guys a visit sometime in May. Kathy has a week of vacation coming up. Would that be convenient?"

"Can I get back to you on that?" Quinn asked, hating the need for duplicity.

"Sure. If that doesn't work, we'll go on a cruise or something."

"You don't sound too excited by the prospect," Quinn observed, clutching at something banal they could discuss.

"I'm not. I don't do well in that type of setting. Too crowded. Too confined. But Kathy loves cruising."

"I've never been on a cruise," Quinn said.

"You'd hate it," Seth replied, chuckling. "There are lots of fossils, but they're mostly of the human variety." Quinn forced a laugh that came out more like a sob.

"Are you okay, kid? You sound kind of weird," Seth said. "Everything all right between you and Gabe?"

"Yes, we're good," Quinn rushed to reassure him. "I've just been a bit under the weather."

"What you need is a big bowl of extra spicy gumbo. I'll make you a pot next time I'm in town."

"Thanks, Dad. I'd love that. Sorry, but I have to go. Work is calling."

"It was good to hear your voice. Kiss the babies for me." He made a kissing sound and rang off.

Quinn exhaled loudly. She hated keeping the truth from him. He didn't deserve this, but how could she tell him what she'd done? She was about to torpedo Seth's life, using DI Marshall as the warhead. Suddenly, she felt an urgent need for air and exercise. Jocelyn would have to wait. She needed to get out of the house for an hour and go for a brisk walk.

Quinn was just lacing up her trainers when her mobile rang again. This time it was Phoebe.

"Hello," Phoebe said cheerily. "How are you, dear?"

"I'm all right," Quinn lied.

"Good. I just wanted to confirm our plans. I'll be arriving at St. Pancras around two on Sunday. I've already booked a hotel," Phoebe announced, sounding pleased with the arrangement.

Staying in a London hotel was a treat not to be missed. Phoebe always ordered breakfast to be brought up to her room and enjoyed it in bed, like an Edwardian damsel straight from one of the romance novels she liked to read. She said it made her feel posh.

"We can't wait to see you," Quinn said distractedly.

"Will you be having a lot of people over for Mia's birthday?" Phoebe asked. She was clearly eager for a chat, so Quinn returned to the lounge and sat down, realizing this would take a while.

"Just the closest family and friends. Mia is looking forward to seeing Olivia and Vanessa. They're so cute when they're together."

"I bet they are. Does Alex feel left out among all these girls?" Phoebe asked.

Quinn had a feeling Alex was Phoebe's favorite, possibly because he reminded her of Gabe when he was little. He certainly looked like him, and perhaps behaved a little like him as well. Gabe had been a quiet, sensitive child who'd preferred to play on his own. Phoebe always went out of her way to get Alex something special, something that would make him feel less like a middle child and more like the favorite grandchild.

"Not yet. He enjoys playing with them," Quinn rushed to reassure Phoebe.

"What is it, Quinn?" Phoebe asked, her radar as attuned to Quinn's state of mind as ever. "You sound a bit off."

"Do I?" She supposed she should be grateful that the people in her life knew her well enough to tell when she wasn't her usual self, but just then, she wished she could fob them off. However, it wasn't as easy to lie to Phoebe as it had been to Seth.

"Are you all right?" Phoebe persisted.

"If I'm to be honest, not really," Quinn confessed.

"What is it? You know you can always talk to me. Sometimes it's easier than talking to your own mum, or mums, I should say," Phoebe quipped.

Quinn sighed. "Phoebe, I have reason to believe Brett was driving the car that killed Jo," Quinn said in a rush.

"What? Why?"

"Some new evidence has come to light. The case has been reopened by the police."

"So, they believe he left the scene of an accident?" Phoebe asked.

"It's worse than that, Phoebe. They believe he struck her intentionally," Quinn said, the words sticking in her throat.

"But why would he do that?"

"Perhaps he thought he was doing me a favor, given what had happened that day," Quinn croaked, now fervently wishing she hadn't said anything.

"Good God!" Phoebe exclaimed. "That must be devastating for you."

"It is," Quinn said. "I just can't wrap my mind around it. And when I think what this will do to Kathy and Seth..."

"Quinn, Kathy and Seth are not your responsibility. Every parent has untapped reserves of strength to see them through the darkest of times."

"I doubt you've ever had to tap into those reserves," Quinn joked. "Gabe is the perfect son."

"And I thank God for that every day. I'm lucky to have raised a man I can be proud of, but not every parent is so blessed."

"I don't believe it has anything to do with luck. You and Graham are directly responsible for the man Gabe grew up to be."

"I'd like to think so, but there are many kind, decent people whose kids don't turn out well, through no fault of their own. They haven't stooped to murder, mind you, but they can hardly be called successful, or independent even. Take Cecily's son, for example. The man is forty-two and he's sleeping on his mother's sofa. Got a gambling addiction," Phoebe said, lowering her voice as if Cecily could hear her from next door. "Lost everything, including his wife and son. They don't want to have anything to do with him."

"That's a terrible situation, but not quite the same," Quinn said, wishing desperately she could end the conversation and get outside.

"Of course, it isn't. I was only saying, you never know how things will turn out. My heart goes out to Kathy and Seth, Seth especially. To have lost a daughter so soon after he'd found her must have been heartbreaking, but to learn that his son was the one to take her life is probably enough to push the poor man over the edge. But Seth is strong. He's tough. He's so American in the way he deals with problems," Phoebe added, making Seth sound like a gunslinger from a Western movie.

That almost made Quinn chuckle, but not quite. "Look, sorry, but I've got to go."

"Of course. Sorry to have kept you. I'll see you on Sunday."

"Yes. Looking forward to it," Quinn said, and ended the call.

She pulled on her jacket, stuffed her mobile, a ten-pound note in case of emergency, and her ID in her pocket, and left the house.

Chapter 52

When Quinn returned, she felt no better. At least with Drew, she could ask for an update, but now that the case had been passed over to the Met, she was no longer directly involved. She wished she could ring DI Marshall but knew he wouldn't tell her anything. Quinn made some lunch, threw in a load of laundry, and stared at the same page in a book she'd been trying to read for a full ten minutes before finally giving up and ringing Drew. He picked up immediately, his voice surprisingly cheerful.

"Guess you heard the good news," he said. "Dan's got them to reopen the case, and he's heading the investigation."

"Is that because he's the best man for the job or because he's best placed to hide where the information came from?" Quinn asked.

Drew chuckled. "The information I provided will never be used in a court of law, Quinn. I used it to show a direct link between Brett, Jo, and the car. The case Dan builds against Brett will be meticulously documented and supported by legitimate evidence that can be used in a murder trial."

"I hope you're right," Quinn murmured. "Have you heard from him? I can't stand not knowing."

"You are going to have to be patient. This could take months."

"Really?"

"Really. This is not a TV program, where a case gets solved in a few days."

"You haven't answered my question," Quinn said.

"Yeah, I've heard from him. They've impounded the car and have been in touch with the New Orleans PD."

"Why?" Quinn asked, surprised by this turn of events.

"To request Brett Besson's fingerprints and a copy of his psychological evaluation."

"Is the NOPD obligated to comply?" Quinn asked. She had no idea how an investigation involving a foreign national worked.

"They can make things difficult if they choose to, but generally, police officers are happy to help each other, especially in a murder inquiry."

"Is there any chance they might be able to lift his prints off the car more than two years after he'd driven it?" Quinn asked.

"I wouldn't bet on it, but they have to try. That car will be taken apart by a forensic team, and if there's anything to find, they will find it. Quinn, I know this advice will fall on deaf ears, but you should really put this whole thing out of your mind. Concentrate on your own life. If there are any major developments, you will be apprised."

"Will I?" Quinn muttered.

"Yes. If you don't hear it from Marshall, you'll hear it from me. I still have my sources at the station."

"Promise?"

"Promise."

"Thanks, Drew. You're a star."

"That I am," Drew said with a chuckle. "They don't shine brighter than me. Now, I've got work to do, and if I remember correctly, you have children that need collecting."

"Right. Bye," Quinn said. If she didn't leave now, she'd be late.

Drew was right, Quinn thought as she hurried to get the kids. She had to put the case out of her mind for the time being and concentrate on her own life. Mia's birthday was a week and a half away, and she needed to prepare. There were still the cake and balloons to get, the presents to wrap, and the snacks and drinks to purchase. She also had to check with all the invitees to make sure they were still coming. She hoped Logan, Rafe, and their surrogate, Chrissy, would be able to attend. Quinn hadn't seen Logan in weeks and genuinely missed him. She couldn't really say the same for Sylvia, but she'd invited her, nonetheless. Mia was

Sylvia's granddaughter, regardless of how Quinn felt about her birth mother.

She wished her own mum and dad could come. It'd been too long since she'd seen them in person, when they'd come to London the previous summer for a fortnight before heading to Scotland for a week. Strange how spread out her family was these days. She supposed this was the new normal for many people, especially those whose families had as many branches as hers now did.

Once Mia's birthday was planned, Quinn would concentrate on Jocelyn's story. She didn't have time to dither if Rhys hoped to turn the narrative into a Christmas special. She still had no inkling how the ring had come to be buried in Hertfordshire but meant to find out. She'd miss Jocelyn once the case was done, Quinn thought as she took her place by the gate, waiting for the children to be brought out. She identified with the young American woman, maybe because, at the moment, she felt as lost and unsure of what was to come as Jocelyn had. At least she had a good man by her side, unlike Jocelyn, who seemed to have inspired admiration but not real love in the men who'd desired her.

She had been truly beautiful, but Quinn wasn't sure if the men in her life saw her as merely ornamental or if they had taken the time to get to know her. They certainly treated her like a prize to be won. Everyone from Ben Wilder, who was convinced Jocelyn had feelings for his brother, to Captain Denning, who seemed determined to break down her walls with his brand of brash charm, had sought to possess her, but how many of them had really cared for her? It seemed that even her brother had been happy to leave her to her own devices at a time when a woman alone was far from safe.

Quinn smiled brightly when she spotted Alex, then Mia. Mia was clutching her favorite giraffe toy, and there was a daub of green paint on her cheek. She saw Quinn and waved happily, then broke free of her teacher and ran to her mum. Alex followed suit, and the three of them took a moment to enjoy a group hug.

"Come on, guys. Let's go home," Quinn said, feeling lighter for the first time in weeks.

Chapter 53

August 1777
New York City

It was in the last week of August that Thomas invited Jocelyn to take luncheon at a quayside tavern just off Beckman's Slip. As they drew near the tavern, Jocelyn had to take out her handkerchief and hold it over her mouth and nose, but it did little to block the smell of fish and rotting vegetables coming from a nearby market, and the acrid stench of sweat and piss that permeated the air. Overheated sailors, their faces glistening with perspiration, crowded the docks, while several army officers, who had to be cooking alive in their wool coats, were supervising the loading and unloading of the ships. They were barking out orders and hurling insults at the exhausted men, who paid them little heed as they maneuvered heavy crates and rolled barrels onto the waiting ships.

"What are we doing here?" Jocelyn demanded. "Surely there are plenty of other places we could have gone."

"It wasn't my choice," Thomas said apologetically. "Come on. Nearly there."

The Dock House was small and dim, the interior smelling of sun-warmed wood, spilled ale, and fish stew. At least half the tables were occupied by sailors who'd come in for a cool drink and a meal. Some talked loudly among themselves, while others sat in silence, presumably too hot and tired, having been laboring since dawn, to do more than lift a tankard to their parched lips. There wasn't a single woman in the place, not even a serving wench. A grizzled, balding man behind the counter spotted them and tilted his head toward a door at the back. Thomas nodded and steered Jocelyn through the crowd at the bar.

Behind the door was a small private parlor. It faced the back of the building, so it was much quieter and cooler, the room decorated with velvet curtains to keep out the heat or cold, depending on the season, and several padded chairs grouped around a rectangular table. Jocelyn supposed the room was used by ship captains or other higher-ranking sailors when they wanted a quiet meal or a place to have a private conversation. At the moment, the parlor had only one occupant, and he sat at the head of the table, nursing a tankard of ale. Richard Kinney smiled at Jocelyn and invited her to sit down.

"You're looking well, if a bit hot," he observed.

"It's hot as hell out there," Jocelyn replied, knowing Richard wouldn't be shocked by such a sentiment coming from a woman.

"It's like hell's very own kitchen," he agreed, loosening his stock a little. His face was flushed, and the linen of the stock was limp with sweat.

"Don't feel you have to suffer on my account," Jocelyn said. "Take off your coat."

Richard threw her a grateful look and removed the coat, breathing a sigh of relief. "I've ordered some food. I hope you like roast beef and potatoes."

Jocelyn wasn't in the mood for a heavy meal, not in this heat, but she nodded. Richard clearly had something other than food on his mind if he'd invited her there. She'd thought Thomas would join them, but he excused himself and went to have a pint at the bar, probably to keep an eye out for anyone who might show too much interest in whoever was dining in the private parlor and to give them some privacy.

A few minutes later, the man she'd seen earlier brought two plates of roast beef and a pitcher of ale. He set them on the table and left without saying a word. Richard eyed the food with obvious appreciation. "I'm starving," he said. "Haven't had a proper meal in weeks. The wife took our girls to see her folks. They have a farm in New Jersey. It's nice for them to be out in the fresh air, and there's a lake nearby," he added wistfully. "My father-in-law takes the girls fishing when the weather is fine."

"That must be lovely," Jocelyn said. In her mind's eye, she could see this lake, its mirrorlike surface reflecting the leafy trees that promised cool shade on a hot day, the air filled with birdsong and the smell of grass and wildflowers. And in the distance, a sturdy white farmhouse with chickens pecking in the front yard, an orange cat dozing in the sun, and a great red barn, the paint vibrant against the blue of the summer sky. She'd give anything to spend an afternoon in such a place, to shed her persona like a snake sheds its skin and just be the girl she'd been before her parents had died and before the war had begun, when her life had been peaceful and happy.

"Jocelyn, you're doing a stellar job," Richard said, startling her out of her reverie. "Your information has been instrumental in planning some of our operations."

"Thank you," Jocelyn said, smiling with pleasure. "I'm glad I'm able to help."

Richard nodded and continued to eat. Jocelyn took a bite of her own food, wondering why he was stalling. Richard wasn't the type to start from afar, but he hadn't asked her to come all this way just to tell her she was doing well and break bread with her.

Finally, he put down his knife and fork and faced her across the table. "Major Radcliffe seems to like you," he said. "It's not every employer who invites his maidservant to dine with him and regales her with stories of his youth."

"I think he's just lonely and wants to talk to someone who's not military personnel," Jocelyn replied.

"And you like him." It wasn't a question, more a statement of fact.

"He's been good to me," Jocelyn replied carefully. She pushed away her plate, the smell of the meat suddenly making her queasy.

"Jocelyn, we need you to get closer to Major Radcliffe. We believe an attack on our troops in Pennsylvania is imminent. If we had a clearer idea of which direction that attack will come from and when the British mean to strike, we'd be better prepared." Richard's gaze was intent, his mouth pursed.

Jocelyn felt as if a bucket of scalding water had just been upended over her head. Her breath came in short gasps, drops of sweat sliding down between her breasts as her stomach threatened to empty itself of its contents.

"Are you suggesting I become his mistress?" she asked incredulously.

"A man will reveal many secrets in his least guarded moments," Richard replied, his gaze still pinning her to the spot. "The information you obtain can save countless lives."

Jocelyn sucked in a shuddering breath. "You are asking me to trade my body, my very honor, for information."

"I am not asking, Jocelyn. I'm suggesting. No one can make that decision but you."

"No one has the right to ask that of me," Jocelyn snapped. "I am risking my life for the cause, but I will not go to his bed and allow him to—" She couldn't even bring herself to say the words. The very idea was repellant.

Richard nodded and turned his attention back to his food. He ate in silence for a few moments, allowing Jocelyn time to compose herself. "Captain Denning is young and handsome," he said, finally glancing up from the plate.

"And that makes it more acceptable, does it?" Jocelyn demanded, outraged.

"Is your virtue not worth the lives of hundreds of men?" Richard asked, all pretense at sympathy and understanding now gone. "You might even enjoy it," he added, smiling at her in a way that made her blood run hot and cold at the same time. "Don't you get lonely, spending night after night by yourself? You weren't so fussy before," he said softly.

"What?" Jocelyn asked, uncomprehending.

"Come, Jocelyn, surely you indulged in an affair or two in your theater days. What beautiful young actress doesn't? You had

253

so many admirers, and a woman on her own can always benefit from such an arrangement."

Jocelyn stared at him, understanding dawning. Richard had asked her to spy for the cause for that very reason. He'd hoped she'd be seduced by the major and pass back the kind of information a man would only reveal in bed, but since she hadn't, he was now asking her outright.

"A few months ago, you advised me not to draw attention to myself. You said you'd pull me out if I ever felt threatened, and now you're asking me to prostitute myself to these men," she hissed, so angry she could barely breathe.

"Things have changed, Jocelyn. If the British take Philadelphia, the war is as good as lost. General Washington's army is all that stands between us and a crushing defeat, and if that army is decimated in battle…"

"You can't seriously suggest that the only thing that stands in the way of a Continental victory is the refusal of one woman to spread her legs for the enemy." She didn't care if she was being crude; she simply couldn't bring herself to agree to what Richard was proposing.

"As I said, only you can make that decision."

"My decision was made before you lured me here. I will not do what you ask. I will try to find out what I can, but it won't be through prostitution."

Richard pushed away his plate and took a long pull of ale. "Any information you can provide us with regarding the planned attack is invaluable. I'm sorry if I've offended you, Jocelyn. That was never my intention. There are others," he said, his gaze sliding away from her for a moment, "who are willing. Both men and women. They're prepared to make a sacrifice for their country."

"Does General Washington know you encourage his agents to barter their souls?" Jocelyn asked. She couldn't believe the gall of the man.

"It's not something that's openly discussed, but sex and espionage have always gone hand in hand."

"Have they?" Jocelyn demanded angrily.

"You know they have."

"Thank you for luncheon, Richard," Jocelyn said as she tossed her napkin onto the table. "I think it's time I returned home."

"Think on what I said," Richard said, making no move to get up. "If you change your mind, we will be grateful. If not, then we will continue as before. Nothing has changed."

Everything has changed, Jocelyn thought as she marched from the parlor, pushed her way through the taproom, and stepped outside into the infernal heat.

"Are you all right?" Thomas asked as he caught up with her.

"Did you know about this?" Jocelyn demanded, taking her anger out on the poor man.

"I do not know what you spoke about," Thomas replied.

"Are you sure about that? Did Richard not encourage you to exert pressure on me?"

"Pressure to do what?"

"To invite myself into the major's bed. Or Captain Denning's. Or both," she exclaimed, feeling a bit hysterical.

Thomas looked genuinely shocked. "He asked that of you?"

"He did. I assumed you were in on the plan."

Thomas shook his head vehemently. "I wasn't. I'm sorry, Jocelyn. I would never ask that of you, or anyone else. Please tell me you refused."

"I have, but he made me feel like a traitor, a coward, someone who puts their own selfish needs before the lives of others."

"He crossed the line, Jocelyn. I cannot and will not defend his methods or his treatment of you." Thomas looked genuinely distressed.

"Has he ever asked you to do something like that?" Jocelyn asked as they walked toward Broadway Street. Thomas was a good-looking young man, the type of man women noticed and flirted with shamelessly.

"No."

"And if he had?"

Thomas colored, averting his gaze. "Jocelyn, it's different for men. A man can take many lovers and still be considered a decent fellow, while a woman is expected to remain pure until marriage."

"So, you're saying you would do it," Jocelyn prodded.

"I suppose I would," Thomas confessed. "If I knew it'd make a real difference."

"Even if the woman was old enough to be your mother?"

"Some older women are quite attractive," Thomas replied lamely.

"You're disgusting," Jocelyn spat out. "The lot of you. You'd stick your cock into anything that has a heartbeat, and not for the cause, but for your own selfish pleasure. Well, don't expect me to compromise myself just because you would."

Jocelyn began to walk faster, Thomas trotting alongside to keep up with her. "Jocelyn, I never meant—"

"Never meant what?" she snapped.

"Never meant to imply that you should agree. As I said, it's different for women."

"Yes. It is. Now bugger off."

Jocelyn turned her back on him and ran, unable to continue the conversation for a moment longer. She was appalled, but also truly shocked to discover that her compatriots were not averse to getting information in any way necessary. She understood that this was a matter of life and death, and the defeat of Washington's army could spell the end of the rebellion, but she simply couldn't bring herself to entertain the idea of offering herself to Major Radcliffe.

Having returned to the house, Jocelyn retreated to her room, tore off her gown and hose, and lay on the bed in her shift, the linen sticking to her flushed skin. Would it be as easy as Richard had suggested to begin an affair? Jocelyn closed her eyes and tried to imagine kissing Hector Radcliffe. She'd been kissed a few times, but that was the extent of her sexual experience. There were always actresses who took lovers from among their admirers and often relied on their financial support, but Jocelyn had always made her own way, dubious that a permanent relationship could ever be possible.

But it was. Sometimes. Anna Reid had met her partner in just such a way. Carole had been married then and had come to the theater with her husband, Dr. Ford, but the two women had struck up a friendship after Carole had come to see Anna again, on her own this time. They had begun an intimate relationship after Dr. Ford passed away three years ago. Until then, Jocelyn hadn't even known such an arrangement was possible, but Anna and Carole seemed happy, and loved each other as much as any married couple of Jocelyn's acquaintance. Of course, they didn't publicize their romance and allowed everyone to believe that they were simply housemates, sharing lodgings to save on cost and have a bit of company.

Would I feel differently if I were no longer a virgin? Jocelyn asked herself as she fanned herself with a newspaper, stirring the heavy air with little result. Would it no longer matter? It was impossible to know how she might feel if she were widowed or had chosen to indulge in a premarital affair, but the very idea of Major Radcliffe touching her as a lover was utterly bizarre. He was a nice man, educated and polite, but despite his good looks, she wasn't attracted to him in the least.

She then considered Captain Denning. Richard was right, the captain was a handsome man, but he frightened her. She could envision the captain in battle: sword drawn, teeth bared, not a trace of fear in his eyes as he charged the enemy. She couldn't see him losing a fight. Nor could she imagine him being tender with a woman. He'd be demanding in bed, her gut instinct told her. He needed a woman who'd be prepared to match his desire and wouldn't be frightened by his intensity.

Strange how some men exuded that kind of sexual power, Jocelyn thought. She could easily visualize the captain in a state of undress, but the major may as well have been born in his uniform. It was hard to countenance that there was a man's body beneath the smart uniform, or a man's needs masked by the aristocratic façade.

Jocelyn curled into a ball. She'd shared a house with several men for months, but her thoughts had never strayed beyond her daily duties and her true purpose. But now she couldn't help but think of them as men, sexual beings who might see her as something more than an efficient servant. She knew Captain Denning did, but she hadn't given his invitation any serious thought. He was an enemy soldier. But perhaps she shouldn't have dismissed his interest so quickly. She would never do what Richard had suggested, but perhaps she could have supper with the man and learn all she could. Would he be careless enough to share anything with her? Jocelyn tried to picture him in civilian clothes, but it proved harder than she'd thought. His uniform was as much a part of him as his ambition. She didn't know much of the inner workings of men's minds, but she did know Captain Denning planned to go far.

Chapter 54

The following morning, having made up her mind to try harder, Jocelyn smiled brightly at the captain when she brought him breakfast. "Lovely day," she said, even though it was just as hot as it had been the day before, and possibly even more humid.

"Eh, yes," he agreed, obviously taken by surprise. Jocelyn was never one to initiate conversation with him.

"You must be awfully warm in that wool coat," Jocelyn said, genuinely sorry for the man.

"The summers here are certainly brutal," Captain Denning said. "I've always hated English weather, but I do miss it now that I've been here for nearly two years."

"Do you plan on returning to England?" Jocelyn asked, doing her best to appear interested. She had no idea what part of England he was even from.

"Once this war is won, I'm sure I'll be sent someplace else. I do hope to get some leave before my next posting and go home."

"Where's home?"

"Bedfordshire."

"Captain Denning, if you're quite finished," Major Radcliffe said as he strode through the door, "I have need of you."

"Yes, sir." Captain Denning pushed away his half-eaten breakfast and sprang to his feet. "Have a pleasant day, Mistress Sinclair."

"And you, Captain," Jocelyn replied demurely. "Perhaps we can go for a walk one evening," she added softly, hoping the major hadn't heard her brazen come-on.

The captain looked momentarily abashed but gave her a brief nod before leaving the dining room. Jocelyn exhaled the breath she'd been holding. There was no turning back now.

Captain Denning found himself unexpectedly free on Tuesday evening and asked if Jocelyn might like to take the air. Jocelyn was finished for the day and agreed to go for a walk. The temperature had dropped somewhat, the evening pleasantly cool after days of relentless heat. They walked up Broadway, then turned left, heading toward the river. Jocelyn inhaled the briny smell, glad to be out of the house despite her nervousness. The captain walked alongside her, the sharp angles of his face softened by candlelight spilling from the windows of the houses or a lantern from a passing carriage.

"What made you change your mind?" he asked. "About taking a walk with me, I mean."

Jocelyn looked down, unsure how to reply. She didn't want to give him the wrong idea, but at the same time, she wanted him to feel flattered enough to believe she might be interested in him. "I don't have many friends," Jocelyn said shyly.

"You're lonely," he said, looking down at her.

"Sometimes."

"I'm lonely too," he admitted. "Working for the major is an excellent opportunity for advancement, but being quartered in his house isolates me from my regiment."

"Do you have many friends in your regiment?" Jocelyn asked.

"I don't know if I'd call them friends, but a man needs like-minded company in a time of war. It relieves the tension and makes the waiting more bearable."

"Waiting?"

"For something decisive to finally happen."

"Do you think something will happen soon?" Jocelyn asked, her heart fluttering with hope. Could it be this easy to get him to talk?

The captain shrugged. "Possibly."

"Like what?" Jocelyn asked, giving him her best wide-eyed ingenue smile.

Captain Denning smiled. "I can't talk about that. Why don't you tell me about you? How is it that you're not married?"

"No one has asked," she replied coyly.

"I don't believe that for a moment. You must have had dozens of offers."

"Not from anyone I would have accepted."

"What are you looking for in a man?" the captain asked, giving her a sidelong glance.

"Intelligence, charm, gentleness," Jocelyn replied, listing the first three traits that sprang to mind.

"I can offer you two out of three," Captain Denning said softly.

"Which one are you lacking?" she asked, even though she already knew. Was he self-aware enough to recognize his shortcomings?

"I'm not a gentle man, Mistress Sinclair. I suppose some would say that's because no one has ever been gentle with me."

"What about your mother? Was she not loving to you before she passed?"

"I don't remember my mother. I was only two when she died. I was raised by my father, who's probably the harshest man I know."

"Did he beat you?"

"Regularly. He thought it built character," Captain Denning replied without any rancor.

"And did it?"

"I suppose, to a degree."

"Is your father still alive?" Jocelyn inquired.

"Yes, but he's not in good health."

"Who looks after him?"

"My younger sister, Judith."

"And is he as harsh with her as he was with you?" Jocelyn asked.

Captain Denning chuckled. "He adores Judith. She's always been the apple of his eye. Possibly because she rid him of the wife he'd loathed."

"How do you mean?"

"My mother died giving birth to Judith."

"Why did your father loathe your mother?" Jocelyn asked. Her parents had been devoted to each other, and her father had grieved for his wife until his own death. It was difficult to imagine a household that was filled with so much hatred.

"He said she was a whore. I think the reason he'd always been so cruel to me is because he never believed I was really his son. I don't resemble him in the slightest. Judith, on the other hand, is the spitting image of him, so he had no reason to question her paternity."

"Do you favor your mother in looks?"

"I wouldn't know. I've never seen a likeness of her, and I don't remember her clearly." Captain Denning stopped walking and looked down at her. "Forgive me, this conversation has turned rather maudlin. I didn't invite you for a walk so that I could cry to you about the lack of love in my childhood. Let's talk of something amusing."

"Such as?"

"I've no idea," he replied, laughing softly.

"I think it's time we turned back," Jocelyn said. "I have to be up early in the morning."

"Of course. I'm sorry to have kept you out so late," Captain Denning replied. "Mistress Sinclair, can I take you to supper next Sunday? We can go to a respectable tavern where other ladies will be present," he added hastily to reassure her all would be above board.

"Yes," Jocelyn said. "That would be nice. And you can call me Jocelyn."

Captain Denning smiled. "That's a beautiful name. I'm glad you changed your mind, Jocelyn," he said.

Jocelyn looked up at him expectantly, but he didn't say anything. "You didn't tell me your Christian name."

"Sorry. It's Jared," he replied, looking a bit bemused, probably because she was looking at him so intently. He really was attractive. "I very much enjoyed your company tonight," Captain Denning said shyly.

Truth be told, she had enjoyed his company as well, and he had been the perfect gentleman throughout, only taking her by the elbow when a carriage had turned the corner just as they were about to cross the street. Supper with the captain would be a safe enough affair, as long as they were surrounded by other patrons and came straight back afterward.

Chapter 55

As the week wore on, Jocelyn told herself that she'd only agreed to join Captain Denning for supper because he was an invaluable source of information, but in truth, she was lonely and had enjoyed their walk. When on his own, his edges were not quite as sharp, and he had offered her a glimpse of a vulnerability he kept well-hidden when at home. Perhaps she had misjudged him. In any case, their conversation had been a welcome alternative to her sessions with Major Radcliffe. Although attentive and charming, the major was an actor in his own right and, like all actors, craved an audience while he delivered his soliloquy, for he prattled on about his life as if it were the most exciting tale Jocelyn could ever hope to hear.

She missed the company of people her own age, but the only person she got to see outside the major's house was Thomas, who wasn't her friend but simply a conduit of information. Was it disloyal to the cause to spend time with a British soldier? Perhaps, but she never intended her liaison with Captain Denning to go beyond the occasional meal or walk. She would never permit him to take any liberties with her, not even if it meant she might learn something in an unguarded moment.

On Sunday, having made her report to Thomas, Jocelyn returned to the house to get ready. She only had two gowns, one for work and one for church that had been provided by Richard and likely borrowed from some well-to-do matron sympathetic to the cause. They were nothing like the lovely dresses she'd worn before, but they were the type of garments a woman in her position would own. The work dress was an unrelieved gray, but the church gown had an apple-green bodice that went well with Jocelyn's fair hair and served to underline her peachy complexion.

When at home, she tucked her hair into a linen cap, but today she decided to wear her hair uncovered, pinning it up at the back but allowing a few curls to frame her face. The cap made her feel like a drab. Jocelyn gazed at herself in the small looking glass Mrs. Johnson had lent her, surprised by what she saw. There was a glint of excitement in her eyes, and her cheeks were rosy, and not just because of the heat. She was filled with anticipation, excited to spend a few hours in the captain's company.

Jocelyn set down the mirror and sat heavily on the bed. What was she playing at? Captain Denning was the enemy, a soldier who'd kill her countrymen without a second thought. He'd probably kill her if he knew what she was about. She should tell him she felt unwell and call the whole thing off. But even as the rational thoughts raced through her mind, she slowly stood and walked to the door, smiling shyly at the captain, who was standing at the bottom of the stairs, his tricorn beneath his arm.

"Ready?" he asked, returning her smile tenfold. "You look lovely."

"Do I?" Jocelyn asked, her hand going to her hair in a gesture of false modesty. She knew she looked good, just as she knew that he admired her.

"You are beautiful," Captain Denning replied breathlessly. "Shall we?"

He bowed to the major, who'd stepped out of the parlor to see what was going on.

"Where are you two off to?" the major asked, his lips pursing with disapproval.

"I'm taking Mistress Sinclair out for an early supper," Captain Denning replied, his jaw tightening.

The major looked like he was about to rebuke the captain but seemed to change his mind. "Don't keep her out too late," he said in an icy tone.

"No, sir. I won't."

Major Radcliffe glared at Jocelyn, his eyes dark pools of displeasure. Jocelyn averted her gaze as she walked past him and stepped outside into the balmy haze of the late afternoon.

"I think he's angry with us," she said to the captain as they fell into step.

"I can't imagine why," Captain Denning replied, his brows knitted in consternation.

"Is there some military protocol regarding mixing with the help?" Jocelyn asked playfully, trying to make light of the major's obvious anger.

"Not that I'm aware of," Captain Denning replied. "And I wouldn't call this mixing. We're simply going out for a meal. It's not as if—" He went quiet, wisely deciding not to finish the sentence.

Jocelyn looked down, partly amused by his embarrassment and partly wary. She could guess what he'd been thinking, and the idea made her uncomfortable. Perhaps the major had a good reason for his reaction. If her relationship with Captain Denning went beyond friendship, living under the same roof might prove uncomfortable for them both and could lead to the loss of their positions. She didn't think Captain Denning would mind a transfer overmuch, but she would certainly rue losing access to the major and the information he was privy to as a highly placed officer on General Howe's staff.

"Don't worry. I'll smooth things over with the major," Captain Denning said, looking down at her anxiously.

"I can ill afford to lose my position," Jocelyn said.

"You won't. I will formally ask the major for permission to court you," the captain said, his blush turning a deeper shade of pink.

"Is this what this is? A courtship?"

"I would very much like it to be," the captain replied. "I have the greatest admiration for you, Jocelyn. I hope you don't think my intentions are anything less than honorable."

I don't know what to think, Jocelyn thought as she allowed him to take her arm while crossing the street to the tavern on the other side.

She hadn't been to this tavern before. It was called the King's Cross and boasted a slightly different clientele than the taverns just off Broadway Street, which were jammed with tommies and occasionally their unsavory companions. Jocelyn spotted several officers dining together, and there were a number of couples, the women well dressed and clearly respectable, not the type of company one paid for by the hour.

Captain Denning escorted her toward a back parlor, which was divided into four alcoves, the tall backs of the booths allowing extra privacy. He must have reserved a table in advance, since there was only one alcove left unoccupied. Captain Denning led her directly toward it.

"Good evening, Captain. Mistress," the waiter said as they sat down. "Your usual?" he asked, looking to the captain.

"Do you like claret, Jocelyn, or would you prefer something else to drink?"

"Claret is fine," Jocelyn replied. She suddenly wondered if Jared had brought other women here before her and felt a pang of irrational jealousy. The waiter bowed deferentially and went to fetch the wine.

"They know you here," Jocelyn said, watching him.

"I come here nearly every Sunday," Captain Denning replied. "This is the first time I've brought a companion, though," he added, his gaze meeting hers.

"Do you normally dine alone?"

"Yes."

"Don't you find it lonely?" Jocelyn asked.

"I'm quite used to being on my own. During the week, I'm expected to dine with the major, or other officers if we're invited out, so one solitary meal feels more like a reward than a punishment."

"You are not solitary now," Jocelyn reminded him.

He smiled. "By choice."

She felt heat rising in her cheeks. His gaze was so intimate.

267

"I hope you're hungry. They do a good roast beef here," he hastened to add, as though noticing her reaction to his words.

"Sounds good," Jocelyn muttered, although she was heartily sick of roast beef. She should be grateful, she knew. Many people rarely ate beef, as it was too expensive, but she wasn't very hungry these days and would have preferred lighter fare. The waiter returned with their claret, and they both tasted it at the same time, their gazes meeting over the rims of the glasses. Jocelyn was first to look away.

They made small talk until the waiter placed plates of roast beef accompanied by mashed potatoes and peas before them. Jocelyn took an experimental bite and nodded in appreciation. "Very good," she said.

"I'm glad you like it. This is one of the places I'll miss," Captain Denning said.

"Are you expecting a transfer?" Jocelyn asked, surprised by his remark.

Captain Denning set down his knife and fork and looked at her thoughtfully, as if deciding exactly how much to share with her. "Not a transfer exactly, but I suspect we might be moving out soon."

"To go where?" Jocelyn asked, hoping she didn't sound too eager to hear the answer.

"Philadelphia."

Jocelyn worked hard not to allow shock to show on her face. Philadelphia was the Continental capital. The British would have to defeat Washington's army, camped at Brandywine, in order to get anywhere near the rebel-held city.

"Is an attack on Washington's army imminent?" she asked, taking a dainty bite of roast beef just to have something to do with her trembling hands. Captain Denning nodded but didn't elaborate.

Jocelyn thought frantically. She needed to find out more, but to ask too many questions would arouse the captain's suspicion. "Will you be in the thick of it, Jared?" she asked instead, hoping he would take the question as concern for his well-being.

"Not very likely. As an aide-de-camp, my duties are mostly clerical in nature," he replied bitterly. "I won't be anywhere near the heart of the battle."

"Do you wish to be?"

"I didn't become a soldier to make lists," Captain Denning replied. "Or cater to the whims of a vainglorious buffoon," he added under his breath.

Jocelyn smiled in understanding. That was one way to describe the major. "I expect the battle will be bloody, and drawn out," she said, desperate to glean something of value.

"Perhaps not," the captain replied with a shrug.

"How could it not be?"

Captain Denning looked conflicted. He obviously wanted to tell her what was on his mind, but he was conscious of his duty and the need for discretion. His desire to impress her won out, however. "All I can tell you is that if the plan works, the Continentals won't stand a chance."

"What sort of plan?" Jocelyn asked, leaning in closer, her eyes widening as she gazed at him.

"The attack will come from an unexpected direction," Captain Denning said. "Now, please don't ask me any more questions. I can't discuss military strategy, not even with someone as beguiling as yourself."

"I wouldn't understand the intricacies anyway," Jocelyn said airily. "What do I know of military strategy?"

"It's not as complicated as you might imagine. It's all about common sense, really, which many military leaders seem to sorely lack."

"What about General Howe? Does he lack common sense?"

"General Howe was endowed with more than his fair share. I have great respect for his tactics. If we had more men like General Howe, this war would have been won before it even had a chance to begin."

"Do you really think so? Perhaps the conflict could have been avoided if the king had been more reasonable when it came to the needs of his subjects," Jocelyn said, and instantly regretted the unguarded statement.

Captain Denning didn't take offense. "I agree with you. The amount of money spent to fund the campaign against the Americans is probably tenfold compared to the loss in taxes Parliament would have suffered had they been more flexible. But, as I said, not everyone is endowed with common sense, especially not when it comes to politics."

"I see your point," Jocelyn said. To ask any more questions about the upcoming campaign would be risky, so she changed the subject. "Would you like to be stationed in Philadelphia?"

"I'd prefer to remain here," he said softly, his meaning clear. "What will you do if Major Radcliffe decamps?"

"Find another position. I can't afford not to work," Jocelyn said. "Should I be looking already?" she asked, wondering how soon the army would be moving out of New York.

"Not just yet. In a few weeks, perhaps."

"That soon?"

Captain Denning nodded. "General Howe hopes to be installed in Philadelphia long before the winter is upon us."

"He's that confident of victory?" Jocelyn asked.

"He seems to be. It would certainly turn the tide of the war."

Not if you get crushed, Jocelyn thought angrily. *The Continental Army will not be so easy to defeat.* "Perhaps it will turn the tide," she agreed out loud. *In our favor*, she added silently.

Jocelyn pushed away her half-eaten supper. "I think we should be going," she said, once the captain had finished his meal. "It's getting late."

"Of course. I'm sorry. I did promise to have you back early." The captain extracted several coins from his pocket and placed them on the table. "Too bad we don't have time for a sweet."

"Another time, perhaps," Jocelyn said, and meant it. She would accept another invitation from the captain, and not only because he was a valuable source of information. She had enjoyed being here with him.

They stepped into the balmy night and walked in silence for a few moments. "Jocelyn, I hope you don't think me presumptuous, but I would like to see you again. In private, I mean."

"Even if the major forbids it?" she asked playfully, stopping to look up at him.

"He need never know," the captain replied. He reached out and pulled her close, lowering his head to kiss her. His lips were soft, but his arms were like bands of steel. He was no doughy paper-pusher stuffed into a smart tunic. He was strong and fit, and aroused. Jocelyn drew back, taken aback by the intensity of his kiss. She'd never been kissed like that. She'd never allowed herself to be kissed like that, she amended. She took another step back, putting at least a foot between them.

"I'd like to go home now," she said, more unsettled than she cared to admit.

"Of course." Captain Denning offered her his arm. "I won't apologize for kissing you," he added. "Because I'm not sorry." Jocelyn looked down to hide her smile.

"Thank you for a pleasant evening, Captain," she said once they'd entered the house. The foyer was dark, the house quiet, but she sensed that Major Radcliffe was nearby, probably in the library, nursing a brandy as he read one of his beloved books on military strategy.

"Goodnight," Captain Denning said, bowing to her formally.

Jocelyn hurried up the stairs and disappeared into her room, shutting the door behind her and locking it.

Chapter 56

Jocelyn quickly undressed, poured some water into a basin, and wiped away the sweat of the day with a wet towel, then pulled on her cotton shift. Instead of going directly to bed, she opened the window and curled up on the window seat, enjoying the gentle breeze on her still-damp skin. The air had cooled, and she thought she could smell the river and the wonderful scent of roses coming from the garden of the neighboring house. She sighed deeply and stared up at the star-strewn sky, wishing things didn't have to be so complicated.

She had always made a point of being honest with herself, and tonight was no different. The captain's touch had awakened something deep and dark within her, something that had lain dormant for years. She wanted him to kiss her again, to touch her as a lover would. Jocelyn rested her head against her knees and wrapped her arms about her legs. To get involved with a British captain was to go against everything she stood for, everything she was risking her life for. He may be sympathetic to the plight of the Americans, but he would fight to the death to put down the rebellion that had become the American Revolution. How could she justify having feelings for a man who stood on the opposite side of the conflict and who would eventually return to his home in England? Even if he had honorable intentions toward her, there could be no future for them in either country. She would never go to England, and he wouldn't wish to remain in America once his regiment was recalled.

She had to nip her attraction to the captain in the bud, she told herself sternly. She couldn't possibly allow their liaison to continue, but an evil little voice piped up in her head, arguing, cajoling, and reasoning away her doubts. There was still so much to learn about the impending attack. Which way would the troops be marching? How many men? How many cannons? There had to be maps, lists, names of regiments and their commanders. How could she simply walk away from such valuable information?

Tomorrow, she would send a message to Richard, informing him of what she'd learned, but she had nothing concrete.

He'd ask her to probe deeper. Was she strong enough to take such a risk? Could she play her part without becoming emotionally involved?

Who was she kidding? She was already emotionally involved, and this was no longer a part she was playing. This was her life. She'd made her bed, and now she'd have to lie in it. The idea made her chuckle. Her thoughts had turned to lying in beds but not because she was tired. She was wide awake, her body thrumming with unfamiliar desires. She opened the window wider, hoping the breeze would chill her enough to cool the need pulsing deep in her belly, but the evening air was damp and warm, her skin radiating heat that had nothing to do with the August night.

Chapter 57

March 2018
London

Quinn stretched luxuriously and smiled, not in any hurry to get out of bed since it was Saturday. Sunlight was pouring through the window, and it looked to be a fine day outside. She felt more optimistic than she had in days. Now that the case had officially been reopened, a sense of rightness had settled on her shoulders. She'd done the right thing, and whatever she outcome, she would accept it and move forward. Craving a bit of company, she had invited Logan, Rafe, and Chrissy for dinner tonight. Chrissy was due in a few weeks, so it would be nice to celebrate Logan and Rafe's impending parenthood and take this opportunity to spend some time with them before they went down the rabbit hole of first-time parenting.

"What's your plan for the day?" Gabe asked as he pulled her closer.

"I have to order Mia's birthday cake, shop for tonight's dinner, and then prepare. What about you?"

"I thought I'd take the children to the Unicorn Theatre. Alex has been asking to go. And Emma might want to tag along too, if she doesn't consider herself too mature for such childish pursuits," Gabe added with a grin.

"I doubt it," Quinn replied. "By the way, Jill asked if it'd be okay to take Alex and Mia for a sleepover tonight. She thought it'd be fun for Olivia to have her friends over. You don't mind, do you?" Quinn asked.

"They're a bit young to sleep away from home, but this is Jill, so I guess it's all right," Gabe said with a shrug. "I can collect them tomorrow after I meet Mum off the train. She can't wait to see the children."

"And they can't wait to see her. Emma was hoping Buster would be coming along for the ride."

"No, Mum's leaving him with Cecily for a few days. Buster is getting a sleepover of his own, with Cecily's Bertie. He'll be in doggie heaven."

"Well, looks like everyone is set for a fun weekend, then," Quinn said.

"What are you making for tonight's dinner?" Gabe asked.

"I thought I'd make salmon, since Rafe doesn't eat red meat."

"Okay. I'll grab a few bottles of white wine on my way home."

"Thanks," Quinn said as she got out of bed. "I need a cup of tea. Want me to bring you one?"

"No, I'm coming down," Gabe said. "I'll help you make breakfast."

Quinn went downstairs and examined the contents of the fridge, making a mental list of the items she needed to buy while the water boiled for tea. She popped two slices of bread into the toaster, then took out butter and marmalade, hoping against hope that she might enjoy a peaceful breakfast before the kids woke up. Her hopes were disappointed when she heard Mia calling for her. A few moments later, Gabe came down, Mia on his hip. Her dark hair curled away from her head like Medusa's snakes, and she was rubbing her eyes with her fists.

"Madam here is joining us for breakfast. Alex and Emma are still asleep," Gabe informed Quinn.

"All right, then. Would you like some toast?" she asked the little girl.

Mia nodded enthusiastically. "And juice," she said.

"And juice," Quinn agreed.

Just as they were about to sit down, Alex came down. "I want a boiled egg and soldiers," he announced.

"Right," Gabe said, springing to his feet. "I'll make it," he said to Quinn, who'd been about to take a bite of her toast. Mia was already halfway through her piece, marmalade all over her face.

"Are you making Alex an egg and soldiers?" Emma asked as she sauntered into the kitchen. "I want some too." She poured herself a glass of orange juice and took a seat at the table. "I found some tops I like on Amazon. Can you take a look after breakfast?" she asked hopefully.

"At this rate, I'm never going to leave the house," Quinn muttered.

"You go on," Gabe said. "I'll see to the kids."

"Emma, Dad is taking Alex and Mia to a show at the Unicorn Theatre. Did you want to go too?"

Emma made a face. "No. Those shows are for babies. Maybe I can help you cook," Emma offered.

"Sure, if you like."

"What are you making?"

"Salmon with roasted potatoes and steamed vegetables."

"Right. Never mind. Let me know when you're making something I like. Will there be pudding, at least?"

"Yes, there will be pudding."

"I want sticky toffee pudding," Emma announced. "Uncle Logan loves sticky toffee pudding."

"Fine. I will get sticky toffee pudding," Quinn replied, now really exasperated. She set her plate and cup in the sink and kissed everyone in turn. "Have a good day, darlings. I'm off."

Quinn was on her way to the shops when her mobile rang. It was Logan.

"Hi. I'm just shopping for tonight. Salmon okay?"

"Quinn, I'm sorry, but we won't be able to make it," Logan said. He sounded tense.

"Logan, are you all right?" Quinn asked.

"I'm at Middlesex. Chrissy was brought in about an hour ago."

Quinn felt a cold dread seeping into her chest. Chrissy wasn't due for three weeks, and even if she was in labor, she wouldn't have been brought in. She'd have arrived at the hospital on her own, and as far as Quinn knew, Middlesex wasn't where Chrissy had planned to give birth. "What happened?"

Logan's voice sounded raspy, harsh, unlike his usual easygoing self. "Chrissy got into a minor accident this morning on her way to an antenatal exercise class," he said. "There wasn't much damage to the car, but the airbag went off and hit her in the chest and stomach. She began to bleed heavily and called an ambulance."

Quinn's dread intensified. "Do they know what's wrong?"

"She's suffered a placental abruption."

"What does that mean?" Quinn asked. She knew what placental abruption was but wasn't sure if the condition was treatable.

"They're monitoring her and the baby. If the damage is minimal, they might recommend bed rest. If not, a decision will need to be made."

"Oh, Logan," Quinn said, her heart going out to him. "Is there anything I can do?"

"Rafe's mum is here." Logan sounded wistful.

"Did you call Sylvia?" Quinn asked, wondering if Logan wished his own mother was there to comfort him.

"She's in Manchester. Went to visit a friend. She won't be back until tomorrow evening."

"I'll be there in a half hour," Quinn said, and heard the relief in Logan's voice.

"Thank you. I know this is not a life-or-death situation, but I'm feeling a bit fragile," he admitted.

"I'm on my way." Quinn abandoned her shopping trip, hailed a taxi, and climbed in. Unfortunately, the traffic was awful, and it took nearly forty minutes to get to the hospital. It took another ten to finally locate the maternity ward and find Logan and Rafe. Rafe's mother, Rita, was holding Rafe's hand, which Quinn found endearing. Quinn enveloped Logan in a big hug.

"Any news?" she asked.

"Not yet. We're still waiting," Logan said. "Jude's coming."

"What, right now? From Germany?" Quinn asked, wondering how Logan had been able to pull that off.

Logan gave her a watery smile. "He was due leave and decided to take it now, before the baby came and no one would have time for him. He was going to surprise Mum. Well, now the surprise is on him. Mum's away, and I'm here. He landed about an hour ago and is on his way to the hospital."

"Is there anything you need? Can I get you some coffee?"

All three shook their heads. "Just stay here with me," Logan said softly. "Come, let's sit down. I'm tired of pacing."

"Logan, it will be all right, won't it?" Quinn asked. Being a nurse, Logan understood the implications of the situation in ways she never could.

Logan covered her hand with his own. "Yes, it will be all right."

"Then why are you so frightened?" Quinn asked, needing to understand what Logan was going through.

Logan's anxious gaze met hers. "Quinn, I might become a father today."

"What? Today?"

Logan nodded. "Normally, if the woman is close to her due date, they allow her to deliver."

"And you think this will happen today?"

Logan nodded. "I doubt they will discharge her. The bleeding was heavy, and unless it has stopped…" He let the sentence trail off.

As if on cue, a doctor appeared at the end of the corridor and headed straight for Logan and Rafe, both of whom sprang to their feet, their faces anxious. The doctor appeared to be in his forties and had warm brown eyes and dark hair threaded with silver. There was an air of calm competence about him that Quinn found reassuring.

The doctor smiled. "Good afternoon. I'm Dr. Hunt, and I've been looking after Chrissy. She is resting comfortably," he said. "The bleeding has slowed, but given how close she is to her due date, we feel it's best if we deliver the baby."

"Will you be inducing labor?" Logan asked.

"No. In this situation, a cesarean section is the safest option."

"May we be present?" Rafe asked. His face was ashen and his eyes wide with panic.

"Which one of you is the father?" Dr. Hunt asked.

"We both are," Logan replied. "Chrissy is our surrogate."

"Right. Well, I can't allow too many people in theater, so I'll leave it up to you to decide which one of you would like to be there. Once Chrissy has been prepped, a nurse will come to get you."

"Thank you, Doctor," Logan said.

Rafe nodded and sat back down, slumping in his chair as if his bones had turned to rubber. "You go," he said as soon as the doctor left. "You're better at this sort of thing."

"Are you sure?" Logan asked, but Quinn could see the eagerness in his gaze. He really wanted to be there when his son was born.

Rafe nodded again. "Yes. I'm sure. I'm a nervous wreck. I won't be doing Chrissy any favors. I'll be right here, waiting," he said.

Logan pulled Rafe into a hug, and Rafe rested his head on Logan's shoulder, his fair head bowed. "It'll be all right," Logan said. "We're going to become daddies today."

"I know." Rafe's whisper sounded strangled. "I don't think I'm ready, Logan."

"Of course you are. You are going to be a great dad."

"So will you."

"Why don't I take you to the canteen for a cup of tea and something to eat?" Rita said to her son once Logan released him from the hug.

"Go on," Logan urged Rafe. "I'll be fine."

Rafe allowed his mother to lead him away, shuffling next to her like a little boy who'd been forced to leave the playground.

"How do you feel?" Quinn asked, looking up into Logan's anxious eyes.

"Excited, scared, impatient, and overwhelmed all at the same time. I'm feeling so much, I think my heart is going to explode."

"Then you are absolutely ready for this," Quinn assured him. "That's how all new parents feel."

"I'm a little worried about Rafe," Logan confessed, his gaze following Rafe until he got into the lift.

"It's natural to be nervous," Quinn said. Rafe wasn't as tough as Logan, emotionally or physically.

"I know, but I think he feels like a third wheel just now."

"Why would he feel like a third wheel?" Quinn asked, sensing that Logan was holding something back.

He sighed, and his shoulders drooped in a way that wasn't at all reassuring. "Chrissy is the biological mum, and I'm the biological dad. Rafe has no genetic connection to the baby."

Quinn stared at Logan, her brain still processing what he'd just said. "What do you mean she's the biological mum? I thought you'd used a donor egg."

A look of guilt passed over Logan's features. "That's what we wanted everyone to think."

"Logan? What exactly do you mean?"

"Look, we didn't have the money to go through multiple rounds of in vitro. Jude's rehab set me back about twenty grand, and the NHS didn't think we were suitable candidates. There are other, more deserving couples, apparently, who no doubt happen to be heterosexual," Logan said bitterly. "So we decided to take a shortcut."

"What sort of shortcut?"

"Chrissy was willing to be our surrogate. She needs the money to send back to her family in the Czech Republic, so, I had sex with her a few times. Until she got pregnant. And yes, I know it's illegal to pay a surrogate, but no one needs to know she's doing it for money," Logan said, lowering his voice to a whisper.

"You had sex with her?" Quinn echoed. "And you're paying her illegally?"

"It's the easiest and the cheapest way. It only took two months for her to conceive, and there was no worrying that the embryo wouldn't take."

"And Rafe was fine with that, was he?" Quinn asked, unable to wrap her mind around this new scenario she'd been presented with.

"He knows I have absolutely no romantic feelings for Chrissy. I simply took care of business."

"Logan, do you realize that as the birth mother Chrissy has legal claim to the baby whether it's biologically hers or not?" Quinn asked, horrified. "She can take him away from you. She can even take him back to the Czech Republic, and since he is biologically hers, she just might decide to do that. She might change her mind and keep him."

"She doesn't want the baby," Logan said, dismissing her concerns.

"But what if she wants to be a part of his life?"

"Every child longs for a mother, Quinn. If Chrissy wants to be a part of our son's life, we'll welcome it. She is a good person. She would never do anything to hurt us, or the baby."

Oh, Logan, I do hope you know what you're doing, Quinn thought, but didn't say anything. It was too late for recriminations now.

A few minutes later, a nurse came to fetch Logan. He'd have to suit up to be allowed in the operating theater. "Are you ready, then?" she asked, smiling up at Logan, who was at least a head taller than her.

"Yes," Logan said without hesitation.

"Come meet your son, then," the nurse said. "It'll be at least an hour, love," she said to Quinn. "Possibly more."

"I'll be here," Quinn said.

Logan gave her a brief hug and a kiss and hurried after the nurse.

Chapter 58

Once Logan had gone, Quinn settled in to wait for news. Rafe and Rita still had not returned, so she reached for a magazine someone had left in the waiting area and flipped through the glossy pages.

"Quinn!" Jude was still in his uniform, his face tense, his eyes searching hers. A khaki kit bag was slung over his shoulder, but he dropped it to the floor and opened his arms to Quinn. "It's so good to see you," he said. "Are Chrissy and the baby all right?"

"They're delivering the baby via C-section. Logan is with Chrissy. Rafe and his mum went for a cup of tea."

"I could murder a cup of tea," Jude said as he dropped into a chair. "I came straight from the airport. Didn't even have time to change."

"You look very authoritative," Quinn remarked, taking in his uniform and beret, amazed that her drug-addicted, self-destructive brother had turned into this strong, self-assured man whose solid presence was somehow very comforting.

"How's Logan?" Jude asked. "Never mind; don't answer that. I'm sure Logan is fine. It's Rafe who's probably falling to bits," he said, shaking his head.

"He seemed a bit fragile," Quinn agreed.

"I just can't see Rafe having a kid," Jude said. "He's so…"

"So what?"

"He's still a kid himself," Jude explained. "Having a child is a massive responsibility. I think once the dust settles, Logan will feel like he has two children to care for."

"Aren't you being a little harsh?"

"No," Jude replied. "In the army, you learn pretty quick who'll have your back should things go pear-shaped. You know whom you can trust."

"And you don't think Logan can trust Rafe?"

"I think Rafe is great. I just don't think he's ready for fatherhood. I hope that a year from now, Logan won't find himself a single parent."

"I hope not. He really loves Rafe," Quinn pointed out.

"I think Logan misses Colin," Jude said. "Colin was so—I don't know—solid, I guess. In that relationship, Logan was the baby, and I think he kind of liked it that way."

"Colin is getting married," Quinn said.

"Blimey. Is he really? Well, good for him. He's a decent bloke. He deserves to be happy."

"And what about you? Anyone new in your life?"

Jude tried to suppress a smile, but the light in his eyes told Quinn what she needed to know.

"You've met someone."

"Yes. Tamzin. We've been seeing each other for about three months now," Jude confessed. "She's—" His face finally split into a grin. "She's like no one I've ever known."

"You're in love," Quinn said, grinning back at him. She was glad to see that Jude had finally let go of Bridget. Having been his twisted muse and heroin-addicted lover, Bridget had come dangerously close to also being his executioner when their drug-addled sex game had gone too far, but it had been Jude's near-death that had finally given him the push he'd needed to finally take control of his life.

"I am. Tamzin is nothing like Bridget," Jude hastily added. "She really has it together. She's also smart, gorgeous, and willing to lower her standards to go out with a tosser like me," he said, still smiling. "Way out of my league. And so hot."

"Is Tamzin a civilian?"

"No. She's a staff sergeant in the Military Police. I met her during an investigation into the death of a friend."

"I'm sorry. About your friend, I mean."

Jude inclined his head in acknowledgement but didn't elaborate.

"Are you and Tamzin making plans for the future?" Quinn asked, still in awe of this new Jude.

"We're taking things slow. I haven't told Mum about her yet," Jude said, suddenly looking worried. "Looks like I get a couple days' reprieve."

"Why haven't you told her?"

"I don't want her to worry that I'll go and do something rash," Jude said.

"Like get married?"

"Like get married. She's always telling me I'm too young to settle down with one woman."

"I think she's just not ready to share her baby," Quinn said, smiling at him.

"I think you're right," Jude agreed. "But hopefully, she'll be too busy with Logan's baby to pay much attention to my love life."

"Does Logan know about Tamzin?"

"Yes, but I've only just told him. He's happy for me."

"I'm happy for you too. I hope she's the one," Quinn said.

"You know, Quinn, I don't really believe in The One. I believe in The One Right Now. I would like Tamzin to be my future, but if things don't work out between us, then there will be someone else down the line, someone who might be a better fit for the person I will be then."

"That's a very mature attitude," Quinn remarked, surprised by Jude's ability to think so rationally.

"I thought I'd never find another Bridget. I clung to her. She was my first love. But once I was able to distance myself from her, I understood what a destructive influence she had been in my life. I have to be good with myself before I can commit to being someone's husband or father. I need to know that the person I'm with brings out my best, not my worst qualities."

"And does Tamzin do that?"

"I really think she does. I feel stable when I'm with her, and loved," Jude said, looking dreamy. "Even when we've had a row, I know that she still loves me regardless."

"That's exactly how I feel with Gabe," Quinn said. "That's how real love is."

Jude nodded. "Can I stop by tomorrow? I'd like to see the kids and say hello to Gabe. I've actually brought some presents for the kids. I think they'll like them."

"You know you don't have to bring them presents every time you see them," Quinn said with a smile.

"I know, but I want to. It makes me happy. Besides, who else have I got to spend my money on?"

"Tamzin?" Quinn suggested.

"There aren't a lot of places to spend your money on base. When we do go into town, we splurge a little."

Jude was about to say something else when Rafe and Rita returned, carrying two cups of tea.

"Where's Logan?" Rafe asked, looking panicked.

"They've already called him in," Quinn said. "It won't be long now."

Rafe sank into a chair while Rita handed the teas to Quinn and Jude. "Nice to see you again," she said to Jude, but there was no warmth in her tone. She'd probably heard too much about Jude's past exploits from Rafe, who seemed to share an awful lot with his mother.

Jude accepted the tea and nodded his thanks. "Yeah, you too," he mumbled.

The arrival of Rafe and Rita had put an end to the personal conversation, so they all sat in silence, too anxious to speak of trivial things. Quinn leaned back in her chair and closed her eyes, recalling her last foray into Jocelyn's life. She wondered if Captain Denning had been the father of Jocelyn's baby and what had happened to the man. Perhaps he'd died, which would explain why Jocelyn had left New York City. With a child on the way, she would have needed the support of her brother, even if they didn't see eye to eye. The eighteenth century had not been kind to single mothers, especially if the child was born out of wedlock. Had Jocelyn known about the pregnancy when she'd boarded the ship, or had she left New York for other reasons?

Chapter 59

September 1777
New York City

Jocelyn barely saw Captain Denning over the next two weeks. He was either closeted in his office or out, accompanying Major Radcliffe to various meetings. When at home, the major always seemed to be around, coming down to breakfast early and staying up well past the time Jocelyn normally retired to her room for the night. He was as courteous and polite as ever, but there was a watchfulness in him she found unnerving. Did he know something? Did he suspect? Did he think she was using his aide-de-camp to gain access to sensitive information? He hadn't expressly forbidden them to see each other, but his obvious displeasure was directed toward Captain Denning rather than herself, or so it seemed.

Jocelyn and Captain Denning had managed to carve out a few private moments, sneaking out to the garden while Major Radcliffe took his evening bath, which lasted a minimum of a half hour. Mostly they just talked, but their relationship had changed. Their attraction to each other was undeniable, and their stolen kisses left Jocelyn feeling guilty and conflicted. The major's house was no longer a stage where she had to play her part; she was now the playwright, pouring out her feelings and setting the actors up for a final act, in which someone would inevitably be betrayed, and hearts would break.

Going about her chores, Jocelyn kept an eye on the major's study and the captain's office, but both rooms were locked when the men were out and no one but Mrs. Johnson was allowed to go inside, and then only with the major's express permission. Word had come down from Richard Kinney that Jocelyn was to find out all she could about the upcoming campaign against General

Washington's army. She didn't know whether Richard had people placed in other military households and had several sources of information, but she had to do her utmost to find out more, and the only way she could do that was by talking to Jared. She had begun to think of him as Jared, an intimacy she shouldn't have permitted herself, since it made it even more difficult to draw the line between espionage and romance.

"When will you know if you're leaving?" Jocelyn asked anxiously as they sat on a bench in the back garden, their faces gilded by the light spilling from the parlor windows.

"Soon," Jared replied.

"Is an attack on the Continental Army imminent?" Jocelyn asked, her heart thudding.

Jared nodded but didn't elaborate.

"I'll miss you," she said, and knew it to be true.

"I will miss you too, Jocelyn," Jared replied. "But I will come back. I promise."

"Not if you will be stationed in Philadelphia."

"Philadelphia is not so far away. I'll ask for furlough." Jared reached out and took her hand in his. "I wish I didn't have to leave just when we're getting to know each other."

Jocelyn leaned against him, enjoying the solid feel of his arm beneath her cheek. He made her feel safe in a world where nothing was certain. He cared.

"Would you ever consider a life in England?" Jared asked, tilting his head to look at her.

"No. Would you consider a life in America?"

Jared thought about that for a moment. "I might."

"Even if the British lost the war?"

Jared smiled wryly. "I don't care about the war. I joined the army because I needed a career, a path forward that didn't depend on my father's generosity, or lack of it. It wasn't from any deep sense of conviction." He wrapped his arm around her, his expression tender. "Jocelyn, I've never been in love. I'd always assumed I'd remain a bachelor. Stay in the army, climb the ranks, then, if I didn't encounter a musket ball with my name on it, retire and settle down in some small cottage by the sea. I'd never imagined having a woman by my side, or children. But once I met you, all that changed. Somehow, living alone in a cottage by the sea now seems terribly lonely and incomplete. What type of life did you envision for yourself before all this?" he asked.

"I suppose I always thought I would marry and have a family, but then my father died, and suddenly I found myself alone. I'd grown used to being on my own. There's a certain freedom in making your own decisions and not having to answer to anyone, but it's lonely too, and at times, very frightening."

"Can you see your way to not being alone?" Jared asked.

"Depends on the circumstances, I suppose," Jocelyn replied with more seriousness than she'd intended.

"I'm in no position to make promises at the moment, but I want you to know that I'd like to give you everything: home, family, security, and tenderness," he said softly.

"I thought you said you are not a gentle man," Jocelyn teased. He still intimidated her at times, especially when he was in a temper, something that seemed to happen more often these days and was usually the result of a closed-door meeting with the major or a visit to General Howe's headquarters.

"I will be tender with you," Jared said, lowering his lips to brush hers. "You make me want to be a kinder man, Jocelyn. You bring out my protective instincts."

"Jared, we hardly know each other," Jocelyn replied, unable to commit.

"We've lived in the same house for months," Jared said. "That's more intimacy that most couples enjoy before they marry."

"I've lived in the same house as Major Radcliffe and Robert Sykes as well," Jocelyn pointed out, "but I don't mean to marry either of them."

"Does that mean you mean to marry me?" Jared asked. It would have been a playful question had he not looked so darn earnest.

"I don't recall you proposing," Jocelyn replied, inwardly chastising herself for playing along. This wouldn't end well, for either of them.

"Would you?" Jared asked, and she knew he was completely serious.

"I don't know," she whispered. "I'm not in a position to make promises either."

"Then can you promise to wait for me? Say, until Christmas?" Jared asked softly.

Jocelyn stared at him in disbelief. Did he expect the war to be over by Christmas? Were the British really so confident in their strategy?

"Do you expect your situation to change in three months?" she asked instead of giving him an answer.

"I do," Jared replied. "You didn't answer my question," he said, watching her.

"I'm not going anywhere," Jocelyn said. That was as close to an answer as she was willing to give.

"But where would I find you if you were to leave the major's employ?" Jared asked, taking her hand in his.

"I honestly don't know," Jocelyn replied. She supposed she'd stay with Anna Reid for a while, but she couldn't reveal the location of her safehouse to him, not when she was feeding information he'd shared with her to the Continentals. She had never mentioned Anna in his presence, nor would she make him aware of her existence. "I'd get a message to you. Don't worry," she promised. "I'd leave word at the King's Cross Inn."

"Do I have your word on that?" Jared asked, his eyes anxious.

"You do. Now, we'd better go in. I have no wish to give the major any more reasons to be displeased. He's been in a mood," Jocelyn said, rolling her eyes in exasperation. "Same time tomorrow?"

"I'm afraid not. Major Andre is hosting a supper tomorrow in honor of General Howe. I've been invited to attend."

"You're moving up in the world," Jocelyn said, and instantly wished she'd kept quiet. Major John Andre was the head of the British Security Services in North America and had a reputation for being fiercely intelligent, incredibly cunning, and ruthlessly charming, but being a maidservant, Jocelyn wouldn't know that. She did know, however, that he was a very handsome man, having met him once when he'd come to dine with Major Radcliffe, and a perceptive one. He'd watched her from beneath hooded lids as she served at table and had even asked her a few questions about her family and past employment. His gaze had never left her face as she replied, her expression calm, her voice even. She may have been quivering with terror inside, but she didn't think he'd known that. He had complimented her on her looks and thanked her for staying up late to look after the men who'd chosen to linger over their port.

"Hardly," Jared said as he followed her inside. "I was only invited as a courtesy to Major Radcliffe. I think he wants me there."

"Why?"

"Probably to keep me away from you," Jared replied.

"Is he that concerned about impropriety under his roof?" Jocelyn asked, arching one eyebrow. Did the major think her relationship with Jared had taken a less-than-respectable leap? She'd done nothing inappropriate, other than allow a handsome man to kiss her. She was a grown woman, for God's sake, entitled to a few chaste kisses.

"The major is a meticulous man, disciplined and correct in his habits. You and I are a complication he can't control, and that rankles him."

He can control it, Jocelyn thought. *He can simply request another aide-de-camp.*

"He can replace me, of course," Jared said, as if he'd read her thoughts, "but he can't forbid me to see you. You are free to choose who you spend your time with."

"He can dismiss me," Jocelyn pointed out.

"I don't think he will," Jared replied thoughtfully. "I imagine he thinks he's looking out for you."

"Perhaps he is," Jocelyn said playfully. "How am I to know you can be trusted?"

"You can trust me with your life," Jared said, his brows knitting together as his expression grew serious. "Jocelyn, I would do anything to keep you safe."

She nodded, overcome by emotion. No one had ever said anything like that to her, not even her father or brother. "You're a good man, Jared."

"I'm really not, but you make me want to be better."

He held the door open for her, and she stepped inside, wishing the major wasn't so averse to opening the windows. It was hot and muggy and smelled of the haddock Mrs. Johnson had prepared for the major's supper.

"Goodnight, Jared," Jocelyn whispered.

"Goodnight," he said, and kissed her softly on the lips. "For the first time in my life, I'm looking forward to Christmas."

"Don't get your hopes up," Jocelyn said, but her smile told him otherwise.

Chapter 60

March 2018
London

Having stayed long enough to visit with Chrissy and meet baby Max, who had a shock of black hair and a stubborn chin identical to Logan's, Quinn and Jude were ready to leave. Quinn was glad to see that after that brief wobble at the beginning, Logan had taken charge of the situation and was already making plans for taking Max home and hiring a baby nurse for the first few weeks to teach him and Rafe how to care for Max properly and help with the night feedings. He hadn't mentioned what Chrissy's role in Max's life would be, and Quinn didn't ask. Presumably, everything would work itself out in time.

"Do you want to come by?" Quinn asked Jude once they walked out of the hospital into the crisp evening.

"No. I'll just go to Mum's, get out of this uniform, and enjoy some peace and quiet for a few hours. It's been a long time since I've been completely alone. I see fish and chips and a beer or two in my immediate future."

"Well, enjoy. I'll ring you tomorrow."

"Will do," Jude said, and headed toward the nearest Tube station.

Quinn decided to splurge on a taxi. She hoped Gabe had organized something for dinner. She was too tired to cook and was starving, having missed lunch. Quinn let herself into the house, tossed her bag onto the console table in the foyer, kicked off her shoes, and walked into the lounge. The spicy smell of curry emanating from the kitchen made her mouth water. Gabe must have picked up a takeaway on his way home. Through the door, she could see the table, set for two, and a bottle of red wine and glasses in readiness on the worktop. A bunch of yellow tulips stood in pride of place on the table, the whole scene like something out of a magazine. Husband of the Year was kipping on the sofa but woke up the moment Quinn walked in.

"Hi," he said blearily, and sat up, running a hand through his hair. "All right?"

Quinn had called him several hours ago, but they hadn't spoken since Gabe had texted to tell her that he'd dropped off the children at Jill's.

"More than all right. Hungry and tired, though," Quinn said. "It turned out to be a very emotional day. Sylvia was sorry to have missed Max's birth. She really wanted to be there for Logan. She's coming back from Manchester tomorrow."

"Where's Jude?" Gabe asked.

"He went back to Sylvia's. He just wanted a few hours to himself."

"Good, because I only got enough food for us," Gabe said ungraciously.

"Curry smells amazing," Quinn said, her stomach rumbling. "Are you ready to eat?"

"We should probably heat it up. It's been sitting out for an hour."

"I'll just pop it in the oven for a few minutes," Quinn said, "but first, I have to tell you about Max. Oh, Gabe, he is so sweet. He looks just like Logan. Here, I have a photo," she gushed as she pulled her mobile out of her back pocket. She held out the phone to Gabe, who reached for it slowly.

Quinn expected a smile at the very least, but what she saw on Gabe's face was shock. He seemed to be staring just past her shoulder, and Quinn felt a sudden cool breeze on her back. She shivered in her thin jumper. Had Gabe forgotten to close the patio door?

She stood and turned around, and came face to face with Brett, who was standing directly behind her, a wicked-looking blade in his hand.

"Hey there, sis," he said pleasantly.

Quinn opened her mouth to reply, but no words came out. She backed away but realized there was nowhere to go when she felt the low coffee table press against the backs of her calves.

"Stay where you are," Brett ordered Gabe, who'd sprung to his feet. "Now, sit down and put your cell phones on the coffee table where I can see them," he said. "Don't test me, Gabe," Brett snarled when Gabe made no move to comply and looked meaningfully toward Quinn.

"Do as he says," Quinn said. She barely recognized her own voice. It was shaky and hoarse. She sat down and laid her mobile on the table. Gabe followed suit. Quinn could almost feel the tension coursing through him, but he remained silent, his angry stare fixed on Brett.

Just then, Rufus exploded into the lounge, barking like mad, his tail wagging at the promise of a new friend to play with. He must have been upstairs in Emma's room. Rufus made straight for Brett, eager to play, but Brett kicked the dog so hard, Rufus went flying across the lounge and landed with a thud after he hit the wall. He whimpered pitifully, then bared his teeth in a snarl, but remained where he was, too frightened to try again.

"Get out," Brett hissed.

Knowing what was good for him, Rufus hobbled out of the lounge and headed for the stairs, his tail between his legs. Quinn's heart hammered painfully against her ribs, but she did her best to keep calm. As long as she knew the children were safe, she could still breathe.

"What are you doing here, Brett?" Gabe asked gruffly.

"Came for a flying visit," Brett replied. He stood over them, knife clasped in his hand, the skull ring they'd seen on the CCTV clearly visible. The light of the lamp glinted off the steel blade, which was long and thin. And deadly.

Quinn forced herself to meet Brett's gaze, daring him to say something, to explain his presence in their house. He looked down at her, an odd expression on his face. It was almost wistful,

297

as if he were remembering the good times they'd had, except that there hadn't been any.

"I had a good life before you came along," he said at last. "Ruining lives seems to be a talent of yours." Quinn didn't reply.

"I had parents who loved me, friends, hobbies. I was going to go to college, party for four years, then decide what I wanted to do with my life. I was happy. But then you showed up out of the blue and started poking your nose where it didn't belong, digging up the past. Filming," Brett added with disgust. "And no one will touch me now that I have a criminal record. Even my own parents look at me and wonder if they've raised a monster," Brett said miserably. "But it was all your fault. You never stopped to think how I might feel about what you were going to reveal. Or Dad. Sure, he told you it was all right, but it wasn't easy for him, you know, coming to terms with what you'd so carelessly spewed to the world. It's not fun, being biracial in Louisiana, especially not in prison. People are not so open-minded there, and I have the scars to prove it."

"Maybe you got your ass kicked in prison because you tried to kill your sister and her unborn child," Gabe snapped.

"You shut up, or she gets it," Brett said, pointing the knife at Quinn.

"Brett," Quinn said in a conciliatory tone. "I've apologized to you and told you I should have been more sensitive to your feelings."

"Yeah, only when you thought you were going to die and would have said anything to get me to let you out. And now you've had the investigation into Jo's death reopened, with me as the star suspect."

"Why would you think that?" Quinn asked carefully. She hadn't mentioned anything to Seth, so how in the world would Brett have found out about an investigation taking place in England, and so quickly? It'd only been a few days since DI Marshall had called her with the news.

"My lawyer tipped me off. He has contacts in the NOPD. Seems they've received a request for my fingerprints, DNA profile, and psych evaluation."

"That's got nothing to do with me," Quinn lied, praying he'd believe her.

"Doesn't it? You're the only person who'd care, which really makes me question your sanity. The bitch tried to fuck you. Royally. She'd set out to destroy your family. You should be grateful she's dead, not looking for someone to pin it on. Haven't you done enough harm?"

Quinn stared at Brett, nailing him with her gaze. "Did you kill her on purpose?" she demanded. What did she have to lose? Brett wasn't simply going to say his piece and leave.

"Yeah, I did. And now I'm going to kill you. Should have done it right the first time. The world will be a better place without Quinn Allenby Russell and her awesome gift," he said sarcastically.

Quinn felt a shudder of fear. Would Brett really use that blade on her? Did he have what it took to kill someone in such a personal way? It was one thing to lock her in a tomb, and quite another to look her in the eye and stab her. But then, he'd run over Jo. He must have seen her face at the moment of impact, must have heard her screams and seen her mangled body in the rearview mirror. He may have even slowed down to make sure she was dead. He'd never hit the brake, so there had been no tire marks to reconstruct what had happened at the moment of impact.

Quinn's gaze locked with Brett's, and suddenly she knew with unwavering certainty that he would kill her. He was past caring.

"You'll go down for murder. You'll spend the rest of your life in prison," Quinn said, but she knew she was grasping at straws.

Brett chuckled. "By the time the New Orleans Police Department gets off their collective ass and forwards the information, it'll be the middle of next week, and if the bureaucracy in this country is anything like it is in the States, which I'm pretty sure it is, it will take another week at least to issue an extradition order. I'll be long gone by then, and no one will ever find me. The world is a big place, Quinny."

Brett reached into his pocket and pulled out a plastic medicine container. Inside were two black capsules. "For you," he said conversationally.

"What the hell is that?" Gabe demanded.

"Cyanide capsules. It's really amazing what you can get on the dark web these days. You'll be gone in moments. Double suicide. So romantic."

"You can't force us to take them," Gabe growled.

"Yeah, I can," Brett said. "Given the choice between a quick, almost painless death and an agonizing, bloody end, you'll choose the cyanide. And if you don't, I'll carve up your lady right before your eyes. Don't worry; I have all night. No one knows I'm here. And looks like no one's coming to your rescue." Brett shrugged. "The choice is yours. I'm only trying to be gallant here, like a movie villain." He laughed without mirth.

"Brett, please. The children," Quinn moaned.

"Your children are not my problem. You haven't given a thought to my children, who would have grown up knowing their father was not only a half-breed but the guy who'd locked his pregnant sister in a vault and left her to die. Not the family history any kid wants. Now, come on, stop wasting time. Which one of you wants to go first? Do you want to end it now, Gabe, or do you want to hold your wife as she draws her last breath? Knowing you, I'd say you'll play the hero to the end."

Quinn was shaking so hard, her teeth were chattering. All she could think of was her babies. Mia and Alex were young enough to recover in time, but Emma would be scarred for life. She'd already lost her mother and grandmother, and to lose her parents in what she would think was suicide would damage her permanently. If only there was a way to leave word, to explain. Perhaps the police would be able to figure out what had happened, but Brett seemed to have it all planned out. No one would ever know he'd even been here.

How had it come to this? Quinn thought frantically. Why did she think she could go up against Brett? He was diabolical. Even now, there was nothing in his gaze save impatience. He wasn't scared or sorry for the way things had turned out, or even truly angry. He was immune to normal human emotions. All he wanted was to get this over with so he could get out of London. Where did he think he was going to go?

Gabe's thigh vibrated with tension next to Quinn's. She laid her hand on his leg, hoping the gesture would convey how much she loved him and how sorry she was for all the trouble she'd brought into their lives. She turned to look at him, but Gabe wasn't looking at her; he was watching Brett, a look of pure hatred on his face. He looked more angry than scared, which she supposed was better than what she was feeling. This was all her fault. Once again, she'd brought danger into their lives, and this time there would be no dramatic rescue.

Brett exhaled loudly and pushed the pills toward them. "Well?" he demanded. "How long are you going to stall? The cavalry ain't coming, darlings."

Quinn began to shake even harder, her extremities growing cold with terror. Was this it? Was this how it was really going to end? Just this morning, she'd been planning a dinner party, then had welcomed a new member of the family into the world. She'd even been allowed to hold Max for a few moments. And now she was about to die, because of her own stupidity. She should have just let it go, told Daisy to go home and forget what she'd seen. Getting justice for Jo wasn't worth their lives, or the loss their children would feel for the rest of their days.

If only Jude had come back with me, Quinn thought desperately. It would have given them greater odds. She turned to Gabe again and whispered, "I love you, Gabe. I'm so sorry for everything."

"I love you too," he said softly. "And you have nothing to be sorry for. You never really had a choice."

"Well, isn't this sweet? Now, if you're done reassuring each other, can we please get on with this? I'm getting kind of hungry. I think I'll have some fish and chips. That's the only thing you people do well, in my humble opinion. Cooking is definitely not your forte." Brett tilted his head to the side, as if watching something particularly amusing. "Oh, I'm sorry. Did you need a moment to pray?" he asked. "How inconsiderate of me. Go on, then. Say your prayers. Much good they'll do you."

Gabe reached for Quinn's hand and bowed his head. She followed suit, fervently praying to God for some sort of intervention. But none would come; she knew that. They weren't expecting anyone, and if someone had decided to drop by, they'd simply walk away when no one came to the door. They were entirely at Brett's mercy.

"Pray with me," Gabe said. She'd never known him to pray out loud, not even the few times they'd gone to church, but she supposed he needed this last bit of comfort. He'd chosen a prayer from the Old Testament, which, under different circumstances, Quinn might have found surprising, but nothing could shock her tonight.

Have mercy on me, O God, according to Your unfailing love;

according to Your great compassion blot out my transgressions.

Wash away all my iniquity and cleanse me from my sin.

For I know my transgressions, and my sin is always before me.

Against You, You only, have I sinned and done what is evil in Your sight,

so that You are proved right when You speak and justified when You judge.

Surely I have been a sinner from birth, sinful from the time my mother conceived me...

Cleanse me with hyssop, and I will be clean; wash me and I will be whiter than snow...

Create in me a pure heart, O God, and renew a steadfast spirit within me.

Do not cast me from Your presence or take Your Holy Spirit from me.

Restore to me the joy of Your salvation and grant me a willing spirit to sustain me.

Then will I teach transgressors Your ways, and sinners will turn back to You.

Quinn never saw it coming. Evidently, neither did Brett, because when Mia's Barbie computer came hurtling through the air and hit him in the head with surprising accuracy, he lost his balance and nearly fell, the few unguarded moments all Gabe needed to charge his enemy.

Gabe hurled himself at Brett, knocking him to the floor, his fingers closing around Brett's wrist with crushing force. Brett cried out in pain but didn't let go of the knife. He was a few inches shorter than Gabe, but he was nearly twenty years younger and more muscular, no longer the lanky kid Quinn had met in New Orleans four years ago. They grappled and rolled on the floor, shoving aside the furniture and grunting with effort. It must have been only a few seconds since Gabe had exploded out of his seat, but it felt like hours, the struggle taking place in slow motion before it froze into a timeless tableau.

She knew she should do something to help, but she was paralyzed with indecision, unsure if she should try to help Gabe subdue Brett or call the police. She was just grabbing for her mobile when Gabe gasped, his eyes opening wide with shock, the moment exploding into shattering reality when Quinn saw the hilt of the knife protruding from Gabe's side.

She shrieked and dropped the phone from her shaking hand, unable to tear her gaze from Gabe, who wasn't giving in to the pain. His hands were wrapped around Brett's throat as the two men thrashed violently on the floor.

Somewhere in the distance, a siren wailed, but Quinn barely heard it. "Gabe, what should I do?" she screamed. "Tell me what to do."

"Unlock the door," he said hoarsely. Quinn rushed to the door and opened it just in time to allow police officers to stream into the house, weapons drawn.

Someone grabbed her by the arm and pulled her outside. "My husband," Quinn wailed. "He's been stabbed."

"An ambulance is already on its way," the officer said. "Let's get you out of the way."

Quinn couldn't see what was happening inside, but there was a lot of shouting. The radio of the officer who was with her crackled, and she heard loud and clear, "The situation is under control. Send the paramedics in as soon as they arrive."

An ambulance came racing down the street, siren shrieking. Quinn's legs gave out just as the paramedics rushed inside. She sank to the ground and buried her face in her hands, unable to come to grips with the horror she'd witnessed.

"Here you go, love," the officer said as he wrapped a foil blanket around her shoulders. "That's one brave little girl you have."

"What?" Quinn asked, uncomprehending.

"You daughter. She called the police," the officer said.

Quinn shook her head. "She's not at home." Gabe had dropped the children off, and the table had been set for two. She'd assumed Emma had changed her mind and decided to spend the night at Jill's.

"No, she's in her bedroom," the man said kindly. He pressed a button on his com and said, "Get a family liaison officer here."

"Please, I need to see her. She must be terrified," Quinn cried, finally piecing together what must have happened. Emma had probably had her earbuds in, which would explain why she hadn't come downstairs when Quinn returned home. And she didn't much like curry, so Gabe must have given her something else for dinner. At some point, Emma had taken the earbuds out and heard what was happening downstairs, possibly after an injured Rufus had come limping into her bedroom. Dear God, how frightened she must have been, Quinn thought, still amazed that Emma had the presence of mind to use her mobile to call the police.

"Don't you worry. She's in good hands," the officer said. Quinn didn't even know his name. "Let's get you off the ground, shall we?" he said, opening the door of the police car for her and helping her into the front seat.

Quinn hung her head, her thoughts spinning out of control as the images replayed themselves over and over. She saw the knife protruding from Gabe's side, the stain spreading as the blood hungrily soaked into the fabric of his cotton shirt. Quinn was in a daze, her mind refusing to cooperate, her hands shaking so badly, she had to push them between her thighs. She barely noticed when two officers led Brett out in handcuffs and forced him into another police car, but her head snapped up when the paramedics wheeled out a gurney.

Quinn jumped out of the car and hurried toward the gurney, the silver blanket fluttering to the ground. "Gabe!" she cried. "Oh, Gabe."

Gabe gave her a watery smile. He looked pale, and his gaze was glazed, probably with the medication he'd been given for the pain. "I'll be all right. See to Emma." His voice was raspy, but he was alert.

"You knew," Quinn whispered. "You knew she was there all along. Is that why you recited that long prayer, to draw Brett's attention away from what was happening upstairs?"

"I didn't want Brett to hear her voice if she called for help. I was giving her time."

"You saved us," Quinn said.

"Emma saved us," Gabe whispered. He was fading fast, his eyelids fluttering as the meds kicked in.

"Where are you taking him?" Quinn asked one of the paramedics. She wanted to go with him, but she needed to go to Emma.

"Chelsea and Westminster Hospital," the paramedic replied. "You can meet us there."

"Mrs. Russell, let's get your daughter sorted and then I'll drive you to the hospital," the officer said.

"What's your name?" Quinn rasped.

"Scoley. Edward Scoley."

"Thank you, Constable Scoley," Quinn said. "Thank you," she whispered as an impenetrable blackness closed in on her, the shock of the past hour finally catching up to her. The last thing she felt before she passed out was Constable Scoley's arm around her.

When Quinn came round, she was stretched out on the sofa. There was no sign of the cyanide pills, but a dark red stain was clearly visible on the carpet. Gabe's blood. She wished someone would have covered it up so Emma wouldn't have to see her father's blood pooled between the fibers.

Emma was huddled in the armchair, her face deathly pale, her eyes wide with anxiety. Rufus sat at her feet, quiet for once. A young woman perched on the arm of the chair, presumably the family liaison officer, her hand clutched in a death grip by Emma's childish fingers.

"Emma, my brave girl," Quinn exclaimed. She sat up and opened her arms, and Emma erupted from the armchair and hurled herself at Quinn, burying her face in Quinn's neck.

"I was so scared," Emma sobbed. "I didn't know what to do."

"You did exactly the right thing," the family liaison officer said gently.

"You did," Quinn rushed to reassure her. "You saved our lives."

"I should have called sooner, but I hid in my room and told Rufus to be quiet. He was hurt," Emma cried. "I tried to hear what was going on. I couldn't understand what was happening." Quinn stroked Emma's head, desperate to reassure her. "Mum, is Dad going to be okay?" Emma pleaded.

Quinn looked at the officer over Emma's head. "He's already in surgery," the woman said.

"Can you take us to the hospital, please?" Quinn asked.

"Of course. Is there anyone you'd like me to call for you?"

"No, thank you."

"Are you sure? A family member? A friend?" the officer tried again. "You shouldn't be alone right now."

Quinn was about to decline but changed her mind. "Please call Jude Wyatt and Drew Camden."

"You got it."

A few minutes later, Quinn and Emma were escorted to the police car, which took them to the hospital.

Chapter 61

Emma held tightly to Quinn's hand as they walked into the hospital and took the lift to the right floor. Quinn asked for an update on Gabe's condition but was asked to sit down and wait until a doctor could speak to her. She sank into a plastic chair, too worn out by the events of the day to keep upright for much longer. Quinn and Emma sat side by side, silent and terrified, waiting to hear news that could change their lives forever.

Soon, a young Asian doctor stepped out of one of the rooms and approached them. He looked calm and relaxed, which Quinn found reassuring.

"Mrs. Russell, my name is Dr. Chan. I was called to A&E when Mr. Russell was brought in. I'm a nephrologist," he explained. Quinn wasn't sure what that was but didn't think this was the time to ask. "He is still in surgery, I'm afraid. The blade punctured his right kidney and nicked the renal artery."

"What does that mean?" Quinn asked in a whisper, wishing Emma weren't there to hear this.

"It means he's lost a lot of blood and might lose his kidney as well. It's too soon to tell."

"Dr. Chan, what is the prognosis?" she asked as calmly as she could, for Emma's sake.

"We have every confidence that Mr. Russell will make a full recovery," Dr. Chan said, smiling warmly at Emma, who was pressing herself to Quinn's arm. "A person can live a long and healthy life with one kidney. It will be a long wait, though. Perhaps you should go home. Someone will call you as soon as Mr. Russell is out of theater."

"No, we'll stay," Quinn said. Emma nodded in agreement.

"I will update you as soon as I know more," Dr. Chan said. "I'm in contact with the surgical team."

"Thank you, Dr. Chan," Quinn said, and watched as he walked away, feeling like a young child whose mother had just left her behind. The helplessness and fear she'd experienced today brought flashbacks of being locked in the tomb, and she reached into her bag and fished for her phone, desperate to hear her mother's voice.

"Darling, what a lovely surprise," Susan Allenby exclaimed when she picked up. "I was just thinking about you. Are you getting ready for Mia's birthday?"

Quinn opened her mouth to reply but burst into tears instead, sobbing her heart out into the phone until she was finally able to speak. By that time, her father was also on the line, talking to her in a soothing tone and assuring her that everything would be all right. Between the two of them, her parents were able to get the full story, their exclamations of horror and praise for Emma's bravery echoing down the empty corridor.

After a few minutes, Quinn passed the phone to Emma, who was eager to tell her grandparents her own version of events. It may have been wrong to lay this at her parents' door, but talking to them had released something inside her, and she was finally able to gather her wits and focus on getting through this.

"They're coming," Emma said as she handed the phone back to Quinn.

"What?"

"Grandma and Grandpa are coming tomorrow," Emma said, and smiled for the first time that evening. And Quinn smiled back, no longer feeling like an abandoned child.

"You still have to give your statement to the police," Emma reminded her as they continued their vigil. Quinn had been too distraught to give a statement back at the house. Her gaze had kept straying to Gabe's blood as she pictured him all alone at the hospital, keeping an eye on the door in the hope that she would come, if he was even conscious at the time. She had promised to give her statement first thing in the morning and wouldn't budge on that.

"Yes. I will do that."

"Will they put Brett in prison, do you think?" Emma asked. Some of the color had returned to her face, and now her natural child's curiosity was beginning to reassert itself.

"Yes, they probably will," Quinn replied.

"Here or in America?"

"Here, I should think. That's where he committed the crimes." By now, Emma had heard all about Jo's death, since Quinn had had to explain to the police why Brett had shown up at their house wielding a knife.

"Will he be charged with murder?" Emma asked, surprising Quinn with the maturity of the question.

"I don't know, Em. The law is complex, and there are degrees of murder and attempted murder."

"That's what Grandma Phoebe says," Emma replied wisely.

"She does?"

"She likes to watch crime shows," Emma said. "Sometimes she tells me about them on the phone. She has no one to talk to except Cecily, and Cecily only likes *The Great Pottery Throw Down* and *The Baking Show*."

"I thought Grandma Phoebe liked only romantic comedies," Quinn said, noting the absurdity of having this conversation while Gabe was possibly losing a kidney.

"She does, but she likes murder too."

"I'm not so sure she'll like it as much after today," Quinn muttered.

"You should call her," Emma suggested. "She'll want to be here for Daddy. She'll knit him socks."

"Grandma Phoebe doesn't knit," Quinn replied.

"She really should try to be more grandmotherly," Emma observed. "She doesn't like to bake or knit or tell stories about the past."

"That's because she was almost a communist once," Quinn replied, trying to suppress a hysterical giggle.

"What's a communist? Do they like to bake?"

"I'm not sure."

"Do they live in a commune?" Emma continued, now in full flow. "Was Grandma Phoebe a hippie?"

Quinn knew Emma was babbling because she was scared but was glad of the interruption when Jude and Drew arrived almost simultaneously.

Drew limped down the corridor, while Jude covered the distance in long strides, his anxious gaze never leaving Quinn's face. Emma jumped up and ran down the corridor, straight into Jude's arms. He held her close and then bent down to whisper something in her ear. Emma looked up at him with shining eyes and smiled shyly, then slid her hand into his, and they walked the rest of the way together.

"I'm so sorry," Jude said once he reached Quinn. "How's Gabe?"

"I don't know," Quinn replied, tears clouding her vision.

"Is there anything I can do?"

"Just stay with us for a while," Quinn said, her voice breaking. Emma had managed to distract her with all her questions earlier, but reality had reasserted itself as soon as she saw the men exit the lift.

"Of course, as long as you need."

"Jude, this is Drew Camden. I don't think you two have ever met," Quinn said.

"No." Jude held out his hand, and Drew grasped it.

"Can I have a moment with your sister?" Drew asked.

"Em, what do you say we go find some snacks? You must be hungry," Jude said. "And your mum hasn't had any dinner."

"All right," Emma agreed in a small voice, but she still looked secretly pleased, making Quinn wonder what Jude had said to her earlier.

"Come on. Let's go," Jude said.

"I'll be right here, darling," Quinn assured her when Emma gave her a questioning look.

Drew dropped into the chair next to hers and exhaled deeply. "Jesus, Quinn. What a cock-up!"

"That's the understatement of the year," she replied.

"There was no way for Brett to know about the request from the Met. It was confidential."

"Seems his lawyer has a contact in the New Orleans Police Department."

"I hope the bastard will be disbarred for what he's done, and the officer who told him should be made an example of, very publicly, and dishonorably discharged without a pension."

"You won't hear an argument from me," Quinn said. She suddenly felt very tired and wished she could climb into bed and hide under the duvet until her world returned to normal, but that wasn't an option. She looked at Drew. He looked gray and tired, and as sullen as a storm cloud.

"What happened wasn't your fault," Quinn said.

"Wasn't it?" Drew retorted.

"Drew, I'm a grown woman, and I knew the risks when I called you. If this was anyone's fault, it was mine."

"Yes, it was," Drew agreed, stunning Quinn into silence. "But you had no choice. How could you go on living your life as if nothing had happened? Even if Jo hadn't been your sister, you still would have come forward, because that's who you are."

"An upstanding citizen, you mean?" Quinn quipped, but the joke fell flat.

"For lack of a better description, yes. When you see a wrong, you have to right it," Drew said. "You would have made a good copper."

That made Quinn smile. "Somehow, I really can't see that, but thank you. It means a lot coming from you. Drew, what will happen? Is there any chance Brett might go free? He'd broken into the house and threatened us, but he only stabbed Gabe once Gabe lunged at him, so he could claim self-defense. With a good lawyer…" Quinn's voice faltered.

"Quinn, he's not going anywhere. I was going to tell you tomorrow, but now's as good a time as any. DI Marshall has been able to connect Brett to the rental car. He located CCTV footage of Brett driving the car just before Jo was killed. It seems that Brett did some evasive maneuvers after he struck her, but not before. He drove directly to her house from the hostel, and there are several frames where his face is clearly visible, as well as his ring, which he was wearing at the time of his arrest this evening.

Also, they've done an extensive forensic work-up on the car. As you might expect, there was nothing on the bumper or the tires, and no fingerprints on the inside, but the forensic team was able to find traces of Jo's blood and tissue behind the registration plate and on the underside of the bumper, since that part of the car would have come into direct contact with Jo when she was struck. Thankfully, they were both screwed on tight, so no cleaning agents got in during the washes. The police now have enough to conclusively prove that the car was the one used in the hit-and-run."

"So, he'll go down for murder?" Quinn asked, her heart leaping with hope.

"Most likely he'll be charged with leaving the scene of an accident, since I'm sure he'll claim that's what it was, and involuntary manslaughter, but he'll also be charged with attempted murder," Drew added. "DI Marshall has the cyanide capsules in his possession, and there's Emma's account of what happened. She heard everything Brett said to you."

"Will a statement from an eight-year-old girl who was hiding upstairs be enough to convict him?" Quinn asked.

"Probably not, but the recording she made on her phone will go a long way to proving his guilt," he replied, grinning broadly.

"She recorded the conversation?" Quinn asked, incredulous.

"She sure did. You have one smart kid there," Drew said. "She forwarded the recording to the detective who arrived at the scene and he, in turn, sent it to DI Marshall."

"Has Brett called his parents?"

"He hasn't been granted his phone call yet, so no. They have no idea what happened tonight. At least I hope they don't," Drew amended. "Quinn, may I offer you a word of advice?"

"Sure," Quinn replied, her mind still on Kathy and Seth.

"Please, seek professional grief counseling, especially for Emma. People tend to say they're all right and think they will not suffer long-lasting effects, but they do. Every time."

Quinn nodded. "We will. You have my word."

"Would you like me to sit with you for a while, or would you prefer a moment alone?"

"I'm really not sure. I feel like my soul is hovering just above us, watching tonight's events from a distance. I can't seem to reconcile myself to the fact that this actually happened, and that Gabe and I might have been dead had Emma changed her mind and gone to Jill's instead of remaining at home."

"Gabe risked his life to save you," Drew said gently.

"I know," Quinn said, a sob erupting from somewhere deep inside her. Drew put his arm around her and drew her close, holding her until the weeping subsided.

Quinn hastily wiped her eyes and plastered a smile on her face when she saw Emma and Jude coming down the corridor, Emma's hands full of colorful packages.

"We got one of each," she announced as she showed Quinn her loot. "Take whichever ones you like."

Quinn wasn't very hungry but reached out a took a bar of chocolate, though she didn't bother to open it. She'd save it for later. All four of them went quiet and watched Dr. Chan as he came toward them. He looked grim.

"Let's take another walk, Em," Jude instantly said.

"No. I want to hear what the doctor has to say," Emma said. "I'm old enough."

"Of course," Jude agreed after Quinn nodded to him.

"How is Gabe, Dr. Chan?" Quinn asked. She felt breathless once again, her anxiety coursing through her veins like poison.

"He's going to be all right, but the surgeon has made the decision to remove the kidney. It couldn't be saved." He looked at Quinn with great sympathy. "Mr. Russell will be in theater for another two hours, at least, and then you won't be able to see him while he's in recovery. May I suggest that you go home and get some rest? Your daughter looks exhausted," he added under his breath. "I will call you once they transfer him to a room. You will not be able to see him before then."

Quinn opened her mouth to argue but changed her mind. As much as she wanted to be there for Gabe, she was shattered, and Emma looked done in. Going home for a few hours seemed a good idea.

"Thank you, Dr. Chan. I'll wait for your call," Quinn said.

"I'll take you home," Drew offered. "I brought my car."

"I'm coming with you," Jude announced as they walked toward the lift. "No arguments," he added.

"I'm so glad you're here," Quinn said.

Jude put his arm around her and gave her a reassuring squeeze. "I'm not going anywhere."

Quinn balked when they returned to the house. Flashes of what had happened left her shaky and tearful.

"Go upstairs," Jude ordered. "I will clean up," he said, diplomatically not referring to the blood by name.

Emma swept Rufus, who'd come limping into the foyer, into her arms and hugged him tight before running upstairs to her room. Rufus would need to be seen by a veterinarian, but he didn't seem badly hurt.

"What did you say to her?" Quinn asked.

"When?"

"Earlier. When you got off the lift."

"I told her that if she were in the army, she'd get a Victoria Cross, and that's the highest honor awarded only to true heroes."

Quinn nodded. "Thank you."

"You never need to thank me, Quinn. Now go and get some rest. Leave your mobile here. I'll wake you when Dr. Chan rings."

Quinn handed over her mobile and trudged upstairs, where she stripped off her clothes and stepped into a hot shower. She wished she could wash away her fear, guilt, and disappointment, but just feeling clean would do. She dried off, pulled on Gabe's T-shirt, and climbed into bed.

She thought she'd fall asleep as soon as her head hit the pillow, but sleep wouldn't come, horrible images and ever-multiplying fears crowding her mind. Having given up on sleep, Quinn reached for the ring. Delving into the past was the only way to quell her fears for the future.

Chapter 62

September 1777
New York City

Having seen Major Radcliffe and Captain Denning off, Jocelyn returned to the parlor and sank into the major's favorite wingchair. Major Andre's supper would last for several hours at least; these types of gatherings always did. There would be various courses, exquisitely prepared and served with all the pomp Major Andre's staff could muster, accompanied by countless bottles of wine, then port and cigars in the library. By the time Major Radcliffe and Captain Denning returned, they'd be nearly insensible with drink and fit only for their beds. They'd have sore heads come morning and carry on like bears woken from their winter sleep.

The ground floor was quiet and dim, only the light of Jocelyn's candle dispelling the shadows of the parlor. Mrs. Johnson had retired directly after taking an early supper, and Private Sykes had gone up to his attic bedroom, glad not to be needed tonight. He had a cold and had been sneezing and blowing his nose all day, and annoying Major Radcliffe so much that he'd dismissed him and told him to take himself somewhere where he wouldn't have to see him. John had bedded down in the stable so he'd be on hand once the men returned and the horses would need seeing to, so the coast was clear. This was the perfect opportunity to discover something about the impending attack on Washington's army. From the snatches of conversation Jocelyn had overheard, it would commence in a matter of days, so this was her last chance to alter the course of events, if what she did could be described in such grandiose terms.

Jocelyn stood and reached for the candleholder, her mind made up. She approached Jared's office first, simply because it was the nearest door, and tried the knob. Locked. She then went across the corridor and tried the major's study. Also locked. She sighed. It would have been so much simpler if either man had forgotten to lock his door, but she wasn't that lucky. Jocelyn considered her options. She could either try to pick the lock, which might damage the mechanism and arouse Major Radcliffe's suspicion, or try to get Mrs. Johnson's keys off her. The housekeeper always wore the keyring at her waist, only taking it off when she retired and got undressed for bed. Jocelyn had seen the keyring often enough to know which key fit which door. She could find her way inside Mrs. Johnson's room easily enough under one pretense or another, but she could hardly take the keyring without the older woman noticing. Unless she took just one key, Jocelyn thought, and smiled to herself.

Mrs. Johnson had planned to have a bath after the men had gone, a luxury she permitted herself once a week. Jocelyn had helped her carry several pitchers of hot water into her room in preparation. She'd luxuriate in the tub until the water grew cold, which gave Jocelyn at least another ten minutes in which to remove the key to the major's office from the keyring. Even if she didn't return the key in time, Mrs. Johnson wouldn't notice one key missing as she prepared for bed, and Jocelyn could pretend to have found the key in the corridor, as if it had somehow come off the ring, and hand it to her in the morning. That was about as good a plan as she could hope to come up with.

She stopped by the airing cupboard and took out a clean towel, then knocked on Mrs. Johnson's door and entered the room, thanking her lucky stars the woman hadn't locked it. Mrs. Johnson was already in the tub, which was discreetly placed behind a screen.

"Who's there?" she called, her voice reedy with astonishment that someone would enter her private quarters without being invited.

"Only me, Mrs. J," Jocelyn replied. "I was just putting away the fresh towels and thought you might need one."

"I have a towel," Mrs. Johnson replied. "But thank you all the same, Jocelyn. Just leave it on the bed."

"Enjoy your bath," Jocelyn called out as she quickly located the right key and slid it off the keyring. She held the other keys tight so they wouldn't make a clinking sound and alert Mrs. Johnson to the fact that she was doing anything other than placing a towel on the bed. Jocelyn pocketed the key and left the room, closing the door with enough force to let Mrs. Johnson know she'd gone. Then she returned to Major Radcliffe's study and looked around, her heart hammering in her chest as she fitted the key into the lock and opened the door.

She slipped inside and closed the door behind her, making a beeline for the carved mahogany desk, which, like the rest of the study, was pristine, the surface polished to a shine. Only an inkwell, a matching cup filled with pens, an ink blotter, a letter opener, and a stick of sealing wax were neatly arranged in the righthand corner, where the major could reach them easily.

Jocelyn set down the candleholder and went to work, pulling open the top right drawer. Inside were the major's diary, a stack of thick, creamy paper, and an extra bottle of ink. She tried the second drawer. This one contained a folio filled with correspondence. Jocelyn leafed through the letters, but most of them contained nothing of interest, dealing mostly with the requisitioning of supplies, orders, and receipts. It seemed most of the major's work centered on inventory and logistics. How boring that must be, Jocelyn thought as she shut the drawer and opened the one beneath it. It contained several ledgers.

Frustrated, Jocelyn pulled open the drawers on the left side of the desk. More useless lists, papers, and requisition forms. She was about to give up when she opened the bottom drawer. There was a rolled-up map and more lists, but the date at the top of the first page was recent, so she studied the notes carefully, her heart fluttering as she realized these lists pertained to the upcoming campaign. The first detailed the provisions, horses, wagons, and other items needed to supply an army on the march. The second list dealt with ammunition, the numbers frighteningly high. Jocelyn unrolled the map and studied it carefully. It was a detailed map of the northern colonies marked with several hand-drawn lines and arrows. Jocelyn's brows furrowed in concentration as she tried to comprehend what she was looking at.

The lines began in and around New York, crossed New York Bay, and stopped at Red Bank, New Jersey. Then new lines spread out from Red Bank, pointing toward Head of Elk in Maryland. Jocelyn's mouth dropped open. If she understood the map correctly, the British Army would not be marching toward an engagement with Washington's army. The soldiers would be delivered to Maryland using troop ships and then attack from the south, taking the Continental Army by surprise. It was a clever plan that was sure to work if no one got wind of the details of the campaign. Jocelyn quickly rolled up the map and replaced it in the drawer. She had time to run to the tavern and pass on an urgent message before the men returned home.

She had just shut the drawer and was about to leave when the door opened and Major Radcliffe strode into the study, his face set in lines of anger, his eyes narrowed with suspicion.

Jocelyn took a step back, her heart hammering and her breath coming in short gasps. Her mind raced furiously for an explanation she could offer, but nothing sprang to mind. She had no right to be in his study, and they both knew it.

"The door was unlocked," the major said as he shut the door behind him and advanced further into the room.

"I… I needed a sheet of paper to write a letter," Jocelyn stammered.

"Did you now?" the major asked conversationally. "And how did you get in, Jocelyn?"

"The door was unlocked, as you said."

"I doubt that." His gaze fell on the key lying on the nearly empty desk. He couldn't miss it. Had she put it in her pocket, its absence would have given credence to her lie, but now she was caught red-handed.

"Where's Mrs. Johnson?" Major Radcliffe barked.

"In the bath," Jocelyn replied as she came around the desk, her hands at her sides to show the major that she hadn't taken anything.

He crossed the room in two strides and grabbed her by the shoulders, shoving her against the desk. The wood bit into her lower back as she leaned away from the major, who looked enraged. All pretense at civility was gone, replaced by cold fury.

"What were you doing in my study, Jocelyn?" he asked, his words clipped and menacing.

"I needed a sheet of paper," Jocelyn replied lamely.

The slap that followed took her by surprise. Her head spun to the side, her teeth rattling with the force of the blow. There was a ringing in her ears as the major grabbed her chin and forced her to face him again.

"What were you doing in my study?" he growled, his dark gaze boring into her.

Jocelyn remained silent, her gaze meeting his, their noses almost touching. She'd thought his brown eyes were soft and soulful, but now they were like dark holes, the pupils dilated and his breath hot on her face. He was staring at her, his breath quickening as he pinned her hips to the desk with his body. Jocelyn felt his arousal against her thigh and shuddered with revulsion.

"Please let go of me, Major Radcliffe," she pleaded, her voice quivering with apprehension. "I had no right to be in your study. I was snooping," she muttered. "I'm sorry."

He didn't react to her words. He was panting now, his fingers like steel clamps around her arms. "You're not going anywhere. You were spying. You are a rebel spy," he hissed.

"I'm not," Jocelyn protested, but it was no use. She had no plausible explanation to give him. Something had made him return to the house before the carriage got too far. He may have forgotten something, or he might have had a premonition. It didn't matter. What mattered was that now she was at his mercy.

"Please, Major," Jocelyn begged, but her pleas fell on deaf ears. He spun her around and pushed her down on the desk. She cried out in alarm when his hands pushed up her skirts, his thighs holding her in place. She tried to fight back, but the major slammed her head against the wood, momentarily stunning her.

"You've been toying with me for months, you little harlot," he panted. "Pretending to like me, to respect me." His voice was gravelly as he shoved his knee between her legs, forcing them to part. "You've been playing me for a fool, encouraging Captain Denning's attentions to make me jealous. I treated you like a lady, but you're nothing but a cheap, lying whore," he spat out. "And you will be treated as such. Tomorrow, I will have you arrested for spying. Do you know what the penalty for spying is?" he demanded hoarsely as he slid his fingers inside her, letting out a deep sigh of satisfaction as if he'd dreamed of doing that for some time. "Hanging," he murmured in her ear as he bent over her. "That's right. You'll be dead by noon tomorrow, Jocelyn. It would be a damn shame not to avail myself of something that should have been mine," he grunted as he guided himself inside her, pushing hard.

Jocelyn felt a searing pain as he breached her maidenhead, his engorged shaft stretching her until she thought he'd rip her apart. He grunted with satisfaction. "And a virgin to boot," he panted. "A double pleasure." He thrust into her again and again, his hands gripping her as his hips slammed against her.

Jocelyn's cries seemed to arouse him, loosening his tongue. The things he said were obscene. He told her exactly what he was doing to her in the crudest terms possible, his breathing ragged as he promised to do it again and again before she was taken away in the morning. He loosened his grip as he spilled himself inside her.

"Thank you, my dear. That was most gratifying," he said as he finally pulled out, releasing his hold on her.

Jocelyn crumpled to the floor, her skirts cascading down to cover her nakedness. Major Radcliffe had taken out his handkerchief and was wiping himself, his seed mixed with her blood.

Jocelyn hadn't heard the door open, nor had she realized they were no longer alone.

"Is everything all right?" Jared asked. "I was waiting in the carriage…" His voice trailed away as he took in the scene, his horrified gaze fixing on the major's shriveled cock and the bloodied handkerchief in his hand.

The major's head snapped back, his wig falling off, as Jared punched him hard, then again. The major fell backward, his breeches still unlaced, his manhood hanging out as Captain Denning grabbed him by the lapels and lifted him up, his face twisted with rage. "You bastard," he hissed, then brought his knee up to hit the major in the groin.

Major Radcliffe let out a blood-curdling shriek and collapsed on the floor once Jared let him go. Blood gushed from his broken nose, dripping onto the carpet as he lay curled up like a shrimp, howling with pain, his hands between his legs.

"You're going to hang right alongside her, you idiot," the major roared. "Sykes!" he cried out. "Help me!"

Private Sykes exploded into the study a few moments later, his hair disheveled, his shirt hanging out of his breeches, his musket in his hands.

"Seize him!" Major Radcliffe bellowed as he tried to staunch the flow of blood with his sleeve. "He struck me."

Private Sykes took in the scene and blanched, as if unsure what to do, but he had no choice; he had to follow the major's orders. He bashed Jared on the side of the head with the butt of the musket. Jared sank to his knees, a trickle of blood snaking down the side of his face as he lifted a hand to his head. He looked stunned, his glazed gaze turning to Jocelyn, who lay on the floor, her cheek pressed to the cool wood as tears slid down her temple and into her hair. She was trembling, her insides quivering after the major's assault. From the corner of her eye, she saw Mrs. Johnson, a shawl held tightly over her nightdress. She stood in the doorway, her mouth open, her eyes wide with horror.

"Oh, dear Lord," Mrs. Johnson exclaimed as her hand came up to cover her mouth.

Having recovered somewhat, Major Radcliffe scrambled to his feet and tucked himself into his breeches before rounding on Jared with the help of Private Sykes. It took a few minutes, but they managed to subdue him and tie his hands behind his back with a tassel tie-back from the curtains. Major Radcliffe grabbed him by the arm and dragged him toward the door while Private Sykes brought up the rear. Mrs. Johnson moved out of the way, her gaze still fixed on Jocelyn as understanding of what had happened finally seemed to penetrate her befuddled brain.

"Jocelyn," Jared called out desperately.

Jocelyn couldn't move. She was glued to the floor, her body like a boneless sack of meat. She couldn't bring herself to speak, so she shut her eyes and allowed herself to drift.

"Mrs. Johnson, return to your room. Now!" the major ordered.

The older woman must have obeyed because Jocelyn heard the key turn in the lock, and then she was alone. She remained where she was. What did it matter now? Come morning, they would come for her and she would hang, just like Nathan Hale, just like so many others. She'd never get her message to Richard, nor would she see Jared again. The major would make sure of that.

After a time, the candle burned down, near-darkness descending on the room silvered by moonlight. Jocelyn finally managed to sit up. She leaned against the desk, resting her head on her knees. Her thighs were slick with blood and Major Radcliffe's seed, and her head ached so viciously, she felt sick. She crawled toward the wastepaper basket and emptied her stomach, vomiting until there was nothing left. She wished she were dead. At least if she were to die now, she'd die on her own terms, not in front of a jeering crowd. She'd heard that people's bowels let loose at the time of hanging. The final humiliation inflicted by a body that couldn't process the shock of what was happening.

Jocelyn's head snapped up, her mind finally growing more alert. What was she thinking? She had to try to escape instead of

324

sitting here and wishing for death. A surge of energy shot through her veins, forcing her to take stock of her situation. She was in a locked room, yes, but the study was on the ground floor, the window easy enough to open. She supposed Major Radcliffe had forgotten about that and assumed she was safely contained until morning.

Jocelyn hurried toward the window and tried to open it, but it was stuck fast. Major Radcliffe never opened the window in his study and, swollen from heat and humidity, the frame was glued to the windowsill. Jocelyn ran to the desk and grabbed the letter opener. It was sturdy, the metal shaped like a dagger. She inserted the tip between the window frame and the windowsill and used the opener as a lever. Nothing happened. She tried again, moving the opener bit by bit and trying to break the seal that had formed during months of disuse. It must have taken her an hour, maybe more, but eventually she managed to loosen the frame.

Jocelyn placed her hands on the top of the window frame and pushed up with all her might. This time the window budged, and she was able to raise it a few inches. It took three more tries, but at last, she was able to open the window nearly all the way. She looked down. It was a drop of about ten feet, but she could do it. She threw one leg over the windowsill, then the other, and gripped the sill as hard as she could, slowly lowering herself until she was hanging down, about two feet between her feet and the ground. Jocelyn let go and landed with a soft thud.

The air was cool and fresh, the night full of mysterious sounds. Jocelyn crept toward the back gate that was used to deliver firewood and foodstuffs to the kitchen. She unlatched the gate and slipped out, breathing a sigh of relief when no one followed. She shut the gate behind her and hurried down the street, praying all the while not to encounter any drunken soldiers or anyone else intent on doing her harm. Once away from the house, she began to run, desperate to get away.

The pitch dark of night began to give way to the murky gray of morning when she banged on Anna's door, calling for the older woman to let her in. Anna opened the door, her face pale with fright. A dark braid streaked with silver snaked over her shoulder, a threadbare shawl draped over her nightdress.

"Jocelyn, what is it? What's happened?"

"Help me. Please," Jocelyn whispered, and went down in a heap, her legs no longer able to support her.

Chapter 63

March 2018
London

Quinn dropped the ring when Jude poked his head into the bedroom.

"Quinn, Dr. Chan just called. He said Gabe's out of surgery, and you can visit him now."

"Thanks," Quinn said. "I'll be right down."

She came downstairs to find a cup of coffee and a sandwich waiting for her.

"You have to eat something before you go," Jude said. "Do you want me to drive you? Emma will never know if I step out for an hour."

"I'll take an Uber. Emma's too young to be left alone."

"All right. Ring me when you get there," Jude said once Quinn finished her meal.

"I will."

"The Uber is outside," Jude said fifteen minutes later. He handed her a coat, her bag, and her mobile. "All right?" he asked.

Quinn nodded. "I'll talk to you later."

"Don't worry about Emma. I'll look after her."

"I know you will."

Quinn was grateful that the Uber driver didn't feel a need to chat. It was just past 5:00 a.m. and the streets were deserted, most windows dark as they drove past office buildings and private residences. She should have been exhausted, but the coffee had revived her and the prospect of seeing Gabe lifted her spirits. He'd be groggy and confused, but he was alive; that was all that mattered.

Leaning back against the seat, Quinn allowed her mind to drift for a moment, her thoughts returning to what she had just witnessed. She hadn't expected to be confronted with such brutality, particularly perpetrated by a man who'd seemed so pleasant and correct in his dealings with others. She'd seen people pushed beyond the point of endurance but didn't think this was the first time the major had taken out his fury on a helpless woman. He'd been successful at hiding his true nature, but it had come out nonetheless, and if Quinn had to guess, she'd bet that he'd been able to get away with it every time. No wonder Jocelyn had been so traumatized, but there was more to the story. Quinn would have to wait to find out the rest.

She thanked the driver and hurried toward the entrance of the hospital, where the night porter demanded to know what she was doing there at such an ungodly hour. Visiting hours would not start for a while yet. Quinn explained, and he waved her through. She took the lift to the appropriate floor and approached the nurses' station.

"I'm here to see Gabriel Russell," Quinn said. "Dr. Chan said I'd be allowed to visit with him."

A middle-aged woman with spiky red hair smiled kindly at her. "He was just brought up half an hour ago. He's asleep, but you can sit with him. He'll be happy to see a familiar face when he wakes up."

"How is he?" Quinn asked.

The woman must have seen the anxiety in her eyes because she rushed to reassure her. "The surgery went well, and he's stable. Don't you worry, love."

Quinn thanked the nurse and walked along the corridor until she found the right room. Gabe had been assigned a double-occupancy room, but the other bed was empty, so he was on his own. Quinn pulled up a chair and sat down, drinking him in until she felt reassured that he was indeed stable. Gabe was hooked up to an IV and several other monitors, but his face looked peaceful, and his color was good. He was breathing evenly, and his heartrate was steady. Quinn reached out and took his hand. It was warm but limp. His fingers did not curl around hers, nor did he respond in any way. That was all right, though. She had no wish to disturb him, only to feel a connection with him.

She sat like that for a long time, just watching him sleep, until the sky began to lighten in the east, dawn fast approaching and the sun rising on another day, a day neither of them might have lived to see. This would also be the day she'd have to tell Phoebe that her son had lost a kidney and inform Seth that his son was in police custody. Some part of her wanted to wait, to let Seth find out on his own, but she owed it to him. He was her father, and the news that his son had not only willfully killed his other daughter but had tried to murder Quinn and Gabe would bring Seth to his knees. He wasn't an overly introspective man, preferring to deal with facts rather than suppositions, but Quinn was certain he'd ask himself the impossible questions, like whether there was anything he had done as a father to set Brett on the path he'd chosen. Any parent would.

Would Seth set aside his own feelings and try to help Brett, or would he let him face the consequences alone this time? Quinn couldn't begin to guess. The very thought of Brett made her feel ill. She hadn't focused on the details last night, having been too shocked and scared to notice the little things, but now her mind was cruelly playing back the tape, forcing her to pay attention to things she'd have preferred to ignore. Brett had been wearing latex gloves, and the hood of his sweatshirt had been pulled up to cover his hair. He hadn't sat down or come into contact with anything. Had the police found Quinn and Gabe dead this morning, there would have been no forensic evidence linking Brett to the scene. He'd thought everything through and had chosen a poison that would kill swiftly, ensuring there'd be no dramatic rescue.

As with Jo, this was no crime of passion. He'd had less than a day in which to set his plan in motion, but he'd done so quickly and efficiently, and would have got away with it. And as he had pointed out, by the time DI Marshall would have issued a warrant for his arrest and gone through the proper channels to have him extradited to the UK, he'd be long gone. A person who had cash could always go off the grid, especially in places where it was easy to disappear. He'd mentioned once that he'd go to Thailand if he ever decided to get away from the States. Perhaps that had been the plan.

"Quinn," Gabe muttered. His voice was barely audible, but he was awake and lucid.

"I'm here. How do you feel?"

"Like I've been run over by a lorry," Gabe replied, giving her a feeble smile.

"You are going to be all right," Quinn assured him. There was so much she wanted to say, but now wasn't the time. She didn't want to upset him or remind him of last night, in case his brain had somehow managed to dull the sharpness of recent events.

"Where's Emma?"

"She's at home, with Jude."

"My mum," Gabe muttered.

"Don't worry. I will ring your mum."

Gabe's eyes cleared a little as he grew more alert. "Do they have enough to charge him?"

Quinn nodded. "They do. He's not getting off so easily this time. DI Marshall has found evidence of Jo's murder as well. Brett is going down, Gabe."

Gabe sighed and closed his eyes. He looked tired and ill.

"Go back to sleep," Quinn said softly. "I'll be right here when you wake." If DI Marshall wanted a statement, he'd have to come to her. She wasn't leaving Gabe on his own, not for such a long stretch of time.

Quinn briefly considered going in search of a cup of coffee but changed her mind. Instead, she reached for the ring and slipped it onto her finger, eighteenth-century Long Island materializing before her eyes.

Chapter 64

November 1777
Long Island

Jocelyn buried her face in her hands, trembling violently as she recalled the horror of that night and the look in Jared's eyes as he was hauled away, his arms wrenched behind his back, his face covered in blood, his fate sealed. The weeks that followed had been a blur, made bearable only by Anna's unwavering support and quiet understanding. Jocelyn had been desperate to remember her past, but now that she did, she wished she hadn't. Only a few days ago, she'd believed that she might have been part of a close family and wed to a man who loved her. Today, she knew better. And she owed the Wilders the truth. She could no longer keep up the pretense in the hope that the truth, once discovered, would be palatable.

The Battle of Brandywine, fought on September 11, had been lost, her part in trying to change the outcome no longer important. If the Wilders chose to turn her over to Lieutenant Reynolds, so be it. She no longer cared. She was all alone, carrying a child conceived in an act of violence and hatred. She didn't blame the baby. It was innocent in all this, but she'd be lying if she said she felt any love toward it.

Forcing herself to her feet, Jocelyn made her way downstairs, where Hannah was washing up after supper, and Ben and Derek sat by the fire in the parlor, talking quietly. Josh must have gone to bed, which was just as well, since this wasn't a story for a young boy.

"May I speak to you all?" Jocelyn said, her voice quivering as she forced out the words. Once she told them the truth, there'd be no going back. She realized she didn't want to leave. She felt safe here and cared for.

"Of course," Hannah said. "Are you quite all right, Alice?"

Jocelyn shook her head. "No," she replied. *I don't think I'll ever be all right again*, she thought as she took a seat at the table and waited for the others to join her.

"My name is Jocelyn Sinclair," she began. "I was an actress at the John Street Theatre before the war began."

"You've remembered. How wonderful," Hannah exclaimed, but the look on Jocelyn's face silenced her. "I'm sorry. Do go on."

And she did. She told them everything, from being recruited by Richard Kinney, whose name she didn't divulge, to the day she'd boarded a ship named *Peregrine* bound for Virginia, where she'd intended to stay with Greg until she felt ready to face the world again.

The Wilders stared at her in horror, even Derek, who'd already known part of the truth.

"My dear girl," Hannah exclaimed. "What you have been through. Oh, if only I'd known."

"You've been the soul of kindness, Hannah. I could never repay you for the care and understanding you've shown me."

"You sound like you're leaving," Ben said, his gaze searching her face anxiously.

"I can't put you out any longer. I will make my way to Virginia, to my brother's house."

"Alice, eh, I mean Jocelyn," Hannah said, the name strange on her tongue. "What of your young man?" she asked quietly.

"Court-martialed for assaulting a senior officer and sentenced to hang," Jocelyn replied, her voice flat. She could barely get the words out, much less allow herself to focus on what they meant. "Anna saw it in the paper."

"Oh, I am sorry," Hannah cried, her eyes shimmering with tears.

"Jocelyn, you don't need to leave," Derek said, reaching out to take her hand. "You are a part of this family now. Please, don't go."

Jocelyn nodded, tears threatening to fall again. "I need some air," she choked out, and fled outside. She ran as far as the stile and stopped, panting as the memories assaulted her once again. Now that she recalled Major Radcliffe's assault, she couldn't get it out of her mind. She could feel his hands on her hips, his swollen cock inside her, robbing her of her innocence and dignity with every savage thrust. And now she carried his child, a child who'd be a constant reminder, especially if it was a boy.

The wind had picked up since the afternoon, and Jocelyn shivered, suddenly realizing she was cold. She wrapped her arms around herself, surprised when a coat was draped over her shoulders. Ben stood next to her, his eyes warm with sympathy.

"You'll catch your death," he said quietly.

"I should have died in that shipwreck," Jocelyn said vehemently. "I'd have been better off."

"No, you wouldn't have. Jocelyn, you're beautiful and clever and strong. You will get past this, in time."

"Will I?"

"You will if you have love and support," he said. Jocelyn experienced a sinking feeling as she looked up at Ben. He'd come out here for a reason.

"You might not think this is the right time, but it is exactly the right time," he began.

"Ben..."

"Please, let me speak. Jocelyn, I will look after you and the baby. I will love it as if it were my own. I will make you whole again."

"Ben, I couldn't possibly say yes. Not now."

"Why not?" Ben demanded. "Do you like me, Jocelyn?"

"Yes."

"Do you trust me?"

"I do," Jocelyn admitted.

"Do you believe I will treat you with kindness and respect?"

Jocelyn nodded.

"Then why can't you give me a chance? Many a marriage is based on less."

"Ben, your mother—"

"My mother knows how I feel about you. She will be happy for us."

Jocelyn shook her head. "I can't. I'm not ready. I thought I could agree to a marriage and learn to love my husband, but I'm damaged, Ben. Broken."

Ben placed his hand over hers on the stile. "How about this? I will give you my ring as a token of my love. Wear it for a spell. Give yourself time to come around to the idea. If, by Christmas, you still feel that you can't accept me, I will take it back, and I will not trouble you again. You don't really want to go to Virginia, do you?" he cajoled.

"No," Jocelyn admitted. "I don't."

"You don't have to tell anyone your real name if you don't want to. You can become Alice Wilder. You can start a new life. With me."

Ben took the ring off his finger and placed it on hers. The ring slid off and fell into the grass at their feet. Jocelyn bent down to pick it up. "It's too big."

Stepping behind her, Ben undid the clasp of her chain and threaded it through the ring, then put it around her neck. The ring hung next to the silver cross she wore.

"There," he said. "Now, you are wearing my ring."

"Ben," Jocelyn began, but he shook his head, silencing her.

"Until Christmas, Jocelyn. No one has to know except us." Ben seemed confident that she'd come around. Jocelyn wasn't so sure.

"Let's go back inside. Your hands are freezing. Tomorrow is Thanksgiving," he reminded her. "I think we all have something to be thankful for this year. I know I do."

Jocelyn nodded and allowed him to lead her back to the house, his hand on the small of her back. He was already acting like a husband, she thought, but the observation did not put her off. Would it be so terrible to be a part of this family? Ben was so solid, so strong. He'd love her, and he'd love her child, she was sure of that. His word meant everything to him. And Derek would marry his Lydia and move to town. It'd be best for all involved. For a brief moment, she had thought she might be able to love Derek, but what she had felt was a need for support and protection from someone who didn't crowd her or make her feel beholden.

Derek had been as good as his word. He'd helped her and guided her toward regaining her memory, but he didn't love her any more than she loved him, and the look of horror in his eyes when she'd described the rape had convinced her that there could never be a future for them. He'd never be able to get those images out of his mind, nor would he be able to care for the child when he knew the truth of its parentage.

"Get some rest," Ben said. "Tomorrow will be a better day."

"Yes," Jocelyn agreed. She trudged up the stairs and walked into her room. Instead of going to bed, she stood by the window, looking out over the moonlit landscape, her hand going unwittingly to her stomach.

"We'll be all right, you and I," she said quietly. "We'll be all right, no matter what."

Chapter 65

December 1777
Long Island

Despite her misery, Jocelyn had managed to enjoy Thanksgiving. It was the first time in a long while that she'd felt like part of a family. Everyone was so kind and careful of her feelings. Jocelyn had thought Hannah might resent Ben's feelings for her. What mother would want her son to a marry a woman who'd been despoiled and now carried her rapist's child? But Hannah was more protective than ever, treating Jocelyn like the daughter she'd never had. Jocelyn was touched by her sensitivity and grateful to have a home with the Wilders, for however long she might need it.

As the weeks passed, she began to feel more resigned, but there were times when she longed to be alone with her turbulent thoughts. She took daily walks, strolling across the fields and through the woods at a brisk pace until she regained some semblance of calm. Her memories came rushing in as soon as she was alone or blew out the candle in hopes of falling asleep without the horrible images replaying themselves in her mind. Ignoring them wouldn't work, so she had to face them and come to terms not only with what Major Radcliffe had done but with the loss of Jared. She'd cried over him while holed up at Anna's, but now that she'd recalled his death, the grief was as fresh and raw as if he'd died yesterday. There were so many things she'd never had a chance to tell him, so many feelings that no longer had an outlet.

Unsure of his feelings for her, she'd kept Jared at arm's length, believing he would leave her behind as soon as he was posted elsewhere, but he'd loved her, really and truly. He'd given his life for her, because as soon as he'd raised a hand to Major Radcliffe, he must have known what the outcome would be. He hadn't hesitated, and he'd have killed the man had Private Sykes not intervened. And now Jared was gone, and she had a chance at a new life, with Ben.

Jocelyn subconsciously reached up and took hold of Ben's ring. It felt warm from its proximity to her skin, the etching bumpy beneath her fingers. What was she to do? Ben had offered her a home, stability, and affection. But what did she have to offer him in return? Could she love him? Would she enjoy his attentions as a wife should? And what of the child? Jocelyn thought as she quickened her steps, her mind returning to the same questions every time she went for a walk. Would either of them be able to love this baby without reservation? She hoped so.

Letting go of the ring, Jocelyn lowered her hand to her stomach. At this stage, the child didn't feel real to her. She wasn't showing yet, and it was too soon for the baby to move. The sickness had abated, and Jocelyn felt more herself, stronger and more energetic. She had a few weeks before her belly would begin to swell and the child inside would make itself known. If she refused Ben, she'd have to go it alone, with no one to turn to for comfort or financial support. She couldn't go to Greg now.

Dear God, what would he say if he knew what had happened to her? If she knew Greg, he'd probably think she had brought this on herself. And she had, to some degree. She'd betrayed the major's trust and had played him for a fool. Her actions didn't excuse his brutality toward her, but he would have had her arrested and executed, of that she was certain. She was lucky to be alive. That was twice she'd cheated death. Didn't things come in threes? she mused as she entered a thickly wooded stretch of the path.

The trees were bare, the branches reaching for the sky like skeletal limbs. Before they knew it, Christmas would be upon them. She had to decide, but despite all the reasons she had for marrying Ben, her heart rejected her decision. It struggled and ached, and refused to comply, holding out like a stubborn donkey.

Jocelyn stopped walking and stood still, listening. She thought she'd heard something. No one ever took this path. It was too far away from town and didn't lead anywhere. Jocelyn laughed at herself. It was probably a rabbit, or even a squirrel. She'd never been fearful and had no reason to be afraid now. She resumed walking, but her spine was rigid, and her ears attuned to the sounds around her. Suddenly, the copse seemed full of noises, and she hurried home, eager to get warm and have a cup of tea by the fire.

She was almost out of the woods when a figure stepped out in front of her. He wore a black coat and a tricorn that was pulled low over his eyes, but she'd recognize him anywhere. Jocelyn took an involuntary step backward, her breath catching in her throat.

"Hello, Jocelyn," he said conversationally, taking a step toward her.

"Major," Jocelyn replied, wishing desperately someone would come along, preferably someone armed.

"I didn't think we'd meet again, but imagine my surprise when Private Sykes told me he'd seen you at a tavern."

Jocelyn gasped. She'd hoped Private Sykes wouldn't mention seeing her, especially since he'd seemed to accept her denials of having met him in the past, but clearly, she hadn't been convincing enough.

"Finding you took a bit of time, but here I am."

"What do you want?" Jocelyn asked. She was shaking with fear, but her voice sounded clear and strong.

"What do you think I want?" Major Radcliffe asked. He seemed to be enjoying himself.

Confused, Jocelyn didn't reply. If Major Radcliffe had come to Milford to arrest her, he wouldn't have been skulking in the woods, out of uniform and without backup. Had he come on his own, he would have engaged the help of Lieutenant Reynolds at the very least to help bring her in and would most likely have arrested her publicly, not on an isolated path through a wintery wood.

Her trembling intensified as the reality of her situation dawned on her. Major Radcliffe had no intention of placing her under arrest. He wanted her silenced. She had the power not only to accuse him of rape and vindicate Jared for defending her but to let it be known that she had been spying under his nose for months, making him look like a dupe and possibly even an accomplice.

Jocelyn looked beyond the major's shoulder, debating if she had any chance of outrunning him if she managed to get past him, but she didn't think so. Despite his love of food and drink, the major was fit and strong, and he'd catch her in moments. Her only chance was to grab a stout branch off the ground and wield it like a club, but there was nothing nearby except a few thin twigs. Not even a good-sized rock. The major was armed with a pistol, and she had no doubt he had a dagger at his hip. He'd come prepared and had waited for an opportunity to catch her alone.

"I'm with child," Jocelyn said, her gaze unflinching. "Your child."

The major looked momentarily surprised, but then his eyes narrowed, and his mouth twisted with derision. "And you think that makes any difference?" he asked. "As far as I'm concerned, that's all the more reason to snuff you out. You're a liability, Jocelyn, a loose end that needs tying up."

Jocelyn didn't argue. His mind was made up, and nothing she said would make a difference. Jared had said that Major Radcliffe was a meticulous man, and he was. As he'd pointed out, Jocelyn was a loose thread, which, if pulled, could unravel the entire fabric of the major's life.

"Get on with it, then," she said, thrusting her chin forward in a last-ditch effort at defiance. She wouldn't beg for her life. She'd die with dignity.

"You are brave; I'll give you that," Major Radcliffe said. "In another time and place, we might have had a different ending, you and I."

He said something else, but Jocelyn wasn't listening to him. She looked up at the sky, suddenly aware of just how much she wanted to live. She was young. She would have had so much living to do had things been different. She recalled Jared's kisses, and her heart squeezed with loss. Would they be together in death? Probably not. They hadn't belonged to each other, not truly. They hadn't been man and wife, only two young people who had, despite all the obstacles placed between them, succumbed to a mutual attraction and let their guard down enough to let love in. It would have blossomed had they been given time, possibly even lasted forever, but now she'd never know. It was as over for her as it was for him.

Out of the corner of her eye, she saw the major reach for the pistol and point. *I'm coming, Jared*, Jocelyn thought as Major Radcliffe fired. She barely registered the sound of the shot, her attention caught by the startled birds that had erupted from the trees, their wings beating wildly against the clear blue sky, their squawks panicked and surprisingly loud. She felt a visceral pain as the lead ball tore through her chest, searing its way toward her heart. The world tilted, her vision blurring as she fell backward, having been nearly lifted off her feet by the impact. She landed on her back, her head snapping backward, her eyes still open as she gazed at the sky. She gasped for breath, her hand going to her chest. Hot, sticky blood covered her fingers and bloomed on the lace tucker.

The last thing Jocelyn saw was the major's impassive face as he leaned over her and yanked off the chain around her neck. He slid off the ring and placed it on his finger, then threw the chain into the brown blanket of rotting leaves. And then the world went dark.

Chapter 66

March 2018
London

Quinn buried her face in her hands, desperate to get the last image of Jocelyn out of her mind. All she saw was the shock on the young woman's face, her body jerking as the bullet entered her chest, and then she was falling, as if in slow motion, her arms outstretched, her mouth open in a silent scream.

"No," Quinn moaned.

"Quinn, what is it?" Gabe asked. She must have woken him, and now he was looking at her with concern, as if she were the one in a hospital bed. He did look a little better, his gaze brighter and more alert. How long had she been in a daze?

"Oh, Gabe," Quinn whispered miserably and placed the ring on the bedside locker, desperate to break the connection.

"Tell me what you saw," Gabe invited. "Tell me the story."

"He shot her," she whispered. "Major Radcliffe shot Jocelyn. The child was his," Quinn said, unable to hide her disgust. "He attacked her when he found her in his office, rifling through his papers. He thought she'd hang, so no one would ever know, but Captain Denning tried to intervene. Major Radcliffe had him court-martialed for assaulting an officer. He was hanged."

Gabe looked confused, having missed a large chunk of the narrative, but nodded all the same, his expression thoughtful as he tried to connect the dots, a task made more difficult by the strong painkillers coursing through his bloodstream.

"And he took Ben's ring. I suppose he wanted a souvenir of his handiwork."

"He took the ring?" Gabe asked, clearly still lost. Quinn nodded, her mind numb with shock.

"So, then the remains couldn't be those of Ben Wilder," Gabe said, verbalizing what Quinn was just beginning to grasp. "The major must have been wearing Ben's ring at the time of his death."

"Yes," Quinn agreed, brightening. She found it fitting that someone had bashed the major's head in and then buried him in an unmarked grave. "Yes," she said louder. "The skelly is not Ben Wilder."

"This explains how Ben's ring came to be in England. Major Radcliffe must have returned home. Do we know if he came from Hertfordshire?" Gabe asked, growing more animated by the minute.

"No, but I can find out. I'll also see if I can find anything about Captain Denning's court-martial. The poor man. To be executed for trying to protect a woman," Quinn said, shaking her head.

"I'm sure that bit never came out," Gabe said. "Major Radcliffe would have made sure of that. He would have presented the tribunal with a convincing tale."

"What a heartbreaking story," Quinn said, shaking her head. "And it was all for nothing. The Continental Army lost the Battle of Brandywine."

"But they won the war," Gabe reminded her.

"But Jocelyn didn't live long enough to find that out," Quinn pointed out sadly.

"Can you use the ring to see what happened to Major Radcliffe?" Gabe asked.

Quinn shook her head. "The ring never truly belonged to Major Radcliffe. He'd stolen it, so his memories would not be imprinted on it. I'll have to come up with some plausible story for the episode, one that's more palatable than the truth. I'd forgotten what a toll this takes on me," Quinn said, choosing to blame the visions rather than the ordeal of the night before. She couldn't bear to revisit it and was glad Gabe didn't want to rake it all over.

"So, no more cases?"

"Oh, I don't know. Someone somewhere must have had a happy ending," Quinn said, giving Gabe a watery smile.

"People who had a happy ending rarely find themselves with a bashed skull."

"True, but in my book, this was a fitting end for the dear major. He got what he deserved."

"Her certainly did," Gabe agreed. "Quinn, you look exhausted. Go home. They'll take good care of me while you're gone."

"I can't bear to be parted from you," Quinn said through the lump in her throat.

Gabe squeezed her hand. "I'll be here when you return. Promise," he added, grinning. When he looked like that, it was truly possible to believe everything would be all right. "And collect the children from Jill. I want to know that you are all together."

"I'll FaceTime you once I get the children. Your mobile is right here on your bedside locker."

"I'll look forward to it."

Chapter 67

Brett stared straight ahead, refusing to look at the evidence spread out before him on the ugly Formica table. Did every country have the same hideous furniture in their police stations? DI Marshall was speaking, but Brett wasn't listening, his mind on what he would say to his parents when he was finally allowed to make his phone call.

He was under no illusions. They wouldn't come to his rescue this time. He was on his own, not counting the drippy lawyer he'd been assigned, who looked tired and bored. This guy wouldn't know how to make a credible objection if someone had supplied him with *Murder Trials for Dummies*. So far, all he'd done was advise Brett to cooperate. Fat chance. He wasn't giving these morons anything. It was up to them to build a case against him, which they apparently had. Between the forensic evidence, Quinn's statement, and some recording they kept mentioning, he was really and truly fucked. And to think that he'd gotten rid of Jo to help Quinn. This was positively the last time he'd do anyone any favors. From now on, he was out for himself.

He was forced to look at DI Marshall when the man slammed his hand on the table to get Brett's attention. Brett met the man's triumphant gaze, and fingers of apprehension walked up his spine, his body temperature dropping by several degrees.

"Brett Besson, you are hereby charged with the manslaughter of Jo Turing, as contrary to Common Law. You are hereby charged with attempted murder against Quinn Allenby Russell and Gabriel Russell, as contrary to Common Law. And you're also charged with leaving the scene of an accident, just for good measure. Take him down," DI Marshall said to one of his goons. He watched with obvious satisfaction as Brett was hauled out of the room and into a corridor that smelled of reheated food. It had to be lunchtime.

Brett glared at DI Marshall one last time, then allowed himself to be led away. As the old saying went, "It ain't over till the fat lady sings," and this opera had only just begun. And even if they did manage to put him away, there were always mistrials, appeals, paroles, and early releases for good behavior. They might have nailed him for this, but they'd never find the others, Brett thought confidently.

Chapter 68

Christmas Eve 1777
Long Island

"Can I help?" Jocelyn asked as she walked into the kitchen, where Hannah was hard at work mashing potatoes.

"Absolutely not. You are to sit down and rest. Doctor's orders."

"I feel well, Hannah," Jocelyn protested, but knew it was pointless. Everyone had been treating her like an invalid these past few weeks, and with good reason. She had recovered physically, but she was still fragile in both body and mind.

"If you are not going to rest, then get some air. You are as pale as the moon. Dr. Rosings did say you should take short walks."

Jocelyn balked at that. She hadn't left the farm since the fateful day she'd met Major Radcliffe in the woods, not even to attend church. But Hannah was right. It was time.

Draping a cloak over her shoulders, Jocelyn stepped outside. A gentle snow was falling, the landscape the dreamy lavender of a December twilight. She lifted her face to the sky, closing her eyes and letting the snowflakes settle on her nose and cheeks. She was so lucky to be alive. Despite his training and rank, Major Radcliffe had proved to be a poor shot. He'd missed her heart by at least two inches, unwittingly saving Jocelyn's life. The bullet had passed right through, leaving a clean exit wound. Jocelyn might have still bled to death out there in the cold had Derek not come looking for her, suddenly certain that she needed his help. He'd lifted her off the ground and run all the way back to the farm, calling to Josh to fetch Dr. Rosings without delay. They'd saved her. Again.

Jocelyn began to walk slowly, carefully putting one foot in front of the other. She was still afraid to leave the farm. Knowing that Major Radcliffe was out there somewhere was terrifying, but she couldn't live in fear. She had recovered, and come the new year, she'd have to decide what to do.

Jocelyn's hand subconsciously went to her stomach. The major had done her a favor, really. She'd lost the baby, probably from shock. It had bled out of her while she lay unconscious, freeing her from a lifetime of being reminded of the worst day of her life.

Now she was free to start again, and she would, as soon as she found the courage to leave Milford. She couldn't stay here, not now. And she wouldn't be taking Ben with her. He deserved better than a woman who used him as a shield against the world. He deserved love.

Jocelyn took a deep breath of the chill air, filling her lungs. She wouldn't go far, not today, but tomorrow, she'd go further, and the next day, further still. She laughed out loud, the sound dissipating in the stillness of the afternoon. She'd cheated death three times. She must be invincible, she thought, amused. Maybe she had nine lives, like a cat.

Her humor evaporated when she saw two men in the distance, her breath catching in her throat. Jocelyn peered through the falling snow, trying to make out the men's features. Derek had been away for nearly a fortnight. He hadn't told her where he'd gone, and both Hannah and Ben had been tightlipped. Jocelyn hadn't pressed them. It was none of her affair. Hannah would be thrilled to have him back for Christmas, though, and he had promised he'd try to get back in time.

As the men drew closer, Jocelyn breathed a sigh of relief. The man on the right was definitely Derek. She'd recognize him anywhere. The man on the left had his hat pulled down low over his eyes and seemed to be looking down as he listened to something Derek was telling him. But then he looked up and stopped, his gaze fixed on Jocelyn, a joyous smile spreading across his face.

Jocelyn let out a cry. She wasn't supposed to run, but she didn't feel the ground beneath her feet. She was flying on the wings of disbelief, crying tears of joy.

Jared sprinted toward her and caught her in his arms, spinning her around as he held her close. They were laughing and crying and tripping over each other in their haste to speak. Derek had gone on, leaving them to enjoy their reunion. There would be time later to thank him for what he'd done for them, for it was clear that he'd gone in search of Jared. He must have known somehow that Jared hadn't been hanged. Perhaps he'd heard something while in New York.

Jocelyn buried her face in Jared's chest, breathing in the damp wool scent of his coat. She'd never imagined she could be this happy. Jared took her hand and sank down to one knee in the snow.

"Jocelyn Sinclair, will you do me the honor of becoming my wife?" he asked, his eyes shining as he looked at her. "I did ask you to wait till Christmas."

"I will," she whispered, overcome with emotion. "I will!" she cried into the swirling snow.

"And will you come away with me?" he asked once he was back on his feet, his hand on hers.

"To England?" Jocelyn asked, suddenly apprehensive.

Jared shook his head. "We can settle anywhere you like, even Canada, if you so desire."

"Will we be safe?" Jocelyn asked, the old fear resurging.

"Major Radcliffe has returned to England. He won't be back."

"What happened after that night?" Jocelyn asked, even though it hurt to speak of it.

"Mrs. Johnson and Private Sykes came forward to testify on my behalf. They weren't permitted to attend the court-martial, but their statements were taken and presented during the trial. They saved me from the noose," Jared said, his eyes moist with emotion.

"Once the truth of what happened that night came out, Major Radcliffe was in disgrace."

"The army held Major Radcliffe accountable for what he did to me?" Jocelyn asked, shocked that anyone would care.

"Not officially. He was sternly reprimanded, but he was tried in the court of public opinion and didn't fare well. The whole episode was an embarrassment, since the story made the rounds among the senior officers. They love their whores, but they do have a sense of honor and believe the transaction should be consensual. Plus, there was the suggestion that you had been spying for the Continentals, which made the major look rather injudicious. He was dismissed from General Howe's staff and viciously ridiculed for his part in the affair, so much so that he was forced to resign his commission."

So, it had been revenge, Jocelyn concluded, not fear of discovery that had prompted the major to wish to kill her. He'd been humiliated and disgraced and had been forced to walk away from a career he'd invested years into. No wonder he'd wanted to see her dead.

"Did you feel betrayed when you found out I'd been spying?" Jocelyn asked, looking up at him. She needed to see his face to know if he was telling her the truth.

"Maybe a little," Jared admitted. "But I also felt admiration and respect. It takes great courage to do what you did. Radcliffe never suspected a thing. I think he was blinded by your beauty," Jared said softly, gazing down on her. "So was I."

"How did he find me all the way out here?" Jocelyn asked. It wasn't really important, but she needed to understand in order to put the whole sorry business behind her.

"Mrs. Johnson had left her position, but Private Sykes was never reassigned. He should have been, given the circumstances, but he remained at Major Radcliffe's house until the major resigned his commission toward the end of November. Derek said Sykes had recognized you at the tavern."

"Yes, Radcliffe did mention that it had been Sykes who told him, but how did he connect me to Milford?" Jocelyn asked.

"The proprietor of the tavern may have known Derek from previous visits, or Derek might have even dropped a casual remark to the boy who'd looked after the horses while you were inside. I don't know for certain, but Radcliffe managed to connect the dots and find your hideout." Jared was silent for a moment, then asked what had clearly been on his mind. "Why did you think I was dead?"

"Anna told me you'd been hanged for assaulting your senior officer," Jocelyn replied.

"But I wasn't. I was cleared of all charges."

Jocelyn sighed heavily. "Perhaps she thought it'd be easier for me to leave if I thought you were dead. She never said so outright, but she didn't approve of me getting involved with a British officer."

"Was she the one who talked you into going to your brother's house?" Jared asked.

"Yes and no. Anna and Carole looked after me at a time when I needed a woman's care and understanding, but I couldn't stay with them forever. Once I felt more myself, I decided to leave New York, but I had to wait until it was safe for me to leave the house. By mid-October, the search for me seemed to have stopped, so Anna booked me passage on the *Peregrine*. I arrived just before departure and went directly aboard. It was a cold day, so no one thought it strange that I was wearing my hood up. I hid belowdecks until the ship sailed."

"And then the storm broke," Jared said.

"Yes. We were only a few hours out of port. It was terrifying," Jocelyn said. "Not only because it seemed clear the ship wasn't going to make it, but because I was all alone. I had no one in those final moments."

"You've been through so much," Jared said, reaching for her hand and bringing it to his lips. "You are the strongest woman I know. The strongest person," he amended.

"I didn't have much choice in the matter," Jocelyn replied with a shrug. "I did what I had to do to survive."

"This, us, really is a miracle," Jared said, his eyes full of wonder. "To think that we are together again after everything that happened. And we will stay together from now on," he said, smiling happily.

"Jared, are you still in the army?" Jocelyn asked. Jared was wearing civilian clothes, but he might be on furlough.

"I resigned my commission and have been working as a shipping clerk these past few months. I have enough savings to set us up with a small concern of our own. We can open a shop or an inn, or anything you think would guarantee us a good living. Just don't ask me to farm," Jared said, smiling down at her. "I'm not cut out for farming."

"Neither am I," Jocelyn said, grinning.

They had reached the farmhouse, and not a moment too soon. Jocelyn's cheeks burned with cold, and she could no longer feel her feet.

"Shall we?" Jared asked, nodding toward the door.

Jocelyn nodded but made no move to go indoors. She lifted her face up to his, desperate for one more kiss. "Happy Christmas, my love," she whispered as his lips came down on hers.

**

Later, after dinner, Jocelyn followed Derek outside to fetch more firewood, leaving Jared to regale Josh with stories of great battles. Derek waited for her to catch up.

"I can't thank you enough for what you've done for me. For us," Jocelyn amended.

"You don't need to thank me," Derek said, smiling down at her. "I was happy to do it. So, what now?" he asked.

"We will get married and start a business of our own," Jocelyn said dreamily. "Somewhere far from here. What about you? Will you finally marry Lydia?"

"No," Derek said simply. "Lydia is beautiful and accomplished, but I don't love her, not in the way that matters. I'm going to leave too."

"And go where?" Jocelyn asked.

"I've decided to join the Continental Army," Derek said sheepishly. "I thought I could avoid taking sides, but I had made up my mind long ago. It's time I proclaimed my allegiance to the world."

"Your mother will be heartbroken," Jocelyn said.

"Perhaps, but I'm a grown man, and I have to do what I think is right. I will sign over the farm to Ben and make my way to Philadelphia."

"God be with you, Derek," Jocelyn said as tears prickled in her eyes. "If not for you…"

"If not for me, you'd never have been shot," he replied huskily.

"If not for you, I would not be this happy."

"It's my Christmas present to you. Now, give me one in return. Stay alive, get through this war, and be happy."

"I'll do my best. I'll send my new address to your mother. Perhaps one day you'll write to me."

"You have my word," Derek said. "Now, go back inside before you get ill. Your intended is waiting for you."

Jocelyn stood on tiptoe and kissed Derek's cheek, then turned and ran back inside, toward her new life.

Chapter 69

April 2018
London

"How was it?" Gabe asked when Quinn walked into the bedroom, looking a bit worse for wear. He was propped up on several pillows, a book he'd just finished lying on the bedside table next to a plate of biscuits left there by his mum, and a bottle of painkillers. He hadn't taken any, even though he was still in some pain. But it had been a week since the surgery, and he was determined to get back to normal within the next few days. This lying in bed and being waited on hand and foot was highly overrated, especially when the waiters in question were his and Quinn's mums, who wouldn't give him a moment's peace and carried on as if he might snuff it at any moment.

"A roaring success," Quinn replied, plopping down onto the bed. "I'm exhausted."

The house had been filled with the sounds of happy children, frazzled adults, and mad barking emanating from an overexcited Rufus, but finally it had grown quiet.

"Mia was thrilled with her birthday."

"Tell me everything," Gabe invited.

"Well, if you're sure you want to know. The zoo was a madhouse. Olivia managed to wander off, nearly giving Jill and Brian coronaries. She was eventually apprehended by Jude near the monkey cage and brought back kicking and screaming. Apparently, monkeys are the coolest and Jude ruined her entire day.

"Vanessa threw a fit because her balloon flew away, and Rhys paid some lucky woman twenty quid for her toddler's balloon, which the toddler in question had no intention of parting with. Mayhem ensured, but he didn't care because Vanessa was happy and that's all that matters.

"Baby Max slept through the whole thing, lovely boy that he is. And Chrissy showed up, which was unexpected since she just had a cesarean a week ago. She was clearly in pain, but I think she wanted to have this memory of going to the zoo with Max since it seems she's set to return to the Czech Republic next week."

Quinn took a deep breath and continued, ignoring Gabe's bemused stare. "Having saved the day by replacing the balloon, Rhys decided to harass me about the case. He demanded an update, once between the lion enclosure and the mandatory bathroom stop, and then again while I was searching for the birthday candle, which had been lying next to the cake all along."

"And did you provide him with one?" Gabe asked, his mouth twitching as he tried not to burst out laughing.

"I did. Katya is thrilled that Major Radcliffe got his just deserts and thinks he should be reburied in a septic tank, and Rhys is practically giddy with the prospect of the Christmas proposal I'd suggested. Fits right into his plans for the Christmas special. Nothing warms the cockles of the collective British heart like a happy ending."

Gabe's eyebrows lifted comically. "Sorry, did I miss something?"

"I decided to fudge the truth a little and give Jocelyn and Derek a happy ending," Quinn admitted guiltily. "Who's to say she didn't survive the shooting?"

"And you think Jocelyn and Derek would have made it official if she did?"

"There was an undeniable connection between them, and with Captain Denning gone, who's to say Jocelyn wouldn't have acted on it?"

"No one at all," Gabe concurred. "An engagement would indeed make for a happy ending if Derek Wilder was prepared to raise Major Radcliffe's child as his own."

"We'll assume he did. The ratings will go through the roof."

"And speaking of children, how did ours acquit themselves today?" Gabe asked, smiling. "No lost balloons or attempted escapes?"

"Our children behaved magnificently," Quinn added. "Alex even offered his own balloon to Vanessa, but apparently it was the wrong color, so his chivalry went unappreciated. Emma said she's never having kids, but I think she might change her mind in about twenty years."

"And our parents?" Gabe asked, trying hard not to laugh because it hurt.

"On their best behavior, or as near as. Your mum served the pizza, and my parents cut and dished out the cake. It was splendid. And they even helped me clean up."

"Where are they now?" Gabe asked, wondering why it was so quiet downstairs.

"My parents and your mum went back to the hotel. I think they've forgotten how hectic a two-year-old's birthday party can be. They're knackered. And they wanted to give us a bit of space."

"That's very considerate of them. And have you spoken to Seth?" Gabe asked, no longer smiling. Kathy and Seth were a sore subject these days, and Brett's name was never mentioned at all, for the sake of everyone's sanity.

"He called to wish Mia a happy birthday."

"How was the conversation?" Gabe inquired.

"A bit tense. He's understandably devastated, but he's going to stand by me, Gabe. He's made that clear."

"I'm glad to hear it. And Sylvia?"

"She's all about Max these days, but she did get Mia a lovely present and invited her for a sleepover if we allow it. Do we allow it?" Quinn asked.

Gabe shrugged. "Maybe in the summer, when we can use a break from all this family togetherness," Gabe joked. "Where's the birthday girl?"

"She's in the lounge, surrounded by a pile of gifts," Quinn said, sighing like a woman who'd just climbed a very tall mountain and reached its peak.

"Which one is her favorite?"

"The dollhouse, I think. She asked for it to be brought up to her room. Jude took care of it."

"I'd like to come downstairs for a bit," Gabe said, already making to rise.

"Are you sure that's wise?" Quinn asked, instantly concerned.

"Quinn, I'm fine. Really. I'll take it easy and sit on the sofa," he promised.

"All right," Quinn said. "But I'm going to help you down the stairs."

"If you must."

"I must," Quinn insisted.

Once downstairs, Quinn settled Gabe in the armchair, and he held out his arms for Mia to climb into his lap. She pressed herself to his chest and looked up with those dark, soulful eyes.

"I missed you, Daddy," she said.

"Did you have a nice birthday?" Gabe asked, blinking away the tears that suddenly clouded his vision.

"Yes." Mia nodded vigorously. "I like giraffes."

"I know, darling."

He was about to ask about the glories of the dollhouse when Alex appeared in the doorway, Quinn's bag in his hands. He pulled out a toy car Quinn must have put in there sometime during the day and allowed the bag to drop to the floor. A silver ring fell out and rolled across the hardwood floor, coming to a stop once it hit the wall. Car forgotten, Alex sprinted after the ring and picked it up, bringing it close to his face to study the object.

"Alex, can I have that back, please?" Quinn said as she approached him, but Alex didn't seem to hear her. His gaze had clouded, and there was a frown on his little face.

"Jocelyn," he whispered. "Pretty."

Gabe felt something break inside him, his hand instinctively wrapping tighter around Mia as he watched his son. He had no illusions. Mia would probably also have the gift, or the curse, as he'd come to think of it. He'd do anything to protect his children from the ugliness and pain they would see, but it wasn't in his power to stop the visions. A new generation of psychics had been born, and it would be up to them to decide how to use their ability.

After experiencing the disturbing memories that were her mother's only legacy to her and learning of the events that had led to Brett's arrest, Daisy had decided to sell the camera and avoid using her ability, much as Jo had. Daisy wouldn't allow the visions to interfere with her life or draw her into the lives of the dead. Instead she was focusing on the future and preparing to start university in the fall to pursue her interest in architecture. Perhaps Alex and Mia would be just as wise when they became old enough to make their choice. Only time would tell.

Epilogue

Christmas 1777
Hertfordshire, England

Hector Radcliffe retired to the library after dinner and poured himself a tot of brandy, then reconsidered and added another three fingers' worth. It was Christmas, and he was all alone, his mood on this most benevolent of days dangerously volatile. He'd come to visit his old Eton friend Howard Lowell at his country estate, but although Howard had been glad to see him and happy for Hector to stay for a few weeks, he'd made his excuses and gone to spend Christmas with his fiancée's family in London, leaving Hector on his own for the holiday.

Normally, Hector wouldn't have minded. It was a large, comfortable house with extensive grounds, an impressive library, and a well-stocked liquor cabinet, but this year he had really craved company, needing someone else's voice to drown out the morbid thoughts in his head, some of which seemed to have taken up permanent residence in his skull during the ocean crossing.

Hector tossed back the brandy and considered pouring himself another. Who'd care if he was drunk? It wasn't as though he had to behave himself in polite company. And he was feeling sorry for himself. He was nearly thirty-five, unmarried, disgraced, the career he'd dedicated his life to in tatters. He could hardly blame Jocelyn Sinclair or Jared Denning for his misfortune. It was his fault, and his alone. He should have arrested the duplicitous bitch and put her under lock and key. Instead, he'd given in the to the desire that had been tormenting him for months. He'd lost his head. Again. He'd worked so hard to control himself, to follow society's rules, but there were times when something took over, a force more powerful than his self-restraint, and then he was lost.

He couldn't control it, couldn't even rein it in long enough to think things through. There had been that doxy in Southampton

358

and then the serving wench at a tavern at West Point. He'd strangled the doxy to keep her from screaming, and the other one wouldn't be making any complaints. He'd paid her off to keep her quiet. But his desire for Jocelyn had been his downfall. He'd have gladly taken her as his mistress, would have showered her with affection and gifts, but she'd had no interest in him. She'd wanted Denning. Hector had been mad with jealousy, his desire for her poisoned with his need to possess her, to bring her to her knees.

Well, he'd done that, but it had given him no pleasure. The fear and disgust in her eyes had been enough to shrivel his manhood, which was why he'd taken her from the back, so as not to see that face. And Denning... He'd done what any honorable man would do in his position. He'd protected a woman. *Too bad he didn't hang*, Hector thought furiously. Denning would never forget what he'd seen, would never allow Hector to sleep peacefully at night. He'd not only been a witness, but a victim, and now he was the victor. He was out there, alive and well, in possession of knowledge Hector would have killed to suppress.

He reached for the ring on his left hand and turned it round and round, an unconscious habit that had formed since he'd taken the ring off Jocelyn in that Long Island wood. He hadn't enjoyed killing her. He'd still wanted her, and she'd been carrying his child. Had the situation been different, he might have asked her to marry him, but Jocelyn wouldn't have him, not after what he'd done and the consequences that had followed. His desire for her had destroyed him, and he would destroy her in turn, wipe that impudent look off her face and silence her forever. But it was her defiance that was his last memory of her. He'd been more afraid than she was, and that rankled.

Hector gave in to the urge and poured himself another brandy, his thoughts still on Jocelyn. She'd been so beautiful, so graceful, he recalled, his fingers still stroking the ring. His mind conjured up the image of her pale thighs as he bent her over the desk, his swollen cock sliding into her virginal tightness. He felt a stirring of desire, his shaft growing hard and straining against the fabric of his breeches. He hadn't had a woman since his ship had docked in Southampton. He was long overdue. Hector tossed back the rest of his brandy and got to his feet, going in search of Maggie. She was a comely wench and certainly not an innocent. She'd do.

Hector crossed the tiled foyer and made his way downstairs to the kitchen. Maggie would be alone, clearing up after dinner. The kitchen was the perfect place. No one would hear them there.

Maggie turned at the sound of his footsteps. "Did you need something, sir?"

Hector's gaze slid to her breasts, which looked pillowy and inviting. He had a mind to suckle them before taking her. Maggie took a step back, as though alerted by the hunger in his eyes.

"Don't be afraid," Hector said softly. "I won't hurt you." But he would, and he would enjoy it, he thought as he reached for her. He wrapped his arm around her waist and pulled her close, his hand cupping her breast as he bent to kiss her.

Maggie pushed against him, her panic an aphrodisiac. "Please stop," she pleaded as she managed to break free. "I'm betrothed to Henry."

"The groom?" Hector asked, amused. "Then you know all about rolls in the hay," he quipped, and went for her again. He pinned her against the stone wall and pushed his hand between her legs, gratified when his fingers slid into the warm moistness of her quim. She did want him then.

"Come now," he panted. "I'll make it worth your while. Give you a start in life." He pushed his fingers deep inside her, anticipating how good it would feel to fuck her.

He never saw it coming. The cast-iron skillet met his head with a sickening thud. Hector loosened his grip, momentarily surprised that Maggie had had the temerity to strike him. He'd show her who was master here, he thought drowsily as he staggered sideways, grabbing desperately for the pine table. His fingers just missed the table edge, and then his knees gave way and he was falling, Maggie's terrified face the last thing he was to see in this life.

Hector was still conscious when Henry came running in. Hector heard them whispering but couldn't find the strength to move. His head tolled like a church bell, and his limbs felt as thick and heavy as an iron cannon. He tried to move his tongue, but it seemed to be stuck to the roof of his mouth, and although his eyes were partially open, he couldn't see anything but murky shadows swirling above him.

"Oh, Lord Jesus, you've bashed his head in," Henry whispered, looking down in horror. "There's so much blood."

"Henry, pull yourself together," Maggie ordered, sounding like a general going into battle. "And get the shovel."

"What for?"

"We'll bury him in the woods behind the house."

"And what are we to tell the master?" Henry demanded.

"We'll tell him Mr. Radcliffe has gone. Took himself off. The master will never question it. Let's strip him naked and bury the bastard, and then we'll get rid of his possessions and sell his horse. No one will be the wiser, and he owes me for the distress he's caused."

"I do love you, Maggie," Henry said affectionately. "You are a rare woman."

"And you're an exceptionally strong man. Now, get his sorry carcass out of here and start digging. I'll clean up the blood."

Maggie began to say something else, but Hector didn't hear her. Jocelyn's face floated before him, her clear blue eyes looking at him with the purest of love.

"Come, Hector," she said. "I'm waiting for you, my love." And he went.

The End

Notes

I hope you have enjoyed the Echoes from the Past series. It was hard to say goodbye to these characters, but I feel that their story is done, at least for now. I hope you will check out some of my other books, in both the Historical Romance and the Victorian Mystery genres.

I love hearing from you, so please post a review if you've enjoyed the book, or even if you didn't.

If you'd like to join my mailing list, please subscribe at
http://irinashapiroauthor.com/mailing-list-signup-form/

You can also find me at www.irinashapiroauthor.com and on Facebook at https://www.facebook.com/IrinaShapiro2

Made in the USA
Coppell, TX
23 March 2022

75407001R20215